Eva Leigh

Temptations OF A Wallflower

The Wicked Quills of London

AVONBOOKS

An Imprint of HarperCollinsPublishers

This is a work of fiction. Names, characters, places, and incidents are products of the author's imagination or are used fictitiously and are not to be construed as real. Any resemblance to actual events, locales, organizations, or persons, living or dead, is entirely coincidental.

AVON BOOKS
An Imprint of HarperCollins*Publishers*
195 Broadway
New York, New York 10007

Copyright © 2016 by Ami Silber
ISBN 978-0-06-235866-0
www.avonromance.com

First Avon Books mass market printing: May 2016

Avon Trademark Reg. U.S. Pat. Off. and in Other Countries, Marca Registrada, Hecho en U.S.A.
Avon, Avon Books, and the Avon logo are trademarks of HarperCollins Publishers.
HarperCollins® is a registered trademark of HarperCollins Publishers.

Printed in the U.S.A.

10 9 8 7 6 5 4 3 2 1

A tempting thought...

Sarah's gaze drifted back to the hedge maze. Could she drop her fan? As they both bent to retrieve it, she might whisper to him an invitation to meet her there in a few moments. And then . . . She could taste those gently curved lips of his. Oh, she'd experienced a few chaste kisses before, but never anything she truly desired. But she wanted to kiss Mr. Cleland. She craved feeling his mouth against hers and seeing if her imagination was correct about him.

He, too, looked at the maze. Was he thinking the same thoughts? Did he want to savor her? A delectable thought, one that made her feel both languid and powerfully alive all at once.

Their gazes met. He turned gorgeously pink.

He *was* thinking of kissing her!

By Eva Leigh

TEMPTATIONS OF A WALLFLOWER
SCANDAL TAKES THE STAGE
FOREVER YOUR EARL

Coming Soon

FROM DUKE TIL DAWN

To Zack, who never doubts

Acknowledgments

Thank you, as always, to my agent, Kevan Lyon. Much gratitude to my editor, Nicole Fischer, as well as Caro Perny, Pam Jaffee, and the whole team at Avon Books. A special thank you to the Avon Books Art Department, for giving me the most incredible covers I have ever seen.

Thank you to Meredith Levy. You're amazing.

Conventional wisdom says that the Internet wastes time, and that it doesn't foster interpersonal relationships—but without the support, encouragement, and general awesomeness of my friends online, there is a high degree of likelihood that this book wouldn't have been written. Specifically, thanks to my Facebook misandrists, and to the Loop That Shall Not Be Named.

Thank you also to my #1k1hr folks, for helping me get this book written, including, but not limited to: Carolyn Crane, Cynthia Eden, Rhonda Helms, LB Gregg, Heather Lire, Judith Leger, and Katie Reus.

Thank you to Briana Proctor, Timitria Cozier-Bobb, Elizabeth Walker Blumenfeld, Lizabeth S. Tucker, Cecilia R. Rodriguez, Valerie Halfen, Kay Sturm, Pat Elliott, Crystal Holloway, Melody Brooke May, Tina

Burns, and Carolyn Jewel for your advice on how to be a rake. Clearly, you know your rakes!

Many thanks to Julia Quinn, Sarah MacLean, Elizabeth Boyle, Laura Lee Guhrke, and Caroline Linden for guidance about titles.

Chapter 1

*In late summer, London sweltered. Worse—
the city grew exceedingly dull as the hot months
dragged on. All my usual lovers had gone to the
country, leaving behind boors with an appalling
lack of knowledge of female anatomy. I decided
that I would take my leave of London and seek
pleasure somewhere in the green of the country.
Thus resolved, with thoughts of lusty rustics in
my mind, I had my trunks packed and set off in
my carriage for a pastoral escape. Too intent
on finding relief, I paid no heed to warnings of
highwaymen who prowled the roads. Perhaps
I should have given those warnings more
regard . . .*

The Highwayman's Seduction

London, 1816

Too much time had passed since Jeremy Cleland had
last been in London. A few months in the country
made quite a difference in a man's life. As Jeremy
rode in his father's carriage to the family's Mayfair

mansion, he felt every inch the humble vicar that he'd become.

Streets seemed dizzyingly congested, sounds ricocheted like bullets from close-set buildings, and the pervasive smell of soot and smoke cloaked the avenues.

He didn't precisely *mind* all the sensory commotion. After all, he'd spent his youth traveling back and forth between London and various country estates. That included the Hertfordshire mansion that served as the seat of his father, the Earl of Hutton. Yet being the earl's third son had its advantages—and many burdens. Granted, the earldom had been gifted to Jeremy's father due to service to the Crown as the nation's moral paragon, but the impact of the title remained the same.

The carriage turned onto Berkeley Square, and it was such a marked contrast from Jeremy's little rural parish of Rosemead that he gave a strained laugh. What would Mr. Kinross, the church sexton, think of the soaring marble and stone mansions that housed dozens of servants but only one family? Likely Mr. Kinross would shake his head and spit tobacco onto the ground, muttering about citified gentry. Bad enough that the sexton already looked at Jeremy with suspicion. If the old man knew precisely what kind of wealth gleamed in the vicar's background, he'd never listen to a word Jeremy said, let alone attend his sermons.

Jeremy was getting closer now to Hutton House. As the distance shortened, concern churned in his gut. What had prompted his father to summon him from Devonshire? Father's letter had been opaque, revealing nothing. And, if Jeremy wanted to be perfectly honest— which vicars were supposed to be, anyway—he wasn't precisely looking forward to seeing the earl again. Not the warmest or most effusive of men, his father. He took his title and responsibilities very seriously, which meant that his offspring were largely means to an end. But they were also extensions of the earl—his representatives to the world at large.

Jeremy didn't envy his brother John the obligation of being heir. Jeremy also didn't have the terrifying uncertainty of being second son, like his other brother, Mark. That left Jeremy the burden of embodying the earl's morals, and his father was a greater taskmaster than the Church.

In his early years, Jeremy hadn't known precisely what he wanted to do with his life—only that it involved helping people. So many charitable organizations needed figureheads and organizers that he had been certain he would take his place there. But his father had had other plans. The earl had made it clear that if Jeremy didn't go into the Church, his allowance would be reduced to nothing. With that threat, Jeremy hadn't possessed much choice but to do his father's bidding and become a vicar.

There was a positive side to it—he did get to help people, only without the freedom he'd dreamed of as a boy.

Upholding a scrupulously moral appearance remained his foremost obligation, serving as an example for not only everyone in his parish but also to the world at large.

Yet, to his highly provincial parishioners, trips to London weren't precisely considered virtuous.

Still, he couldn't deny his father, though he had no

idea what the earl wanted. Now he rode in a phenomenally expensive carriage, pulling up outside an extraordinarily old, costly home in one of the most exclusive neighborhoods in the world. Doubt assailed him. What did his father want with him now?

Long ago, Jeremy's closest companion had been his wild cousin Marwood. Yet the earl hadn't approved of the association and had forbidden Jeremy from seeing Marwood except at family gatherings. As always, the threat of disinheritance had been given. Too young to make his way in the world, Jeremy had done as his father had demanded. He hadn't liked it, but what choice had there been?

Beaten-in habits died hard. Years later, Jeremy still rushed to his father's bidding. His income from his living was modest—he could ill afford to refuse the earl, especially on a financial level.

When the vehicle stopped and a footman opened the door for him, Jeremy stepped down and smoothed the front of his clerical jacket. Compared to the liveried servants, he looked severe and dour.

Jeremy mounted the stairs and had barely raised his hand to the door before it opened and Jeffries, the butler, silently escorted him in.

Soaring marble archways comprised the foyer, designed to intimidate the visitor. Even though Jeremy had grown up in this very home, even he felt a little small and gauche as he gazed up at the crystal chandelier.

"My favorite son!" a female voice called out from the top of the winding staircase.

Any sensation of not belonging dissolved immediately when Jeremy beheld his mother descending the stairs, her arms open.

When she stood before him, he kissed his mother on her cheek. "You say that to all three of us," he murmured.

"Yes, but I mean it with you," she answered with a smile.

"And you say *that,* too." He took her small, powdery hands in his.

"I can't be accused of favoritism," Lady Hutton replied, sniffing. "Though," she added conspiratorially, "you certainly received the bounty of the looks. You're the image of your father. No wonder he stole my heart." She sighed. "How the other girls envied me when he made his suit. I held him off, you know, just for appearance's sake, but I couldn't wait too long, lest he find another gel to take my place."

Jeremy had heard this story his whole life, but he always indulged his mother. "As though any girl could replace you," he answered, as he usually did.

Lady Hutton tapped him playfully on his arm. "I didn't realize the Church required vicars to flatter old women."

"I am, in all things, scrupulously honest." He bowed. "A hazard of the profession."

"Oh, but you were ever a truthful boy," she said with an almost despairing shake of her head. "Used to sneak off to go swimming in the middle of the night, then came running to us full of confession."

He hadn't abandoned his habit of midnight swimming. The pull of the water along his body, the burn of his muscles, the moonlight and liquid isolation.

Sometimes he felt it was the only thing that kept him from descending into bored melancholy.

A vicar's life was, if anything, marked by quiet, solitary routine. The pinnacle of morality was a lonely place to be.

"You were marked for the Church from an early age, my darling," his mother continued. "Your father wouldn't have it any other way."

And she hadn't protested, either. "Fortunate, then, that I didn't become a lion tamer."

"You have the souls of your parishioners to tame and guide," Lady Hutton answered. "A much more noble and dangerous endeavor."

The butler, standing nearby, coughed quietly.

"Oh, all right, Jeffries," Lady Hutton said with a roll of her eyes. She sighed again. "'Tis a sad day when a mother cannot spend five minutes with her son—whom she hasn't seen in an eternity, mind you."

"I promise hours of unexpurgated time alone over tea," Jeremy said. "After I see what Father wants."

"He's in the study with Allam," his mother replied with a wave of her hand. "Neither of them has said a word to me about this matter. But you know how those brothers can be. Silent as wolves."

"Wolves howl, Mother."

"Mute wolves, then." She shooed him off. "Go on, then. See what he wants. The sooner you get that out of the way, the sooner we can talk. About finding you a wife, specifically."

Jeremy fought the urge to roll his eyes. Marriage always beckoned. Wives were crucial for vicars, helping with the duties of the parish, but his needs and desires also burned with an unseemly heat. Nightly, he prayed to withstand the fires of his own body's demands. He'd banked them for so long that they threatened to burn him from the inside out. As the son of the highly moral Earl of Hutton, Jeremy couldn't avail himself of actresses and demimondaines. And vicars certainly didn't. Which left him a seething, simmering volcano of need.

How likely would it be that he'd find a good, sweet, patient woman with a siren's sexual appetite? Not likely at all.

Loneliness had made itself too common in his life. Its constant emptiness was a hunger that could never be satisfied.

None of this would he tell his mother, of course. They might be close, but they weren't *that* close.

"This way, please," the butler intoned.

"I know the way to the study, Jeffries," he answered with a smile.

The servant bowed. "As you wish, Master Jeremy."

With a last kiss for his mother, he headed toward the study.

An uneasy energy pulsed along Jeremy's neck as he contemplated what, exactly, necessitated the presence of his uncle, the Marquess of Allam. Perhaps it had to do with Allam's son, Cameron, Viscount Marwood. Recently, Marwood had married—a commoner who was also a *playwright,* of all things. Allam couldn't be happy about that.

Reaching the door to the study, Jeremy tapped lightly. His father's voice called out for him to enter.

Jeremy took a deep breath. Being called before his

father had never been a pleasant experience as a boy, and little had changed. Dread pooled coldly in his belly.

He stepped inside.

The room was paneled in dark wood, full of books and gravitas. An acre of desk occupied one corner; his uncle sat in front of it. His father stood behind the desk, a slim book in his hands.

Lord Hutton strode forward as Allam rose. Jeremy took turns shaking their hands and murmuring greetings. The two brothers held themselves with the same proud, upright bearing, and both wore their age remarkably well.

Jeremy did indeed feel as though he gazed at himself through the lens of time whenever he looked at his father. They both had the same long faces, the same bright blue eyes. Even, God help them, the same curly blond hair. Yet for some reason, women found their hair extremely charming, so Jeremy had little cause for complaint. Still, where Jeremy saw curiosity and openness in his own eyes, his father's were much harder, more demanding.

He couldn't help but feel that his father was sizing him up, taking his measure. The earl bragged to many about having a son in the Church—his virtuous son, the future archbishop. His father's scrutiny reminded Jeremy that he needed to remain constantly vigilant, lest his halo slip or tarnish.

"Had a good journey, I hope?" his father asked.

"Passable roads," Jeremy answered, "made all the better by the services of your carriage."

Lord Hutton nodded, though the excellence of his vehicles was never in doubt.

"Good to see you, my boy," Allam said jovially, thumping Jeremy on his back.

At twenty-eight, Jeremy could hardly be called a boy anymore, but he accepted his uncle's compliments and returned them with his own. Genuine pleasure lit within him to see the older man again. "It's been too long," he said. Marwood's wedding had been small, and quickly performed. There hadn't been time for Jeremy to come in from Rosemead for the event.

"Indeed it has. You must come for dinner," Allam enjoined. "Though," he added darkly, "I cannot guarantee the presence of my eldest son."

"I'm sure he's quite busy," Jeremy said diplomatically. "When my parishioners are newly married, the first few months keep them remarkably . . . occupied."

His uncle's look darkened, and he grumbled under his breath.

His father asked, "A drink? Something to eat? It's a long way from Devonshire."

"I promised Mother tea after our . . . meeting."

"Good lad," Lord Hutton said stiffly. He never offered praise without sounding uncomfortable.

"Perhaps we should get to it, Hutton," Allam suggested.

"Yes, of course. Have a seat, please."

"May I stand?" Jeremy asked. "My legs are cramped from the journey." Though being tall made for an advantage when leading services, it had its drawbacks as well, including discomfort from long carriage rides. He now walked to the fire to warm himself.

"As you like." The earl stood as well, though Allam, leaning on his cane, took a seat.

"You came a fair distance," the earl said, "so I shall come right to the point." He held up the book in his hand. "Are you familiar with the . . . I hesitate to call her an author . . . with the *person* known as the Lady of Dubious Quality?"

"Of course he wouldn't be," Allam interjected before Jeremy could answer that he was, in fact, acquainted with her work. "The lad's a *vicar*. Why would he read such filth?"

Jeremy said nothing. Not very long ago, when he'd visited Cam to offer some counsel, his cousin had actually given him a copy of *The Highwayman's Seduction,* the latest erotic offering from the Lady of Dubious Quality. It was the first time Jeremy had ever heard of the woman or her novels—but not the last.

Underneath his bed, in a hidden, locked chest, he now possessed every single one of the Lady's books.

Another secret he would never tell anyone.

"Why indeed?" His father chuckled. "Forgive me, Jeremy. I shouldn't have assumed that you, of all people, would know about wicked, indecent books."

"No need for forgiveness," Jeremy answered. He clasped his hands behind his back and gripped his fingers tightly.

"These . . . scribblings . . ." his father continued. "They are full of the most vile, reprehensible imaginings. Nothing but fornication. They undermine the very foundations of English morality. The same morality that I have been defending so scrupulously for decades." He puffed his chest. "Our virtuous and upstanding King George himself thanked me for my efforts with my earldom."

Jeremy knew full well that his father's title had resulted from the earl's constant campaigning against brothels and courtesans appearing in public. Jeremy had been told so over and over again his whole life.

"I'd no idea a single book had such power," he said.

"The Bible has power, does it not?" Allam asked. "And it is but a single book."

"But it is *the* book, Uncle. Not a minor footnote in the chronicles of literature."

"Literature?" the earl demanded. "Pah!" He shook the volume in his hand. "This is an abomination, is what it is. And it is hardly a footnote. These books are wildly popular. They cannot keep them in stock at the booksellers'."

"However we may disagree with the content of these works," Jeremy offered, "we must congratulate the author on her success. It takes a considerable amount of courage and determination to thrive in the field of publishing."

"I shall do no such thing," Lord Hutton growled. "There is nothing to be lauded in the peddling of ribald smut."

There would be no arguing with his father. The man had made up his mind, and to change it would be a feat even the Lord would struggle to accomplish.

"In what way does this relate to me, Father?" Jeremy asked. A faint prickling of fear hurried up his spine. Great God, had his housekeeper discovered the chest of forbidden books and reported it to Lord Hutton? Disaster.

"This person, this so-called *Lady*." His father paced. "She hides behind a pseudonym. Clearly, she is trying to shield herself from scandal. Which must mean that she possesses some rank or position within the community. But she must know that she cannot hide forever. She will not."

He continued, anger tightening his words. "If she insists on corrupting English morals, she must know there is a price to pay."

"That price is . . . ?" Jeremy wondered.

"Her identity," Allam said.

His father went on, "And *you*, Jeremy, are going to discover who she is."

Chapter 2

The roads were clear, and we traveled on into the night. I had just fallen into a doze when the carriage lurched to a stop, and I heard those unmistakable words:
"Stand and deliver!"

The Highwayman's Seduction

For a moment, Jeremy could only look back and forth between his father and his uncle. Yet both men's stern expressions made it plain that no one spoke in jest.

Finally, Jeremy asked, "Why me?" He spread his hands. "Of all the people to investigate the identity of this author—which I still don't understand the purpose of—I cannot see the reason for having me take on this matter. I'm only a vicar."

"That's precisely why you are the ideal candidate for the job," his uncle answered.

"Other people have tried to learn this *woman's* identity," his father continued. "To no avail. But as you come from a high moral position, you should be able to get further than anyone else."

Jeremy fought a wince at the words "high moral position." He was no better than any other human. With the same faults and frailties, the same needs and desires. He only worked harder to disguise them. But he could never say that to his father. At all times, he had to be better, more virtuous than an ordinary man.

Still, it was clear his father and uncle had discussed this subject at length and prepared a strategy for recruiting Jeremy to their cause.

"I still cannot fathom why I must be the one to lead this investigation," Jeremy pressed.

His father's expression turned grim. "There are whispers in court and in Parliament. My star as England's moral leader is fading. Especially with Prince George and his dissolute circle setting the tone for our times. The obliteration of the Lady of Dubious Quality would see my star shine again."

"Then oughtn't you be the one to discover her identity?" Jeremy wondered aloud.

The earl's look soured further. "I'm too old for such work. It takes a younger man. A man of my family. That can only mean you."

"As the heir," Allam continued, "John cannot involve himself in the task. He has responsibilities of his own. Same with Mark."

"But you," his father went on, gesturing toward Jeremy, "my son, a *vicar,* you are the perfect man to take on this task."

Jeremy pondered this rationale. "This . . . Lady of Dubious Quality," he said slowly. "Is there a specific rationale for exposing her?"

"Once her identity is revealed," his father explained as though talking to a dim child, "the scandal will be so tremendous that she will be forced to stop writing her lewd books, and we'll put an end to her once and for all."

He continued, "Think of your cousin Marwood. And his friend Lord Ashford. Both of them married down."

Allam grimaced and looked away.

"How did the Lady of Dubious Quality cause that?" Jeremy asked.

"She may have influenced their decisions to wed beneath them. I've heard from others that she often writes of the classes . . . *intermixing.* There is nothing good to be gained by such seditious ideology."

"Chasing after a writer of, ah, prurient literature would take me away from my parish and my duties to my parishioners," Jeremy pointed out.

"You're a bright lad," Allam noted. "It shouldn't take you more than a few weeks to learn who our mystery scribbler is. Make some inquiries. Talk to her publisher. Booksellers. It should hardly be enough time for your parishioners to notice."

"There's that curate of yours, Mr. Wolbert," his father said. "He can take care of things while you're away."

Mr. Wolbert was a good man, if a trifle young and inexperienced. Shouldering the Sunday services and managing the rest of the responsibilities that came with the job might do him good.

"If there's any reluctance on your part," Lord Hutton continued, "consider this: I'll increase your allowance if you uncover the Lady's secret." He took a step forward, his hands spread. "You'd like that, wouldn't you,

Jeremy? Doing whatever it is that you want. Perhaps the Church isn't your cup of tea. Perhaps you'd like to venture into other areas, or even live the life of a country gentleman." His father's tone became more coaxing. "All those possibilities could be yours."

His mind whirling, Jeremy crossed his arms and stared off into the distance. The life of a leisured gentleman held no appeal, yet if Jeremy had more money in his pocket, he wouldn't be dependent on his income as a vicar. He'd have the freedom denied him from an early age, freedom to go where he wanted, do what he pleased. There were innumerable charities and benevolent organizations with which he could work without being limited by his Church-ascribed role.

Certainly none of Jeremy's letters home had indicated how dissatisfied he'd become of late with life as a vicar. Oh, he managed his duties fine. Did them well, even. He fielded the usual number of complaints from parish busybodies who were perpetually disgruntled. Mr. Engle was never satisfied with the lilacs that grew in front of the church and wanted them pulled up to make way for sturdy juniper. Jeremy often had to mediate between neighbors Mrs. Litchfield and Mrs. May over disputes about whose goat belonged to whom.

Overall, he'd been made to feel welcome and had been readily taken into the community. He'd been to numerous dinners at his parishioners' houses, and he was frequently positioned next to their marriageable daughters at these meals. Mr. and Mrs. Allen, in particular, seemed eager to pair him with their girl Adeline.

The last visit from the archdeacon had gone very well, too. No professional concerns marred his experience.

His father couldn't know, but in truth, Jeremy was busy but bored numb. He found himself staring off into space instead of deep in prayer at church. He'd set off to pay visits, and then discover himself sitting beside his favorite swimming pond instead.

Guiding people toward realizing their best selves fulfilled him, but that comprised a minor component of his work. Most of the time, he felt constrained, hemmed in. That tight vise would grip him when he had to listen to Mr. Edgar complain about his gout, or when a young couple dithered over the name for their new baby.

Everyone—especially his father—expected him to behave a certain way, to be a particular type of man. Was he that man? He didn't know, especially as of late.

He searched for something, but he didn't know what it was.

Would money solve the problem? What his father offered was appealing, but that wasn't what pricked Jeremy's interest now. Learning more about the Lady, however . . . that was an exciting, tantalizing prospect. He'd read all her books—now he could discover more about her and the dark, seductive world she embodied. And perhaps, when it was all over, he could at last have the liberty so long refused him. He could travel, see the world, help those both here in England and abroad.

The fire popped, and he realized that he'd fallen silent for several minutes. Glancing up, he saw his father and uncle staring intently at him, awaiting his response.

"I'll do it," he said. He had a strong suspicion that the "Lady" was, in fact, a man. It would be a simple matter to track him down.

"Excellent," his father said. His stern face cracked a smile as he came forward to shake Jeremy's hand. "Whatever you need is at your disposal."

"I shall keep you informed," Jeremy answered.

"And while you're in town," Allam added, "please come to a garden party Helena and I are hosting tomorrow. It's a bit chilly, but the last of the flowers are out, and Helena wanted to take advantage of them before the blossoms are gone."

"Sounds delightful," Jeremy said.

"There should be a nice selection of suitable young women there, as well." His uncle waggled his eyebrows.

"Given that I'm on the hunt for the Lady of Dubious Quality," Jeremy replied drily, "I'll likely be too busy to go wife hunting."

"Never too busy to find yourself a bride," his father said firmly.

Well, that was a battle Jeremy had no interest in fighting right now. How could he search for a woman to share his life with when he didn't even know what he wanted anymore? Much as he craved the companionship, he doubted he could ever find a woman who would truly understand his own complexities—especially when *he* didn't understand them.

"I shall see you tomorrow," Allam said.

Jeremy's quest would start then. He'd venture into the realm of temptation, and perhaps, in the process, he'd learn more about himself.

It was a beautiful autumnal day, full of golden sunlight and elegant talk, but Lady Sarah Frampton craved nothing more than a quiet place inside, some paper, and a quill. She'd made her way indoors from the Marquess of Allam's festive garden party, seeking solitude.

Pushed by an unstoppable urge, she eased her way through groups of people—an easy feat, since very few paid her much attention. There had to be somewhere in the marquess's London home that was unoccupied. Somewhere where she could be alone and give rein to the needs that demanded to be met. But *where*?

A gentleman of middle age appeared in front of her. She recognized him as Sir William Lewis, who, she had learned from her mother's circle of acquaintance, was a baronet who had recently decided he needed a wife and had come out of country isolation to hunt for a bride.

"Capital day, Lady Sarah." As he looked at her, his healthy red face had the same air it might have if he were to examine a strange animal brought to him by his hunting dogs. "This is quite a gala. Puts our country assemblies to shame."

"I'm sure those gatherings have their own appeal, Sir William," she offered.

He shrugged. "Suppose so."

They fell into an awkward silence.

"Enjoying the Season?" Sir William asked. He clasped his hands behind his back, and she could easily picture him as a country squire, tramping over hills with his gun under one arm and his hounds trotting beside him.

"There's so much to enjoy," she answered, which didn't actually answer the question.

"That there is." He glanced around the garden. "It's all so different from back home."

"I'm very interested to hear about your home," she said sincerely. Right then, the country sounded delightful. Fresh, open. Quiet. Where a woman could be alone and not be subject to a hundred measuring gazes.

"Not much to tell," he said with another shrug. "Farms, fields. Sheep." He seemed disinclined to speak any further on the topic, and it wilted like an untended crop.

Well, not everyone was a born conversationalist. She wanted to give Sir William the benefit of the doubt. Perhaps he, too, preferred the life of the mind. "Do you have a library at your country estate?" she pressed. A well-read man held pride of place in her estimation.

"Got a Bible and an almanac," he said after thinking about it for a moment.

She suppressed a sigh. "Ah. Well, if you'll excuse me."

"Of course!" he exclaimed almost with relief.

She hadn't walked more than a few steps when she overheard another gentleman speaking with Sir William.

"Don't bother with that one," the man said. Sarah recognized his voice as Lord Pennerly, a young buck eagerly searching for a wealthy, titled bride.

"Why not?" Sir William asked.

"Pretty enough, in an odd sort of way. Got that nose on her, and that overlarge mouth."

"True," Sir William mused.

"She's *the Watching Wallflower*. Only observes, never participates. Always watching, thinking."

"Don't like the ones that think too much," Sir William huffed.

"No one does," Lord Pennerly answered. "And she's the worst of them. Find yourself a nice, sweet, *sparkling* girl, Sir William. You needn't squander your efforts on the Wallflower."

"My thanks for the advice," said the older man, and they both drifted off to find more *sparkling* females.

Sarah didn't even bother blushing or feeling humiliated. Things like that happened with far too much frequency for her to feel anything beyond mild irritation anymore.

A handful of guests lingered in a corridor leading off the terrace. Here, in the dim passage, people engaged in flirtatious conversation, away from curious, speculative eyes. Too engrossed in their own interests and dramas to notice one slightly tall wallflower skulking away from a garden party, no one paid Sarah any attention as she passed. She was glad at this moment that, to the *ton,* she was unremarkable. Had she been a diamond of the first water, and one of the lights of the Season, surely she wouldn't have had as much freedom. And freedom—and the chance to write—was what she desired.

Bypassing the retiring room at the end of the hallway, she turned a corner. The kind of solitude she needed wouldn't be found amongst a bunch of gossiping women fussing over their gowns and hair. Instead, she glided down another, smaller corridor, testing doorknobs, the metal rattling softly beneath her gloved hand. Many were locked.

At last, one door gave way. Sarah peered inside. The curtains were pulled back, revealing a snug, unoccupied room.

Sarah slid inside and shut the door behind her. Unfortunately, there was no lock, but she supposed it might look especially suspicious if she opted to barricade herself inside a private room. Drifting farther inside, she kept one eye on the door as she perused her surroundings. There was a bookshelf with a few slim volumes, a settee, and, as she'd noticed, a little lady's desk.

No other invitation was needed.

Sarah sat down at the desk and opened her reticule. She pulled out a few sheets of paper folded into quarters, along with a small silver pencil.

Relief surged through her, like the sweetest balm. She took a moment simply to luxuriate in the sensation of holding a writing implement, blank paper in front of her. Heaven. Exactly what she'd been craving all day.

After a moment, she began to write.

> *Lady Josephina surveyed the garden party with a sharp, predatory eye. She couldn't stop the smile that curved her wide, sensuous lips. Sarah also smiled, much like her heroine. The story's possibilities opened up like a corridor filled with doors, each of them swinging wide to admit her to another place, another world. Where to go next?*
>
> *So many men to choose from! Which one would come home with her to share her bed? Or perhaps she might select more than one lover. After all, she was a woman of expansive appetites. Seldom could she find satisfaction in the arms of a lone man.*

Oh, this would be a good one. Sarah could already tell. Her pencil flew across the page, muting the sounds of the chatter in the background.

Beneath her red satin bodice, her breasts grew tight and heavy. Josephina enjoyed the hunt as much as a lioness did, but it was in the satiation of her hungers that she found true satisfaction. Besides, her bed was large enough to accommodate an entire orgy if she so desired. She knew this from firsthand experience. There had been those Spanish sailors . . .

The tension that knotted Sarah's shoulders and coiled in her stomach slowly spiraled away. She closed her eyes and let the warm, comfortable sensation drift through her. At last, she could be her true self.

Lady Sarah Frampton. The Duke of Wakefield's daughter. The Watching Wallflower. She was all of these things, and none of them. For her true identity was known to her readers as the Lady of Dubious Quality, author of several extremely successful and popular erotic novels.

No one at the marquess's garden party knew. Not a single person. Including her own mother.

Precisely the way Sarah needed it. Should anyone find out that the Lady of Dubious Quality was, in fact, Lady Sarah, the scandal would be devastating. Even a man as powerful as her father might not be able to help her weather such a storm. The family might not be received by others, while she would be cut off from all of Society, forced to flee to the country or abroad. Perhaps she'd have to assume a new name, since all decent people would have nothing to do with her, knowing that she was the author of salacious novels.

And yet, despite the fact that she knew she courted danger by writing and publishing such work, Sarah couldn't stop herself. She might as well give up eating and drinking. Writing was *essential*. She'd known it from the age of four, when she'd learned how to hold a pen. Her parents had often had to take away her quill and paper and chase her outside to play, or else threaten her with no paper for a week if she didn't put down her pen and go to bed. And when she hadn't obeyed, and they had taken away her foolscap, she'd written in the end papers and margins of her books.

Sarah scanned the sheet in front of her, smiling ruefully to herself as she read what she'd written.

Everyone wanted her to be decorative, useless and virginal, but penning erotic stories pushed blood through her veins. If only Lord Allam's garden party was as debauched and free as Lady Josephina would have liked. If only Sarah could be as liberated as her heroine. Her sensual education had started only a few years ago when a certain book had fallen into her hands by mistake, but ever since then, her eyes had been opened, and the world was entirely different. Yet Lady Sarah had a reputation to preserve, so, rather than experiencing the sensual realm in real life, she freed herself with writing about a woman on a sensuous hunt, searching for the perfect sexual prey.

After using a small knife to sharpen her pencil, Sarah began to write again.

She had heard that Lord E. had a most impressive—

"Sarah? Sarah?" The doorknob rattled.

Damn.

She barely had time to shove the paper into her reticule before the door opened. Her mother sailed into the room.

"What are you doing?" Mama demanded. "Writing? What have I said about that?"

"It's just a garden plan." Sarah hated gardening and scrupulously avoided it.

Lady Wakefield made a tsking sound of displeasure. "You shan't find a husband scribbling in rooms, all alone."

In truth, no fewer than four offers of marriage had been presented to Sarah in her first two years out. And Sarah had refused every one of them. But neither she nor her mother would discuss that—it was too frustrating.

Her mother sighed. "You're spoiled by your father. Too many books ruin a girl's mind. Not to mention reading causes wrinkles, just here." She pointed to the corners of her eyes.

"You have no wrinkles, Mama," Sarah pointed out.

"Because the only thing I'll read is *La Belle Assembleé,*" her mother said proudly, "and even then, I make sure I don't peruse it for more than ten minutes at a time. You'd be wise to follow my example, Sarah."

"I'll try." There were many days, especially when Sarah was younger and believed in—and wrote—fairy tales, that she hoped herself to be a warrior queen from a mythical realm. Perhaps she was a foundling. Yet she and her mother bore a striking resemblance to each other . . . appearance-wise. And she had her father's love of reading to prove that she was, in fact, an ordinary girl, not a fierce monarch wielding an enchanted sword rather than an embroidery needle.

"Come now," her mother snapped. "We'll return to the party at once and make ourselves agreeable. I saw how you walked away from Sir William."

It was useless to protest. Lady Wakefield would only goad and harangue Sarah until she agreed. Perhaps soon, in another few years, her mother would finally accept defeat and realize Sarah would never marry.

With an internal sigh, Sarah rose from the desk. She secretly patted her reticule, making sure that her writing was safe. After giving the little room one last, longing glance, she followed her mother toward the garden in the back.

"Honestly, Sarah," Lady Wakefield protested as they walked, "I cannot understand why you don't give potential suitors any encouragement. The years are ticking by, my dear."

A fact Sarah was counting on. Telling her mother outright that marriage would never happen was impossible—Lady Wakefield would only see that as a gauntlet thrown down, a challenge to be met. Her efforts to pair her only daughter off would become unendurable.

They finally reached the terrace outside, and Sarah and her mother gazed out at the assembled guests.

"Smile, darling," her mother said in an undertone. "You look far too serious and, well, *literate*."

"I'll endeavor to appear more vacant," Sarah replied. Her mother shot her a sour glance.

Sarah looked out over the party full of Society's finest male specimens. Nearly all of them were titled. A good many had decent fortunes. Most still had all their teeth and hair. A few were known to be fond of their drink and gambling. The majority of them would make for acceptable husbands—after all, love wasn't a requirement of marriage.

But what of passion? What of fire? She'd read and written so much of all-consuming hunger, that magnetism that pulled two bodies together and made it impossible to part. Could Sarah ever find such a thing for herself, or was it exclusive to the pages of novels? Her new character, Lady Josephina, couldn't be the only woman to know it.

None of the men in this garden had the allure of the heroes from her books. None of them made her feel that intangible, ravenous physical need. The only desires she truly felt now were those to write, but when it came to sensual urgings, she felt . . . uninspired. The men she encountered didn't stir her blood. Certainly never enough to give up what little power she had. Once she was married, she became a man's property. She'd never be able to write again.

Now, as Sarah gazed around her at the charming garden scene, words formed in her head to describe it.

The Marquess of Allam always threw a wonderful garden party, thanks in large part to the efforts of Lady Allam. The garden itself was a jewel tucked away from the busy Mayfair streets—French doors opened from the house onto a wide, paved veranda, with a spacious terrace leading down to gravel-covered paths. Though it was late in the season, some hardy blooms still made their appearance along the walkways, and here and there stood silent, mossy statuary, gazing out with sightless eyes at the parade of London's most fashionable elite.

Small tables were arrayed throughout the garden, little islands of conversation where guests could take their rest and enjoy the plentiful refreshments. Autumnal sunlight shone down in pale splendor.

Sarah took a seat on a hard little iron chair with the widows and matrons, an array of iced cakes and tea set on a table before them. Her mother wandered off somewhere to maintain her status as one of the older set's most charming and influential women.

While Sarah appreciated a fine garden as much as anyone else, she longed to be back inside, at her desk with pen in hand, either writing her newest tale or else working on her edits for her latest book. Her publisher could barely contain his fiscal excitement over the Lady's next work—*The Clean and the Filthy,* about the amorous adventures of a laundress. That rewrite wasn't going to be completed with her stuck at a garden party.

Sarah was uninterested in trying to drag out pointless conversations with gentlemen she had no desire to meet. Considering how many of their gazes flicked over her with barely any notice, she didn't think any of them wanted to meet her, either. Sir William scrupulously avoided her gaze. Sitting as she was with the more mature women, her place on the shelf as a spinster looked decidedly certain.

With her practiced scribbler's eye, she looked

around at the assembly, seeking food for her Muse. Men and women milled about the terrace and down into the garden itself, exchanging conversation deftly. The air glinted with bright talk. Gazes danced like butterflies fluttering on the cool breeze.

To one side was a hedge maze—a convenient place for a tryst. The lilac bushes were also thick, making for a good location to sneak a kiss . . . or something more. Given the way some of the faster set looked at one another, the possibility was a distinct one. She could well imagine it now. The woman in the pink gown would brush up close to a gentleman, pretending to drop her fan. When he'd retrieve it, their fingers would brush. Once, twice. A shared look, fraught with meaning. Their gazes would glide over toward the maze. Shared understanding. Then the woman would float into the maze and await her soon-to-be lover.

Lady Josephina could find a lover in a maze . . . Sarah tucked that idea away for later.

If only Sarah could skip marriage and go straight to being an adventurous widow. Then, at last, she could do precisely what she pleased—write, take lovers— away from the strict confines of what Society expected of her. Perhaps if she went away to America and reinvented herself . . . but that would mean losing her family and everything she'd ever known.

"Does anyone have need of spiritual counsel?" one of the matrons next to her murmured slyly.

Another older woman snickered.

Following the other women's glances, Sarah looked toward the top of the terrace, where a man was stepping out onto the flagstones.

A newcomer had arrived.

His simple clerical black highlighted the beauty of his long, sculpted face and high cheekbones. His lips weren't precisely full, but they held a surprising degree of sensuality for a man—especially a man of the cloth. Even from a distance, his blue eyes shone like warm tropical seas. His clothing also served to emphasize his lean, tall body, as well as the width of his shoulders and narrowness of his hips. The curls in his blond hair seemed to beg for a woman's fingers, urging them to tease and play.

He looked around at the assembly with a careful gaze, a hint of reserve in his expression. Whoever he was, he wasn't precisely pleased to be here, but neither did he reject the setting. Like her, he seemed to be cautiously testing.

But he did not shine with a holy light. If anything, he radiated an earthy quality.

A story formed in her mind, like shards of pottery assembling themselves into a whole. He was the product of a nobleman's tempestuous affair with a strolling actress. A man who had seen much sin and wickedness in the world. Rather than follow in his mother's footsteps by living on the stage, the stranger sought goodness and a sense of purpose by taking up clerical orders. Yet he struggled every day with his mother's hot blood urging him to give in to the sensuality that pulsed through him.

"I hope we won't be treated to a sermon," a matron near Sarah muttered.

"Maybe if I give him a donation for his church, he'll leave us alone," said another older woman.

"Oh," sighed a matron, "it might be amusing to sully a man of the cloth."

The women tittered amongst themselves. Then they caught sight of Sarah and smothered their laughter. She fought a sigh. She had that effect on people—always dampening their amusement or excitement, as if her status as an unwed woman of excellent reputation meant she couldn't appreciate such sentiment.

I want to live, too!

But who could she say that to? How could she break the golden tether that bound her in place? Impossible.

Lord Allam strode up to the clerical man—he was too young to be that high up in the Church hierarchy, so that must make him . . . a curate? A vicar? Ah, now she remembered. As Lord Allam shook the man's hand, she recalled that her host's nephew was a country vicar. Though she'd never met the man before, she knew him by reputation as a serious and scholarly fellow. No one had ever told her how bloody handsome he was, however.

Sadly, he wasn't a highwayman or a pirate. Good looking as he was, the vicar couldn't compete with the men of her fantasies. He had probably never heard of half the sexual acts she wrote about—more the pity. Furthering their education together could be interesting.

She shook her head, dismissing the thought. If anyone was to show the vicar the ways of the flesh, it wouldn't be her, a duke's unspoiled daughter.

Lord Allam took the vicar around, introducing him to various guests. Sarah watched the newcomer closely, seeing how he seemed to give everyone particular regard, as if each person with whom he spoke had been the most engaging and interesting one he'd ever met. His smile was luminous, filling his face. No wonder this man was in the Church.

At last Lord Allam reached the collection of chairs where Sarah and the matrons sat. The women continued to sit as the vicar bowed.

"Ladies," said Lord Allam, "may I present to you my nephew, Mr. Jeremy Cleland."

Learning their names, Mr. Cleland bent over the women's hands one by one. At last he reached Sarah.

"Lady Sarah Frampton," Lord Allam said. "My nephew."

Sarah extended her hand. Mr. Cleland took it.

He wore no gloves, and though she wore hers, she was engulfed in warmth the moment his fingers clasped hers. A current pinged through her body, hot as summer.

They both went still. His eyes widened, as if he, too, felt that sudden spark, that unexpected heat. Mr. Cleland seemed frozen with shock. As though the truth of himself surprised even him.

Perhaps everything she'd imagined for him, all that sensual potential, hadn't been entirely her imagination. Maybe it was real and alive within him.

She cleared her throat, struggling to regain her balance. "Where is your parish, Mr. Cleland?"

"Rosemead, Lady Sarah, in Devonshire." He had a velvet voice, low in register, that stroked along her neck and up her calves.

"You must consider London a dreadful pandemonium after the pleasures of the country."

"I find the greatest collection of demons to be here,"

he said with a smile, tapping the center of his chest with his free hand.

"How very true."

He still grasped her hand in his. They realized it at the same time. She and Mr. Cleland broke apart like the severing of a silk cord.

The women nearby looked from Sarah to Mr. Cleland, and back again, clearly intrigued. As if they, too, finally saw what Sarah had known all along. This man was much more than his simple black clothing. It merely hid the fires that blazed within him.

"If you'll excuse me," Lord Allam said, "I must see to my other guests."

Once he had gone, Sarah was left with Mr. Cleland. They regarded one another with curiosity, each trying to gauge the other after their strange, brief moment. There seemed no accounting for it. They had just met.

Maybe he saw what she recognized. Perhaps the heat that smoldered within each of them called out to the other, like to like.

If she hadn't been trapped by propriety, she would have asked him what it was that he sought. What drove him, pushed him. A faint tension rose up in him, as if he, as well, struggled with something internally—a decision to be made, a desire suppressed.

Mr. Cleland leaned down. "Would you care to stroll in the garden with me, Lady Sarah?"

"It would be my pleasure." She never accepted such offers, but the response leapt from her mouth before she could think twice.

He offered her his arm.

To her shock, she stood and took it.

Chapter 3

My heart pounded and I could scarce catch my breath. I pressed a hand to my chest, waiting in an agony of terror as I heard the jingle of the highwayman's spurs as he approached my carriage. I felt the sword of Damocles hanging perilously above my head. What would he do to me?

The door to my carriage opened suddenly. A man with a cloth covering the lower half of his face stood there, a pistol in his hand. But his hazel eyes widened when he beheld me. His free hand slowly came up and tugged down his disguise—revealing an exceptionally handsome face. He had a sensualist's mouth and coin-clean features. His raven-dark hair was pulled back into a queue. Indeed, I'd never beheld a man so attractive. My fear began to dissolve . . .

The Highwayman's Seduction

Tall as Sarah was, Mr. Cleland stood taller by half a head. It was oddly comforting to find herself finally looking up into a man's eyes, rather than down at his hairline—though she mostly enjoyed not having to stare up at anyone. Even so, it felt strangely nice to for once be smaller than, to be worth protecting and shielding.

Not that Mr. Cleland would defend her against an attack by a band of brigands. Bandits and buccaneers were in short supply in Mayfair, for one, and she doubted that a vicar knew much by way of sword fighting or fisticuffs. But there went her writer's imagination again, inventing things that could never—would never—happen.

Still, as they walked sedately together down one of the garden paths, she could sense in him a kind of barely restrained physicality. He certainly didn't move like a soft scholar. Rather, he had a lean grace, muscular and economical. His arm beneath her hand was delightfully solid and firm. Thinking of it, the clerical black clothing he wore rather suited him, hinting not at moral reserve but at a sort of secret danger.

"What brings you to London, Mr. Cleland?" she asked, breaking the silence.

He hesitated, then said, "Visiting family."

Interesting, that pause. As though he had another agenda. But vicars were supposed to be upright and honest, the epitome of truthfulness. He had no reason to evade her question. She was likely just spinning tales once more, seeing things that weren't truly there.

She started to speak, then stopped. Why did she hold herself back? He was a vicar. She could be herself with him. He had nothing to gain by their acquaintance, nor she with his. All artifice could be, in essence, lost, and nothing would suffer for it. What was the point of empty politeness? It served no purpose other than to fill time with shallow words and hollow gestures.

Liberated from her hesitancy, the words flowed freely.

"An interesting choice for a younger son," she said. "The Church."

His brows rose at her frankness, but he didn't look affronted. Instead, he seemed intrigued. "My brother is a barrister, but there's too much arguing in the law."

"Don't care for conflict, then," she noted.

"Not for its own sake, no." He appeared thoughtful. "There are clerical disputations, but they exist to make people's lives better. The law seems engineered to be as complex and difficult as possible. It supports itself. It couldn't exist unless it wanted to muddle everything."

She matched his pace down the path, but she didn't pay attention to the flowers and statues around them. "Then one could fashion change from within, if one so desired it."

"I'm but one man," he pointed out. "It would take much more than I could possibly effect to dismantle hundreds of years of tradition."

"The tradition of muddling," she said with a smile.

"The very one." He smiled back at her, engulfing her in warmth. Gracious, did the man have a lovely smile.

"What of soldiering?" she asked.

He shook his head. "Much as I like the idea of defending my country," he said, "I have no desire to order men around. Especially if that means commanding them to face their own deaths." He glanced at her. "Forgive me. That was . . . indelicate."

She waved her hand. "No reason to apologize. In all

honesty," she confessed, taking up more of the spirit of candor, "I appreciate you not shielding me from such matters. Most men think women cannot manage to hear anything that might suggest unpleasant—even ugly—truths."

"It's my experience that women are far stronger than men," Mr. Cleland said, guiding them around a dry fountain.

She contemplated this. "How so?"

"They shoulder the burdens of life and death much more gracefully than men."

What a surprise to hear anyone, especially a male, say such a thing. No one had ever voiced such an opinion to her before. "I imagine that, as a vicar, you must see a lot of the harsher sides of the world."

He tilted his head in acknowledgment. "Sickness and, yes, death. But I also see its beauty. Marriages and births."

"This must all seem frivolous to you." She glanced back toward where the party continued, a riot of bright colors and empty conversation.

"On the contrary. Darkness and light exist side by side. We can't have one without the other."

She laughed. "My goodness, you sounded very vicar-like just then."

He grinned in response. "I did, didn't I? Can you write a letter to my archbishop and let him know?"

"'Mr. Jeremy Cleland conducted himself with the utmost vicarish behavior in the midst of a godless garden party.'"

"Beautifully phrased, Lady Sarah."

She couldn't stop her own grin. "I have some skill

with a quill." As soon as the words left her mouth, she wanted to grab them back and secret them under a rock. She couldn't very well *brag* about her writing. Ladies didn't boast, and certainly not about the erotic novels they penned.

"You write?" he asked.

"A little," she murmured. "Trifles." It galled her a little to have to hide what she labored so hard over, but circumstance necessitated false modesty. "Nursery rhymes for my nieces and nephews." Which wasn't entirely untrue. She had written a few little bits of childish doggerel for the amusement of her elder brothers' children.

Still, she waited for Mr. Cleland to say something about women knowing their place, or how it wasn't proper for ladies to engage in intellectual pursuits.

Instead, he only nodded. "An enviable skill. I have to write a sermon every Sunday, and it's like swimming the Atlantic every time. Cold at first, then exhausting after a while."

No lecture? No sidelong look of censure?

What an interesting man.

"Yet you make the swim every week," she pointed out.

"So I do," he agreed amiably. "You'd think I'd have developed some muscles after all that exercise, but I feel like I flounder every time."

"Somehow, I doubt that." She felt the strength of his body. He had to provide his congregation with spiritual comfort and guidance. Just a few words with him and she knew. Sharp mind, honed wit and intellect. And there was that extraordinary face of his, so full of beauty and sensuality all at once. How had the women sitting with her earlier not seen it? Surely others had to.

Together, they fell into a companionable quiet, making their way slowly up and down the paths. Sarah glanced toward the hedge maze, her imagination spinning. Wouldn't it be delicious to steal a kiss from Mr. Cleland? He did have a lovely mouth and was handsome as . . . well, as sin. Talking with him held its share of pleasures. He didn't act like other men, trying to curry her favor. Nor was he dismissive. He listened to her, treated her as though she had worthwhile opinions.

For the first time in . . . she couldn't remember when . . . she enjoyed conversing with a man. Exhilaration moved through her. As though she was waking up from a long sleep, to blink happily in the sun.

"Do you enjoy reading, Lady Sarah?" he asked.

"Very much," she answered. "Sentimental novels are my favorite, though I'm not supposed to say so."

"Why not?" he wondered with genuine surprise.

"Because they aren't edifying or educational. Because they teach me to expect things out of life that aren't really possible."

He made a scoffing sound. "Rubbish. Not the books, but those opinions. There's nothing wrong with a little escape. And there's certainly nothing at fault with teaching someone how to hope for a better life."

"So you aren't going to press me with some spiritual texts? Things that teach me the value of patience and humility?"

He laughed, and the sound was like brandy, rich and full. "Saints preserve me from moralizing literature.

While I do read my Bible every day, I find myself particularly fond of the novel *Waverley* and the poems of Blake."

"The battle scenes in *Waverley*," she said, excitement rising at mention of the book. "I swore I heard the gunfire and smelled the blood and powder."

"Have you read *Guy Mannering,* by the same author?" he pressed with equal excitement.

"I even saw it performed as a play at Covent Garden earlier this year," she exclaimed.

He looked blissful. "That must have been wonderful."

"'Wonderful' is a paltry word compared to the experience."

"How I envy you," he said, a touch of wistfulness in his voice.

Now it was her turn to laugh. "I'm hardly enviable, Mr. Cleland."

His expression shifted to thoughtfulness. "I wonder why you might say that."

"I have . . . everything a woman could want," she acknowledged.

"Such as?"

"Wealth, position. If there's a material thing that I desire, I simply have to ask, and it's mine." She shook her head. "And I'm grateful for these things. I truly am. And yet . . ."

"And yet . . . ?" he prompted gently.

"It comes at a high price," she admitted.

"What is that price?"

She considered this. Never before had she spoken so openly to anyone. Not her friends or her family. But here, now, to be with this man, and to consider the foundations of her life, was both odd and deeply right. At last, she said, "Freedom."

He contemplated her perceptively. "Must be very restricting," he murmured. "The responsibilities of your position in Society. Not to mention the fact that you're a woman." He blushed a little at that word.

It was a charming—but also gently erotic—blush. Her own cheeks warmed.

He continued, "You haven't the liberty that a man in your place might have."

"Indeed, no." She gave a small, strained laugh. "You must think me dreadful to take issue with my admittedly fortunate circumstance."

He fell briefly silent. "I know a little about having one's role be predetermined." They stopped walking, and she gazed up at him. Cool sunlight carved hollows in his cheeks and gilded his eyelashes. "Being a vicar means I must be a model to everyone in my parish. I have to be more pious, more humble, more self-sacrificing. I have to be better at everything while also being deferential. I certainly cannot admit to being an ordinary human man."

Their gazes held at that word, *man*. Awareness of him sizzled. His height, his physicality. That suppressed desire. Her own body warmed in response.

She tilted her head to one side, imagining what it had to be like to live such a restrained life. "Sounds exhausting."

"Not unlike being a duke's daughter, I imagine." He smiled at her, and that lush warmth continued to gather through her.

"I never would have thought I'd have much in common with a vicar," she said with a laugh.

"Nor I with you," he answered, his smile softening. "But here we are, in this garden."

"So we are." Strange how the world worked, that she would discover a man such as him on a day that had started out so perfectly ordinary. It was almost . . . miraculous. Did miracles happen? She went to church as a matter of form, not faith, though the ritual gave her comfort. Still, it was a revelation to learn that men of God were mortal, just like everyone else, with the same needs and frustrations anybody might experience.

She ought to have imagined as such. In her mind, she often imbued people with hidden motivations and secrets. He was no exception.

"And does your . . . wife . . . feel as you do?" She inwardly grimaced at her lack of tact, but she needed to know whether or not he had someone in whom he could confide. It seemed a shame, a right shame, that he should be alone in this world.

"No wife, I'm afraid," he said with a self-deprecating grin.

A strange relief shot through her. She reasoned that it was because it wouldn't do to flirt with a married man. "Stick around the London Season long enough," she replied. "An earl's son, with a living? You'll make someone a fine catch."

"I'm just a humble country vicar," he answered. "Hardly the stuff of a doting mama's dream for her daughter."

"You might be surprised." Without a doubt, she and Mr. Cleland could never be a match. Even if she wanted to marry, he stood too far beneath her to warrant any possibility of courtship. Duke's daughters and vicars—

though they might be sons of earls—made for an improbable, mismatched pairing.

A vicar could never be married to a woman who wrote anonymous erotic novels, either. The very idea was ruinous.

But damn and all the other curse words she wasn't allowed to use—she *liked* Mr. Cleland. The way his mind worked, how he spoke to her like a person of equal intelligence, the sensual quality within him. It wasn't all her writer's fancy. Something burned in him, and it lured her closer, closer, drawn toward the mysteries of this man. Even Lady Josephina wouldn't find someone half as interesting in her adventures.

And . . . he was exceptionally attractive. In a way she'd never experienced with another man before. She'd met handsome gentlemen in the past, but Mr. Cleland lit a spark within her, low and hot.

A shame, really, that Sarah couldn't have been someone else. Because if she had been . . . she might have given him serious consideration.

But that was never to be. She was who she was, and he was who he was, and they would have to be friends—nothing more.

So absorbed was she in this thought that she didn't hear footsteps approaching until they were almost upon her. Turning, she saw her mother coming down the path, wearing a pinched expression.

"There you are," Lady Wakefield said impatiently. She nodded at Mr. Cleland, barely acknowledging him. Sarah felt a small stab of shame at her mother's rudeness. But a vicar didn't warrant much attention. "This sun has given me a headache. It's time to go."

"Yes, Mama." Before the words had left her mouth, her mother had spun on her heel and stridden off back toward the main house.

Sarah offered Mr. Cleland a remorseful smile. "I'm so sorry."

"Nothing to apologize for," he said easily, and it was clear he meant it. He bowed. "It was a genuine pleasure to meet you, Lady Sarah."

"I feel the same way." They smiled at each other, for a long time neither, it seemed, willing to move away.

"Now, Sarah," her mother called out over her shoulder.

Sarah sighed. Her gaze drifted back to the hedge maze. Could she drop her fan? As they both bent to retrieve it, she might whisper to him an invitation to meet her there in a few moments. And then . . . She could taste those gently curved lips of his. Oh, she'd experienced a few chaste kisses before, but never anything she truly desired. But she wanted to kiss Mr. Cleland. She craved feeling his mouth against hers, and seeing if her imagination was correct about him.

He, too, looked at the maze. Was he thinking the same thoughts? Did he want to savor her? A delectable thought, one that made her feel both languid and powerfully alive all at once.

Their gazes met. He turned gorgeously pink.

He *was* thinking of kissing her!

"Now, Sarah!" her mother snapped, waiting.

"I must go." Turning, she walked toward her mother. Who would talk to him now that she was going? Yet he had such an easy manner that he'd find no difficulty securing more conversation.

Lady Wakefield stood on the terrace, waiting. She

looked confused. "I'd no idea you had need of religious guidance."

"I don't," Sarah answered.

"Then why bother spending time with that man?"

"Because he intrigued me."

Surprise crossed Lady Wakefield's face. "You honestly wanted to talk with him?"

"I did. He's . . ." Earthy. Intelligent. Unique. "Interesting."

Her mother stared at her for a moment. "Good gracious, you were actually *considering* him?"

Though it was an impossibility, Sarah said, "I might have been."

Lady Wakefield clicked her tongue. "Interesting or not, he's no match for you."

"We got along rather well, actually."

Her mother's lips thinned. "That's not what I meant."

"I know." Sarah took her shawl from the servant who offered it to her, then adjusted it around her shoulders. Oddly, she hadn't felt much of the cold when she had been with Mr. Cleland.

"Don't squander further time with him. He's useless."

The harsh word made Sarah recoil. A protest hovered at her lips. But arguments were pointless with the duchess.

Sarah glanced back toward the garden, where, to her surprise, the vicar remained alone. Instead of looking at the flowers or statues, however, his face was tilted upward, and he contemplated the pale sky, the sunlight painting him brightly.

Was it a shame or precisely right that a man of the

cloth should be so extraordinarily good-looking? When would she see him again?

Wouldn't it make for an interesting Lady of Dubious Quality novel to have a vicar for a hero?

These questions haunted her long after she climbed into the carriage and headed for home.

Chapter 4

"Sir," I gasped, "you have quite terrified me!"

"That is the very last thing I should like to do to you, ma'am," he answered with a voice like rough silk.

"And what is it that you would do with me?"

"I could never say such things to a lady," he answered. He tucked his pistol into his sash. I noticed then that he had large, broad hands, callused from holding the reins of his horse. How might they feel on my bare flesh?

"Oh, sir," I answered, "I am no lady. Not in the truer sense of the word . . ."

The Highwayman's Seduction

One couldn't mention publishing in London without thinking almost immediately of Paternoster Row. Even a man as unfamiliar with the modern city as Jeremy was knew this. Publishers crammed together down the street, the air alive with the flow of ideas and words. Nearby was the bustle of Spitalfields Market and the dignified splendor of St. Paul's.

The lively market and its surroundings interested

Jeremy far more than the cathedral, but he felt obligated to spend a few minutes inside, hat removed, his head bowed in solemn contemplation of the task before him. Did the Lord intervene when it came to concerns of salacious literature? Jeremy rather doubted it. Surely, there were greater concerns for the Prime Mover than a handful of inexpensive—though popular—lewd novels.

Once back on the street, Jeremy donned his hat and headed north, toward Paternoster Row. Buildings pressed in closely, radiating with commercial importance. Here, the sacred and the profane were printed side by side, coexisting in the eternal dance of business. There might be art between the leather-covered bindings, but what concerned the serious men of the publishing world was the inarguable truth of money.

Seeing the books brought Lady Sarah's face into his mind. Did she ever come to this part of the city? Most likely not. A duke's daughter had little call to involve herself in the world of masculine trade, though he had a suspicion that she might actually enjoy seeing where the many books she read came from. He wanted to show her this place, to watch her as she explored a new realm, far away from the confines of a life that hemmed her in on every side.

Jeremy had no business thinking of her—a vicar could never cast his thoughts so high as to consider a duke's daughter in any way other than a possible patron.

She had been utterly unexpected, a lovely surprise in the midst of what he'd anticipated to be the usual Society routine. No denying she was a pretty young woman, her soft brown hair slightly curled, her clear gray eyes shining with insightful—almost frightening—intelligence. Her looks were more emphatic than gentle, with those straight eyebrows, assertive nose, and full lips, yet she held an undeniable appeal.

She wasn't like the other soft, easily understood girls, as straightforward as roses. Lady Sarah was more like a tall wildflower, found growing in the secret places of the forest, hidden from the eyes of man but possessing a beauty that belonged to no one but herself.

He'd never thought about the constraints placed upon the daughters of the elite, but she had shown him her diamond-encrusted manacles. And now that his eyes had been opened, it was impossible for him not to feel a thread of . . . pity? Empathy? He wasn't certain.

But he felt it. Something . . . intangible. Linking him with her. A confidence shared only by themselves.

Oh, but the man in him responded to far more than her wit or her insight. He'd found himself staring at her petal-pink lips and wondering how they tasted. His gaze had touched along the column of her neck. What would her skin feel like? Did it have a scent? Despite her virginal demeanor, there was an untapped eroticism in her, in the way she turned her face to the sun or absently brushed back a lock of hair, her fingers lingering for a moment to rest upon her own flesh. He couldn't have imagined those seconds at the end of their time together, when he'd looked at the maze in the garden, thinking of what it might take to lure her in there for a stolen touch—and she had been staring at the maze, too, her own eyes filled with wanting.

Did he wish her to be that rare gem that all men dreamed of but never found? The sensual virgin, eager for a man's touch?

He glanced at his reflection in one of the windows. A man in the staid garments of the Church looked back at him. He might think of Lady Sarah, might wonder what kind of lover she could be, and fantasize about her many tastes and textures, but she would always be a dream, forever out of reach. Even though his father was an earl, Jeremy had little fortune besides what he earned from his living. Duke's daughters didn't consider vicars as potential husbands. He and Lady Sarah were simply too far apart. He might as well court a constellation.

Not the most happy thought, but it brought him back to Earth. He was in London for a reason, and that reason wasn't the futile attempt to woo a woman who'd have nothing to do with him.

Still, he couldn't help the excitement rising up in him at the thought of when he might see her again. Between Lady Sarah and searching for the Lady of Dubious Quality, the tedium of his recent existence had certainly transformed into something exciting and stimulating.

Checking the address he had written down on a scrap of paper, Jeremy searched out one particular sign. He dodged crowds of soberly dressed men, as well as wagons carting off books to be sold all over the city and the country. Compared to Mayfair, the noise here was terrific. How could anyone concentrate on the printed word when the audible one held so much sway?

At last, he came to a sign that read STALHAM & SONS. From the outside, it appeared to be an ordinary business, with a bay window fronting the street. Jeremy peered through the glass, cupping his hand to see better. Men bent over rows of desks, stacks of paper piled up all around them. A lad in a cap and ink-stained apron rushed back and forth, delivering sheaves of paper, hauling them away, and generally looking harried. At the far end of the chamber within was a glass door leading to a private office. But the window was smudged and not particularly clean, so Jeremy couldn't make out any further details.

A man carrying a paper-wrapped bundle started to enter the front door, then stopped. "Can I help you, Vicar?" he asked.

"Yes, actually." Jeremy stepped away from the window. Sometimes there were certain advantages to being in the Church, including a small amount of deference from the laity. "I'm looking for the man who runs this business."

"Mr. Stalham Jr., you mean." The man frowned. "What do you want to see him for?"

"I'm afraid that's something I can discuss only with him."

The man shrugged. "Suit yourself. Follow me, then, Vicar."

Jeremy did as the fellow suggested, trailing after him into Stalham & Sons. A few of the clerks looked up from their desks as Jeremy entered.

"We getting into printing sermons and tracts, now?" one wag commented.

"Somehow," Jeremy commented, "I doubt that one book is going to keep you off the paths of vice."

"Oi, he's got you, Drew," another man laughed.

Drew scowled and returned to his work.

"This way, Vicar," said the first chap, who guided Jeremy down the rows of desks to the office at the end. The name LAWRENCE STALHAM JR., PUBLISHER was painted on the door in gold leaf.

All in all, the place looked prosperous and respectable. No signs of lambs being sacrificed to unholy gods, or naked women dancing in a frenzy of pagan madness. They could be printing cookery books and gardening instructions.

Jeremy's guide tapped on the door.

"What the hell do you want, Jones?" shouted a man inside.

"Got a visitor for you, Mr. Stalham."

"Too busy for visitors," came the answer.

Jones looked apologetic, but Jeremy held up his hand. He tried the doorknob and found it open, then let himself in.

"Even for me?" he asked Stalham.

The older man—a decent-looking fellow in a slightly rumpled jacket and waistcoat, his cravat undone—widened his eyes when he beheld Jeremy.

"What's he doing here?" Stalham asked Jones, pointing his finger at Jeremy.

"Why don't you ask him?" Jones answered.

"And I'd be more than happy to answer that question," Jeremy said, "in private."

The publisher raked his fingers through his thinning hair, making it stand on end, but then he shook his head. "All right, come in and shut the door behind you, Vicar."

"Thank you, Mr. Jones," Jeremy said, giving the man's hand a shake.

"Put in a good word for me," Jones replied. "With Him."

"I shall."

With that, Jones strode away, leaving Jeremy still standing outside Stalham's office.

The publisher waved. "Come in, Vicar, and take a seat. Is it 'Reverend'?"

"Just 'vicar' or 'Mr. Cleland' is fine." Jeremy closed the door, then sat down. Like the rest of the business, Stalham's office appeared perfectly ordinary, with galleys for books heaped up on tables, and manuscripts piled here and there. A miniature of Stalham's wife adorned his desk, along with some correspondence. But there were no signs proclaiming the Lady of Dubious Quality's identity, no letters with her (or his) signature announcing who she (or he) might be.

Stalham caught Jeremy's inquisitive gaze and returned it with a puzzled look.

"We're not in the market for religious works, Mr. Cleland," the publisher noted, interlacing his fingers over his stomach.

"Sermons for my parish are the extent of my writing endeavors."

"Then what brings you to Stalham and Sons? My family runs a respectable business and has done so since the time of our monarch's father."

"There are those who might say that what you publish isn't entirely respectable," Jeremy noted.

From his pocket, he pulled out *The Highwayman's Seduction*.

Stalham's eyes went wide again. "Didn't know the clergy read our humble little books." He leaned forward. "Life in the parish getting a little dull, eh, Mr. Cleland?"

Though it was the truth, Jeremy maintained his collected demeanor. He had been given deportment lessons as a child, after all.

"I would like," he said coolly, "to know more about this Lady of Dubious Quality."

"What about her?"

Was that a clue? Was the author truly a woman, or was Stalham merely trying to throw him off the scent?

"Who is she?" Jeremy asked.

A corner of the publisher's mouth turned up. "Want to meet her?"

"I simply want to know her identity."

"Why? You could be trying to get her to find religion and stop writing her books."

"Call it intellectual curiosity," Jeremy said. "It has nothing to do with faith. I merely want to know what kind of person could pen such works."

"You aren't going to shut her down?"

Jeremy couldn't outright lie, so he offered, "I'd like to talk with her." Which was true. What made someone write such works, especially if they had so much to lose by being discovered? It had to be some kind of compulsion. Unless they needed the money that badly. Perhaps whoever it was might be a commoner. Or an impoverished noble.

Whoever it was, Jeremy needed to understand that desire, that drive. Perhaps something could be learned there, though he wasn't certain what. Vicars and authors of smut generally had little to unite them.

Yet the world was a strange and mysterious place. It shifted and changed from moment to moment, revealing connections that might never have been seen before. Consider himself and Lady Sarah. They were two people with very little in common, yet it turned out they shared an attraction and a potential bond.

Lady Sarah wouldn't think much of him if he revealed his true reason for coming to London—as though it might taint him somehow. Perhaps, if their paths ever crossed again, she would ignore him or be cuttingly polite and distant.

A pain stabbed in the center of his chest. His fingers rubbed absently at his heart. His health was good, so why did he feel this ache?

Was it . . . the thought of losing any connection with Lady Sarah? She seemed to be one of the true bright spots here in the city, and he was loath to lose her light.

"Talk?" Stalham asked.

"Talk," Jeremy echoed. He hoped God would forgive him the omission. It was for the greater good, he hoped.

Stalham scratched at his face. "Even if I wanted to tell you who the Lady was—and I don't, because she sells more books being anonymous—I couldn't."

"Why not?" Jeremy demanded.

"It's all done through secret channels, you see." Stalham stood and paced to one corner of his office, hooking his thumbs into his braces. "She routes all her manuscripts through a fourth party."

"Who?"

"No idea." Stalham shrugged. "Once I tried to have the chap that delivers the manuscripts followed, but he shook the tail—that is, he lost the man I had follow him."

"You must have tried more than once," Jeremy deduced.

"Half a dozen. All came up empty. I even hired me a Bow Street Runner to get the job done." He shook his head. "To no avail. They couldn't find her. Whoever she is—"

"Or he," interjected Jeremy.

"Or he," Stalham allowed with a nod, "they don't want to be found. They're damn—I mean, quite— careful."

On that, Jeremy had to agree. The steps taken by the Lady to protect her identity were indeed elaborate. It would take a considerable amount of thought and deduction to ferret her out. Yet, far from deterring him from his goal, he found his excitement and interest growing, like a spark that wanted to burn hotter and higher. This was a world of which he knew little—a slightly lurid realm of the senses.

Who was she? Why did she want to protect herself so badly? Idle curiosity shifted, became stronger.

How long had it been since he'd been truly challenged, since his mind had been fully engaged in a pursuit, something beyond his constraining parish duties?

Too long.

"Afraid I can't be much more help to you, Mr. Cleland," Stalham continued. "But, as I said, even if I knew who the Lady was, I wouldn't tell even you, a man of God. The sales of her books help put my children through school and keep my wife in new gowns, so I'd be a blasted fool to give up my golden goose."

A knot of regret formed in Jeremy's stomach. He didn't want to keep Stalham's children from their education, and if finding out the Lady's secret meant the end of that, Jeremy wasn't certain how he could shoulder the guilt. But his father and uncle relied on him to see this task through. He couldn't let them down—because the earl would never permit it. And Jeremy had to consider the good he could accomplish if, given the freedom of more money, he could establish his own charitable organizations. Perhaps he'd assist the widows of men killed in the war, or help returning veterans find employment. Surely that had to outweigh the benefit of a few prurient books.

"Thank you for your time," Jeremy said, rising. He shook Stalham's hand. "Yet you ought to consider publishing something a little more . . . wholesome. It might help out when it comes time for a tallying of accounts." He looked heavenward.

Stalham laughed. "Oh, I'm too far gone for that, Mr. Cleland, but I thank you for your concern. Include me in your prayers."

"I will," Jeremy promised. Given how many inveterate sinners he met here in London, it would take him a full two hours to get through his evening prayers. He prayed for himself, most of all, a man too much on the edge of dissolution. His encounter with Lady Sarah had him kneeling at his bedside for a long, long time the previous evening as he'd tried to stop thoughts of her from filling his mind.

Jeremy exited Stalham's office, then made his way

back through the main room full of desks, where writers and clerks watched him with more curiosity. He smiled and nodded as he went, then emerged onto the street. Setting his hat back on his head, he glanced up at the sky. It was hazy and stained with coal smoke, with a faint sun struggling to pierce the urban gloom.

He'd hit a temporary obstacle, but he would prevail. In that, he was determined.

Chapter 5

*"It would take a great deal of convincing
to prove to me that you weren't a lady," the
highwayman said.*

*"Then step inside my carriage, sir," I replied,
tracing my fingers along the neckline of my
bodice, where my breasts strained against the
silk, "and I shall show you."*

The Highwayman's Seduction

The smell of butter and vanilla perfumed the air, and
the atmosphere was alive with the chatter of dozens of
happy women—and a handful of men. The cakes themselves were works of art, elegantly frosted with flowers
and curlicues, geometric shapes and elaborate fantasias
constructed entirely from sugar. In the window was a
tiny pastoral scene completely fashioned in sugar, and
on a table was a reproduction of Vauxhall, everything
edible.

It was impossible for Sarah to go to Catton's re-
nowned bakery and sweet shop and not have her
imagination stirred. The owner and head baker was a
woman, and Sarah couldn't help but feel a certain kin-

ship with any female who dared make her way in a male-dominated field.

Sarah sat at a little table with her mother, an array of cakes and tea spread before them like a jewel box laid open. Picking up one small frosted delicacy, Sarah admired its intricate piping.

"It's almost too beautiful to eat," she murmured.

"Nothing is too beautiful to eat," the duchess answered. She bit into her cake, and Sarah did the same.

Though it was sweet, it didn't overwhelm her with cloying flavor. Rather, the orange sponge cake slowly evolved with sensory detail, evoking Mediterranean skies, sun-filled courtyards, and the strum of a guitar as ladies drifted in and out of dusky shadows.

"We should have gone to Gunter's," her mother said, surveying the bustling shop. "It's much more fashionable."

Sarah glanced around. Catton's could barely contain all of its customers. A queue formed out the door, and footmen bustled in and out with the shop's signature pale blue boxes tied with brown satin ribbon.

"Catton's is on the verge of stripping Gunter's of its title as London's most popular sweet shop," Sarah pointed out. "Isn't it better to be on the leading edge of fashion, rather than one of its followers?"

"I suppose so," her mother sniffed. She took a bite of her lemon cake and couldn't disguise her look of pleasure. "Well, the food's superior here, at any rate."

"Which reflects well on your taste," Sarah added.

"Oh, enough," the duchess said with a smile. "I know when I'm being patronized. And by my own daughter."

"We're nothing if not familiar with each other's little

tricks." Sarah also smiled. Irritating though her mother might be, there were times they actually enjoyed each other's company, like two shipwreck survivors finding a moment's amusement in between trying to cannibalize each other.

Sarah gazed at the cakes displayed so magnificently along one wall of the shop. There were cakes of every sort—everything anyone could ever want in an alchemy of butter, flour, sugar, and eggs. Little placards described the filling and icing of each one. Orange and lemon, of course, as well as nuts, seeds, dried fruits. A flavor to suit every personality.

If I were a cake, what kind of cake would I be?

Something with a pale, fluffy icing. Hiding a rich, dark interior. Secretly decadent beneath an inoffensive exterior.

And what of her mother? Fruitcake—rich and sweet, sometimes a little too much to take. She'd have an elaborate icing, though, given Lady Wakefield's taste for extravagant hats.

Sarah's glance fell on a couple enjoying a fruit ice together while the woman's maid sat nearby. A courting couple, still excited by the blush of newness. What must that be like? To look forward to seeing someone, to have each moment alight with anticipation and pleasure?

Sarah hadn't seen Mr. Cleland in four days, though she had attended several social gatherings around Town. Each time she had hoped to run into him, but disappointment had inevitably followed. She shouldn't expect a vicar to attend assemblies and tea parties—though he was an earl's son, and he might have had entree to these events. But he hadn't been at any of them. She'd scanned the corners of rooms and chambers' alcoves. All to no avail.

Instead, she would spend her time against the wall, alone save for her mother's company, like always.

It was strange . . . this urge for something besides her writing. This need for more. More of *him*.

If Mr. Cleland were a cake, what sort would he be?

No, he wasn't a cake at all. He'd be something savory and complex. Like a stew, full of many ingredients. Seemingly simple, but capable of complicated, intricate flavor. Something that seduced without trying, all through its own earthiness.

"What are you smiling about?" the duchess asked, breaking Sarah's musings.

"Food," she answered.

"What about it?"

"It's about more than sustenance," Sarah said. "If we only wanted nourishment, we wouldn't have invented so many kinds of food. Like bread, for example. We have dozens and dozens of types, each of them with different flavors, different textures. Clearly, we want more out of our food than just nutrition. We want pleasure and experience."

Her mother stared at her for a moment, a curious, puzzled look on her face. Then, after a pause, she said, "Too many books, too much time at your desk. It's created a maze in your brain from which you cannot escape."

Despite the duchess's words, Sarah's fingers itched again with the need to get back to her quill. What if she wrote a story about a baker, a shop owner, who seduced her patrons through her food? All the emotions the baker felt would be translated into the food she prepared, and one need only sample a bite before being overcome with melancholy, or joy, or lust. There would be scenes where lovers fed each other, or else ate off each other's bodies in a delicious bounty of sugar and flesh. It would be very sticky, but that would be part of the pleasure.

Or perhaps, in her exploits, Lady Josephina could take a baker as a lover. The idea held potential.

"Woolgathering again." The duchess sighed, but not entirely with despondency. "My little dreamer."

"Lady Wakefield! Lady Sarah!" A woman's voice rose above the chatter of the shop.

Looking up, Sarah saw three people approach them—two well-dressed ladies and an equally resplendent dandy. She recognized them as members of the fashionable set, approximately her age but seldom inclined to give her much notice, unless it was to subtly tease her with wit as dry and flavorless as old, stale pastries. She never teased back. It was difficult to fight a sigh at seeing them. The afternoon had been largely an enjoyable one.

"Why, Lady Donleigh, Lord Lynde, Miss Green." Sarah's mother gave a polite smile and nod in greeting as the newcomers bowed and curtsied. "A pleasure."

"You crave something sweet?" Lady Donleigh asked, eyeing the assortment of cakes in front of them.

"Yes, well, I find Gunter's to be a bit *de trop*," Lady Wakefield answered. "The tastes here at Catton's are much more forward thinking, wouldn't you say?"

"Of course," all three agreed at once.

Sarah smiled into her napkin. If these three were cakes, they would be inconsequential fairy cakes, prettily iced but tasting of nothing.

After exchanging pleasantries about the nature of everyone's health, Lord Lynde said, "It's actually quite fortunate that we ran into you here. In two days' time, we plan on attending an exhibit of Oriental art. A private collection on Mount Street that's lately been open for viewing."

"Fascinating," said the duchess, though it was clear she found the notion anything but. To Sarah, however, the idea seemed quite intriguing. She'd read quite a bit about the Orient, especially writings about the secret sexual practices performed by certain individuals. She would have liked one of her characters to be educated in these erotic arts, but her knowledge had been limited by the scope of her reading materials. An exhibition of Asiatic objects and paintings would add more fuel to her creative fire.

"Might Lady Sarah accompany us?" Miss Green asked—though she directed the question to Lady Wakefield and not Sarah herself, as though asking if a dog might come out and play in the park.

Sarah didn't expect the invitation to be directed at *her*. Certainly not from these people, who seemed to enjoy carefully, delicately tormenting her.

"It might prove . . ." Lord Lynde coughed to cover a snicker. ". . . educational."

The other two women giggled.

Sarah didn't like this at all. Much as she wanted to see the Oriental art, something seemed awry. The invitation. The snide laughter. It didn't add up to anything she had an urge to be involved with.

Yet before she could politely decline, her mother spoke.

"Of course Sarah would be delighted to join you!" the duchess exclaimed, beaming.

"Mother, I don't think—"

"Perhaps this could be a way out of that cerebral maze of yours," her mother whispered under her breath.

Sarah answered in a low voice, "Yes, but I don't think they really expect me to go with them to the exhibit."

"They wouldn't offer if they didn't want you to accompany them," the duchess said primly. "Now be a dear and say yes."

The iron in her mother's tone said that there would be no refusing the invitation.

"I would be . . . overjoyed," Sarah finally said to the expectant trio.

"Excellent!" Lady Donleigh clapped her hands. "I'll send the address to you, and we'll all meet there on Thursday."

"Sarah cannot wait," her mother said.

With a few more exchanges of polite nothingness, Lady Donleigh, Lord Lynde, and Miss Green took their leave.

"Now I know how conscripted soldiers feel," Sarah muttered once she and her mother were alone.

"Nonsense," Lady Wakefield said crisply. "It will be an enjoyable afternoon. Get you out of the house and, most importantly, out of your daydreams."

Sarah preferred it in her daydreams. Those dreams fed her purse. They inspired and impelled her. They were lurid and lascivious and wonderful. The world bent to her will in her imagination.

And there, she could keep company with people she wanted to be with . . . such as the alluring Mr. Cleland.

The idea occurred to her later that afternoon. Why *shouldn't* she spend time with someone who actually interested her? If she was going to be dragged along as an object of amusement for the fashionable threesome, oughtn't she find a way to make the experience a little more endurable, more enjoyable? Her characters lived far outside the realms of conventional behavior. In fact, she had written a scene where her amorous washerwoman visited a dockside tavern all on her own—and found two randy sailors to play with. Lady Josephina also didn't care about what Society thought, taking lovers from both high and low ranks.

What if Sarah also disregarded Society's rules, just this once? Could her real life and her dream life blur together, for one afternoon?

Her plan wasn't at all respectable. It was, in truth, a little fast, a little racy. Her heart sped up at the mere thought. Yet she was willing to chance a tiny bit of scandal for herself. It was nothing compared to the scandal of her identity being revealed, after all.

So she went to her desk, sat down, and wrote. Once it was finished, she reread it, grimacing.

Such a dull, prosaic piece of writing. She was constrained by politeness, unable to tell Mr. Cleland about imagining everyone as food. Certainly, she couldn't tell him about the idea she had for a sensuous, magical baker. The alchemy of the kitchen.

All these notions, she longed to tell him. But it was impossible. They didn't know each other that well.

Even if they did, an unmarried woman never spoke of such things to a single man.

God—what if she sent him one of her manuscript pages instead, such as the scene when Lady Josephina amused herself with the stable master? Mr. Cleland's servants might rush in to find him having an attack of apoplexy on the floor of his drawing room, the paper clutched in his hand.

But no, she was certain she was sending him the right letter.

After reviewing the missive once more for spelling errors, she sanded it, then folded it up. Sarah sealed the letter and handed it to a footman.

"Shall I await a reply?" asked the servant.

She considered it. It might be impertinent of her to send the invitation, but it would be even more so if she expected an immediate response. "Not unless he asks."

"Yes, my lady."

The footman bowed and left. Sarah sat and fretted. Would Mr. Cleland reject her bold invitation? How might he react? With shock, repulsion or . . . excitement? There had been a shared heat between them at Lord Allam's garden party. Or perhaps she'd only imagined it. Perhaps all she'd experienced had been his politeness, or the courtesy he showed everyone. Yet by writing this letter and overstepping her bounds, it was possible she'd ensured that Mr. Cleland wouldn't want anything to do with her.

Would he send a reply right away? He was a vicar. Certainly he would be prompt in his correspondence, unless he wasn't home and something else claimed his attention. In that case, she'd likely have to wait.

She paced the length of her sitting room. Writing could distract her. Lady Josephina had tired of her footman, as well as the stable master, and was seeking diversion elsewhere. Who might she encounter next? Perhaps a change of scenery from London . . .

The words were eager to leap off Sarah's quill, but she couldn't find the necessary place in her mind to concentrate. Strange. Writing had always proven a comfort to her, a ready source of solace. Not now. Words tumbled over themselves, refusing to be sorted out.

Heavens, but she hoped this was a temporary condition. It had to be. Otherwise . . . No, she wouldn't contemplate it. A writer unable to find comfort in words was a dreadful creature.

The words could wait just a little while. At least until the footman returned. They'd find their way back to her. That, she had to believe.

Finally she heard a careful, measured tread on the floor outside. She twisted her fingers together, wondering. Had Mr. Cleland answered? Would she have to wait for his response?

There was a knock at the door, and Sarah bid whoever was outside to enter. The door opened, and the footman appeared.

Sarah tried to school her features to look as impassive as possible. "Yes?"

"For you, Lady Sarah." He held out a small letter that bore no seal. After handing it to her, the footman bowed and retreated out the door.

Alone, she examined the missive. Her name was written in a surprisingly bold hand across the front. She'd expected him to write in thin, spidery letters, or with very careful, deliberate penmanship. But here again, Mr. Cleland proved he was far more than his sober exterior would indicate. She pictured him at his desk with a quill in hand, hesitating slightly over his words, but with an overall sense of purpose.

Oh, but she was delaying. She did and did not want to see his answer. She'd survive, surely, if he said no. Wouldn't she? The disappointment would be sharp and cutting—or so she imagined. She hadn't wanted anything this badly in a long, long while. Would she be able to endure it should he reject her? She prayed so, but the whole experience was new and not entirely pleasant.

Best to get it over with. She opened the letter.

Lady Sarah,

I would be most honored to accept your invitation. In truth, I've done little but think of our conversation at my uncle's house, and was most pleased to have received your correspondence. Do send me the details, and I will eagerly await you.

I remain,
Yours, &c.
Jeremy Cleland

Happiness rose up within her, bright as morning. It was a fresh, unfamiliar feeling—one she'd only known in connection with her writing. But now the emotion soared up, unfettered. Should she feel this way? Relieved and joyful? And all for such a simple exchange of words.

Jeremy. Jeremy. She liked the sound of his name, and even whispered it to herself. Yes, it suited him well. If only she could call him by his Christian name rather than the more formal "Mr. Cleland." She wished he might call her by her own name without the honorific "Lady" in front of it—yet that was too forward and intimate for people who had met but once. If she was a character in one of her books, she would be bold and call him by his first name. She'd insist that he do the same with her. Bringing an intimacy between them.

Yet she wasn't one of her characters. She wasn't Lady Josephina. This was reality.

Still, she held his first name close to herself, like a secret.

He would accompany her to the exhibit. Perhaps the fashionable trio might object to him being there. And yet . . . what did it truly matter what they thought? What value was their opinion? Perhaps she could learn from her own books and be daring. She could go after something she wanted. She'd pursued her writing career, after all. Now she could be bold in another part of her life.

Having Jeremy at the exhibition was for herself alone. Where once she might have dreaded the day, now she looked forward to it with the excitement normally reserved for working on a new story. Now, if only for a few hours, she might be the heroine of her own tale.

Chapter 6

At once the highwayman obeyed, climbing eagerly into the carriage and shutting the door behind him. The space within the vehicle was quite small, but it didn't matter, as soon the stranger and I were in each other's arms, caressing one another everywhere. He was strong and solid as an oak, and the instrument in his breeches was just as thick. Never were two people so frenzied, so eager for touch as we were that night. I wasted no time in reaching for his instrument of passion, taking it in my hands and . . .

The Highwayman's Seduction

Jeremy had awakened that morning in a fever of impatience. The afternoon couldn't come quickly enough. And now here he was, only five minutes away from seeing her again. He thought his heart might puncture a hole in his chest from beating so fiercely. All the other young women he'd met had seemed so pallid by comparison. Never speaking their minds. Without that blaze of intelligence or curiosity. Deprived of hidden sensuality.

He stood outside an elegant town home on Mount Street, while her letter continued to reside snugly in his pocket. He'd read and reread it a dozen times between receiving it and today. The words never changed, and he'd memorized them. It didn't stop him from touching the paper she had touched, trying to find hidden meanings in the loops in her penmanship, some secret message disguised in an admittedly restrained, almost dry, letter.

The missive hadn't seemed much like her. Much more contained, less expressive than he would have anticipated from the woman who had spoken with such candor, moved with such unconscious sensuality. Whatever the letter did or didn't reveal, he'd been pleased to receive it. His father had even remarked on Jeremy's high mood after the correspondence.

"Got a grin on you, my lad," the earl had said sternly at breakfast that morning. "Isn't seemly in a man of God."

"Sorry, Father." Jeremy had tried to hide his good spirits after that, though it hadn't been easy. Jeremy knew all about wearing a professional demeanor like clerical robes. Though he was in London, away from his parish, he had to remember he couldn't be entirely himself in the city. Not around his father, anyway.

Why was he so excited? It wasn't as though his association with Lady Sarah could lead to actually courting her. Yet he couldn't make himself see reason.

As he continued to wait, three extremely well-dressed people approached the town house. Two women and one man, all of whom could have stepped from the pages of a fashion magazine. They seemed well aware of their magnificence as they posed and preened in the pale sunlight.

"My goodness," one of the women, a blonde, whispered loudly to her companions. "A vicar. *Here*."

"He's just a priest," the brunette woman answered, not bothering to lower her voice. "Not a panther."

"But what is he doing *here*?" the blonde pressed. "There isn't a church for a quarter of a mile."

"Maybe he's looking for souls to save," the man drawled. "Yours is stained enough, Lady Donleigh."

"Hush, you beast!"

Jeremy pointedly didn't look at the three people as they spoke. Apparently, they thought being a man of God meant he was deaf, like a young man gone old before his time. Either that, or they simply didn't care that he could hear them talking about him so blatantly. Neither option particularly appealed to him.

"I say, Vicar," the man said, approaching, "are you lost?"

Jeremy turned and saw that the man was not only well dressed but handsome, as well. "Thank you for your concern," he answered. "I'm waiting for a friend."

At least he thought he might be a friend to Lady Sarah. He wasn't really certain, since they had only shared a few moments in a sunlit garden.

Yet he did know her. Understood her a little. A young woman with a hidden vein of sensuality, constrained by her role in Society.

"A friend?" the man repeated, as though vicars couldn't possibly have friends.

Just as he spoke, a very elegant carriage with a liveried footman perched on the back and a crest upon the door pulled up alongside them. The footman jumped down from his roost and opened the carriage door. He reached in and took a woman's hand to help her get down from the vehicle.

Lady Sarah. She wore a pale green muslin paired with a darker green spencer, with matching ribbons on her bonnet. The color made her glow with soft vitality, her lips rosy pink, her eyes alight. Having escaped its pins, a curl of pale brown hair trailed down her neck. Jeremy caught a glimpse of embroidered clover on the ankle of her stocking and had to force himself to look away from that enticing curve.

She looked delicious. And he was headed straight for hell, the way he wondered about her long legs encased in silk stockings, and whether or not her garters were green, to match the ribbons on her bonnet.

"Am I late?" she asked.

Jeremy checked his pocket watch. "It's just two minutes past two o'clock."

She beamed, and her smile warmed him. "Excellent. I should hate to think I kept you waiting for long."

The dandy had been watching this exchange with a puzzled frown. "There's a connection here?"

"Lord Lynde," Lady Sarah said to the man, "may I present Mr. Jeremy Cleland."

The two bowed at each other, falling back on politeness. Lady Sarah introduced the blonde as Lady Donleigh, and the brunette as Miss Green. Everyone bowed and curtsied, which seemed rather ridiculous, given the way they had been talking about Jeremy moments earlier. Now, suddenly, he seemed to possess significance.

"I hope you don't mind," Lady Sarah said to the

threesome. "I invited Mr. Cleland to join us today. It *is* a cultural activity," she offered by way of explanation.

For some reason, the elegant trio looked a little mystified, glancing back and forth between them. Lord Lynde spread his hands in a *Now what?* signal. Lady Donleigh, the elder of the three, shrugged. They gathered close for a minute, whispering.

Jeremy looked at Lady Sarah. She looked puzzled by the behavior of her friends. Though they both gazed at each other in bewilderment, he liked looking into her eyes and sharing even this moment of connection.

Finally, Lady Donleigh said, "It sounds like a capital idea." She fought a giggle as she said this.

"Yes," agreed Miss Green, snickering. "Capital."

Something was clearly going on here. What? He wanted to take Lady Sarah somewhere else, somewhere away from these people and their sly looks and hidden agendas, but societal demands to remain polite at all times bound him.

"Shall we go inside?" Lord Lynde suggested.

"Let's," Lady Donleigh said gleefully. She took one of Lord Lynde's arms, while Miss Green took the other.

Lady Sarah turned back to her carriage. It was then that Jeremy noticed that her maid waited in the vehicle.

"Please stay with the carriage," she said to the maid, then turned back to him.

Jeremy offered Lady Sarah his arm and exhaled when she placed her hand on his sleeve. Her hand was a light but burning presence upon the fabric of his coat. Just the barest of touches. There were layers of fabric between them. Yet her nearness beside him, and how she smelled faintly of jasmine, thrilled.

Sarah smiled up at him. Her smile wavered as she glanced toward the trio walking up the steps to the town house.

"Come on," called Lady Donleigh—clearly the leader of this group.

Was it his imagination, or did Lady Sarah square her shoulders and draw up her chin, as though preparing to meet an adversary? No, it hadn't been his idle fancy. She really did look prepared for some kind of battle.

"Let's go," she said to Jeremy. Determination firmed her words.

Together, they climbed the stairs.

Entering the foyer, Jeremy's eyes adjusted to the dimness of the interior. A servant took his hat and placed it with a small collection of other hats sitting atop a long, narrow table. Lady Sarah handed the footman her bonnet, giving Jeremy a fuller glimpse of her profile and the curve of the back of her neck.

"The gallery is upstairs," the manservant intoned, gesturing toward a winding staircase. Already Lady Donleigh, Lord Lynde, and Miss Green stood waiting for them on the landing, their eyes strangely hectic with suppressed merriment.

"They're up to something," Lady Sarah murmured quietly to him.

"Perhaps we should leave," he offered.

Her chin came up another notch. "Let's see what they have planned. I know we can face it."

Many other people in her position would have turned tail and fled, but she refused. She might be a genteel lady, but one with a hidden backbone of iron.

He escorted her up the stairs, liking the feel of her on his arm as they took each step, well-matched in height and pace. He usually had to shorten his strides to accommodate a woman, but not with Lady Sarah.

Typical landscapes adorned the walls of the stairwell, but Jeremy didn't pay them much mind. He was fuzzy-headed from having Lady Sarah so close.

He struggled to converse like a normal human being. "Admittedly, I know very little about the East," he confessed.

"Likewise," she said with a self-deprecating smile. "But I've always longed to travel there. Just the names of the places sound so wonderful. Peking. Baghdad. Bombay. Wonderful things must happen there."

"We'll have to resort to using our imaginations," he answered.

"My imagination has a considerable capacity," she replied, her smile growing slightly more secretive.

What did that little smile mean? And what, exactly, *were* the limits of her creativity?

They finally reached the landing, where the trio exchanged barely suppressed grins. "It's just this way, Lady Sarah, Vicar," Lord Lynde said, waving them toward a nearby long gallery.

A dozen people milled through the exhibit, all of them likely denizens of St. James and Mayfair, judging by their fine clothing and upright posture. They milled in couples or alone, men and women. The women were all accompanied by men.

Paintings and sculptures were arrayed in the gallery, the sheer curtains drawn to keep damaging light to a relative minimum. Placards describing each piece were mounted beside the artwork, and a few gentlemen examined them using spectacles or quizzing glasses. People spoke in low voices, as befitting a museum, though it was a privately owned collection.

"What do you know of the owner of these pieces?" Lady Sarah asked Lady Donleigh.

"Only that he is a man of particular tastes," Lady Donleigh answered. "As you shall see."

"Indeed, most particular," echoed Miss Green.

Not much of an answer.

"Please," Lord Lynde said, gesturing them forward. "See for yourself." He seemed on the verge of laughing aloud, scarcely restraining himself.

Frowning, Jeremy escorted Lady Sarah to the first displayed painting. Together, they peered at it.

"Chinese," she said quietly, tapping the description on the placard. The faces and dress of the people depicted in the artwork revealed that it hailed from the Far East.

Jeremy started, and stared. Dear *God* . . .

The painting showed a woman playing some kind of stringed musical instrument that rested on the ground. A man sat just beside her. They were in some kind of garden pavilion, draped with flowers. But Jeremy's gaze went straight to the middle of the painting. The female musician's robes had fallen open, revealing her bare breasts, pointed with cherry-colored nipples. And the man seated behind her was currently in the process of gently pinching those nipples.

Jeremy tore his gaze from the painting to stare at the other artwork. The larger paintings and sculptures showed couples in various states of nudity, displaying acrobatic skills as they coiled their bodies together, limbs entwined, heads thrown back with expressions of ecstasy.

Good Christ—it was an exhibition of erotic art.

"Oh, my," Lady Sarah breathed beside him, apparently reaching the same conclusion.

Jeremy threw an accusing look over at Lady Donleigh and her companions. All three of them had their hands pressed to their mouths, trying to smother their laughter.

Two emotions hazed his vision. Anger on behalf of Lady Sarah, that these three jackasses would dare insult her like this, using her obvious virtue and lack of experience as the brunt of their crude joke. If only he could stride over to Lord Lynde and plant his fist right in the nobleman's face, then bodily shove the women out onto the street.

But he couldn't deny his other reaction. Pure, unadulterated lust. It roared in his ears and taunted him, as though throwing his own appetites back into his face. His cock surged to attention. Thank God he wore black rather than white breeches, so he didn't treat everyone to the sight of his rousing erection.

He quickly returned his gaze to Lady Sarah. Her cheeks were stained pink, her eyes wide, her lips slightly parted. She looked astonished but also . . . intrigued.

"They've had their jest," he whispered to her, after clearing his throat. "Time we leave."

"That's what they want," she said after a moment. She glanced over at her three so-called friends. "To see me run out, my face on fire. Or else they want me to swoon with the shock to my fragile sensibilities."

The three seemed to be waiting for something. Jeremy wished he wasn't a vicar so that he could pick up a nearby painted porcelain vase and smash it down on Lord Lynde's head, followed by a punch to the man's gut.

"How bloody *dare* they?" he growled.

She exhaled. "They dare because I'm an easy target. Haven't you heard? You will soon enough. I'm called the Watching Wallflower."

He longed to curse roundly. Damn Society. Damn everyone. Her honor demanded defending.

The hell with it. He started to take a step toward her three tormentors.

"Don't," she said quietly, fiercely. "I won't give them the gratification, and you shouldn't, either."

"I've got to *do something*," he said through clenched teeth.

"Prove them wrong," she answered lowly. She looked him full in the face. Hope and fury and courage wavered in her expression. "Stay with me."

"You aren't . . . you aren't going to leave?"

"Not if it pleases them to have me do so," she said. "Besides," she added, almost conversationally, "it's interesting, the art. Informative."

As informative as having all the secret hungers of his heart and body displayed for all the world to see.

"So, will you?" she pressed. She continued to gaze up at him, her heart in her eyes. "Stay?"

Refusal was his first impulse. He wanted to drag her out of there, away from those sniggering buffoons, away from this place that celebrated all things carnal and sexual. Things that she oughtn't, as a young woman of quality, see. Really, the insult the threesome had presented to her would have to be addressed. Jeremy had no skill with pistols or swords, but he'd gotten into a scrape now and then, and hoped he could at least challenge Lord Lynde to fisticuffs. He'd beat that dandy into a smear on the ground. It would be more problematic and require other means of redress with Lady Donleigh and Miss Green, but he'd find a way.

The artwork spurred dangerous thoughts, too. He already thought of her too much in a sensual way as it was. It would tax his every ounce of self-control to look at people engaged in bedsport, Lady Sarah standing right beside him, without it shaking him deeply. He was only a man, after all. A man with boundless desires that he tried desperately to ignore.

So, no, he didn't want to stay. But looking down at Lady Sarah, he saw something in her eyes—defiance, and a kind of plea. *Don't make me face them on my own,* she seemed to be saying, her gaze determined.

"Yes," he said at last. He could deny her nothing. "Yes, I'll stay."

Chapter 7

Oh, reader! The way the highwayman and I shook the carriage with our enthusiastic sport. We thoroughly ravished each other, using a multitude of creative postures to accommodate what limited space we had. Indeed, my highwayman was a most imaginative and vigorous lover. He quite took my breath while pleasuring my body. We hadn't the patience to undress completely. He lifted my skirts to my waist, revealing my . . .

The Highwayman's Seduction

Sardonic amusement filled Sarah at what was supposed to be a joke. Her erstwhile friends thought that they were scandalizing her with this erotic art. Little did they know . . .

She would not give those fools the satisfaction of leaving. She must prove to them, to herself, and to Jeremy that she wasn't someone to be toyed with, the way a cat batted at a baby bird fallen from the nest. She had her own claws. And, by God, she would skewer Lady Donleigh, Miss Green, and Lord Lynde in her next story. A trio of nincompoop aristocrats who die awfully in a horrible boating accident.

There was some gratification in this, but not enough. No, she had to show them that she was made of stronger stuff than they'd imagined.

The joke was on them. Seeing this artwork *benefitted* her. Made her more powerful as a writer. They had no idea she was the Lady of Dubious Quality, but at the very least, Lord Lynde must have read her books. The girl he deceived was none other than the woman who made his cock hard. Now she had the means to torment him even further.

Most of what she knew of sex came from books. A few of those books were illustrated, but not nearly enough. She'd had to make do with her thoughts to envision sexual acts. Here, in this gallery, she had the images presented to her, ready to be savored. Ready to be hoarded by her imagination to use later.

She could use a scene very like this one in one of her books. Lady Josephina might visit a gallery showing erotic art. She would meet the handsome gallery owner, and then they would act out the scenes. That could do very well.

Oh, in another world . . . she and Jeremy would race, hand in hand, back to her pristine bedroom. There, they'd throw the room into chaos as they played out the pictures. Their bodies would grow damp, fevered, their limbs supple as they tested out pose after pose, straining themselves to the utmost in their exploration.

She mentally shook herself. No. That could never happen.

Yet . . . here they were. Standing beside each other.

The limits of her hungers stretched and strengthened with him so near. He, who was both pure and deeply—perhaps unknowingly—carnal.

She wanted him to stay with her. She needed it. Needed him, in a marrow-deep way that made her ache.

So she'd stared up at him, rebellious and also imploring. His own blue, blue eyes fixed on her face. So much conflict lay behind his gaze, so much uncertainty, but also, yes, a thread of wanting, of hunger. For her? For something more? Whatever that need was, she craved it.

"Yes," he said. "Yes, I'll stay."

Relief nearly staggered her with its power. It was so much better to show up those fools with Mr. Cleland at her side, rather than attempt it on her own.

"Thank you," she whispered. It was a paltry thing to say when he'd given her so much more than simply a few moments looking at smutty art.

Together, they turned back to the picture of the woman playing a stringed instrument, her lover plucking at her nipples. The soft colors of the scene highlighted its lush, charged sexuality. What must it be like to be engaged in an activity while being the object of seduction? She could be sitting at her desk, writing peaceably, but then her imaginary lover would come in and trail kisses down her neck while his hands caressed her breasts. She'd try very hard to keep writing, but it would be impossible when her fantasy lover moved lower, to go beneath her desk and kneel between her legs, and then his curly blond hair would brush the insides of her thighs as he—

"Very, ah, pretty," Jeremy offered.

"I wonder that she can pay attention to what she's doing," Sarah answered, her voice slightly breathless. Heat and slickness gathered between her legs, and she fought to keep her thighs from brushing together. Warmth bloomed in her face. It was a marvel she didn't glow.

He looked at her for a moment, as though surprised she still hadn't fainted dead to the floor. But then he nodded.

"Perhaps she's composing a song," he said, his deep voice slightly rough.

"Something to fit the moment." What would that song sound like? Though Sarah could play piano with some skill, she had no real gift for music. But still, a song inspired by passion . . . now there was an idea. A musician who drew creativity from sex. Each composition providing a musical retelling or accompaniment to an act of love.

"Shall we . . . move on?" Jeremy suggested.

Sarah glanced back at Lady Donleigh, Miss Green, and Lord Lynde. They wore stunned looks on their faces, as though astounded that she hadn't fled in virginal terror. Let them gape.

Drifting away from the painting, she glided toward the next piece of artwork on display. Jeremy's lanky, sleek presence warmed her as he stood close. They stopped at a lovely, verdant landscape, filled with intricately crafted trees—each leaf seemingly painted one at a time with a minuscule brush.

"This must be here by mistake," she murmured. "I don't see—" *Fucking,* her mind filled in for her, but she'd never say that word aloud.

"In the . . ." Jeremy coughed. ". . . lower right corner."

Sarah bent closer, peering at the artwork. "You must have very good eyesight."

"I do."

Sure enough, half hidden by the branch of a tree, a couple embraced one another. The embrace wasn't entirely shocking, but the couple's state of partial dress was more so. It was also evident that the man in the scene had a rampant erection.

"Imagine doing that, right out in the countryside," she said, mostly to herself. She'd written scenes that took place in the out-of-doors. A farmer and the washerwoman. A lady and her groom. But it was one thing to write about something, entirely different to see it enacted before her very eyes. If one made love outside, anyone might walk by and see. The risk of being caught seemed like it would be an exquisite thrill.

"Have you ever . . . ?" she found herself asking.

He looked at her with violent alarm.

"Come across anyone," she hastily amended. At his continued silence, she murmured, "I'm sorry. I oughtn't ask such personal questions."

"Well, I—ah—" His voice was nearly an octave deeper. "Once, I walked into a stable and saw two young men hurriedly straightening their clothing. They'd been . . . enjoying themselves."

She'd read about amorous encounters between people of the same sex, but everything was rumor and other people's experiences. Still it came as a double surprise: firstly, that people truly did engage in such behavior, and secondly, that Jeremy would confide in her about it.

He seemed to think the same thing, giving a soft, incredulous laugh. "I'm sorry. Never in the depths of my most fevered dreams did I think I would say such things to you."

"I'll tell no one," she answered, humbled by his trust. "Besides, I think you and I, we rather understand each other. Don't we?"

He gazed at her for a moment, and she felt it all the way to her toes. "We do. To an extent."

"No one can know someone completely." She thought of all the secrets she carried, a trove of confidences that sometimes weighed more than bars of gold, yet she would never willingly part with any of her burden. What mysteries did he carry? It seemed like a great many, perhaps ones he might not even be aware of.

"We're each of us enigmas, especially to ourselves," he answered, as if reading her thoughts. "That might be our life's work—to unlock those mysteries."

"Oh, but mysteries make things so much more interesting," she said. It seemed odd and not quite real to be having this conversation with a vicar in front of a Persian miniature painting of two lovers fondling each other. And yet, when it came to Jeremy, she wanted everything as extraordinary as he was. As unexpected and remarkable as the man himself. "And some of them are best left unsolved. Otherwise, everything becomes featureless and dreary."

"But what of the thrill of the hunt? The pursuit of . . . knowledge." That word in his mouth, with his rich voice, seemed imbued with possibility.

"Let us seek, then," she conceded, "but always have something left strange and unknown to us."

He inclined his head in agreement. Yet there was a flush in his cheeks, as though he was still under the influence of the sexual artwork displayed not but a few feet from them.

"I should think that a stable would be an excellent place for an assignation," she said conversationally.

His cheeks darkened further. "I wonder how you might even know of things like that."

"I read," she said, knowing she sounded coy and enigmatic. She bent close to study the delicate, sensual painting, biting her lip in concentration.

He seemed to go very still. She glanced at him through her lashes. His gaze ricocheted between the artwork and her, never resting. His breath came at an accelerated pace.

Did he picture her in the scenario before them? Was he the man, in his imaginings? It was a dreadful thing of her to wonder, yet she couldn't help herself. Because when she saw the painting, she thought of them, together.

They hardly knew each other, yet her body didn't think so. It wanted him. *She* wanted him. The realization hit her as she stood there, placidly examining erotic artwork. She'd written pages and pages of it, and she'd longed to know what sex was and experience it for herself, but this was the first time she'd desired a specific man. Craved his touch. Wanted him in her bed.

She should leave. Forget about Lord Lynde, Lady Donleigh, and Miss Green—they could have this victory for now. She ought to go and not look back. There was nothing to be gained by tormenting herself with what couldn't be.

Remain? Go?

Hearing their suppressed laughter firmed her spine. Stay.

This was where she belonged. Here, with him. If not for her own selfish desires, then . . . for her writing. In the future, who knew? She could use this all. This helpless longing. This ravenous need for one person.

She walked away from the painting and heard him follow. A statue of a couple caught her attention. The male figure was much larger than the female. He sat cross-legged, and the woman was in his lap. Straddling him. They wore rather serene expressions. Were they merely cuddling?

Only when Sarah looked closer did she see that the man's penis was erect and partially sheathed within the woman's body.

Beside her, Jeremy saw it at the same time. He gave a startled grunt, as though hit in the stomach.

She thought she heard him curse under his breath.

"Should we go?" she ventured.

He shook his head, though his expression was pained. As if he suffered physically. His voice was raspy. "She's very . . . limber."

Pleasure rose up anew at his continued presence. He could have made excuses, invented an appointment that called his attention. But no, he stayed. For her.

It was an odd thing for a knight valiant to do—look at lewd art. Yet by so doing, he proved that he wouldn't back down in the face of obstacles. He remained strong and steadfast. Her heart brightened.

"She must stretch beforehand," Sarah agreed. Yet she gazed at him, wordlessly communicating her thanks.

By mutual, silent agreement, they did not linger long at the statue. They walked rather quickly from piece to piece, their conversation limited. Yet he remained with her the whole time.

At last they returned to Lady Donleigh, Miss Green, and Lord Lynde.

"Commendable," Jeremy said, his voice cutting. "An extraordinary showing."

"I . . . I . . ." stammered Lord Lynde.

"It's rather an interesting aspect of art," Jeremy continued, speaking over the faltering man. "Whatever the subject matter may be, it reveals more of us than it does itself. For example, it showed that Lady Sarah is a woman of uncommon courage."

She went giddy and hot, dizzy and elated.

But Jeremy wasn't done. "It also," he went on, "revealed that you three"—he skewered the trio with his bright blue gaze—"are better suited to the nursery than respectable Society."

All three gaped in response.

"Lady Sarah," he said, turning to her. "It's been my privilege." He bowed low, one hand pressed to his chest.

"Mr. Cleland," she murmured. "Thank you."

"The pleasure was mine, I assure you." With that, he turned and strode from the room.

She heard his footsteps on the stairs, then his low voice as he retrieved his hat from the servant in the foyer. The front door opened and closed.

He was gone.

"The artwork has been educational," Sarah said, looking at the three gaping people. "But, aside from

Mr. Cleland, the company has been juvenile." With that, she turned and walked away.

As she made her way down the stairs, she thought of what Mr. Cleland had done. That defense of her . . . no one had ever given her the same honor.

Yet . . . had she pushed him too far? Was he utterly disgusted by her? Dear God, she hoped not.

She wished she would see him once more. It would be for the best if they never crossed paths again. Yet her mind and body couldn't be dissuaded.

Lord help her, but she was in deep, deep lust with a vicar.

The fast walk home did nothing to calm Jeremy. His cock remained a thick, insistent presence in his breeches. Walking with an erection as big as a tree wasn't an experience he longed to repeat, but he needed to find some way to calm himself, and a hired carriage ride back wouldn't help.

He practically ran. Yet when he reached home, he felt no more at ease than when he'd been with Lady Sarah at the gallery. Once inside, he nearly threw his hat at the waiting footman, then took the stairs two at a time to reach his room.

Having confirmed that his chamber was empty of servants, he quickly locked the door behind him. He staggered to the bed and gripped one of the posts. With his other hand, he groped for the buttons of his breeches.

He groaned aloud when he grasped his cock. Had he ever been this hard, this demanding? Had he ever been as tempted as he'd been at the gallery? He'd wanted to pull Lady Sarah into a waiting closet, gather up her skirts, and thrust himself into her as she bit his shoulder to quiet her moans.

Jeremy stroked himself. God, to do the things to her that were shown in those paintings! To open her bodice and take those soft, silken breasts in his hands, play upon her nipples—were they pale or dark? Or to fuck her outside, in the sunshine, beneath the branches of a sheltering tree. She would be luminous in the sunlight, partially dressed, hot and responsive as he sank deep into her sweet, tight depths.

Or to have him sit upon the floor, as in that Indian statue, and she would mount him, ride him . . .

With only a few hard strokes of his cock, Jeremy's release tore through him. He clenched his teeth to keep from shouting. He bowed with the force of it.

For a moment, he could only stand on shaking legs. Rousing himself, he cleaned up and tucked his now sated penis back into his breeches. It might be satisfied, but Jeremy wasn't.

He staggered to a chair next to the fireplace and sank into it. Resting his head in his hand, he cursed himself. Oh, he pleasured himself quite often. He couldn't survive unless he did. But always he constructed fantasies with faceless women, careful to never call to mind anyone he knew. Never before had he pictured one woman in particular, thought of all the wicked, depraved things he wanted to do with her.

It felt wrong, so very wrong, to invoke Sarah like that. To use her in that way. But, God preserve him, he couldn't help himself.

When it came to Lady Sarah, he was utterly lost.

Chapter 8

When we had at last exhausted ourselves, we sat quietly, holding each other.

"Do you often make a habit of seducing the men who seek to rob you?" he asked me.

"Do you often make love to the women you steal from?" I returned.

He grinned. "Never."

"This is a novel experience for me, as well."

"Perhaps we might see one another again," he offered.

"A dangerous game."

"Ma'am, I am not afraid of danger."

Ah! He was too delicious, as dark and wicked as Mordred, and I unable to resist his roguish charms.

The Highwayman's Seduction

Frustration remained Jeremy's constant companion. He ached for Lady Sarah—and could do nothing to assuage that need.

At the least, he had something with which to distract himself. After a subdued supper, Jeremy retired back to his room to contemplate his current task. Thank God he had his search for the Lady of Dubious Quality.

Alone, he sat by the fire and picked up a copy of *The Highwayman's Seduction*. There had to be clues to her identity buried somewhere within the text. He had to do his utmost to read it with an aloof eye, unmoved by the salacious contents. Not an easy task, but if anything could have been gained by this afternoon's exercise in self-indulgence, it was that the edge of his desire had been slightly blunted.

The fire burned low in the grate, casting dancing shadows but providing enough light by which to read. Keeping his mind fixed on its purpose—and not allowing his thoughts to drift toward Lady Sarah *at all*—he began to peruse the book's contents.

Reading the novel with a more distant perspective, the author's voice caught him. It didn't merely relate the story or provide thinly veiled scenarios that easily gave way to sex. Instead, there was actual artistry involved.

What would it be like to discuss the Lady of Dubious Quality with Lady Sarah? They'd spoken so openly about sensual matters at the art exhibit. Surely, she'd be intrigued by this book. Intrigued and . . . aroused?

It was too much to contemplate, so Jeremy forced himself back to his goal.

Whoever the Lady was, one thing was certain: she was literate, educated. Which didn't necessarily guarantee that she was of gentle birth. English education continued to evolve, and it was entirely possible that whoever posed as the Lady was someone of common blood.

Though a considerable part of *The Highwayman's Seduction* took place in some unnamed part of the countryside, including the highwayman's lair, Jeremy's interest perked up when the action briefly moved to London. Something in this location might give away even the smallest crumb of information.

"Hold a moment," he murmured to himself.

The heroine of the book observed the way the sunlight shone on a statue of Eros riding a porpoise. Jeremy knew that statue. The small, unremarked-upon sculpture stood in a hidden corner of the city. Considering how vague most of the locations were in the rest of the novel, surely there had to be some relevance to citing this particular place. Maybe the Lady of Dubious Quality actually frequented this spot.

He'd go there in the morning and perform some reconnaissance. Anything was better than the minimal amount of evidence he had to go on. He could perform his task and not think of Lady Sarah or her lively eyes or soft lips. Not once.

But as he undressed and climbed into bed, her image continued to dance behind his closed eyes. Her bravery today continued to resonate through him. Her strength, and her perceptiveness. She was no wilting blossom. No pallid flower. She reminded him more of a lioness, tawny and proud. No one's fool.

Thoughts of her tormented him all the way into a restless sleep.

Jeremy stood contemplating the statue of a young boy riding atop a porpoise. He glanced around at the small courtyard that contained the statue. Quiet homes ringed the sculpture. Perhaps he'd have better luck out on the street. He crossed a narrow lane, then emerged onto a busy urban intersection.

Late-morning traffic crowded the streets. Jeremy dodged a dray loaded with kegs of beer, then wove between more wagons, carts, and carriages. The din was considerable, and crowds pressed close on every side. He'd grown too familiar with life in the country, its slower rhythms, its soft sameness from day to day, change ruled not by the clock but by the sun and shifting seasons.

He rather missed the chaos and excitement of London, yet he ought to be grateful for his comfortable living, his secure employment. *Ought to* being the operative words.

"Out of the way!" someone shouted.

Jeremy leapt up onto the sidewalk just in time to keep from being plowed down by a hired carriage barreling toward him. Not much respect for a man of the cloth here in the city. As evidenced by the way Lady Sarah's awful acquaintances spoke to him, he wasn't entirely seen as man. Neither lion nor lamb. Which left him adrift.

He was here now, in the midst of the city's businesslike madness. He stood on the corner and looked around, hoping for something, some mote of knowledge to fall upon him.

He saw a grocer's, a mercer's shop, an office conducting some kind of business, as evidenced by the clerks hustling in and out with sheaves of paper. Not especially revealing.

His gaze caught on one storefront. J & C McKIN-

NON, BOOKSELLERS. Jeremy snapped to attention. That might prove useful. The Lady revealed through her writing that she was well read. Did she frequent this bookshop?

Carefully, he crossed the street and approached the shop. Shelves stood out front, offering leather-bound volumes for perusal. The cost for each book was written in pencil inside the cover. He paused to look over the shelves. The volumes they held covered a wide range of subjects, from scientific inquiry to sentimental novels. On the pavement, a gentleman and a lady were busy reading, neither of them paying him any mind. He surreptitiously scanned their faces. Could either of them be the Lady of Dubious Quality? The man was middle-aged, with a round nose and wisps of white hair peeking out from beneath the brim of his hat. He seemed like someone's kindly uncle—but that wouldn't impede him from secretly writing erotic books. Anyone could be the author. Anyone at all.

The woman was also middle-aged, with ash-blonde hair and a soft, comfortable look. She appeared to be reading a book about interior design. Might she have penned salacious novels?

Perhaps he ought to inquire with the proprietor of the bookshop. See if anyone was a regular customer, and, if so, what kind of books they commonly bought.

He stepped across the threshold, entering the shop, and was met with the smell of leather, paper, and a faint sugary scent, as though someone often enjoyed tea and cakes while reading. Which seemed a perfect way to spend a day.

In fact, had he not been on an objective from his

father, the bookshop would have been a wonderful place to spend many hours. More shelves lined the walls and formed a maze, all of it full to bursting with rows upon rows of books. There were books on the shelves, on the floor, stacked onto tables and covering every available surface. A large orange cat curled up on a pillow, dozing, beside a heap of books. It was a bibliophile's paradise.

First he needed to track down the proprietor, who'd abandoned the desk by the door. Jeremy straightened his shoulders and called to mind all the religious authority he could manage in order to glean the necessary information.

He turned down an aisle and stopped short.

"Lady Sarah!" he said automatically.

For there she was, looking perfectly edible in a peach gown with a dark blue spencer over it. She glanced up in surprise at hearing her name. But the moment she saw him, surprise gave way to something far warmer.

Pleasure burst in his chest. Would she be glad to see him? He'd given the three fashion plates a set-down the other day. But had she wanted his cutting candor?

He stepped closer, yet gave her enough of a respectful distance. It wouldn't do to crowd her.

"Are you following me?" she asked with a teasing glint in her eye.

"Spycraft is not one of my skills," he said. Then, "I feared you might be angry with me."

"Why would I?" she whispered.

"Because of yesterday. I was . . . abrupt with those people."

She shook her head, soft curls framing her face. "They deserved it."

Another surge of relief rushed through him.

"Besides," she murmured, "it's I who should wonder whether or not you'd be upset with me."

"No reason to," he answered at once.

"There's every reason. I . . . pushed you too hard."

He felt his face redden at that, but not for her reason. Words like *push* and *hard* took on much more salacious meaning to him when she said them.

"I should have known that what I asked of you wasn't appropriate," she said regretfully.

"It's your friends that should apologize," he replied. "What they did was inexcusable."

She gave a rueful, angry laugh. "They are no friends of mine, and after that trick they pulled yesterday, I've vowed never to speak to them again."

After a moment, she glanced up at him through her lashes, looking shy and lovely. "Then . . . there are no resentments or feuds between us?"

"None," he said quickly, stepping nearer so that only a dozen inches separated them.

A smile bloomed on her face, easing the worry that had tightened her features. "I cannot tell you how pleased that makes me."

"And your pleasure is mine." He realized too late how that comment might be read more than one way, and her eyes widened. "That is . . . I meant . . ."

"I know what you meant." She laughed again. The sound rang like a bell deep in his chest.

They stood in sociable silence for a moment, and he smelled the delicate jasmine fragrance that followed her wherever she went. It shamed him to consider how he'd invoked her yesterday when touching himself.

Could she see what he'd done? Was it written on his face? He'd been overcome with desire for her. Helpless before the ravenous beast of his need.

"What brings you here?" she asked, unaware of his thoughts.

"I'd heard about this bookshop from my father." The lie came too quickly. But he couldn't very well tell her the exact nature of his visit. A fine woman like Lady Sarah likely knew nothing of the Lady of Dubious Quality.

She frowned. "I didn't think Lord Hutton was familiar with a place like this. It's not precisely known by the gentry. It's more a favorite of prosperous bankers and brewers."

"Yet you're here," he pointed out.

"Because the McKinnons are the best booksellers in London," she answered with a curve of her mouth. "Their book selection is incomparable."

"Perhaps it was someone else who recommended this shop," he prevaricated. "Difficult to remember. What do you read now?"

She held up the cover. "A treatise on knot tying."

"And here I didn't take you for a sailor," he said with a smile.

"Perhaps I'll ship off to tropic seas."

"Careful," he warned. "It's said that those tropics can lead to all sorts of wild behavior."

"Does that include talking with vicars?"

He grinned. "Most assuredly. Everyone knows vicars are stepping stones to wild, drunken orgies." Good God, had he actually said the word *orgy* in her presence?

At that moment, a tall fellow with deep-set eyes appeared beside them. He carried several volumes in his hand. "Lady Sarah!" he exclaimed with pleasure. "Back again."

"I've brought a friend," she said.

Was that the right word to describe him? He did feel warmly toward her, but not all of his urges were platonic.

"Oh, a friend! How lovely!" The man turned to Jeremy. "She's here at least twice a week. Always reading about different things. Novels, philosophy, art."

"Then you supply books to all tastes?" Jeremy asked, assuming the man was the proprietor.

"Indeed," the tall man said. "Whatever a body could want, we can get it for them. Speaking of which," he added as he glanced at Lady Sarah, "your special order has arrived. It's in the back. All wrapped up nice and secure."

A furious blush spread across Lady Sarah's cheeks. "I'll pick it up later," she muttered.

The proprietor looked over at Jeremy. "Of course! Another time." He cleared his throat. "I can help you with something, Vicar?"

There was no way that Jeremy could ask about other regular patrons in front of Lady Sarah without looking suspicious. "Just enjoying your shop," he said instead.

"Let me know if you need anything. Just ask for McKinnon." With that, the man bowed and took his leave.

The air between Jeremy and Lady Sarah seemed charged, ripe with potential. Or perhaps he only wished that was the case? It prickled along his flesh, and there was answering interest in her eyes. Did Lady Sarah think of him the way he thought of her? Part of her was secretly sensuous, and certainly after the art exhibit yesterday, she wasn't entirely innocent. The engrossed way she'd looked at the exhibits, the questions she'd asked . . . she might be a virgin, but she wasn't entirely virginal.

She had that quality of mind that so intrigued him: open yet assessing. Astute, but appreciative.

Surely she saw how much she affected him. A part of her seemed to welcome that interest.

Could he take it further? An impossible desire. If he dared presume to court her, he'd be laughed out of her father's house.

She broke the spell between them by checking a small jeweled watch pinned to her spencer. "Oh, blast," she muttered. "I have to go."

"May I walk you home?" he offered immediately, unwilling to let her go.

"My carriage is waiting," she said regretfully. Then she brightened. "I can give you a ride home." She added in a confiding tone, "My maid is with me, so you needn't worry that I'll ask you to do anything scandalous again."

More the pity.

He ought to stay at the bookshop and ask McKinnon his questions. But the offer of being alone with Lady Sarah—despite the presence of her maid—was too good to refuse.

"A lift home would be most welcome," he said.

After collecting her maid, who had been reading volume two of a gothic novel, they climbed into her carriage outside. In a trice, they were heading back to Mayfair.

They swayed with the movement of the vehicle, and for several minutes they traveled in silence. The maid stared deliberately out the window, making herself fade into the background. Given the length of Jeremy's legs, he worked to keep from brushing them against Lady Sarah, but it wasn't easy.

"How long do you plan on staying in London?" she asked. "I imagine your parishioners cannot spare you for long."

"I have a curate to oversee things whilst I'm away," he answered. "As to the length of my visit . . ." He shrugged. "That's yet to be decided."

"I'm going to be impertinent again, I'm afraid, and tell you that I'm going to the Imperial Theater tomorrow night. To see a new burletta by the writer Mrs. Delamere. Oh, didn't she recently marry your cousin, Lord Marwood? I guess that would make her Lady Marwood."

"Indeed, but how is that impertinent?" he wondered.

"Because I hope to see you there," she replied, smiling.

He'd had no plans to go to the theater. "There's a very good chance that I will be in attendance."

Her smile widened. "Excellent. Have you seen anything by Mrs. Delamere?"

"I've been away from the city for too long."

"You'll enjoy her work," Lady Sarah vowed.

"If you do, then I'm sure I will."

"Ah, flatterer!" But there wasn't any censure in her voice.

"Men of God don't flatter, Lady Sarah," he intoned.

At that, she laughed. "Very vicarish words, Mr. Cleland."

He laughed with her. "Then my work is done."

As they continued on toward home, his heart loosened. What was this sensation? Pleasure. Joy. Excitement. A host of emotions that brewed potently within him.

He craved these new sensations, powerfully. And yet . . .

Jeremy cursed what could never be.

Chapter 9

"I must go now," the highwayman said regretfully. "But before I do . . ." He reached out and plucked the diamond and pearl ring from my hand. "A memento."

Before I could protest the theft, he was gone. I leaned out the window to see him riding off into the night, like a phantom, his long greatcoat flying out behind him.

"My lady?" the coachman called to me. He emerged from the woods, throwing off the ropes that had been used to bind him.

"Drive on," I said. "But we'll stop at the next town." If my highwayman frequented this region, perhaps someone in the village might have an idea as to his whereabouts. I wasn't ready to let my wonderful lover slip through my fingers . . .

The Highwayman's Seduction

So much potential here in the theater for her writing! Flirtations, scandals, cuts direct, and whispered promises, all behind the veneer of a social night out to see and be seen. Sitting in her family's private box at the

Imperial Theater, Sarah surveyed the crowd excitedly. Numerous places for amorous encounters existed here, too: the boxes themselves when the lights dimmed, in one of the retiring rooms, or even backstage, hidden behind painted scenery while the performance was ongoing. The possibilities were numerous and delightful.

She could have Lady Josephina start an affair with an actor and they could . . . no. Actors were a feckless lot, hardly the stuff of rich sexual fantasy. They were likely too obsessed with themselves to be very talented as lovers. She smiled to herself, thinking of an actor watching himself and not his partner in a mirror as they made love. How dispiriting.

No, Sarah decided that Lady Josephina would be traveling to Oxford to visit her nephew at university. Then, Lady Josephina would meet her nephew's classical theater professor—a sober but attractive man possessing a secret sensuality. It could lead to some very thorough and focused lovemaking . . .

The performance had yet to begin, and people were seating themselves in the pit or in the boxes as the orchestra warmed up. She fanned herself against the stifling heat from so many people and lights. But another kind of heat pulsed just beneath the surface of her skin.

She'd see Jeremy tonight. It thrilled and terrified her to have had him observe her book on knot tying. Let him think her interest was purely nautical.

She oughtn't look forward to seeing him this much. Theirs was an association that couldn't go very far. But her heart, mind, and body remained obdurate, craving him with an unseemly hunger. She'd no one to whom she could confide this need. Certainly not her mother.

Of her few friends, she didn't trust any of them not to gossip. Best to keep her feelings to herself and let her quill be her outlet for everything she could not allow herself to do.

The duchess sat beside Sarah, while her father was absent, as he didn't much care for the theater. Lady Egerton, her mother's friend, had positioned herself just behind them, and she chatted with Mrs. Boyle, her companion.

"What's on the bill tonight?" the duchess asked.

"A burletta by Mrs. Delamere . . . I mean, Lady Marwood," Sarah answered, consulting her program, "followed by comic songs and acrobatics."

"I do like a good comedic tune," the duchess said. "And acrobatics. Pity we have to sit through the first part."

"Don't you care for the burletta?" Mrs. Boyle asked. "Lady Marwood is quite celebrated."

"Her tragedies are finely written, but too gloomy," her mother replied. "Life is difficult enough without forcing ourselves to endure someone else's suffering."

Sarah's stories celebrated the earthy, joyous part of life and left it at that. No need to worry about practicalities or how her characters would go on for the rest of their lives. No, she happily wrote about sex, knowing that her readers would get to enjoy themselves whenever they picked up one of her books, leaving the cares of the mundane world behind, if only for a few hours.

Sarah gladly shouldered the responsibility. She'd no desire to write "serious literature." It was too often moralizing, or crammed full of sorrow. Escape had its own important value. She would never flatter herself into thinking she could change the world, but she didn't want to. That task would be left to other writers, other minds. She wanted only to entertain, and counted herself lucky that she had the opportunity to do so.

"It's hard to believe," Lady Egerton exclaimed, "that the playwright married Lord Marwood!"

Sarah's mother sniffed. "A topsy-turvy world we live in, when a viscount marries a commoner—and a writer, at that."

Sarah thought it all quite romantic, frankly.

Their voices hushed as the curtain to their box was swept aside. A darkly handsome, Byronic-looking man stepped inside. He looked every inch the rogue, with his long black hair, piercing eyes, and sensuous movement. Viscount Marwood, the very man they'd been speaking of and London's most notorious rake. Well, he *had* been a rake, until he'd proposed to Mrs. Delamere onstage, and the playwright had accepted him. They'd married not that long ago. If only Sarah had been in the audience the night of the proposal, she could have seen the drama unfold before her very eyes.

The viscount didn't seem entirely glad to be in a theater box with older matrons and a wallflower, yet he quickly covered his lack of enthusiasm with a smile and bow.

"Ladies," he murmured. "My greatest pleasure."

"Lord Marwood," the duchess said, inclining her head and offering her hand. The viscount took it and pressed a kiss to the back of her knuckles. "My felicitations on your, ah, recent nuptials."

"Thank you, Your Grace. I am delirious with happiness," Lord Marwood said without a trace of irony.

While Sarah might have normally been intrigued by a man so infamous, she paid him no mind. Not when Jeremy strode in behind him, wearing all black, his curly hair swept back to reveal the clean contours of his face.

Sarah's heart hammered. She half-rose from her chair, then sat back down, fanning herself.

"May I present my cousin," the viscount said, waving toward Jeremy. "Mr. Jeremy Cleland."

Jeremy bowed, the movement elegant and restrained. "An honor," he said. His gaze immediately went to Sarah, and she couldn't make herself look away.

She found her voice. "Will you join us for the performance?"

"Much obliged," Lord Marwood said before Jeremy could answer, "but I have my own box, and my bride awaits me." He said this with a glow of happiness. "Though," Lord Marwood added, glancing over at his cousin, who continued to gaze at Sarah, "I can spare Jeremy."

"Oh, but we don't want to keep family apart," Lady Wakefield said airily. Sarah wanted to kick her.

"Nonsense," Lord Marwood answered with a wave of his hand. "I'm sure Jeremy would relish the chance to get away from an old sinner like myself."

"Sin is contagious," Jeremy said, nodding.

"Let him stay, Mama," Sarah said quietly but urgently to her mother.

Her mother sighed, as though put upon. Clearly she felt that entertaining Jeremy was a waste of time. Yet she said, "Very well. Do sit, Mr. Cleland."

"Maggie and I shall see you after the performance,"

Lord Marwood said with a chuckle, then disappeared.

Jeremy took a seat just behind Sarah. She could sense his rangy, warm presence like a fire at her back. But she kept her gaze firmly on the stage, as if testing herself. Could she spend at least ten minutes in his presence without actually looking at him?

"Lady Sarah," he murmured. His breath, lightly scented with tobacco and whiskey, fanned gently against her neck.

"Mr. Cleland," she answered. "It still shocks me that Lord Marwood is your cousin. Rather a diverse family tree."

"Since Marwood's married," he said, "his mania for the theater has been replaced with a mania of an entirely different kind. One that seems to make my cousin very happy. Poor bloke."

"Why 'poor'?" Sarah asked, turning around in her seat. Blast, she hadn't lasted nearly as long as she'd hoped, but she was rewarded by looking upon him again. She glanced quickly at her mother and was happy to see that Lady Wakefield was too engaged in conversation with her companions to notice Sarah's own discussion with Jeremy. "Surely, as a man of the cloth, you believe in the sanctity of love."

"I do," he said at once, holding up his hands. "I believe love is a true, beautiful, and solemn thing."

Their gazes met and held, a current of heat passing between them.

"But not too solemn, I hope," she pressed. It was grim to think that Jeremy would be the sort of man to extinguish the candles, get completely under the covers, pull up her nightdress just enough to get the deed done, and then apologize afterward for sullying her.

"There's joy in it, too," he amended. "But where Marwood's concerned, before he married I doubt he knew what it meant to love. Beyond the physical act of it," he added, then blushed both adorably and carnally. Perhaps he wouldn't be a staid lover, after all. He rested his hand on the back of her chair, and she felt the brush of his knuckles between her shoulder blades.

More heat filled her. This was a dangerous conversation to have with him. Were she ever to marry, the most she could hope for was esteem and perhaps a mild, weak sort of affection. Love was the stuff of plays and novels—though her own books seldom mentioned that emotion. Lust motivated her characters, not love.

Yet with Jeremy . . . she dreamed of things she'd little hope of ever knowing.

Sarah wished . . . oh, she wished for many things. All at once, the strangest desire to tell him every secret surged forward. Partially because he was a man of the cloth. But more because he was *him,* with that openness of heart that felt so genuine and enfolding. She wanted to confide in him, let him know that she was the Lady of Dubious Quality. Much as she enjoyed holding that mystery to herself, she wanted to share it with someone. Her hidden triumph.

But if he knew, what might his response be? He wouldn't greet the news with excitement and approval. He could be disgusted, or angry. Even if he did, astonishingly, accept her as a writer of erotic books, his role as a moral leader of the community would be jeopardized by the knowledge. He'd have to turn his back on her.

"I've seen far more happy brides than unhappy," he continued.

"There must be something to the institution, then," she answered.

"Most likely," he said, a corner of his mouth turning up, "or else we wouldn't keep getting married. We need someone with whom to share our most intimate thoughts."

The word *intimate* sent a shiver through her.

Another intimate secret threatened to spill, one she had to bite back forcibly. Perhaps it was the way Jeremy inspired thoughts of confession. Perhaps it was the understanding and confidence they shared. But she longed to tell him something about herself. Something no one knew.

She had invited Jeremy to the theater tonight, but she could never invite him to her next destination. In three days' time, she was to visit a clandestine club, one that specialized in masked revelry. Often, part of the entertainment included people making love on stage. Through her publisher she'd heard that occasionally members of this club liked to enact scenes from her novels. The notion was thrilling, to know that her writing impacted people so much that they would want to re-create her work, live and in the flesh.

The idea of going to see it was impossibly scandalous. Her, a duke's untouched daughter, venturing forth incognito to a gathering known for actual sexual performances was unheard of. Devastating to her reputation.

And yet the possibility was far too enticing. She could not resist it, as much as she could not resist the pull of writing. The danger of it. The risk. Her life was so circumscribed, so regimented and quiet—she needed that element of chance. It was as if, by taking risks, she regained control over herself.

But if Jeremy found out . . . then, surely, he would never want to see her again.

Pain filled her, sharp and caustic.

Pushing away the urge to divulge her secrets, she focused instead on what she and Jeremy could speak of. Even the precarious topic of love was more acceptable than her carnal writings, or discussing covert masked societies with staged sexual acts.

"Perhaps Lord Marwood can learn from his cousin's example," she offered.

His alluring blush deepened. "He's a sight more experienced than I."

"It would be difficult to find anyone who could top him for experience," she noted with a smile.

Jeremy chuckled at that, the sound like napped velvet against her flesh. She leaned back, pressing his hand against her skin. He glanced over at the point of contact but did not move away. A secret touch, its knowledge shared only by them.

His cousin would be an excellent model for one of her characters. Sensuous, worldly. A veteran of the bedroom. Yet Lord Marwood interested her not at all. Far better to write of a man like Jeremy, one who discovered and learned his potential. And there was so much promise in him . . . they could learn things together. Explore the realm of the senses. Explore each other.

Her pulse thrummed at the thought, and her body cried out silently, *Yes, please!*

"I like the way you speak your mind, Lady Sarah," he murmured softly.

"I like to speak it," she answered. "Though I don't often get the opportunity."

"That's a shame."

"I thought women were for decorative purpose, not to opine their thoughts and feelings," she noted.

He shook his head. "I find that men who believe that are petty creatures, fragile and afraid."

"You aren't? Doesn't the Bible teach us that women should be docile and biddable?"

"The Bible is a remarkable document," he mused. "It can be interpreted many ways, and reveals as much about whoever reads it as it does about the Book itself."

"Do you have a favorite chapter or verse?" she wondered.

"I'm rather fond of the Song of Songs, myself." He spoke, his voice as liquid and hot as silken flame, his eyes never leaving hers. "'Thy lips, O my spouse, drop as the honeycomb: honey and milk are under thy tongue.'"

Breath whooshed from her, stolen as if by an invisible caress. "'His mouth is most sweet,'" she quoted. "'Yea, he is altogether lovely. This is my beloved, and this is my friend, O daughters of Jerusalem.'"

They stared at each other for a long while, their gazes holding. His hand remained at her back, his fingers gently brushing against the flesh just beneath her nape. She felt herself falling, falling, into a whirlpool of desire.

At that moment, two young bucks entered the box. Sarah recognized them as Mr. Gregory, a baronet's son, and Mr. Lovell, heir to a somewhat impoverished viscount. They were handsome enough—the darker Lord Gregory being of average height and just starting to paunch, and the fair Mr. Lovell thin and attractive in a reedy sort of way. Both of them had only this year started shopping for brides, or so her mother had told her after one evening's soiree.

Jeremy removed his hand. The absence of his touch was a palpable thing, and she craved its return.

"My ladies," both men intoned in unison, bowing. "And sir," Mr. Gregory added perfunctorily, glancing at Jeremy.

A round of greetings and introductions followed the men's entrance.

"You're looking as fresh as morning," Mr. Lovell said to Sarah's mother.

"Indeed, Your Grace," seconded Mr. Gregory. "Is this your first Season out?"

Lady Wakefield laughed appreciatively at the mild flirtations.

"And Lady Sarah," Mr. Gregory continued, turning to her, "it will be hard to watch the performance with your light shining so brightly in the theater."

"You are very kind," Sarah answered with a wan smile. She might be somewhat pretty, yet she was no gleaming beacon of loveliness. Such compliments only reinforced to her what she could never—and did not want to—be.

"He isn't kind," Mr. Lovell insisted. "He speaks too weakly of your charms."

His companion shot him an angry glare, and Sarah herself wasn't much inclined to look kindly on

Mr. Lovell. Compliments were like sweetmeats thrown by the handful. They did nothing to sate hunger and only made her stomach ache.

"Are you a habitué of the theater, Lady Sarah?" Mr. Gregory said, seemingly eager to impress.

"Not regularly, no," she admitted. "Though I think Mr. Cleland here will enjoy Lady Marwood's work. Especially now that she's related to him."

Neither Mr. Gregory nor Mr. Lovell even glanced at Jeremy. He must have rated very little in their limited vision, which made her unease around the two newcomers shift into something tight and angry. How dare they dismiss him? How small-minded of them.

"The performance is about to begin," Sarah said coldly. "If you don't mind . . ." She glanced toward the entrance to their box.

"Yes! Of course!" Both young men stumbled over themselves in their haste to be agreeable. "Perhaps we'll see you afterwards."

"Perhaps," she said with deliberate vagueness.

Shortly, the two gentlemen were gone. Sarah's mother exhaled loudly.

"Sarah . . ." she said in a warning tone.

"They were being rude to Mr. Cleland," Sarah answered angrily.

"Little boys distracted by their own reflections," he murmured. "Hardly worth noting."

"Their behavior was intolerable," she answered, her throat tight. "If they insist on treating others like rubbish, then I'll do the same."

Her mother's expression was rigid, and she gave Sarah an unmistakable *We'll talk about this later* look.

No doubt Sarah's reputation as a wallflower would only be enhanced by her treatment of the two young men—they'd likely talk about how she was a terrible conversationalist, awkward and rude—but she couldn't bring herself to care. Anger on Jeremy's behalf boiled, even if he seemed to think the incident hardly worth noting. He wasn't a milquetoast. Far from it. But he possessed a far more forgiving nature than she.

Lady Wakefield turned back to face the theater, effectively giving Sarah a chill shoulder.

Jeremy leaned forward. "You're familiar with those two men," he whispered.

"Fortune hunters," she answered softly but bitterly. "They come around every so often, trying to woo the duke's daughter. It's my dowry they find so worthy of fulsome praise."

"They should consult with the king's physicians," he said tightly. "For surely if they cannot see your value beyond the monetary, they must be mad."

His words touched her, but they didn't undo what she knew to be true. "It's been five years since I came out," she replied. "Five years, and I've learned that no honeyed phrases are given to me without an ulterior motive."

"Then that's a damn shame." He reddened at his hard language, and they both looked over at Sarah's mother. Fortunately, Lady Wakefield was too engrossed in watching the theater fill and talking with her friends to be much concerned with Sarah's conversation.

Seeing that they had some privacy, he continued, "You ought to be courted, wooed. For yourself, not for your fortune."

He ran a fingertip along the flesh between her sleeve and her glove, and she barely resisted moaning aloud at the clandestine touch.

She couldn't withstand him. Not when he said such things, or when he touched her as though she was something precious and rare. Something in her softened, the barriers around herself caving in, leaving her unprotected and vulnerable. Yet she welcomed those feelings with him. Had it been anyone else, she'd fear manipulation. But she sensed with Jeremy that every word he spoke came from a place of perfect honesty. He said nothing he didn't mean. And to hear herself spoken of in such a way . . . she felt herself sliding deeper and deeper into a terrifying emotion.

"It's a futile exercise on their part," she said, steering her thoughts away. "Seeking me as a bride."

"The young girls of my parish have me half convinced that women seek only to become someone's wife," he noted. "You aren't the same?"

She contemplated mouthing the countless platitudes she'd used to pacify others in the past. When the right man came along. When the time was right. Any of a dozen delaying tactics. But Jeremy deserved more than empty platitudes. He deserved as much truth as he gave her.

But what was the honest answer? It baffled even her. "I cannot say," she finally admitted.

That was the strongest response she'd ever given, revealing how little she knew what the future of her heart might hold. Being with him made her reconsider exactly what she wanted. He made her consider things that couldn't be.

Now, uncertainty fogged everything.

"Better to be alone than suffer with someone merely enduring me for the sake of several thousand pounds."

His expression turned thoughtful. "A woman who sees the world as you do . . . who has intelligence and courage . . . you deserve more. If you were mine . . ." he whispered, but to her dismay he did not finish the thought. He shook his head, as if the very idea was beyond him. "'Thou art beautiful,'" he quoted, "'O my love, as Tirzah, comely as Jerusalem, terrible as an army with banners.'"

Those velvet ties between them knotted more firmly. Her heart to his. How would she ever sever them?

Music rose in a crescendo, signaling the beginning of the performance. Sarah turned back to the stage, hoping to lose herself in other people's happiness and sorrow.

She was the Duke of Wakefield's daughter. A marriageable prize, despite her status as a wallflower. Any titled gentleman would be eager to marry her. Except one that cared for her, truly cared.

Chapter 10

Country villagers were a taciturn lot. They didn't want to divulge their secrets and hoarded them like jewels. But I was not without my own resources, wielding my charm and charisma like weapons to obtain my objective. Every man likes to have himself flattered by a pretty woman— and words flowed freely when eyelashes were batted and an ankle was discreetly revealed. No journeying hero of the old tales ever underwent such trials as I did.

With my arts thus deployed, at last I learned the location of the highwayman's lair. He was something of a hero to the townspeople, as he often donated a portion of his plunder to the needy and destitute— though he did retain a substantial amount for himself, the scoundrel. I also learned his name: Jacob Clearwater.

Determined to retrieve my stolen ring (and, I must admit, in order to see him again), I hired a horse and set out on my own in search of Jacob's den . . .

The Highwayman's Seduction

It hadn't been very long ago that Jeremy had stood in front of his cousin's door, interested to know about the identity of the Lady of Dubious Quality. At that time, his own inquisitiveness had been the sole motivating factor to learn who she was. He'd been curious to know what sort of person felt compelled to write such salacious material, when his own life had been so circumscribed.

But when he'd gone searching for answers, instead he'd provided Marwood with guidance. And now, Cam—the quintessential rake, ever free and generous with his affections—was married. The world was full of wondrous, miraculous things.

Today Jeremy was back at his cousin's door. His question remained the same, however.

At his knock, Strathmore, the butler, answered. When Jeremy asked to see Marwood, he was summarily escorted to his study.

He found his cousin seated behind a desk, somewhat incongruously industrious with notebooks, correspondence, and folios of what looked like agricultural reports. Marwood rose with a smile at Jeremy's entrance, extending his hand.

"You're home," Jeremy noted, coming in and shaking Marwood's hand.

"My apologies," his cousin answered. "I'll creep out the back door and hide in the garden until you leave."

"I never expected such a domestic scene." Jeremy nodded toward the masses of paperwork, his gaze alighting on the recently used quill lying on the blotter.

"If you must blame someone," Marwood said cheerfully, "blame Maggie. It's her polishing influence."

"She ought to be canonized." Jeremy took a seat in front of the desk, and Marwood sat down opposite him, steepling his fingers and looking almost, but not entirely, civilized. Even in some things, the remarkable Lady Marwood couldn't quite work magic.

It was astonishing. Marwood, who'd never met an actress or widow or opera dancer he hadn't adored, had finally found one woman with whom he wanted to grow old. Jeremy would have vowed upon every Bible in his church that such a marvel could never happen. And yet . . . it had. Against every prediction. Marwood was a man who'd had his first kiss at age seven. Years of kissing—and more—had followed. Yet he proudly wore a wedding band now.

Such a thing happened for a rogue like his cousin. What did it mean for Jeremy?

Lady Sarah's clear, strong presence nestled snugly within the confines of his heart. Her keen intelligence, coupled with an innate sensuality, was a rare and precious combination, one he'd never truly encountered before.

But that door had to be closed. It couldn't happen. Country vicar. Duke's daughter. Never to be.

Instead, he now focused on his goal and what brought him to his cousin's home.

"Ah, but Maggie's no saint." This Marwood said with a fond, though slightly lascivious, smile. "I was very disappointed you didn't perform the ceremony, of course."

"Except all I knew of your marriage was a polite letter informing me that it had already happened."

His cousin spread his hands. "When am I ever polite?" he countered.

"The letter was from your wife."

Marwood grinned. "I was afraid you'd show up drunk to the ceremony."

"For *your* wedding, there's such a thing as too much sobriety."

"Now," his cousin said, "with courtesy dispensed with, I can ask you what brings you to my door."

"It's a confidence that must be kept between us," Jeremy insisted.

"Of course," Marwood answered at once.

From his pocket, Jeremy removed his copy of *The Highwayman's Seduction*. "Remember when you gave me this?" He placed it on the desk and slid it toward Marwood. Too late, he realized that the book was in slightly worse shape than when his cousin had given it to him. It bore the telltale signs of numerous readings.

Marwood picked up the book. His eyebrows lifted. "Enjoyed it, did you? Want more? Just a moment. There are some around." He searched the drawers of his desk.

Jeremy cleared his throat. "I've got them."

His cousin grinned. "Sly dog! Here I thought you were ready for entombing."

"Save the pennies on my eyes for later. Right now, I need to know more about the book's author."

Marwood leaned back in his seat. "The Lady of Dubious Quality."

"I need to find out who she, or he, is."

A corner of his cousin's mouth turned up. "Oh, she's definitely a woman."

"You sound confident of that assessment," Jeremy noted drily.

"Because the Lady shows a tremendous understanding and concern for how women feel pleasure," Marwood explained. "Men are more interested in their own gratification."

"Doesn't speak well for our sex," Jeremy observed.

"Not much does," Marwood agreed brightly. "Why do you want to know who the Lady is?"

"I've got reasons that I cannot reveal." Being evasive pained him, but his rakehell cousin would never agree to locating her if it meant ending the Lady's books. There was always the possibility, however slim, that Marwood could also reveal Jeremy's secret agenda to someone—his bride, perhaps—and that could circulate back to Lady Sarah. Which Jeremy couldn't have.

"That's your prerogative, of course," his cousin replied. "What have you done so far to track her down?"

"I've been to her publisher and went to a bookshop I thought she might frequent." He shook his head at this list. "Neither lead has taken me anywhere fruitful."

Marwood crossed his arms over his chest, looking pensive. "There is a possibility . . ." he said after a long pause. "Might be a little dim, but it could work."

Jeremy leaned forward. "At this point, I'll take any direction I can get."

"Every now and then," his cousin explained, "there's a masked club, a secret society, that meets in a house in Bloomsbury." He looked at Jeremy pointedly. "What I tell you, you cannot tell another soul. Nor," he added, "can you use this information to shut down this secret society."

"I won't," Jeremy said immediately.

"They're actually meeting in just a few days' time."

"And what do they do there?" Jeremy wondered.

His cousin stared at him. "I'll be honest with you, cuz. People like to go there to have sex," he said bluntly. "With strangers."

Sitting back, Jeremy absorbed this information with a touch of shock. It wasn't truly a surprise that such places actually existed. London was a worldly, sophisticated city with worldly, sophisticated citizens who had probably seen, and done, more things than he could ever imagine.

"I see," he said after a moment, striving for a level of sangfroid he didn't quite possess. "Have you ever been there?"

"What do you think?" his cousin answered with a smile.

"I think I'd rather not know."

"Good lad. They like to have entertainments at this club," Marwood continued. "People performing sexual acts in front of an audience."

Jeremy's face and body nearly went up in flames. To take something so incredibly private and make it public . . . it . . . excited him. He couldn't dream of making love in front of an audience, but watching something like that, seeing it happen before his very eyes while he stood nearby . . . would be an exercise in sensual torment. Wondrous sensual anguish.

Would Lady Sarah be excited by something like that? By his very interest in it? Or would she be appalled?

"I see," Jeremy said again, his voice a thick rasp.

"Sometimes the acts are improvised," Marwood went on. "And sometimes they stage scenes. From the Lady of Dubious Quality's books."

Jeremy's eyebrows went up. "Oh."

"Perhaps," his cousin mused, "just perhaps, the lure of such a thing might draw the Lady out. The idea of seeing her work performed live might be too much for her to resist. She might be there. And you could go, too. Catch her in the act, as it were."

Shooting to his feet, Jeremy declared, "I'm not going to any masked orgy."

"Come now, Jeremy, if it really is that important for you to find her," Marwood chided, "this isn't the time to fall back on your vicar's prudery."

How could Jeremy explain? Prudishness wasn't the issue. His whole body burned with the thought of it. His own reaction to the prospect alarmed him. It was . . . frightening. Alluring. Calling to all of his buried hungers, his hidden desires. Unfettered sexuality. Freedom. What if he was lost to it? What if it consumed him and he couldn't find his way back?

"That's . . . it isn't . . ." Jeremy paced the length of the carpet, trying to marshal himself. His thoughts. His riotous body.

Marwood got to his feet and came around the desk. He seized Jeremy by the shoulder, holding him steady.

"Be at peace, cuz," he said soothingly. "It's just a night. One night. And right now, if you truly want to locate the Lady, it's the best chance you have of doing so. If she isn't there," he continued, "perhaps someone at the club will have information about her. That's all you have to do. Beard the lion in his den, and then emerge unscathed."

Could he? Would it be possible? He didn't have to participate in anything. Just look around, ask a few questions, and leave. He could hold temptation at bay for a little while—vicars did not participate in covert sex societies. If word somehow got out that he'd not only attended but also actively taken part in the club, the consequences to his reputation would be disastrous.

It would be like visiting another country. He didn't have to become a native of that land, merely visit, and then return to the life that he knew. Staid and reserved. No one would have to know.

"Very well." He exhaled. "If that's the best option, I'll go."

His cousin grinned. He was altogether too invested in Jeremy's descent into the underworld. "Wonderful."

"I just need the address," Jeremy continued.

Marwood stepped back, releasing his shoulder. "Hold a moment. You can't go like that."

"Like what?" Jeremy frowned.

"Like a walking sermon," his cousin explained. "You'll never fit in that way." He waved at Jeremy's simple black clerical clothing. "No one will act naturally around you. At the very least, you'll have to change your clothes."

"To what?"

"No ecclesiastical black, for one thing. You can be a little more exuberant in your choice of colors."

"I don't have anything else," Jeremy complained.

"Tomorrow, go to my tailor on Jermyn Street," Marwood said. "Tell him you're my cousin. He'll have you fitted with something in a trice. Don't worry, old man, you can still wear dark colors, but please, lose the black."

"I can't afford to have a suit of clothes made up in a day," Jeremy exclaimed.

"Don't worry about the cost," his cousin assured him. "I'll pay any price to sully my uncorrupted cousin."

Jeremy was going to object, but, hell, if receiving one suit of clothes meant finding the Lady, then he'd accept it. Marwood was appallingly wealthy. Such a thing meant nothing to him. Even so, Jeremy vowed to himself that he'd pay his cousin back.

"So my wardrobe is settled," Jeremy said decisively. "That means I'm ready to go."

"This is just the beginning!" Marwood threw wide his arms. "You'll need a mask."

"I haven't got one lying around," Jeremy answered wryly.

"Just a moment . . ." Marwood strode to his desk and rifled around in the drawers for several moments. "Aha!" he cried, pulling out a half mask.

"What are you doing with a mask in your desk?" wondered Jeremy.

"If you have to ask . . ." His cousin handed the item to him. It was ink-blue leather, with finely wrought gold embroidery around the edges. "Be sure to wear that," Marwood continued as Jeremy pocketed the domino. "Don't shave for a few days so you have some stubble. And slick back your hair," he commanded. "Darken it, as well. The color's too distinctive."

His head spinning, Jeremy removed a notebook from his inside pocket. "Just a moment." He scribbled on the pages with a pencil. "Don't shave," he muttered as he wrote. "Hair. Darken." He glanced up to see his cousin laughing.

"Only you would take notes on how to attend an orgy," Marwood said with a shake of his head.

"It's a considerable amount to remember," Jeremy muttered. "So, my ensemble and appearance are taken care of. I'm prepared."

Marwood held up his hand. "Easy on the reins, cuz. We've taken care of the externals. But it's the internals that are equally important at an event like this one."

Jeremy's brow furrowed. "What are you blathering on about?"

"It's not blather if it comes from decades of experience," his cousin answered good-naturedly. He tapped Jeremy in the center of his chest. "How you conduct yourself at the club is as important as, if not more so than, how you look."

"I'm not going to assault anyone, if that's what you're concerned about," Jeremy snapped. "I'm not going to read anyone passages from the Bible, either."

"You want to fit in, don't you, so you don't draw unwanted attention to yourself?" At Jeremy's nod, Marwood continued. "Then it's important for you to act like you belong there. And that means acting sexual and confident."

Jeremy drew himself up to his full, not inconsiderable, height. "I can do that."

His cousin looked dubious. "Can you? You're probably a virgin."

Face hot as a furnace, Jeremy said, "I'm not. There was . . ." He cleared his throat. "One woman."

Marwood rolled his eyes. "How many years ago?"

After a long pause, Jeremy answered, "Five."

His cousin heaved a sigh. "All right, old man, let's discuss how to act like a rake."

Jeremy grimaced. "Must we?"

"We must," Marwood insisted. "Approach it like you would a theosophical conundrum. Besides, perhaps afterwards you can use what I tell you to find yourself a nice, wicked little vicar's wife."

"I won't do that," Jeremy insisted at once, but inside, he paused. Could he? Use his cousin's skills at seduction to secure himself a woman? The only woman he wanted was Lady Sarah, but he couldn't have her. Still, it would be nice to approach her with more confidence, more self-assurance, instead of feeling as though he was blundering and lumbering around her like a bear in a clerical collar.

"Are you going to take my advice or not?" Marwood pressed.

Jeremy exhaled. "Bestow it upon me, O wise one."

Marwood pointed to a chair by the fire. "Have a seat, and take copious notes."

Deciding it was best to humor his cousin, Jeremy sat in the suggested chair and held up his notebook, poised at the ready.

Seeing that he had Jeremy's full attention, Marwood clasped his hands behind his back, assuming his most professorial manner and tone. "First of all," he intoned, "you have to know that you can give a woman the best night of her life."

"Seems an odd way of starting a conversation," Jeremy said, looking up from his notes. "'Pleased to meet you. I can make you see stars in bed.'"

Marwood made a scoffing sound. "You don't *say* it, dunderhead. You think it. You *feel* it. Then it shows in your face, your movements." He planted his hands on his hips. "Let me see your best smoldering look."

"What?" Jeremy set his notebook on his knee.

"Just *do* it."

Jeremy attempted to smolder, imagining he was channeling all the sexual energy of Lothario and Casanova and Byron at some distant point across the room.

"You look like you want to murder someone," Marwood exclaimed in disgust, and Jeremy deflated. "Imagine that you're looking at someone you desperately desire, someone whose skin you long to feel, someone you want so badly, every part of you hurts. And you're trying to communicate to her that making love to her would be the pinnacle of your worthless existence. Can my virtuous cousin attempt to imagine such a woman?"

Jeremy imagined trying to impart to Lady Sarah through looks alone all the pent-up longing he felt for her. Letting her know just how much he desired her. How greatly he wanted to worship her body for as long as she would let him. That she would become the sole object of his universe if only she gave him the chance.

"Jesus," Marwood muttered. "I didn't think you had it in you."

Jeremy shook his head, coming back to himself.

His cousin continued, "It almost makes me think . . ." He peered at Jeremy. "As if you were thinking of a specific woman when you gave that look."

At once, Jeremy said, "There's no one." He didn't want Marwood considering Lady Sarah in any way.

"Shame," his cousin said. "A woman would want to be looked at that way." He smiled. "If I wasn't married, related to you, and inclined toward the amorous company of women, you'd have me in a heartbeat."

"Thank God for all those 'ifs,'" Jeremy said wryly,

but inside, he exulted. Perhaps it wasn't impossible for him to play the part of the rake, after all. He only needed to imagine every woman he came across as Lady Sarah. Of course, he wouldn't *act* on any of the signals he would be sending out, but it was good to have a plan. He wouldn't be swimming in completely uncharted waters.

"You've got your smolder down," Marwood continued. "That's good. But it's about more than the lure of sexual satisfaction. You must remember that every woman you encounter is a human being, with thoughts, feelings, and ideas of her own. Treat her with respect, never as an object for sating your lusts. There is no such thing as a conquest. Conquering is for bullies. A seduction is for both parties, not just the man's gratification."

Oh, all this was good. Jeremy wrote hurriedly, trying to keep pace with his cousin's advice.

"Take your time," Marwood went on, fully warmed to his topic. He paced back and forth, expounding. "Nothing is less appealing than a man who's in a hurry. Which brings me to my other point—"

"Slow down!" Jeremy exclaimed as his pencil flew across the notebook page. "I can't keep up."

"Look lively, damn it!" his cousin barked. "Genius doesn't dawdle."

After stretching his hand to relieve a cramp, Jeremy continued taking notes. "Go on."

"My other point," Marwood said with a pointed look in his direction, "is to leave a woman wanting. Never give her everything she desires all at once. Women like the chase just as much as men do, and if there's anything they cannot abide it is a desperate man. A man who clings like wet muslin is just soggy, not seductive."

"How on earth am I supposed to remember all this?" Jeremy asked when his cousin paused.

"You've always had a scholarly bent," Marwood decreed. "Only this time, you'll be studying something useful."

Jeremy shot him a dry look, then shook his head. "I'd no idea seduction was such an art."

Marwood raised one finger. "Depend on it, my lad. It's not a truncheon but a sword, to be wielded only by the most skilled men and women. It shows you the measure of my esteem for you that I consent to share this advice at all."

Jeremy inclined his head. "I am deeply honored."

"As you should be," Marwood said solemnly. Then spoiled the whole effect by grinning. "I don't want to overload your brain and bollocks with too much information at once. I think this is a good starting point."

"Let us hope so," Jeremy remarked, rising. He shook hands with Marwood. "My many thanks for the gift of your knowledge."

"Pleasure is my business," Marwood answered. "Well, it was. Now I concentrate all my business on one woman." But he said this with obvious devotion to his bride.

Jeremy's head swam with the surfeit of knowledge and experience imparted to him by his cousin. But if anyone knew the dance of the sexes, it was Marwood, a certified dancing master.

Marwood gave Jeremy the address in Bloomsbury, as well as the secret knock and code for the door, then escorted him toward the foyer.

Jeremy stepped back onto the street, but his buoyant enthusiasm soon faded. It was one thing to feel the giddy possibility of sex and seduction when safely ensconced in his cousin's study. Quite another to put it into practice. In a short time, he'd visit this secret club and test out his newfound knowledge. His notebook rested in his pocket, heavy with importance. It was a notebook that only his eyes would ever read.

He was truly in it now, the darker realms of the senses and animal hungers. His life had split in two—he wasn't simply a vicar anymore. He was a vicar with a clandestine mission to infiltrate a secret hedonistic society. It thrilled him to contemplate doing something so dangerous, so outside the realm of his circumscribed life. Here was the freedom he'd been forbidden—risky, delicious freedom. He could take a step closer toward discovering the Lady's identity, while pushing the limits of his own existence.

He fervently hoped Lady Sarah didn't find out about any of it.

Chapter 11

*The following night, I set off in my pursuit of
Jacob Clearwater. I left the village and plunged
into thick woods, guiding my horse into a
deep vale. Ahead, shielded by trees, I saw an
old stone ruin, overgrown with ivy and full of
secrets, like a sorcerer's lair.*

*Someone was within, judging by the glow of
a fire. I left my horse behind and crept forward
on foot. Peering through one of the windows, I
beheld Jacob's den. But no one was within.*

*Suddenly, I was grabbed from behind by
muscular arms. "You took a hell of a chance,
coming here," a familiar voice growled in my
ear. Excitement thrummed through me as I
managed to turn around.*

*"You have something that I want," I said, then
kissed him . . .*

The Highwayman's Seduction

She didn't recognize herself.

Sarah stared into the mirror, and a stranger gazed
back. A liberal application of cosmetics had trans-

formed her face, making her appear more angular, older. She had taken extra care to change the shape of her mouth with lip rouge, since that was the most visible part of her visage. A gold silk mask covered her upper face, obscuring it from view.

If someone recognized her tonight . . . the consequences would be disastrous. Unmarried virgins didn't escort themselves to secret masked gatherings. She did, though. Starting tonight.

The clock on her mantel chimed just midnight. Fortunately, her mother and father had spent the evening at home and had gone to bed an hour earlier. In a state of nervous excitement, Sarah had pled a headache and stayed in her room. With her parents entirely certain that she was abed, she could creep out of the house without detection. It was a fast run down the back stairs, through the mews, and to the waiting carriage. She just needed to be fleet of foot and pray the servants kept their silence. They had all been persuaded with money into complicity, including the coachman. Thank God for her additional income as the Lady, which helped her afford the numerous bribes.

Her pulse throbbed. Could she do this? Over the past few days, she'd taken special precautions—even selecting a false name should anyone ask. Between her disguise and careful planning, she ought to be untraceable. But there was always a possibility of detection.

She stood back from her mirror and paced to the mantel. The carriage waited for her. But it wasn't too late to back out. She could remove her cosmetics, doff her mask and cloak, and climb into bed with none the wiser.

Yet *she* would know that her nerve had failed her.

This was her chance to live a life like her characters'. To be as bold and daring as Lady Josephina. As Sarah had always longed to be if given the chance. If she stayed at home, would she look back on this moment with remorse? Raking herself over the coals with what might have been?

The night outside was thick and dark, the moon obscured by a haze of clouds. It was precisely the sort of night for assignations and adventures. *Her* adventure. At last.

Before any more doubt could shackle her, she grabbed her cloak, pulled up the hood, and drew open the door to her room. She made certain the hallway was clear before shutting her door and slipping down the silent darkened corridor. Her dancing slippers barely made a sound on the carpet or when they padded softly down the stairs.

With only a few lights burning dimly, everything in her home was shrouded in shadow. More than once she'd gone down to the library in the middle of the night when the rest of the house had been asleep, but that had felt entirely different from tonight. At worst, if she'd been caught in the library, she might have received a mild scolding from her mother about catching a chill. Yet if her parents saw her this evening, completely disguised, sneaking out of the house—she'd never have a moment's freedom again.

But she wouldn't turn back. Not now.

Walking speedily, she hastened to the back of the house. After double-checking that no one was in the stairwell leading to the kitchen, she scurried down.

She nearly yelped when she saw a tired maid sitting at a table, pillowing her head on her folded arms, but the girl's breathing remained deep and steady in sleep.

After waiting a moment just to be certain the servant wouldn't stir, Sarah slid from the kitchen out the back door. She hurried into the mews alongside the house. Her heart jumped to see the carriage waiting for her, a lone driver perched on the seat. The horse's breath steamed in the cool night as it pawed the ground.

Seeing the animal's exhalation convinced her that this was all very, very real. She was truly going to do this.

Catching sight of her, the driver secured the reins, then jumped down to help her in. Sarah reached into her reticule and produced a coin, which she slipped into the driver's hand.

"Speak of this to no one," she whispered.

"Aye, Lady—I mean, miss."

"Madam," Sarah corrected him. Even in disguise, a young, unmarried woman could not travel alone at night. "Mrs. Chalbury."

"Yes, madam." The young man carefully helped her into the carriage.

She sat down with a rustle of silk, pulling her cloak close. The driver shut the door, and the carriage swayed as he climbed up into the seat. He called softly to the horse. Then they were off.

The carriage rocked as it drove down the dark, empty streets. A few stragglers were out on their own. Some people pulled carts, and a handful of drunken men tottered along the road, leaning on each other. But for the most part, London was quiet.

She had never been out at this hour on her own. The city felt huge, laden with possibility. She could just keep going in the carriage, roll on into the night and not stop until she was far from home, far from what anyone expected of her. Liberation tugged at her. It would be so easy . . . she could write anywhere. She pictured a snug little study on a Scottish island, a view of gorse leading down to a roaring sea, with all day to write and no one to disturb her or drag her anywhere she didn't want to go.

And . . . if she was spinning fantasies . . . Jeremy would be there, too. He'd come in to see how she was faring, bearing a cup of tea. No, it was her dream. Let him come with glasses of wine. But they'd set their wine aside as they drank from each other, instead. He'd lift her up out of her chair, and set her on the edge of the desk, then slowly lift her skirts . . .

She shook herself. Now was not the time to indulge in such flights of imagination. Though the club was known for catering to sensual whims, she needed her wits about her. It would be unfamiliar territory, an obscured part of the map, and for her own safety she had to treat the endeavor much as an explorer would. Eyes open, hands to herself.

At last the carriage drew to a stop outside a house in Bloomsbury. The den of iniquitous indulgence looked like any other house on the block—three floors, a columned entryway, even a tidy garden out front. All the curtains within were drawn, and very faintly, the trill of music rose above the stillness of the night. If she were to write such a place, it would be ablaze with light and laughter—though that wasn't very discreet.

"This it, madam?" the driver called down uncertainly.

She checked the address scribbled on a scrap of paper. "It is. Drive on, about five blocks from here."

"Yes, madam."

When the carriage stopped the requisite distance away, she opened the door and stepped down.

"Wait here. I shouldn't be above an hour." There was always the chance that someone at home might discover her missing. She didn't want to tempt fate by staying out too long.

"As you wish, madam." He didn't question her rationale, but it was all part of her carefully thought-out disguise.

She left the carriage behind and approached the house on foot. All was quiet. Hardly any noise disturbed the sleeping neighborhood. Sarah climbed the front stairs and gave the secret knock at the door. She had only learned of this place from her publisher, who'd had half a mind to shut the whole operation down, but she'd assured him in a letter that having aficionados stage scenes from her work could only help increase sales, not hurt them.

Her heart thudded as she gave the coded knock again. *Tap. Tap tap. Tap.*

After a moment the door opened, and a slim, black-haired woman stood before her, looking gorgeous in a bloodred mask and matching gown. Her skin was a lovely, deep-golden hue, revealing mixed heritage. She said nothing, only stared with sharp green eyes at Sarah.

"I've come for the plums," Sarah said breathlessly.

"We haven't any," came the low reply.

"Peaches will suffice."

It was an exchange from her novel *Alone with the Rogue*. Sarah exhaled when the woman stepped aside, the coolness in her expression giving way to a warm smile. "Welcome. I am Amina."

"I'm Mrs. Chalbury." Sarah almost stumbled over the false name, but she'd practiced saying it over and over at home so that there would be hardly any hesitation.

Amina held up a finger. "Other than myself, we use no names here."

"Sorry," Sarah mumbled, feeling like a green fool.

But Amina only continued to smile. "Don't concern yourself. It's a common enough error for newcomers. May I take your cloak?"

"No! I mean, I'd rather keep it." Keeping the hood up provided Sarah with an extra measure of disguise, and a barrier between her and what she was about to witness.

Amina nodded, as if this was a perfectly ordinary thing to do. "This is your first time, yes?"

"It is," Sarah admitted.

Amina's smile widened. "Your first time costs nothing, but if you return, there is a fee. There's nothing to fear here. We all abide by the same rules. There is to be no forced contact. All participation is optional. Those who wish to engage may do so, but if you prefer to simply watch, that is also perfectly acceptable. We've had men and women attend our salon many times who have done nothing more than drink negus before going home alone."

Sarah exhaled in relief. "That's good."

"Please," Amina said, gesturing toward the corridor behind her, "make yourself comfortable. If you've any questions, or if you object to anything you see here, find me."

"I will," Sarah vowed.

"You're amongst friends here. Friends with an appreciation for the Lady of Dubious Quality."

A thrill of excitement worked up Sarah's spine to hear herself referenced. She almost blurted, *That's me!* but managed to keep her silence. Trying for her best sophisticated nod, Sarah moved on from the foyer, drifting down the hallway toward the sounds of music, talk, and laughter. It seemed like any other party where one might meet friends and potential suitors.

What if Jeremy saw her here, like this? He wasn't just a gentleman but a vicar. Morality was his chief concern. But she also wondered what it might be like to take him to a place like this. Would he appreciate her compulsion to come here, or would he condemn her choice? He was a man of the cloth, after all.

A doorway opened onto the corridor, and she looked into a large chamber. The candles burned low, and the room was full of masked guests. Some people wore deep jewel tones, others sported cloaks, and a few had on the kind of fancy dress one might have seen at a party thirty years ago. The scent of sweat and perfume pervaded the air—not unlike any other social gathering.

In fact, at first glance, it truly did resemble any number of assemblies she had attended over the years. Servers circulated amongst the guests with trays of wine and cakes. Groups of men and women gathered here and there, chatting and laughing. Through a doorway that looked into another large room, Sarah observed couples dancing—a waltz, she noted. It was, initially, a little disappointing. Not nearly as scandalous as she'd feared and hoped.

But then . . . at further inspection . . . she saw that it was far from an ordinary party. Hands moved liberally over guests' bodies. In corners and even standing in the middle of the room, men and women kissed boldly, openly, in front of everyone. On a sofa, a woman in white sat on the lap of a man in green, her fingers freely toying with the buttons fastening his breeches. Two women were locked in a passionate embrace, their hands and mouths all over each other, and three men in one corner were also kissing and fondling one another.

Sexuality saturated the whole chamber, soaking into her own body. Her pulse raced heavenward when she observed a man slide a woman's bodice down to reveal her breasts. Sarah had never seen another woman's bare breasts before, though she'd written about such scenes often enough. And in another corner, a woman was reaching down into a man's trousers. She fumbled with the fastenings, the action not quite as smooth and effortless as Sarah expected. The woman was about to reveal the man's cock. Here. In public.

Sarah glanced away. She wasn't ready to get her first glimpse of an erect penis. Not quite yet.

No one was actually making love, but they were coming very, very close.

Grabbing a glass of wine, Sarah hurried into the next chamber, where the dancing took place. Here, too, more sensuality imbued the air as the dancers pressed their bodies close to one another's and people kissed deeply right in the middle of the ballroom. She noted with a soupçon of thrilled alarm that a stage stood at one end of the room. With a bed on it. The bed was unoccupied—for the moment.

That's where it was going to happen. The scenes from her books would take place right there. Before the eyes of the entire company.

My God.

She had truly entered into the realm of her books, where reality was fantasy, and fantasy was reality.

Terrifying—and wonderful.

After taking a healthy drink of wine, she continued to watch the dancers move through their paces. The waltz was performed at many assemblies and balls, but not quite as lasciviously as it was here, with the dancers holding each other so closely that there was no space between their bodies. Deeply sensual, this dance. The swaying rhythm, the isolation of each couple becoming their own spinning constellation of two.

She had only waltzed twice in her life. Both times had been lackluster and unremarkable—though she suspected that had more to do with her dull partners than the dance itself. The two men had moved without grace, escorting her across the floor with leaden steps.

Yet here, the carnal nature of the dance reached its apotheosis. Women wrapped their arms around their partners' shoulders, pressing their breasts tightly against male chests. Men clasped women's waists snugly, and sometimes their hands drifted even lower, cupping the women's buttocks close so they were groin to groin. One couple didn't even bother attempting to dance. They merely swayed together in place, stroking each other's bodies, staring into each other's eyes. Sarah was surprised the air around them didn't vibrate with heat.

"A dance, my lady?"

Sarah nearly jumped when a man suddenly appeared beside her with the request. He stood half a head taller than her, nicely filling out his bronze coat, and he wore a matching bronze silk mask. His muscular thighs were encased in black breeches. His lips were voluptuous as he smiled invitingly at her, one large hand extended to escort her onto the ballroom floor.

He would be perfect for an assignation. Young, strapping. Already primed for seduction. All she had to do was take his hand and see where the night would lead.

"No, thank you," she said instead.

"If you should change your mind . . ." He bowed and retreated back into the dimness of the room.

She was alone again.

A sigh rose up from her chest. Even here, in this masked assembly, where no one knew her and she could do and be anything at all . . . even now, she'd consigned herself to the role of wallflower. As if she knew no other way of being. But she did! She knew the realm of her books. There, nothing was impossible, and all whims and desires were indulged. If that existed in her mind, in her imagination, then surely the potential was there in her. She'd freed herself before, when she'd decided to become a working writer. Now she could embody all elements of the Lady.

If only for tonight, she vowed, she would be the kind of audacious, intrepid woman from her novels. She would be a woman who made good earnings from her own ability. She would finally be someone who saw and desired and took, according to her own demands.

The dance ended. Many couples hurriedly left the ballroom floor, seeking shadowy corners, where they immediately fell into each other's arms.

Sarah looked around for the man in bronze, hoping to catch sight of him. She would let him know that yes, she would like a dance. It didn't have to lead to anything further, but she needed to know her capability, her strength.

With the dance floor emptied, the other side of the chamber was revealed. Guests she hadn't seen before emerged from the darkness. Women in gowns that fastened up the front. Men in snug breeches. Everyone masked, anonymous and free in their disguises. A woman laughed riotously. A man had his arms wrapped around two women as they tried to dance to their own music. They seemed antic in their need for freedom, moving with the energy of billiard balls ricocheting across the baize.

Not everyone.

She became aware of him through his stillness. His self-contained vitality. Where others around him spun and staggered, he was leashed power.

He wore dark blue, with a matching blue and gold mask. His dark hair had been ruthlessly slicked back from the hard contours of his face. A faint haze of stubble lined his lean cheeks. He stood tall, sinewy and muscled, surveying his surroundings with a slightly mystified smile, as if surprised and amused. Was he a regular? Was this his first time? Difficult to say.

Whoever he was, he attracted attention. Women hovered around him like bright moths. He wasn't doing much besides standing with a glass of wine. Watching everything with that removed smile. Yet the females floated close by, striving to catch his eye with fluttered fans, even dropped handkerchiefs.

He didn't pay them much attention. Just continued to observe.

A thousand questions pirouetted through Sarah's mind. Who was he? From whence did he come? Her writer's mind flew in a dozen different directions. Was he a bandit? A prince? A sea captain covered in intricate tattoos beneath his clothing? Anything seemed possible. And she wanted to know everything. He gleamed like a black diamond in the depths of night.

She froze when their gazes met across the room. He stood too far away, and the light was too dim for her to make out the color of his eyes, but she felt the sudden heat and intensity of them—all through her body. Everything within her seized and stilled, drawn to one finite point. The room and all its occupants dissolved like sugar in tea. All that existed was her and the man in blue. He started, as if struck by the same bolt of electricity.

What should she do? Approach him? Remain where she was to see if he approached? Indecision pinned her in place.

But he knew what to do. Without breaking his gaze from hers, he set his wine on a passing servant's tray. Then, with sure, deliberate steps, he crossed the room. Heading straight for her.

Chapter 12

"My ring," I demanded. "I want it."

He lifted one brow. "Is that all you came for?"

"You're a clever man," I said, trailing my fingers up his chest. "What do you think?"

"I think," he said, grinning, "that I am growing exceedingly fond of you."

"Then show me," I insisted.

And he did, his mouth finding mine, his hand slipping beneath my bodice to caress my . . .

The Highwayman's Seduction

The man in blue said nothing as he approached Sarah. His gaze remained on her as he cut across the room, sure and purposeful. Nothing stood in his way. Music for the next waltz started up, and couples began to collect on the dance floor.

Her heart lodged in her throat as he came to stand in front of her. Warmth and the scent of leather radiated from his body, invisible and alluring.

Without speaking, he held out his hand. He broke their shared gaze long enough to glance toward the dance floor. An invitation.

Everything seemed to fall into place. She had come to free herself, and this was her moment. This stranger was the man. And she was the woman. To take what she wanted, when she wanted.

She slid her hand into his. Neither wore gloves. It was skin to skin. Her breasts went tight and heavy, and heat pooled between her legs—all from a simple touch.

Wordlessly, he led her onto the dance floor.

He wasted no time on preliminaries. No polite bow at the onset of a dance. No discreet distance between them. He pulled her close against his taut body. Even through the fabric of her cloak and gown, she felt the hard strength of him, sinew and intention. As he held her, she couldn't break from his gaze. She didn't want to. Her breath came hot and quick, and her head spun— all before they had taken a single step.

Who was she? What was happening? Nothing but now mattered.

The dance began in earnest. And he moved. They were as close to each other as two clothed people could be. She felt every twitch, every glide of his body against hers. The music swirled and floated, and they moved in time with it, hips together, this way and that. He was at all times in control, his hand large and hot in the small of her back. He watched her with proprietary need, his gaze on her lips.

It was the closest she'd ever come to making love. She didn't know this man in blue, but they claimed each other.

Yet . . . oddly . . . she felt as if she *did* know him. She could not quite explain or understand it, but something in her recognized something in this masked stranger.

She turned protectively toward it, as though seeking the warmth of the sun in the middle of a cool, rainy day.

Yet he was profoundly *other*. Charismatic, without saying a word.

They turned together, moving as one, moving as though they were meant for this. For each other.

Time slowed. And yet, all too soon, the music came to a halt. Whether the other couples left the dance floor or remained, she had no idea. All she knew was him.

Then he bent down. And kissed her.

His lips were firm and soft against hers. Surprisingly gentle and tender. At first. His mouth slanted over hers, urging her lips to part. Stunned at first, she could only let him kiss her. This was her first real kiss. But then an age-old instinct took over. She needed to claim this thing she desired. She opened for him, letting him in.

It was lush, their kiss. Rich and intoxicating in its naked desire. This was not a kiss of politeness, of well-mannered affection. This was a man and a woman—strangers to each other—united by shared hunger. His tongue swept against hers, searching, and she sucked on it. Her reward was a low growl deep in his chest.

One of his hands cradled the back of her head. The other flattened against the small of her back, urging her against him. She wrapped her arms around his wide shoulders as she pressed against him tightly. It was only a kiss—she'd written about so much more—yet she felt herself lost, dazed, adrift on sensation.

She broke the kiss with a gasp. *Good Lord. Jeremy.* How could she do this with a stranger, a man she'd known less than an hour, when she'd barely even touched the man she truly wanted? Tears burned her eyes at the thought of her disloyalty. How could she face herself, when she'd proven herself to be a faithless lightskirt?

"I—" But she had nothing to say to the man in blue.

She turned and fled the chamber. She had to go. Immediately. Before she did something she would truly regret.

Hurrying down the hallway, she passed a small group of women standing near a table of refreshments.

"It's true," one of them was saying to the others. "I have it on the best authority that someone is here tonight to learn the identity of the Lady of Dubious Quality."

Sarah froze.

"How did you find this out?" another queried.

"Servants' gossip. They said a stranger had come tonight. A man. Tall—wearing green? Blue?"

Sarah's stomach pitched. Heaven help her, had she just been kissing the man who wanted to learn her secrets? No, it couldn't be him. She refused to believe it.

I have to leave. Hastening past the women, she stumbled toward the foyer.

"My friend?" Amina asked with a puzzled frown.

But Sarah had no words for her. She dragged open the front door and hurried off toward her waiting carriage several blocks away. One of the most thrilling and adventurous nights of her life had turned into the very worst. She could only pray that the man in blue never learned who she was. That all her secrets would remain safe.

She hastened into the night, fear and inevitable change chasing her like demons.

His hair curling damply over his collar from his dawn swim at Hampstead Heath, Jeremy paced the paths of his mother's garden, deep in thought. Other than his early morning excursions to the bathing pond to work off a surfeit of energy, he'd gone nowhere in the two days since he'd visited the masked gathering. Instead, he'd haunted the garden that had always given him peace, searching for a measure of elusive tranquility. Yet it didn't matter how many times he strode up and down the gravel walkways. He couldn't be still, couldn't be calm.

Not since The Kiss.

How could he not have known? How could he have blithely assumed that he could go to that gathering without there being some profound change in him? That he could continue on as he always had, ignorant of who he was? Never knowing what he was capable of?

The gravel crunched beneath his boots as he walked briskly past the struggling rose bushes.

His mother had been mercifully ignorant of Jeremy's visit to the masked club, but she had noticed with some gentle reproof at breakfast that he hadn't been sleeping, as evidenced by the telltale shadows beneath his eyes. "Perhaps I should fetch my physician," she'd murmured concernedly.

"I'm just not used to London anymore," he'd answered, but that was far from the truth.

Now, alone in the garden, he pushed his body into motion as his thoughts churned.

He roasted upon the spit of his own conscience.

What had happened had been . . . much more than he'd ever imagined. Awful, wonderful. Liberating. Imprisoning. A host of contradictions that continued to torment him, days later.

He'd never felt as free as he'd been at the masked gathering. As though he could finally loose himself from the checks that held him firmly in place, confining him to a role that never felt natural. The club had been a place of unfettered sensuality. A realm of the senses. And he'd *belonged*. He'd experienced all the things that he normally kept locked within himself. Confidence had surged through him. There hadn't been anything to prove. He could simply *be*.

And it had worked! Women had gathered around him in remarkable numbers. They'd hinted at invitations both silent and spoken.

He'd been intrigued. What man wouldn't be? But none of the women had fascinated him so much as the Golden Woman, as he'd taken to thinking of her. In her gold cloak and mask, she'd looked still, remote, yet alive with sensuous energy. She'd been alone, hardly attracting attention to herself, but he hadn't been able to look away from her. She'd been a lodestone, drawing him forward, obscuring all thought other than the need to be near her. To touch her. See if she'd been as cool and distant as she'd appeared.

He'd been another man as he'd crossed the room to her. He'd transformed as he'd taken her hand and guided her onto the dance floor. Bolder than he'd ever been. Possessed with a self-assurance he'd never had. Whoever this Golden Woman was, he'd craved her with a sudden and inescapable need.

Then he'd kissed her. And just that one kiss had surpassed all his previous carnal experience. She'd been spicy and sweet, utterly delicious. Irresistible with her seeking lips and forthright desire. There had been a moment, a bare moment at the very beginning, when he could have sworn that she didn't know much about the act of kissing. But that hesitation and uncertainty had quickly burned away, revealing naked passion.

Need continued to pulse through him as he turned down the garden path, barely seeing the hedges and statues around him. They were obscured by the storm cloud of his thoughts hidden in the mists of his mind.

Where that kiss would have led . . . What might he have done had the Golden Woman not broken the contact and fled? There had been a second of wanting more, but then she'd left, and he had been on his own. Alone with the growing specter of regret.

That same remorse cut him now with rusty, jagged knives. His hands clenched into tight fists at his sides. He was a cad. A bounder. Worse. Far worse.

Lady Sarah was the one he wanted, not some faceless, nameless woman at a masked orgy.

There had been an intangible quality about the Golden Woman that had called to mind Lady Sarah. Both were watchful, separate. Was that why he'd been so comfortable approaching her in the first place? Yet the Golden Woman wasn't Lady Sarah.

He wanted to apologize to Lady Sarah, but he couldn't tell her about where he'd been and why he'd been there.

It would have to remain a secret, buried within himself. Even the thought of confessing it burned him. He would take this knowledge to his grave, but it would always smolder like a coal within him.

He stopped in his anguished pacing as a thought occurred to him. The Golden Woman and the Lady of Dubious Quality might be one and the same. She'd held herself apart from the proceedings, just as the Lady of Dubious Quality might. She hadn't had the same practiced air about her as the other women, as though she lived a life of the mind more than one given to masked orgies.

My God—it made sense. He went ramrod straight at the thought. He'd come so close, so *very* close to his quarry.

"Brooding is bad for a man's humors," his father's voice said, interrupting his thoughts.

Jeremy glanced over with dismay. Lord Hutton strode toward him, brow lowered. It was an expression with which Jeremy was a little too familiar. What would his father disapprove of now?

"Sometimes it's the only recourse," Jeremy answered, his temper too short for deference.

"Nonsense," his father clipped. "There's always the moderate option."

"Moderation is a luxury in which not everyone can indulge," Jeremy countered.

His father's frown deepened, and no wonder. Jeremy seldom spoke to Lord Hutton this way. But Jeremy was too exhausted and drawn taut to give his father the usual reverence he demanded.

Standing in front of Jeremy, Lord Hutton clasped his hands behind his back and glowered. "Your search for the Lady of Dubious Quality seems to have grown stagnant."

"I've been conducting my investigation," Jeremy said.

His father waved a hand dismissively. "I've seen none of it."

Jeremy couldn't tell his father about the masked society—and the fact that he'd very likely *kissed* the Lady of Dubious Quality. "Nevertheless, it's been carried out."

"I want more progress," the earl insisted. "Whatever it is you've been doing, you'll need to push harder on discovering who this jade is, and soon."

"I'm doing the best I can," Jeremy answered.

"You seem to need further inducement," his father said. "If the prospect of more money doesn't inspire you, then perhaps less might be more motivating."

"What do you mean?"

"If you refuse to do your duty," the earl snapped, "then I refuse to do mine. Unless I see tangible results of your search, unless the Lady of Dubious Quality is found, I will cut your allowance in half."

Jeremy stared at his father, aghast.

The earl continued relentlessly. "I doubt a vicar with a modest living can afford trips to London, much less all those books you are so fond of."

What little freedom Jeremy had suddenly disappeared, choked by his father's threat. "You cannot . . ."

"I can, sirrah, and I will."

With that, Lord Hutton paced away.

The earl's demands always came first. It didn't matter if Jeremy was eight, or eight and twenty. He was a pawn to his father, little more.

He stood in his mother's garden, but he felt trapped, caged. As though the hedges surrounding him were bars, and all he could do was smash against them in frustration.

At dusk, he journeyed back to Bloomsbury. The building that housed the club appeared even more sedate and ordinary as daylight faded. There was no sign of what went on in the evenings. Though the growing darkness conspired to hide details, Jeremy took no chances and wore a suit of russet and brown—old clothing of his that remained at the house—rather than his more sober clerical clothing. It wouldn't do if anyone saw him approach the house in his role as a vicar.

With his father's threat hanging over him, Bloomsbury remained Jeremy's most concrete lead toward finding the Lady of Dubious Quality, who might also be the Golden Woman. So many secret identities, so many disguises.

But she wasn't the only one perpetuating a role. He led more than one life, inhabiting more than one persona. Ever since he'd kissed the Golden Woman, that was even more true. A part of him that he'd kept hidden had been loosened, freed, and now protested being forced back into its cage.

As he mounted the steps to the Bloomsbury house, he glanced around quickly. Making certain that no one was watching, he quickly donned his borrowed blue leather mask. With his disguise in place, he knocked on the front door.

After a few moments, the door opened, and the woman who'd called herself Amina appeared. She wore a mask, though her sumptuous red gown had been replaced by an ordinary muslin dress. She frowned at him as she held the door open.

"There's no gathering of friends tonight," she said, eyeing his mask.

"I haven't come for that." He looked up and down the street. A few pedestrians were out, along with a cart heading home from market. "May I step inside?"

Wordlessly, Amina held the door wider, permitting him to enter.

Once inside, he was struck anew by how typical the house appeared without its exotic, sensuous guests, dim lighting, and music. Any younger son or well-to-do brewer might call this place home. Yet the specter of the Golden Woman haunted this place, as well as the ghost of his other, more liberated self.

That self could not be allowed to stretch and breathe. What would Lady Sarah think if she knew there was some lascivious, lecherous vicar panting after her?

"What is it that you want?" Amina asked without preamble. "We never permit guests inside unless it's the selected night."

"There was a woman here," he answered, cutting to the chase. "Wore a gold cloak and gold mask. It might have been her first time."

"What of her?" Amina folded her arms across her chest. She was really quite lovely, but her eyes held far more knowledge than one would expect in a woman so young.

"I need her name."

At once Amina said, "Absolutely not."

"It's a matter of some urgency," Jeremy pressed. It

felt bitter in his mouth to speak again, but he had to. "I can . . . make it worth your while."

But Amina only shook her head. "Names are never given here. It's one of the reasons why our friends return. They need the security of absolute anonymity."

Though he felt considerable discouragement, he urged, "There's nothing I can do to change your mind?"

"Nothing," she said flatly. "And if that's all you wish to discuss, I must bid you good evening, sir." She gestured toward the door.

Seeing that there was nothing further to be gained by pursuing this line of inquiry, Jeremy bowed and turned to open the door. He felt compelled to add over his shoulder, "As I said, it's an urgent and serious matter. If you change your mind—"

"I will not." Amina's voice was cold. "Now go. And you are not welcome back here again."

"As you wish."

With that, he went out to the stairs and shut the door behind him. Removing his mask, he started down the steps, taking them slowly, wondering what his next move was to be. He clung to a precipice. If he found the Lady of Dubious Quality, he'd have the autonomy he longed for. But if he did not . . . his world would become thimble-sized, strangling him.

Steps sounded from the mews that ran alongside the house. Jeremy turned to see a servant hastily edging forward. "Oi, governor," the man whispered, waving him forward. The man looked around, over his shoulder, and up and down the street. "You want to know about that lady in gold?"

Jeremy hurried over. "I do."

The servant's eyes narrowed. "Information don't come without a price."

"Why would you tell me?" Jeremy demanded.

The man scowled. "She docked my pay for taking something from the wine cellar. Got to earn my blunt back somehow."

Jeremy produced several coins from his pocket, which he held up for the other man's inspection. Bribery wasn't entirely virtuous behavior, but hopefully the end justified the means in this case.

The servant quickly grabbed the money and tucked it away. "I heard," he said in a barely audible voice, "the woman call herself Mrs. Chalbury. That was it. Just Mrs. Chalbury."

Jeremy nodded and wrote the name down in his notebook. A tremor worked through him just to hear it. The mysterious woman had an actual name. It made her more fantastical, but yet more real. "Anything else?"

"She came on foot," the man said hastily.

An interesting detail. Perhaps it meant that she lived nearby.

"Thank you," said Jeremy.

But instead of answering, the servant scurried away.

For a moment, Jeremy simply stood there, absorbing the information. His first real clue in this chase.

His future hung in the balance.

Chapter 13

We disported ourselves with a heat and energy unlike anything I had ever known. We were mythical in our need, ageless in our desire.

When he stripped me of my garments, he did so with an uncommon reverence, as though revealing something precious. His hands and mouth possessed extraordinary talent as he ravished my body and plundered my mind. I, too, worshipped his body, using my many skills and considerable experience to show him that I was a woman he would not soon forget.

I could not resist the allure of his body, and eagerly tasted his . . .

The Highwayman's Seduction

Jeremy searched for Mrs. Chalbury from one London parish to another, yet she eluded him, not appearing on any documentation. The curates and vicars were very gracious, and gave him space in their rectories to peruse the large tomes. Ever hospitable, his colleagues offered him refreshments at each stop. Jeremy drank more tea in a morning than he'd had in a week.

After visiting three churches in the area near the masquerade house with no success, he nearly gave up. But at the fourth church, he found it at last. "Mrs. Mary Chalbury" resided on Gower Street, only a handful of blocks away from where Jeremy was at that very moment.

Right within his grasp. The Golden Woman—and the Lady of Dubious Quality. His goal had almost been achieved. Was he relieved? Disappointed? Perhaps both.

"Find what you're looking for?" the curate asked him as he strode out of the rectory.

Yes, he'd gotten what he was after, but it was a bitter accomplishment. Now he was going to have to reveal her identity to his father.

She'd be exposed, her books coming to an end. And he'd be the instrument of her destruction.

Jeremy immediately headed toward the address on Gower Street, his heart both pounding with excitement and heavy with regret. He hadn't known he could feel both emotions at the same time, yet he did. He barely knew himself anymore, torn as he was between so many different desires.

He wanted freedom. He wanted Lady Sarah. He wanted so many things but had no idea how to attain any of them. If anyone would understand what it meant to be uncertain of one's self, it would be Lady Sarah. She grasped life's ambiguity.

Yet they would never have the kind of intimacy he desired, and so he had to keep his many questions, his many uncertainties, locked away.

A few short minutes later, he found himself standing

in front of the address taken from the parish register.

And stunned everyone around him by laughing aloud.

It was a shop selling women's undergarments.

By God, she'd fooled him. The Golden Woman, the Lady of Dubious Quality, had tricked him. She must have known that someone might go looking for her, and she'd worked hard to obscure her trail.

Still, he had to be certain. He entered the shop, the bell ringing cheerfully as the door swung open.

His face flamed. Mannequins were laced into ribbon-trimmed stays, and countless trays were filled with filmy stockings and sly, satiny embroidered garters. He'd never been confronted with so many underthings. They were everywhere. On countertops, in glass-fronted drawers, draped across tables and display stands.

A pretty redheaded clerk, slightly older than Jeremy, approached him with a bemused expression.

"Is there something I can help you with, Vicar?" she asked. "No one here's in need of saving."

A young girl behind the counter giggled.

"I'm not here on matters of doctrinal concern," he said.

"Then what brings you to my fine establishment?" she pressed.

"Are you Mrs. Chalbury?" he asked.

"I'm Mrs. Hart," the woman answered.

"Does a woman by the name of Mrs. Chalbury live above this shop?"

She shook her head. "There's a tailor above us. No one named Mrs. Chalbury."

"Nor any employees who answer to that name, either?"

"Just myself and Jeanette," the clerk said.

"I see." He turned to go.

"Is there anything else I can assist you with? Something for your wife, perhaps?" She held up a pink garter worked all over with tiny roses.

He could just picture that wrapped around the silken flesh of Lady Sarah's thigh. But then Lady Sarah melded in his imagination with the Golden Woman, and he couldn't tell if he was aroused or confused. "Uh . . . no thank you."

Hurrying outside, he paused to collect his breath. His head spun, and he looked up at the pale gray sky, gathering himself.

She'd led him on a dance, the Lady of Dubious Quality. One where she knew the steps, and he stumbled over his own big feet. Admirable, really, that she'd thought so far ahead, anticipating his moves, knowing how to outwit him. Respect for his intended target grew.

He'd have to find another way of tracing her—though he'd have to ponder the how of it later. If only it was late or early enough for him to go for a swim that he might clear his mind. Instead, he walked with a wide stride back toward his father's house, letting the movement and momentum override the thoughts that crashed against each other.

Two women filled his mind: the Lady of Dubious Quality, also known as the Golden Woman, and Lady Sarah. They were forever apart, yet they occupied his every thought, the beat of his heart and movement of his body. He wanted all of them in different capacities. And he could have none of them.

Everything fell into place when Sarah picked up her quill—the external world dissolved, all questions and concerns evaporated like morning mist the moment the pen was in her hand. She had no doubts about herself or what she wanted out of life. Energy and purpose flowed through her as she sat at her desk, a blank sheet of paper in front of her. The stories were her stories, her breath and pulse.

She'd sequestered herself in her usual spot in the Green Drawing Room. It was an old-fashioned chamber that had been neglected when her mother had remodeled and redecorated the house ten years ago. Few ever came in here. So Sarah had claimed it for herself, setting up a little desk and a goodly assortment of quills and paper to feed her compulsion to write. Her mother always assumed that Sarah spent her time in here either writing letters or keeping extensive journals—never suspecting that the locked bottom drawer of Sarah's desk contained manuscripts for Lady of Dubious Quality books.

Her mother was out shopping today, leaving Sarah in blissful peace. Wasting no time, she'd immediately gone in to work after breakfast. This latest story was coming together nicely, with Lady Josephina and her university professor engaged in a torrid affair. They had made love in his study, as well as in a library.

Would Lady Josephina stay with the professor? Did she settle down with one man? Or would she move on to another lover? The idea of her heroine forever searching for a specific man to satisfy her desires, always on the hunt, never finding a true companion . . . it didn't sound as appealing now as it once had. Perhaps she would find completion in the arms of a single person. The most unlikely man. The professor perhaps, a scholarly man, serious but witty, insightful and thoughtful . . .

A tap sounded at the door.

Sarah quickly sanded her sheet of paper, then slid it underneath the blotter of her desk. "Come in," she called when the evidence of her writing was secreted away.

"A letter for you, Lady Sarah," said a footman, appearing with a silver tray.

"Invitations go to my mother first," she answered.

"This looks like a regular letter," the servant said. "If a trifle big. And it's addressed to you, not Her Grace."

Sarah took the large envelope, frowning. She seldom received much direct correspondence. Nearly all the letters went through the duchess before Sarah looked at them, since most that came to the house during the Season were generally invites to one social gathering or another.

She recognized the handwriting on the envelope as her third-party intermediary who carefully routed all her Lady of Dubious Quality letters to her. The intermediary was a crossing sweep who collected mail for her from a pub in Bishopsgate, and he was well versed in keeping anyone off his trail.

"Thank you, Paul," she said, dismissing the servant.

As soon as he bowed and left, she was on her feet at once, breaking the wafers on the envelope.

One was from her publisher. The other was from Mrs. Hart. She read them both in quick succession. The first alarmed her. The second terrified her.

The coded letter from her publisher informed her that Amina, of the masquerade house, had let him know that a man in a blue mask had been looking for a woman in gold, a woman, he seemed to intimate, who was also the Lady of Dubious Quality.

The second missive came from the proprietress of the shop that served as "Mrs. Chalbury's" residence. Mrs. Hart informed Sarah that, per her instructions, she kept track of anyone searching for a woman by that fictitious name. And a man had, in fact, been in recently, asking after Mrs. Chalbury. What should Mrs. Hart do if anyone was to return and ask more questions?

Sarah immediately hurried to the fire and threw the letters on the blaze. She watched the paper blacken and flake, but it was a futile hope to wish that the fire could erase the danger.

For danger it was. Fear clawed at Sarah, climbing up her throat as she paced the length of the room, back and forth. Someone was searching out her true identity and was coming so close, so terribly close, to discovering the truth.

God—if that was the case? What was she to do? If anyone found out who she was . . . She would be ruined. Cast out from polite Society. Her parents' reputations would be in tatters. Everything would be ripped apart, never to be repaired again.

She had to do something to fix this. But what?

She couldn't think while trapped within the walls of her family's home.

In a moment, she'd rung for her maid and announced that they would be heading to McKinnon's. She'd no desire to peruse books, but it gave her a destination, an objective, since she couldn't just wander the streets of London in a panicked fog.

After donning her bonnet and redingote, and with her maid keeping pace behind her, Sarah quickly made her way down the front steps.

"The carriage, my lady?" her maid asked.

She shook her head. "On foot today."

Her servant didn't look particularly happy with the news that they would be walking, especially since McKinnon's was at least two miles away, but Sarah was too distracted and fearful to do more than allow herself to move. So she strode with long, unladylike paces toward the bookshop, her mind in a fury of agitation.

What was she to do? How could she protect herself with danger lurking so close? Even if she were to abandon writing—which she could never do, since it was so much a part of herself that she might as well cut off her hands—it wouldn't stop the threat that prowled near. As a single woman of good name and sterling virtue, her position was desperately precarious. She had nothing to protect her. Only her parents and their title, but a young woman without a husband was still all too vulnerable.

Was that the answer? Marriage?

If she did take a husband, she would have the protection of his name.

There was one girl who'd been out a few years ago—Miss Crane, the daughter of a country gentleman. Miss Crane had been a bit wild, given to trips to

Brighton and Bath, associating with soldiers and fast company. Rumors had flown about her . . . until she'd taken a husband. She'd been a wild bride, too, but the gossip had almost completely stopped as soon as she'd wed. Miss Crane, now Lady Beauchamp, was never turned away from any door. She was whispered about, but with more amusement than shock and revulsion. Amusement was far less damaging than horror.

In some ways, a wife had more freedom than an unmarried woman. Though she was her husband's possession, she traded one kind of liberty for another. She didn't need to shelter her reputation as much. She wasn't looked at as though she was in constant danger of having her chastity assailed or challenged.

Wives had power that unmarried young women did not.

As Sarah hurried from the west toward the commercial center of London, her thoughts kept spinning, traveling leagues in a second when her feet could only take her a few miles an hour.

Perhaps Sarah would be protected from slander by the asset of being someone's wife.

"My lady," her maid huffed behind her. "Please . . . slow down . . . I can't keep . . . up."

"Sorry," Sarah answered distractedly, trying to shorten her paces.

If she did marry, whom would she pick?

None of the available men that had been presented to her held any appeal. They were shallow, dull. Fortune hunters who wanted nothing more than her substantial dowry. And not a single one of them made her feel anything like her heroines felt with her heroes. No passion. No blaze of need. She couldn't imagine spending fifty years in her would-be suitors' beds. She'd expire of boredom within a decade.

She wanted passion. And she wanted a man who made her feel . . . everything. Alive. Intelligent. Wanted. Was that impossible?

It wasn't impossible with Jeremy. He made her feel all those things. He appreciated her mind, her intellect. And there was no denying that she felt herself powerfully aware of him as a man, and herself as a woman, whenever they were together.

Was he what she needed? Was he the prospective husband she was looking for?

She *was* highly attracted to him. Desired him as she'd desired no one else before. He was witty, scholarly, perceptive. Kind and honorable, but he was no one's easy prey. He'd stood up for her when she'd been insulted, and blazed with barely restrained anger in her defense.

Yet . . . he was beneath her in station. A country vicar with a decent, but still relatively small, living. She was a duke's daughter, expected to marry one of the highest-ranking men in the country.

She couldn't ignore the fact that it would be a huge problem for her to keep writing should she and Jeremy marry. But she *had* to continue penning her stories.

He wouldn't have to find out, however. She had ways of keeping the two identities apart. True, her safeguards had been tested recently, but if she became someone's wife, if she was Jeremy's bride, they might be strengthened by her married status.

Jeremy would never need to know that she was

the Lady of Dubious Quality. She could even take the smallest break away from her writing, just a month or two—though the time apart from it might prove very difficult—to wait for the danger to die down. She could leave London for a time, as well.

Sarah paused to give a beggar a coin, despite her maid's look of disapproval, and continued on her way to the bookshop.

As for Jeremy being beneath her . . . he was the son of an earl, not a commoner. While such distinctions mattered little to Sarah, they did count in the eyes of Society, and she dwelt within those confines. The scandal of marrying Lord Hutton's youngest son would be far less than her taking just any man as a husband.

Besides, her parents were eager for her to marry someone. Far better for her to take a vicar to wed than for her to be unmarried forever. No one wanted a spinster for a daughter.

Sarah drew up short and stared at the front of McKinnon's. Somehow, she'd reached the shop already.

She stepped inside. McKinnon sat at his counter, reviewing an accounting book.

"This isn't your usual day, Lady Sarah!" the bookseller exclaimed.

"I need to ask a favor of you," she said.

"Of course," he answered at once.

When she told him what it was, he nodded slowly but did not press her for details. For that, she was glad. There were irreversible moments in life that needed silence far more than words.

Chapter 14

On a fur blanket, naked, we reposed before the fire, sharing a glass of wine. He stroked my hair and murmured endearments. A fine rain began to fall, sheltering us, as though we were the only two people in England. I had never been so content . . .

The Highwayman's Seduction

As Jeremy walked into breakfast following his morning swim, one of the servants approached him.

"A letter for you, Master Jeremy," the footman said, holding out a small envelope.

He took the letter and dismissed the servant. The handwriting on the front of the missive didn't match that of Mr. Wolbert, his curate.

The letter was from McKinnon, the bookseller, telling him that the book he'd ordered had come in and was ready to be picked up.

To the best of his recollection, he hadn't ordered anything from McKinnon's. It had to be a mistake. Should he write the man back and let him know? Or perhaps he ought to go there himself to inform him of the error.

The clock chimed just half past nine. The day at home stretched before him, stifling. Ever since his dead end with Mrs. Chalbury, he'd been at a loss as to how to proceed with his search for the Lady of Dubious Quality, but if he stayed at home, he'd be subject to more of his father's stern looks.

His mother entered the breakfast room. She offered her cheek for a kiss before approaching the sideboard to help herself to her repast.

"You aren't staying home again, are you?" she asked, setting a rasher of bacon on her plate. "Young marriageable ladies don't simply show up on our doorstep."

That settled it.

"No indeed." He finished his breakfast in a few bites, swallowing a mouthful of coffee to wash it all down. Then he gave his mother another kiss before grabbing his hat. Within a few moments, he was on the street, walking toward the bookshop.

Finally, he reached McKinnon's. It was early enough that the customers were few, both outside and within. The moment Jeremy set foot through the door, the tall bookseller appeared, carrying a stack of leather-bound tomes.

"Ah, Mr. Cleland," McKinnon said, his deep voice drawling. "You've come for your book."

"That's why I'm here," Jeremy replied. "I've no recollection of ordering anything from you."

But the bookseller didn't seem to hear him. "Just a moment, sir, and I'll fetch it for you." He unloaded his burden of other books onto the desk by the front door, then moved off toward the back room, where this mysterious volume awaited.

Deciding it was best to see exactly what this strange book was, Jeremy waited. He nodded politely to two women entering the bookshop arm in arm. They returned the greeting and disappeared into the stacks, whispering about the latest novel from a celebrated author.

McKinnon returned a short while later, bearing a small book bound in dark brown leather.

"Here you go, Mr. Cleland." The bookseller handed him the tome. "It's all paid for, so you're free to take it home."

Truly baffled now—books were expensive, and he didn't prepay for them without making note of it— Jeremy consulted the front cover. It was a thin treatise about astronomy based on the most recent findings of Herschel. Though Jeremy found the subject of astronomy an interesting one as he had almost no understanding of how the cosmos and stars worked, he generally didn't read much on the topic, spending most of his time consulting books of philosophy and theology.

Something was inside the book, forming a slight gap between the pages. He flipped the pages open until he reached the object, then started in surprise when he saw that it was a note, folded into a neat rectangle. His name was written on the note. And it was in Lady Sarah's hand.

He glanced up to see if McKinnon watched him, but the bookseller had vanished in the peculiar way in which tall people could make themselves disappear noiselessly.

Jeremy's heart sped up. What was the meaning of the note? After looking around to make certain he was truly alone, he pulled open the small bit of paper.

Dear Jeremy—

She'd used his Christian name. He traced his fingers over it, imagining her writing out the letters.

He continued to read.

> *Please meet me tomorrow afternoon at the Observatory at Greenwich.*

> Yours, &c.
> *Sarah*

And there, she'd used her first name, as well, leaving off the honorific. What could it mean? There was a strange, laconic urgency to her note. She wasted no time on pleasantries. But then, when one left a secret letter for someone tucked inside a book, a long-winded missive discussing the weather didn't seem quite called for.

But why had she been so secretive about asking to see him? She'd been much more open when inviting him to the exhibition of Oriental art. Now . . . well, he wasn't sure what to think. Only that he'd soon see her again.

He could not wait.

The Royal Observatory at Greenwich stood impressively on the south bank of the Thames. Jeremy walked, then took a wherry across the stagnant river to reach his destination. He hadn't slept well, excitement dancing along his nerves and Sarah's visage appearing behind his eyelids every time he'd tried to shut them. So he'd spent most of the night reading—*not* the Lady of Dubious Quality's work—and writing up plans for a winter festival in his parish. Winter wouldn't be coming for a few more months, but it didn't hurt to be prepared for the season.

The small skiff glided across the river, and Jeremy tried not to breathe in the stink of the water, thick as it was with fetid debris.

The wherry rocked as it approached the small pier just down the river from the Observatory. His own heart rocked with it.

After paying the ferryman, Jeremy climbed up the bank and headed toward the Observatory, standing proudly as it had for the past hundred and fifty years, a monument to man's quest to look beyond himself and the limitations of this strange, small planet. The brick and white stone of the façade gleamed dully in the gray afternoon light, and its domes arched toward the sky. Where was Sarah?

Footsteps sounded, and he turned. His pulse thundered when he beheld Sarah walking toward him, dressed in a dove-gray spencer and pale pink bonnet. Her gaze was fixed only on his face as she neared. It seemed as if years had passed since he'd last seen her, though it couldn't have been more than a week. She looked pale, her eyes shadowed but still impossibly lovely to his mind. He'd come to prize the assertiveness of her features, her unusual, strong beauty. How could anyone mistake her for a wallflower when she stood out from all the other soft, colorless young women?

She was quite alone.

No maid, no mother. No friends. Just herself. Clearly, this wasn't a simple outing.

"Are you by yourself?" she asked, coming to stand in front of him.

He spread his hands. "Entirely. And you?"

"My maid is in the carriage." She glanced toward the far bank of the river. "I had to bribe her silence with a pearl pendant."

She still seemed tense and on edge, so he tried for a scrap of humor. "Secret messages hidden in books. I felt like the king's spymaster. Perhaps being a vicar is an excellent disguise."

She only smiled thinly. "The subterfuge was an unfortunate necessity."

"Something's wrong," he deduced.

"Yes. No." She shook her head. "Might we walk?"

He silently and readily offered her his arm. His already frenetic heartbeat kicked when she placed her hand on his sleeve and held him snug against her chest rather than a polite touch of her fingers on his arm. The soft roundness of her breast pressed against his biceps.

They sedately trod along the paths surrounding the Observatory. When she was ready to speak, she would. But until then, he'd give her what space she needed to collect her clearly disordered thoughts.

"Have you ever considered marrying?" she said suddenly, breaking the quiet.

The question caught him entirely off guard. He said slowly, "I *should*. Many vicars do. They stress that in seminary. That one of our responsibilities is the taking of a wife."

"An odd thing to urge on you," she murmured.

"They tell us it's important for us to have wives to reach out to the community. Makes us models to those around us. Makes us approachable, too, I suppose. Shows that we're human like everyone else."

She mulled this over, her pace easily matching his. "But what do *you* want?" she asked after a moment.

"I always thought that I would take a wife," he eventually replied. "Never really knew when. Or whom." He hadn't known himself well enough to offer his hand to anyone. His own carnal impulses were so intense that he felt he always needed to keep them tethered.

"So there's no one in particular that you'd really want to marry," she said.

He could prevaricate, if not outright tell an untruth. But he couldn't. Not with her. They both deserved better. And he was tired, so tired, of fighting this war inside himself. He could let her know how he felt—and if she didn't reciprocate, he'd find a way to go on. A man with a hole in his chest.

He stopped walking. "There wasn't," he said, gazing at her.

She stared up at him, her eyes wide and lovely. "Has that changed?"

Everything in the world went into one word. "Yes."

He watched the pulse in her throat flutter, and a pink stain rise in her cheeks.

"What if . . ." she began. She swallowed. "What if we were to marry?"

He jolted with the immensity of what she suggested. For a moment, he could do nothing but gape at her, like someone seeing the stars for the first time.

"You and I?" he asked.

She spoke quickly, as though afraid he might object. "We like each other, don't we? We share something . . . a bond. I'm not imagining things. I have a very good imagination, but I'd never concoct a man's esteem for me. I couldn't be so foolish. That's—"

"I care for you," he said, trying to assuage her fear. Fear that touched him, deeply. She was afraid of his answer. Afraid he might say no. "Very much."

"Enough to take me as a wife?" she pressed.

He stared at her. She voiced the very thoughts he'd been afraid to speak. Dazed, he said, "It's not possible. You . . . outrank me. And your parents. They'd be furious at the match."

The color darkened in her cheeks. "I'm two years past my twenty-first birthday. I've reached my majority. Their approval isn't necessary."

"And what of the approval of the rest of Society?" he asked softly.

She made a scoffing sound, and her eyes were bright and hot. "What has Society ever done for me?"

"You're saying," he said, "that you'd have me as a husband? Against all the odds, you want me?"

"What if I said yes?" she threw back at him. "What would you do?"

In response, he wrapped his arms around her. Pulled her close. And kissed her.

Heat exploded through him at the touch of their lips. His mind urged him to go slowly, gently. This was their first kiss. He should be a gentleman, show her respect. But at the brush of her lips against his, the feel of her so close, primal hunger and need roared through him. She was soft. Spicy and sweet. And she responded to him immediately. No fearful, virginal restraint. No uncertainty. She wanted him, as much as he yearned for her. Her mouth opened to his, and she accepted the sweep of his tongue eagerly.

Her body pressed snug against his, soft and curved. The world spun around him.

There was something strangely familiar about the feel of her, the taste. But no—it had to be his lack of experience.

He devoured her, letting her know through this intimate contact that she was all he wanted. And she responded in kind, her fingers curved around the back of his neck, pulling him down, closer, closer. She held nothing back. Her honesty. Her openness. He would take anything she offered him, wanted everything.

At the sound of her moan, he surfaced. Broke the kiss, though it felt as though he was being torn apart.

"We . . ." He panted. "Shouldn't be doing this."

Her eyes opened, shadowed by disappointment. "But I want to," she breathed.

Fire shot along his veins. His cock leapt at her words. "I want to, as well." He forced himself to loosen his hold of her. "But we both know that a duke's daughter isn't meant to be a vicar's wife."

Her fingers slid from behind his neck until her fists curled at her sides. She glanced away, a suspicious sheen in her eyes. "I know," she said on a sigh. "This was my idea. I wanted it so much . . . but it can't happen. I just wish . . . I'd been born someone different. That we could have known one another under different conditions."

"As do I." His throat was raw, his voice a grating

rasp. "We're not eccentrics, my family. Everything we've done has been scrupulously well behaved."

"Mine, too," she said, choked.

"But perhaps that doesn't mean you and I cannot break free," he suggested.

Her gaze gleamed, as though wet with tears. "I shouldn't have suggested this. It was wrong. I was wrong. In the eyes of my kin, in the eyes of Society, I've more to lose. A man may ascend, but a woman cannot follow her heart, no matter where it takes her."

Without another word, she turned and strode away. He could do nothing but watch her go, wanting so desperately to go after her.

He was alone. Again. He'd gone from the pinnacle of his existence to its lowest point in a moment.

Chapter 15

We talked at length, Jacob and I. Dashing as a knight of old, he'd been a cavalryman, riding across the breadth of the globe in service to his king and country. Like all wonderful and terrible things, the war ended. The home he returned to had no use for surplus officers. What choice was left him? The road, and its plunder, beckoned. A highwayman from a cavalryman, his only means of putting food in his belly and keeping the rain from his head. The grim tale pierced my heart. I grew too fond of my highwayman . . .

The Highwayman's Seduction

Jeremy entered Marwood's box at the Imperial Theater. His cousin was preoccupied watching the rehearsal of his wife's latest burletta. But Jeremy could not wait patiently. He needed guidance. Now.

He coughed as a means of announcing himself. Marwood turned around in surprise, but smiled in welcome.

"All the souls here are black as pitch," he told Jeremy. "Too late, old man."

"There's only one soul here that's too far gone,"

Jeremy noted. "I'll pray for you, but it will be like throwing droplets of water on a conflagration."

"Much appreciated." Marwood stood, and Jeremy shook his cousin's extended hand.

"Normally you can crush coal into diamonds with your handshake," Marwood noted. "What's amiss? Aside from the condition of my benighted soul."

Striding over to the railing, Jeremy looked over the theater. His gaze didn't linger on anything in particular but danced around, searching for a calm place to land but finding none. Everything churned in him, a tempest.

He asked abruptly, "How does Lady Marwood's latest work fare?"

"Oh, the usual histrionics between actors—always feuds brewing. But they love each other like a big, messy family." Marwood crossed his arms over his chest. "I have a gnawing in my gut that tells me you're not here to discuss Maggie's most recent burletta."

Could Jeremy speak of this to his cousin? They'd been separated as youths, but now they were grown men. What more could his father threaten him with? After a moment, Jeremy asked, "How did you know that you wanted to marry Lady Marwood?"

The question seemed to catch Marwood off guard. He pondered it for a moment. "Thinking of life without her was impossible. Pretending that I could exist deprived of her was an exercise in futility. Completely impossible."

"And the difference in your stations?" Jeremy wanted to know hotly.

"Didn't matter to me," Marwood said frankly. "So

long as I had her, Society could go hang. Our happiness was at stake."

Jeremy peered closely at him. Then, slowly, Marwood's brows lifted. "There's some lowborn woman who caught your eye."

Jeremy looked down at his flexing hands. "The opposite," he said darkly. "I'm the one that's lower than her."

"My mind spins at the possibility—who is she?"

"Lady Sarah Frampton."

"The wallflower," his cousin exclaimed.

Anger surged, hot and roiling. "Don't call her that," Jeremy snarled. "It's a damn insulting name. She's . . . so much more than that name."

Marwood nudged a chair toward his cousin. "Have a seat, and tell me everything. Spare no detail."

Jeremy turned the chair around and straddled it, his long legs sticking out on either side. He raked his hands through his hair.

"She and I . . ." He exhaled roughly. For a long, long time, Jeremy said nothing, visibly fighting to gather his thoughts and words. Finally, he admitted, "We've gotten very close."

"How close?" Marwood leaned against the railing, folding his arms across his chest.

"Very," was all Jeremy would expound on the subject. "We've . . . kissed." His face reddened.

It looked as though sheer strength of will kept Marwood from clapping and hooting his approval. "I take it the kiss was satisfactory," he drawled. "Never mind. Judging by that febrile blush staining your pure cheeks, it was more than satisfactory."

"She's . . ." Jeremy's voice trailed off, and his gaze went far away. He felt tight and alive and ready to burst just thinking of Sarah—her sharpness, her keen interest in the world around her. The secret earthiness of her.

"Ah."

"She's even suggested that we marry," Jeremy said, his voice shadowed. "Though we both eventually agreed that it couldn't happen."

"I fail to see the problem," Marwood noted. "Unmistakably, the lady wants you—though I have to question her judgment."

Jeremy glowered at him.

Clearing his throat, Marwood continued. "Is she beholden to her parents for their approval?"

"She's of age," Jeremy explained. "Their endorsement isn't necessary."

"What of their blessing?"

He shrugged. "Whether she needs it or not, I cannot say."

"If she makes you happy—"

"She makes me very happy," Jeremy said at once. Confused, restless, but happy.

"Then," Marwood said, spreading his hands wide, as though they encompassed the answer, "do what you need to do." He studied Jeremy closely. "It's not all that simple, eh?"

Jeremy couldn't meet Marwood's gaze. "I've kissed someone else," he gritted.

"What do you mean?"

"I mean that I went to that damn masquerade and kissed another woman," he growled. "A woman wearing a gold mask. I think," he added unhappily, "that she was the Lady of Dubious Quality." He wanted them both—Sarah and the Golden Woman—but he couldn't have them both. Yet it was Sarah who had taken up residence in his mind, his body and heart. The Golden Woman was unmitigated physical pleasure. Sarah was so much more to him.

"And that makes you miserable," Marwood said, confused.

"It . . . lit something in me." Jeremy stared off into the memory. "Something wild. Don't know how to explain it."

"I think I understand." Marwood nodded in consideration. "I've had kisses like that."

Anger and mystification warred within Jeremy. "How can I offer myself to Sarah if I've had thoughts about another woman?"

"Of course you can," Marwood said at once. "Maggie and I didn't come to each other as virgins."

Jeremy stood abruptly, tipping the chair to the floor. "I didn't make love to that other woman."

"But you still feel the betrayal," his cousin noted.

Jeremy could only nod unhappily. He thought of those stolen touches at the theater, of the kiss at the Observatory, and confusion mired him. Could he desire two women? When he truly only wanted one?

Walking up to him, Marwood placed his hands on Jeremy's shoulders and looked hard into his eyes. "Don't confuse what your cock tells you for what your heart wants," he cautioned. "Clearly, it wants Lady Sarah." He smiled wryly. "Not so long ago you were the one dispensing advice, Vicar. The honor's mine now. Though I'm no man of God."

Jeremy exhaled but felt no more certain than he had when first he'd entered the theater box. "I just don't bloody know."

"You want the woman," his cousin said with careful patience. "She wants you. Yes, there will be hurdles to leap, but you've got long legs and a strong heart. There's nothing more to discuss. Marry her. Besides," he added with a wry smile, "taking a bride might repair that dented reputation of yours."

Alarm gripped Jeremy. "What do you mean?"

"I've heard a few things," Marwood answered smugly. "Going into shops that sell women's undergarments, for one thing." Before Jeremy could exact more answers, Marwood continued, "Listen, you once asked me what I was afraid of. Time to ask yourself the same question."

The quill sharpener was poised in Sarah's hand when the door to the Green Drawing Room opened and Jeremy strode in. He looked intent, focused, barely aware of the rain darkening the shoulders of his coat, and hardly attentive to the footman hurrying up behind him.

"I'm sorry, my lady," the servant began. "He just came right in and—"

"That's all right, Paul," Sarah said with as much calm as she could muster. Jeremy's sudden, unannounced appearance rattled her—especially after the way they'd left things two days ago, without a word of communication between them since.

The last few days had been knotted with anxiety and confusion. She didn't believe her own bold actions. Had she actually presented him with the option of marrying her? And he'd gone and kissed her in response—a kiss as melting and powerful as the one she'd gotten from the man in the blue mask. She'd known it would be good between her and Jeremy physically. Actual proof changed everything. They lit the world on fire with the heat they shared. It was as spontaneous and instant as a midsummer blaze.

Had it been her imagination? She'd exhausted herself trying to convince herself it couldn't have been so blistering, so devastating. Yet here he was, stalking into the Green Drawing Room, the center of her most private self. It was both appropriate and strange to have him here. Her palms dampened and her mouth dried, and she couldn't stop her gaze from straying to his lips. The same lips that had tormented her for hours, both awake and asleep.

"Forgive me," he said tightly. "I couldn't wait to be announced."

She set the quill sharpener down with more calm than she felt. "I'm glad you're here." Turning to the footman, she directed, "Please have Cook send up some tea."

But Jeremy shook his head. "Not here for tea."

"Well, I'd like some." At her nod, Paul disappeared to fetch some refreshments. She didn't truly want tea or anything to eat, but it would give her a reason to divert her attention from the tension that filled the room and pushed at the windows.

"Please, sit." Sarah rose and walked toward two chairs facing each other in front of the fire.

At first, it looked as though Jeremy would refuse.

She sensed that he had a goal, but she had no idea what it might be. He appeared to be wrestling with something within himself. After she sat, however, he lowered himself down into a chair. His long legs stretched out before him, and she distracted herself by looking at the gleam of firelight shining on the leather of his tall boots rather than staring into his blazing face.

Nervousness seized her. She twisted her fingers together, listening to the pop of the fire and the patter of gentle rain on the windows. A thousand questions flooded her mind, jostling against each other, making it almost impossible to sit still. She chanced a peek at him through her lashes. She'd never seen him so resolute, his brow lowered, his jaw a hard square line. He did not look like a man on a happy errand. Rather he resembled someone with a purpose, as though there was a tree that had to be felled before a field could be plowed.

"You don't have to say anything," she burst out. "I . . . I understand. It was a thought, a suggestion. I didn't really think that you and I . . . that we . . ."

His blue eyes bored into her. "It wasn't serious then? What you said at the Observatory."

She pushed up from her seat, and he stood, as well. Both of them couldn't be contained. She paced away from him. If he rejected her, how would she bear it? Yet she couldn't hide behind obscuring half-truths. He deserved her honesty—and so did she.

"I did mean it," she admitted. "But," she added hastily, "I don't hold you to anything. We can . . . we can remain friends. If that's what you want." Though she couldn't truly be friends with a man who'd kissed her into insensibility. When she'd want that same kiss again and again, and wish and wonder where it might lead, what it could presage.

"It's not what I want at all," he gritted. "I can't be your *friend*, Sarah."

"Ah." Disappointment rocked through her, scooping her out and leaving her hollow. The burn of unshed tears ached behind her eyes. The polite thing to do was offer her hand to shake, and then part company with him as civilly as possible. But she didn't have much in her to be polite. She wanted to run far away to some dark cavern, where she could weep and howl and lick her wounds. Possibly never to emerge.

He took two long steps and stood in front of her, taking her hands in his. A faint tremor shook him, and he was a burning coal beneath her touch. She stared at their joined hands.

"What I want," he said, his voice deep and low, "is to be your husband."

Her gaze flew up to meet his. "You . . ." But she couldn't finish the sentence. Emotion and disbelief clogged her throat.

"Sarah," he said urgently, the world in his eyes, "if you meant what you said, if you'll have me . . . I want to marry you. I need you as my wife."

He continued, "I care for you, Sarah." He was bright and serious, and impossibly beautiful as he said these words, lit from within. "I hope you'll come to feel for me even a tenth of what I feel for you."

"There's no need to wait for that," she declared. Emotion overwhelmed her, carrying her off in a tide of sensation. "Because I care for you, too, Jeremy. Very much."

They met for a kiss.

She clung to him. Her hands gripped his biceps, and her head tipped back to allow him full access to her lips, her mouth, her entire self. He kissed her hotly, hungrily. A claiming. His hands pressed on the low curve of her back, holding her close, as close as possible. She was lost in him. In the need they created together.

She hadn't known that a second kiss could be better than the first. Yet it was. Because they knew each other now, and heat rose up, instant and assertive, the moment their lips met. That same heat built and built with each stroke of his tongue, each delving and taste.

An insistent need built up within her, centering lowly in her belly and climbing higher, higher. Into her breasts, into her whole body.

She would turn to ashes in an instant, and everything she'd known and felt before this moment had been a pale shadow of experience. But with his hands, his lips, his body, he communicated to her all the need in his heart. All the wicked, wonderful things he wanted to do with her. She had only to say the word, and it would be hers. Everything would be hers.

He broke the kiss with a gasp. "That is a yes."

"It is a yes," she agreed. "If we tell my parents before we wed, they'll try to stop it."

Jeremy's lips tightened. "Your father won't be pleased."

"No," she answered candidly. "Is that troubling?"

The look in his eye firmed with resolve. "Not for myself. But I won't have him hurt you."

"I can't be hurt." She smiled, replete. "I have you."

"The sentiment is appreciated." He cupped her face

between his big, warm hands. "But romanticism has to face certain cold realities."

"Whatever my father does or says cannot matter," she answered. "All that counts is what we feel for each other. And that isn't simply romanticism speaking. It is the unshakable truth."

Jeremy smiled at her, warmth in his eyes. She hoped her own showed confidence and assurance. Because she truly did not know how her father would respond to his only daughter marrying so far beneath her. Winning his approval would be a challenge. One that she wasn't certain she could overcome.

She didn't know, either, if the Lady of Dubious Quality could continue to exist when Sarah became Jeremy's wife. Sarah needed her. She needed Jeremy, too.

They were going to have to make a leap together, hand in hand. But where they landed . . . no one could know.

Chapter 16

"What of you, my lady heart?" he asked me. "I know so little of you."

"You know all of me," I answered.

"That is but one part of who you are," he pressed. "Give me all your treasures."

I hesitated. My life was one marked by privilege and luxury rather than the want and rootlessness that were the hallmarks of his own existence. We were creatures from two very different worlds . . .

The Highwayman's Seduction

"How do you expect me to greet this news, Sarah?" her father demanded, sitting on the other side of his desk in his study. His face was set, his hands clasped in front of him. He regarded Sarah and Jeremy, seated before him. The rain steadily drummed against the windows like impatient fingers.

"With joy, I'd hoped," she answered him as evenly as she could.

"Joy?" Her father exhaled. "By special license, you two have gone and married. There's no joy to be found in such an alliance. Duke's daughters are meant for more than becoming vicars' wives. And you've gone and thrown yourself away, without even *consulting* me."

The wedding that morning had been small and hasty. Two paid witnesses and the priest. A cold rain falling. Sarah had worn one of her better dresses, but it hadn't been a wedding gown with acres of lace. Hardly the stuff of girlhood dreams.

"If you'll forgive me, Your Grace," Jeremy said firmly. "My father is the Earl of Hutton. Your concern about her stooping to marry me is unfounded."

"Is it?" her father challenged. "You are a third son. The likelihood of you inheriting a title is practically nil."

"I have no intention of inheriting," Jeremy countered. "I have a profession, and one that will provide very well for Sarah."

"But not in the manner to which she's become accustomed," the duke returned.

"Which matters not at all to me," Sarah threw in.

"You say that now," her father said pointedly. "With the glow of a newlywed. But what about in a few months' time, or a year, when the bloom is off this youthful fantasy, and you long for London life—its Society, its pleasures and luxuries?"

"Have I once, in my life, expressed a love of those things?" she disputed.

The duke glanced away. He muttered half to himself, "Always secreting yourself in the Green Drawing Room whenever you've got the chance. I don't know what you do in there all day."

"Things that don't require London Society, pleasures, and luxuries," she noted, glancing quickly at

Jeremy. No one could ever know—not her husband, not her family—what she did in that drawing room.

Worry and regret stabbed her. Secrets would follow her into her new marriage.

"And what of all the other suitors that offered for you? You rejected them but wed *this* man?" her father pressed. He looked at Jeremy. "I must speak frankly, sir. We are talking of the fate of my only daughter, and I won't let social niceties stand in the way of her future security. If the wedding took place only this morning, we could obtain an annulment."

Before Sarah could speak, Jeremy said, his voice hard, "Your Grace, all that matters is Sarah, and her happiness. I cannot promise her fathomless wealth like those other men. Nor a houseful of servants and a carriage of her own. I have only my heart, and my constancy. Those things will always be hers."

"Prettily said," her father replied. "But I worry that such sentiment cannot continue through a lifetime together. Status, safekeeping—these are the foundations of a lasting union."

"Then it shouldn't matter that I'm the daughter of a duke and he's a vicar," Sarah interjected. She gripped the edge of the desk in front of her. "The men you spoke of, that parade of Society's finest scions, they cared nothing for me. They looked at me and they saw *you,* Father. Your wealth, your title. I was simply a cypher. A means of acquiring a country estate and a fine entry in *Debrett's.* It wasn't *me* they wanted."

"But I want Sarah," Jeremy continued resolutely. The light from the rain made him glow softly, handsome and unyielding. "It doesn't matter if you approve or not. She agreed to be my wife, and the bond has been sealed before the eyes of God."

Her father rubbed the space between his eyebrows, as he always did when troubled. Sarah and her father had never been precisely close. He was a man of great consequence, so their paths crossed infrequently. She knew him best from the other end of the dining table—a dignified, slightly intimidating presence that required good behavior and polite, somewhat impersonal conversation. She had always been her mother's project, not her father's, so he'd passed Sarah on to the duchess with a distant smile and a pat on the cheek.

This was, perhaps, the longest conversation she'd had with him.

"Father," she said quietly, "I come to you as a gesture of good faith. I'm of age now. I can marry whomever I like. And I did. But I'd hoped that I might have your blessing."

The duke knotted his fingers together. "If you're worried that I'll cut you off—don't. Your dowry and inheritance are secure."

Sarah exhaled, and she was fairly certain that Jeremy did the same.

"However," her father went on, "you are to leave here by tomorrow morning. You will not be welcome back for six months. Correspondence to me and your mother will be unanswered during that time, as well."

Her heart sank. She'd known, logically, that she would live elsewhere with Jeremy, yet to be cast out from the only home she'd ever known was a cruel blow. "But—"

Her father stood. "These are the cold facts, Sarah.

The decision you've made is one I cannot endorse. However," he added, "I am not without feeling. In time, you may be permitted to visit—briefly. That is the best I can do."

"Father," she said, rising, and Jeremy did the same. "You are a duke. You may do precisely as you wish."

Her father's smile was thin and wry. "How little you understand the world, my girl."

"Your Grace," Jeremy said decisively, "whatever you may think of me, know this: Sarah's happiness is my sole ambition."

Her heart swelled at his words, but her father was more obdurate. "If that was the case, Mr. Cleland, you would not have married her."

At this late, unfashionable hour, few riders were out on Rotten Row—only a handful of dedicated sportsmen and women too concerned about exercise to care much for the hours kept by polite Society.

Jeremy's father was just such a sportsman, preferring to take his bay gelding out for a ride when there was little chance of actually meeting someone and wasting time with idle chitchat. This evening, Jeremy joined the earl. The conversation he was about to have wasn't one he particularly looked forward to—but it had to be done.

Riding a spotted gray mare, Jeremy kept pace with his father as they trotted between the rows of chestnut trees, occasionally nodding at a passing rider but mostly keeping to themselves. With tension building inside him, Jeremy felt like a steam engine. He had to speak, but there was still something intimidating about talking with his own father. However, only that afternoon he'd faced the Duke of Wakefield. Surely talking with Lord Hutton couldn't be as daunting. Or perhaps the task of speaking with his father was even more formidable. Jeremy cared for the duke's opinion only as much as it affected Sarah. But his own father . . . he'd always been a large, insurmountable presence in Jeremy's life, ever since childhood. Intimidation, threats . . . this was the currency of the earl's realm.

Jeremy wasn't a boy any longer, though, but a man. And a man who'd married that morning.

Before Jeremy could speak, his father broke the silence. "How fares your task?" he asked, making it sound more like a demand than a question. "The search for that *authoress*."

Damn. Jeremy had been involved with his own life, rather than his father's task.

"It proceeds," he said instead. "She hides herself well. She's extremely intelligent."

"Wily and cunning, rather." Lord Hutton exhaled through his nose. "Which only proves that she cannot continue peddling morally depraved smut."

Jeremy wondered if there was any other kind of smut, but he decided it was best not to quiz his father on the subject. "Have you ever read her books?"

Lord Hutton looked appalled. "God, no! I'd never waste my time with such tripe."

It seemed so easy to criticize something with which one had no experience. Yet this, too, was something that Jeremy opted not to voice.

He had to do it. "I do have some other news," he began. They'd reached the end of Rotten Row and had turned their horses around to begin another lap. "I'm married."

His father pulled up so abruptly on the reins that his gelding danced sideways. "What?"

"I took a wife," Jeremy explained. "Entered into the bonds of holy matrimony. Tied the knot."

Lord Hutton looked uninterested in Jeremy's attempt at wit. "To whom? When?"

"Lady Sarah Frampton," Jeremy answered. "This morning."

Now his father truly looked shocked. "The Duke of Wakefield's daughter?"

"The same."

For a moment, Lord Hutton seemed incapable of speech. He stared at Jeremy, the distance between their two horses seemingly as wide as the English Channel. In all his life, Jeremy had never seen his father appear so utterly at a loss, and it startled him a little to see the older man thus.

"I . . ." Lord Hutton cleared his throat. He never cleared his throat. "I wasn't even aware that you knew Lady Sarah."

There was a considerable amount about Jeremy that his father didn't know. Much more, ever since he'd come to London.

"We've come to care for one another during the time that I've been in London," Jeremy said. "We knew her father wouldn't approve, so we married by special license today."

For a moment longer, Jeremy's father continued to stare at him with amazement. Then his expression shifted to one of reserved happiness.

"My congratulations," Lord Hutton finally said, a small smile creasing his face. It was the first time Jeremy had ever received felicitations from his father—even when he'd been ordained as a priest, he'd gotten a handshake, but that had been all. Not today. A rising feeling of pride awakened in Jeremy's chest.

"You've landed quite a rich catch," Lord Hutton crowed.

Disappointment shot through Jeremy at his father's words. So that's what this was about. Seeing Jeremy not as a man capable of earning the love of a worthwhile woman but as a fortune hunter.

"Her dowry is not why I married her," he said coldly. He nudged his horse into motion.

His father was quickly at his side, looking utterly baffled. "Why else?" he wondered. "The gel's a wallflower of the first water. Hardly much besides her money and title to recommend her."

Fury gripped Jeremy—he'd never felt such rage and disappointment toward his father, not even when he'd forgotten his birthday two years in a row. Those were minor slights, but to insult Sarah . . . that was intolerable.

"Whatever you may think of her," Jeremy said tightly, "she's my wife now." He nudged his horse into a sedate walk. His father rode beside him. "The duke isn't happy with the union."

"Has she been cut off?" His father looked alarmed.

"She's packing right now. The duke wouldn't permit her to stay under his roof for more than a night."

"But what of her finances?" the earl pressed.

"Those are untouched." Yet he'd seen the hurt in Sarah's eyes when her father had made it clear that relations between them from now on would be strained. Curse the man for causing her any pain. But Jeremy would give Sarah a lifetime of happiness, as much as he could possibly bestow, to ameliorate that hurt.

Lord Hutton exhaled. "That's good."

"But I am putting my search for the Lady of Dubious Quality on hiatus," Jeremy went on. "I need to spend time with my new bride."

His father didn't look pleased by this announcement, but he must have realized that to insist otherwise would have been contrary to his own trumpeting of morality.

He mulled over this prospect. Then, "It was a small wedding?"

"Yes. It's better that way." It hadn't felt odd that his father hadn't been there, but his mother would likely be hurt by the suddenness and smallness of the wedding. "Sarah spends the night at her father's, and then we leave for Devonshire at first light."

They reached the end of Rotten Row, and in silent agreement, they guided their horses onto one of the other paths.

"Not going to spend your wedding night with your bride?" His father frowned. "Aren't you impatient to bed the girl?"

Heat crept up Jeremy's collar. He didn't like speaking of this with most people, especially his father. His desire for Sarah came from his heart and body. It was something private and personal between him and Sarah alone. Yet the marriage rites were public, in a way, much as he disliked the idea.

"I want to truly make her my wife soon, yes," Jeremy allowed. He kicked his horse into a lope, riding ahead of his father. "But she needs the night to gather her possessions."

Despite the discomfort of discussing such matters with the earl, excitement and fear danced through Jeremy. Soon he'd take her to bed. Notions of his vicar's morality and responsibility to decorum fled. All he wanted was to give her as much pleasure as she could take. But for the first time, he wished he had more experience besides his one night with the Widow Marley, if only to guarantee that Sarah's first time was good. Better than good. He didn't want her to regret a moment of her life with him, and if that meant the constant pleasuring of her body, then he'd gladly apply himself to the task.

At the least, he'd been reading the Lady of Dubious Quality. The books were a wellspring of information on the physical act of sex.

His body tightened in response just thinking of Sarah's soft curves, her untapped sensuality. The kisses they'd had only hinted at what potential they shared. It could be . . . beyond belief.

"You've got my blessing and compliments," his father said brusquely, catching up. "You've . . . done well for yourself."

The joy and burden of his father's words were like a cloak of iron feathers. Sarah was now Jeremy's—her safety and happiness were his responsibility. For all her enthusiasm, she knew little of what was required of a vicar's wife, and he would have to show her. Doubts continued to assail him and he sent prayers up to the heavens, hoping that his status as a man of the cloth gave him some small preference.

Dear Lord, let me care for her as she deserves. Let her know no sorrow under my roof and in my arms. I will do anything you wish, so long as she is happy.

Amen.

Chapter 17

. . . as he looked up from where he nestled between my thighs.

The night wore on. I was relieved that the rain continued, for it meant that I could not leave Jacob. Yet I knew that soon, it would be time for me to go . . .

The Highwayman's Seduction

The carriage swayed from side to side as it sped down the road. Outside the windows, the countryside unfolded in long, green banners, embroidered with farms and small towns. The sky deepened toward dusk, from pale gray to growing spills of violet, signifying the end of a very long day.

Yesterday had marked the end of Sarah's spinsterhood. Tonight, she would fully become a wife. Here she was, an entirely different person, bound for eternity to another person.

Jeremy sat opposite her in the carriage. He'd actually fallen asleep soon after they'd started out for his parish in Devonshire—a bridal tour was something neither of them desired—and now his head tipped back and dreams danced beneath his eyelids. He must not have slept well last night, to have drifted off so quickly. She hadn't, either. But nerves forced her into wakefulness.

She took advantage of his sleeping state to thoroughly study him. Her husband. A faint golden gleam shone on the clean line of his jaw, proof that it had been many hours since his morning shave. Soon she'd have the opportunity to watch that domestic ritual every day. It would become as familiar to her as brushing her own hair, she imagined. Yet it would always be slightly foreign to her. The province of men.

His mouth opened slightly as he breathed in the steady rhythm of slumber. She resisted the urge to trace her fingers over the curves of his lips. Amazing to think that she could now—so long as they were in private. Shyness held her back. Yesterday, she and Jeremy had been separate individuals. Now they were joined together. Forever. Yet he was still in many ways unknown to her. Would he appreciate her touching him as he slept? Or did he hold sleep to be sacrosanct, never to be disturbed?

The carriage jounced in a rut. Jeremy stirred but did not wake. He murmured, "Sarah," then fell back into a doze.

Her heart seized. God—she must fill his mind the way he inhabited hers. She'd thought of nothing and no one but him, especially in the days preceding their marriage. Would it always be thus—her mind utterly occupied with the sound of his voice, the texture of his skin, the bright blue of his eyes? Or would it fade into something less fiery, more comfortable? She did and did not wish for that. Domesticity seemed anathema to passion.

No way to know until she discovered it for herself. Yet she suspected it would never be calm and ordinary between them. How could it? Not when she burned so hotly for him. Seeing him waiting for her by the altar yesterday . . . so terribly handsome in black, his hair a burnished gold, his eyes shining with undisguised affection . . . the fire that already blazed within her flamed even higher. This man was *hers*. As she was his.

Lady Sarah Cleland. A hybrid of her old and new selves. She took consolation in this as her chest ached with the loss of her parents. The marriage band on her finger proved she was a different woman now. One with a home of her own. Responsibilities. A husband. They'd recited their vows, pledged themselves to each other until the end of time.

But one part of her remained unchanged: the Lady of Dubious Quality. She witnessed and watched the whole day, her keen eye and observational powers always present. She was with Sarah now, eager for the next stage of the journey, accompanying Sarah as they transitioned to married life. But the Lady of Dubious Quality hadn't signed her name on the parish register. Did that mean she was unwed? And would she change because Sarah had?

It all felt both dreamlike and sharply real. This was to be her now.

Her body thirsted for experience.

The mysteries of sex loomed. The Lady had been a good tutor and spinner of dreams. She had guided

Sarah down unknown paths, paths they had explored together. In her thoughts. She'd learn it all soon.

But what if Jeremy got suspicious because of her understanding? Her writing still stood between them. With Jeremy and her under one roof, she would have to be very careful to keep it hidden. He was far more attentive and aware than her parents were, and a considerable amount of subterfuge would be needed to keep her authorship secret. A shadow passed over her heart. They were barely a day into their marriage, and she was already planning to deceive him. A tenuous balance was needed. Nervousness and excitement battled for supremacy.

How much experience did Jeremy possess? Was he a virgin, too? Doubtful. Most men didn't make it to their twenty-eighth year without making love at least once. His cousin, Lord Marwood, had probably taken legions of women to bed by the time he was Jeremy's age. But then, few men were as proficient or dedicated to the pursuit of physical pleasure as Jeremy's cousin. Certainly a vicar wouldn't have the time to bed so many females.

What if . . . one of his pretty parishioners had come to seek him after Sunday services, and the two of them made love atop his desk while he still wore his clerical robes?

Damn Sarah's imagination.

A wave of acidic heat shot through her. She didn't want to imagine him in someone else's arms, flesh to flesh. Yet at the same time, it would be better for both her and Jeremy if he wasn't completely inexperienced.

The carriage bounced again, and this time, Jeremy

woke. He stretched and then opened his eyes. As he beheld her, a sleepy little smile played about his lips, and she wanted to kiss it. But she merely smiled in return.

"Did you have a good rest, husband?" she asked, testing the feel and texture of the word.

"Tolerable, wife," he answered, and grinned. "Made all the better by waking and seeing you." His gaze sharpened, grew hungry. "Come here." He gestured her forward.

"Where? The carriage is small, and there's no place for me to sit."

He patted his thighs. "A comfortable chair is yours right here."

She crossed the narrow space between them to sit on his lap, twining her arms around his neck. He held her close. One of his hands undid the ribbons of her bonnet, and he set the hat aside. He cupped the back of her head as his other hand clasped her waist.

"The seating accommodations in this carriage are most amenable," she murmured.

"It gets better," he said, his gaze on her mouth.

They came together in a lush kiss. Her breasts crushed against his hard chest, and she felt the strain of his muscles beneath the fabric of his coat. His tongue caressed hers. They did not waste time on gentle preliminaries. This was a kiss of claiming. It promised, *Soon we will have everything.*

"I like this kiss better than the one we had after the wedding ceremony," she sighed when they finally broke apart.

"Couldn't do this in front of the Vicar Chumley."

"Surely he's seen such things before," she noted.

"But not from me." He commanded gently, "Kiss me again."

She readily obeyed. As their lips met, his hand skimmed up from her waist, coming to rest just beneath the curve of her sensitive, aching breast. She leaned closer, wanting his touch. With that small bit of permission, he brought his hand up, cupping the fullness of her breast with his large hand. She moaned softly into his mouth as his fingers stroked over the fabric covering her. His fingertips strayed over her nipple, teasing it even beneath her clothing to a ready point that demanded more. Dampness gathered between her legs. She'd written about these feelings before, but experiencing them for herself was revelatory, as though she discovered she could suddenly perform magic.

Reaching for her, his elbow banged into the side of the carriage wall. He groaned, and rested his forehead against hers. The carriage slowed.

"Drive on," Jeremy called to the driver.

The vehicle picked up speed.

"Want you so much," he growled, his eyes closed. "Not enough room or time in a damn carriage."

She'd written about carriage trysts and was eager to try one. But that might have to wait. Yet she felt a thrill at hearing him curse. "We'll have both soon."

"Not soon enough," he rumbled.

"Impatience is a virtue." She squeezed his taut shoulders. "Where do you get these muscles?"

He snorted a soft laugh. "Built like a working man, not a vicar?"

"I'm not complaining," she said quickly.

"Most mornings I swim," he admitted. "Been out to Hampstead Heath when I was in London, but there's a lake near the vicarage that I use when I'm home."

Shock filled her. Here was an important aspect of her husband that she'd had no idea about. What else did she not know about him? If he were a written character, she'd have to decide things such as whether or not he liked his toast pale or dark. If he sprawled in bed or slept in a neat, contained fashion. Small things, but they added up to so much—an entire self she knew little about.

For some time, they sat in companionable silence with her still on his lap. Warmth and a sense of security and comfort crept through her. Yet there was excitement, too. No one could stop them now. They were husband and wife, and if she wanted to sit atop him, then, by God, she would.

"Have you been to Devonshire before?" he asked, continuing to hold her close.

"We went to Torquay once about three years ago," Sarah said, resting her head against his chest. "Mother heard it was becoming fashionable."

He laughed. "I'm afraid Rosemead isn't very *au courant*. Our High Street cannot compete with Bond Street. We have one mercer's shop, though Plymouth is about half a day's ride if you've a yearning for fashion."

"I seldom have a yearning for fashion," she said. "What else can you tell me about my new home?"

"There are a thousand souls who dwell within the parish of Rosemead. We've got a tea shop, a tavern. The mercer's shop, as I said. Raised a respectable militia during the War."

"But the *people*," she pressed. "What are they like?"

He paused thoughtfully. "Some good, some less so—just like London. They prefer things to remain as they've been for the past two hundred years, though the younger folk push for more modernity. My parishioners like it when my sermons are about current events, not just the Bible. Our latest excitement was the establishment of a lending library. The usual farming journals and moralizing books—but there's a secret stash of romantic novels that have been making the rounds. Which I've read to stay abreast of what my parishioners have been up to."

"Very conscientious of you," she said drily. Had the Lady of Dubious Quality's books made it into circulation? Unlikely.

"Indeed, madam," he intoned seriously, "I am quite dutiful when it comes to my responsibilities."

She spoiled the effect by combing her fingers through the curls at the back of his neck, making him purr.

"Will they like me?" she asked, more than half serious.

"How could they not?" He asked this with genuine bafflement.

"Because . . ." She gave voice to the fear that had been nagging at the back of her mind. "I'm not one of them. My father's a duke. I don't want them to think that I believe myself better than them. Like that dreadful Mrs. Elton in *Emma*."

"That's contingent on you," he answered, and she was grateful he didn't try to coddle her or give her a sugary palliative about her inherent captivating charm.

"It depends on how you treat them, how you think of them. They'll know if you consider yourself superior. Most likely, they'll be a little shy around you at first—which might come off as distance. But give them time. They came around for me. Be yourself, and they'll do the same for you."

She exhaled. "I'm more nervous about meeting your parishioners than I was for my debut."

"I'll be beside you every step of the way." He embraced her tightly for emphasis, and some of her fear did drift away, knowing that he was with her. Her ally. She'd never trusted anyone as she trusted him. He would not throw her to the wolves. But he respected her enough to let her stand on her own.

She actually dozed a little, soothed by the rocking of the carriage and by the warmth of Jeremy's arms around her. The next thing she knew, his lips were at her temple, and he whispered, "Time to rise, sweet. We've arrived at the inn for the night."

She stirred, unwilling to break from the delicious heat of his embrace, but at the mention of the word *inn,* she started awake. She'd written dozens of scenes set at inns. Much more than sleeping and eating transpired at these liminal places, private and exotic.

This was it. Mysteries teemed—his body, sex—and she'd soon learn them. Terrifying. And exciting.

She went back to her seat just as the carriage rolled to a stop outside a coaching inn. Peering out the window, she saw it was a neat, comfortable, two-story building, with two dogs playing in the yard and a young groom waiting outside. Once the vehicle stopped, Jeremy immediately disembarked.

"I'll see about a room. Wait here."

Was that a tremor in his voice? Or did she imagine him as nervous as she? Sarah bided her time watching the front of the inn, seeing the warm light of the taproom pushing back the growing evening's darkness, and listening to the cheerful voices within. She marked it all for future writing—though this was *her* story now. After a few minutes, Jeremy emerged from the front door.

"Our accommodations are arranged," he said. "We'll be dining in a private room, if that meets with your approval."

Anyone looking at her and Jeremy would likely spot them at once as newlyweds and guess at what the night's activities would hold. She didn't want to be the object of amused, ribald speculation—certainly not when her every nerve was alight.

"I approve," she said, taking his hand. He led her across the yard, making sure to guide her around a puddle. As she walked, the two dogs trotted curiously beside her, snuffling at her skirts and letting their tongues loll unconcernedly from their mouths. She smiled at them. Nothing bad could ever truly happen in the presence of a dog. They were blessedly good-natured creatures, full of effervescent life. They calmed her a little.

Jeremy guided her inside, where the innkeeper and his wife greeted them both. "Would madam care for a bath first before dining?" the older woman asked.

"After our meal, I think," Sarah answered.

"This way, then," the innkeeper said, gesturing toward another chamber.

A wave of profound bashfulness struck Sarah as she

entered the taproom, feeling every eye upon her. Her face felt bright as a lantern.

One of the men nudged the other with his elbow, and the two chuckled.

"God bless ye on your marriage," one of them said to Jeremy.

How could they tell they were newlyweds? Did she and Jeremy wear signs? Hers would read: *About to be deflowered.*

Her own husband turned a fine shade of red, causing the room as a whole to laugh genially. "My thanks."

"Don't ye worry, lass," a woman said, taking Sarah's hand. "Man like yours'll know how to treat a lady."

"But not be *too* nice about it," another woman said with a grin.

Oh, Sarah was quite certain she'd burst into flames in an instant. "Um, thank you?"

Gales of laughter broke out, and Sarah gently disengaged her hand and walked on. It was a relief to finally reach the private dining room, with its small round table, two chairs, and fireplace.

"What will madam care to drink?" the innkeeper asked.

"Wine." She accepted the seat that Jeremy held out for her and moved to take off her bonnet, then remembered that he'd removed it in the carriage when he'd kissed her. Goodness, at the rate she was blushing, there wasn't any blood left in her body. It was all in her cheeks.

"Ale for me," Jeremy said, sitting down opposite her.

"I hadn't taken you for an ale man," she noted as the innkeeper and his wife left.

"I imagine we've a lot to learn about each other. All our secrets."

The blood that had been so concentrated in her cheeks rushed away.

Now was about discovery. In a few hours, she would be a different woman. A woman who knew what it was to feel the touch of a man. A woman who not only wrote about physical love but had experienced it for herself. Would it change her completely? Would she find the whole thing anticlimactic and underwhelming? She stood upon a precipice, eager and afraid to jump.

Watching Jeremy smile at her in the candlelight, all she knew was that there was no going back. Only forward.

Chapter 18

*He was asleep when I left him, sprawled like
a wolf on the fur blanket. Jacob barely stirred
when I pressed a parting kiss on his cheek. But I
could not leave without claiming my other prize.
Carefully, slowly, I removed the pearl ring from
his finger and replaced it on my hand. Then it
was time to leave, and I parted from that spot
with a heavy heart . . .*

The Highwayman's Seduction

Heart pounding, palms damp, mouth dry, Jeremy
stood in the darkened hallway outside the room he was
to share with Sarah. To give her privacy, he'd lingered
in the dining room while she bathed. It had been a sore
temptation to drink himself either to greater courage or
unconsciousness. But he'd remained temperate, finish-
ing only one pint of ale before heading upstairs. The
men remaining in the taproom had ribbed him mightily, hooting encouragement full of much biologically
impossible advice as he'd walked through. If ever a
man had spontaneously gone up in flames, surely he
would have done so, passing through that gauntlet.

He'd climbed the stairs, feeling half as though he ascended the gallows and half as though he rose up toward heaven. All the while, he silently prayed—perhaps not the most religious usage of prayer, but he likely wasn't the first man to call upon a higher power to aid him on his wedding night. Better to turn to God than beer.

Let me do this right, he'd silently enjoined as the stairs had creaked beneath him. *Let me make this good for her.*

Now he paced back and forth in the corridor. He kept hovering his hand over the doorknob, then turning away and pacing some more, feeling like a beast on a tether. He paused, listening at the doorway. Silence. No sounds of water splashing from her bath, nor the creak of the floorboards as she got ready for bed.

Got ready for bed. Their *shared* bed.

Imagining her sliding between the sheets made Jeremy feel as though he was going to come. Or vomit. Or both. Hopefully not at the same time.

Breathe, damn it! He tried to follow his own command, dragging air into his lungs like he was preparing to dive beneath the surface of the sea.

Other relatively inexperienced men had bedded women. But he didn't care about any of those other men. He was concerned only about himself and his ability to pleasure his wife.

If only he hadn't left his copy of *The Highwayman's Seduction* in his valise, currently inside the room. He could have thumbed through the pages, picked up a few suggestions as to how to proceed. But the highwayman hero of that novel had a sight more confidence than Jeremy possessed.

That's what he needed: confidence. In all of the Lady of Dubious Quality books he'd read, every one of the male lovers had been supremely self-assured, almost to the point of arrogance. They knew that they could give a woman pleasure, and that informed all of their actions, their words. Marwood's advice rang in his ears. Conviction and boldness had been key at the masquerade in Bloomsbury.

He pushed thoughts of the Golden Woman aside. Now was about him and Sarah. His wife. His future.

A door to one of the other rooms opened, and a middle-aged woman emerged. She looked at Jeremy with motherly concern.

"You don't go in there, Vicar," she said, glancing toward the door to his room, "she'll head down to the taproom and find someone else to do her good and proper."

With a pat on his cheek, the woman moved on, chuckling to herself.

Jeremy took a deep breath, straightening his shoulders and broadening his chest. He was a grown man. He was made to give Sarah pleasure. And he would do it . . . now.

He knocked on the door. "Sarah?"

There was a sudden patter of feet, and the ropes of the bed creaked as someone—presumably Sarah—climbed in. The bedclothes rustled.

He hardened like iron.

"Yes," she called. "Uh, come in."

He stepped inside, shutting and locking the door behind him. Sarah was in bed watching him, the covers pulled up to her armpits. Her skin had gone pink all over, concentrating especially in her cheeks. Her eyes gleamed brightly as she observed him come in and pull off his coat.

Sounds from the taproom dimly penetrated through the floor. Men laughed. Someone struck up a tune on the fiddle.

"The bath was acceptable, I hope." He glanced over at the tub full of cooling water and tried not to picture her naked in it—without much success. His cock grew even harder. At this rate, he'd terrify her with the pier piling of his erection.

"The innkeeper's wife put rose petals in the water," Sarah said.

At the mention of the flower, he realized that the air was scented with its fragrance. A few wilted petals drifted in circles atop the surface of the bathwater.

"That was kind of her," he said dully.

"It was," Sarah answered.

Both of them looked everywhere but at each other as conversation guttered out like a candle flame. More sounds continued from below—a shout, a woman singing—and the pop of the fire in the grate sounded as loud as a gunshot.

Would he and Sarah stay like this all night, frozen with apprehension?

Confidence, he reminded himself. *You will make her feel inexpressible pleasure.*

"I'll just have a wash up," he said, tipping his head toward the washstand in the corner.

"Of course," she answered quickly, her eyes darting to the opposite corner.

He walked to the small table, where a pitcher, basin,

and small cake of soap awaited him. A mirror hung on the wall, allowing him a view of Sarah behind him. She kept her gaze firmly away from him, so he took advantage of this and hastily stripped from the waist up. Neckcloth, waistcoat. Then his shirt, which he tugged rapidly from his trousers. All of these garments he set aside on a nearby chair.

He readied the water and washcloth, then scrubbed himself. Neck, underarms, chest. Water sluiced down his torso. The room felt very hot, however, so he didn't mind.

Glancing up at the mirror, he noticed Sarah staring. At him. His back. Her gaze roved eagerly over his shoulders, his arms. She even let her eyes roam lower, to his arse and thighs.

She had no idea that he watched her watching him.

Knowing that she observed him with so ravenous a look, his heart sped up and his cock ached. So . . . his new bride liked what she saw. Rather than be repulsed by his muscular physique—so unlike most noblemen's—she seemed to enjoy his form. Gratitude for his morning swims filled him, and he felt a nice little surge of masculine pride. The desire in her eyes stoked his own.

He didn't want to embarrass her by drawing notice to her attention, yet he didn't want her to stop looking at him as she did.

Pride goeth before destruction, and a haughty spirit before a fall. But perhaps just a little bit of conceit might be a good thing. There was no real harm in it.

So he stretched a little and flexed the muscles of his arms and back, as though unaware of her gaze. Her eyes widened in appreciation. He struggled to resist the urge to preen and pose even more.

She loosened her grip on the covers. The blanket slid down to her waist, revealing her in a ribbon-trimmed chemise. The fine fabric did little to conceal the lush, full shape of her breasts, or the tight little buds of her nipples straining against the linen.

At this rate, he'd be lucky to make it to the bed before exploding.

He turned around, and, to his surprise, she didn't look away. Instead, she continued to stare at his chest and arms. He would have thought an untested maiden like her would have shown more shyness—but her boldness filled him with his own sense of strength. She hadn't looked away from the erotic Oriental art, and now she showed the same daring with him.

His hands strayed to the fastening of his breeches, readying to completely undress.

"Will you blow out the candle?" he asked, glancing at the light on the bedside table.

"Ah, my husband is shy," she returned with a little smile.

He didn't want her believing him timid or nearly as inexperienced as he actually was, sensing that neither emotion created much passion. "Leave it burning," he said, summoning his own bravado.

Her widening smile showed that she did appreciate his courage.

After taking a deep breath, he began to unfasten the buttons on his breeches. This was only the second time in his life that he'd stripped before an audience, and the first time had been mostly in darkness. Sarah watched his movements avidly, her gaze fastened on his stiff fingers as he slipped each button through its hole. The front flap opened. He peeled off his breeches. And then he stood before her in nothing but his smallclothes.

The fabric of his undergarments was very thin. There was little hiding the jut of his erection tenting the linen. His whole body was flushed and aflame. He thought to cover himself with his hands, lest he frighten her. But then he saw her looking straight at his cock, not with fear but with curiosity and excitement. His hands stayed at his sides.

"My wife is not shy," he said huskily.

"Not with my husband, I'm not," she answered, dragging her gaze back up to his face. "I've spent too long in the shadows. Now . . . with us . . . I want everything in the light."

His heart—and other parts of his anatomy—leapt.

He wouldn't keep her waiting—not when he could barely delay another moment. So he padded across the room toward her, his every muscle tight with wanting, his pulse hammering.

She edged over in the bed, making room for him. He let the candle continue to burn as he slid into bed. The sheets were warm from her body, faintly perfumed with roses. He felt big and ungainly as he climbed in beside her, but she merely watched him with that same eager look. They sat side by side, leaning against the headboard. Her near nudity was a tempest in his veins—her long, sleek legs, the curve of her belly, her bare arms. Everywhere was Sarah, filling his senses.

What would Marwood do in this situation? Masterfully take command, sweeping the woman into his arms and claiming her confidently. But Jeremy wasn't his cousin, and never would be.

A moment passed. And then another.

"You've never done this before, either," Sarah said.

He thought, briefly, about prevaricating or overstating his experience. "I have," he replied. Then admitted, "Once."

She exhaled, and her lips curved. "We can learn together. Step by step."

He threaded their fingers together and pressed a kiss on the back of her hand. "God, Sarah—if you only knew how much I want you." His voice was rough. "The prayers I've said . . . I'm afraid of scaring you."

"Fear has no place with us," she said softly. "You aren't alone. I've been waiting for this—for you—for a long time."

He leaned down and, with his free hand, cupped her face, tilting it upward. His mouth came down onto hers. She kissed him back feverishly, hotly, her lips as demanding as his. They devoured each other, consuming and taking. There was no part of him that did not feel and respond to her, urging him to take her, take her swift and hard.

But he would not give in to the commands of his impatient body. He needed to give her more than a fast, graceless fuck.

Taking hold of her shoulders, he guided her down until she lay flat upon the bed. He loomed over her, bracing himself on his forearm, as he continued to kiss her. He stroked his other hand along her jaw, down the column of her neck, playing over the fine curves of her collarbones. Then he let his hand drift lower, between her breasts, where her heart hammered.

He cupped one breast, silken and full, and groaned at the feel of her with so little between them. She gasped into his mouth at his touch, her gasp turning into a moan as he found the stiffened tip of her breast and stroked it. She was so tight and eager, straining against the fabric of her chemise, panting with each caress, each focused touch. Gently, very gently, he pinched her nipple, and her moan deepened.

Jeremy played with her other breast, giving it the same attention. She writhed beneath him, arching upward, wrapping her arms around his neck. Her legs were restless against his, so soft and long as they rustled the bedclothes.

He stroked his hand down even lower, skimming her ribs, her waist, feeling the supple curve of her stomach. Lower still. Until he reached the juncture of her legs. Slowly, he guided his fingers over her mound, until they rested over her folds. Then he simply let his fingers stay there, letting her grow accustomed to the feel of him through the fabric.

His cock ached, and everything felt ready to combust at the slightest movement. He was so close to her. To the very core of her, the center of all her secrets, her most private self. He wanted to delve deep, but he had to keep a tight rein on his hunger.

Slow, slow, he reminded himself. *You're not a damned wild beast.*

She shifted beneath his touch. Pressed upward against his fingers. Her legs opened slightly.

"Yes," she sighed. "Yes."

He caressed her lower still, moving over the fabric of her chemise, until he reached the bare skin of her thigh. Nothing ever felt so soft as she did there. Creamy and sleek and lush. And hot as a fever. He gathered up the hem of her chemise, until she was nude from the waist down.

With more patience than he knew he possessed, he stroked up her thigh. Then found her. That lovely quim. And, Lord help him, did she feel like Paradise. He touched her gently outside her folds, rubbing her, listening to Sarah's responsive sighs and moans. His fingers dipped deeper. He almost came at once, feeling her wet heat. She wanted him. As much as he wanted her.

"I can't wait anymore," he growled. Taking his hand away, he positioned himself above her, settling between her legs. He angled his cock toward her entrance. Then slowly sank in, inch by inch, as her body worked to accommodate him. All he knew was tight, molten heat surrounding him, enveloping his very consciousness.

She stiffened beneath him. Her face was tight and strained.

"I've hurt you," he panted, agonized.

Her eyes were wide and shining as she shook her head. But it was no use. He knew she was in pain. There was no hiding it in her taut muscles, the whiteness of her lips.

He moved to pull out.

"Don't," she said, voice thick. She tightened her legs around him, keeping him lodged within her. "Keep going."

Argument was impossible, not when she felt so blissful around him. She was so tight. So narrow. It took some work to thrust more deeply into her. He sank in and out. Sensation engulfed him. He couldn't last, no matter how much he wanted to.

The climax ripped through him in an instant. He groaned, his head thrown back as he poured his release into her.

He opened his eyes. It was over. They were joined as husband and wife.

But it hadn't been pleasurable for her. Pain and disappointment shone in her eyes, though she smiled bravely at him when he gazed down at her.

He'd had his release, but it hadn't been satisfying. Not the way he'd imagined. She hadn't made any sounds of pleasure. Her face had been tight with pain, not passion.

He made a vow to himself, then and there. He would stop at nothing to give her pleasure, and he would spend his every moment learning how to do just that.

Chapter 19

*I did not continue on my journey to the
countryside. The lush landscape held little
appeal—its very abundance seemed barren
to me. I turned around and headed back to
London. The bustling, crowded city was so
familiar, but changed now through my new
vision. How would I ever return to the life I'd
once known?*

The Highwayman's Seduction

Jeremy rolled off Sarah and she lay on her back, staring at the light dancing across the ceiling. Her body
cooled. She rested her wrist on her forehead, trying
to bank the feelings of disappointment that refused to
abate.

She had hoped for insupportable, endless pleasure.
The kind of pleasure that would drive her mad in its
pursuit. The sort of feelings and sensations she'd been
writing about in exquisite detail as the Lady of Dubious
Quality.

But had it all been a lie she'd told herself? She'd read
so many other people's accounts of sex, and they had

been so rapturous, so blissful. It couldn't all be untrue. Surely, paradigm-shifting ecstasy had to be possible. But not with her and Jeremy. Another wave of regret and disenchantment pulsed through her. They'd shown so much promise, but something wasn't right between them. Was it him? Was it her? Or did they simply not work together?

"You're very quiet," he said, lying beside her and also staring up at the ceiling.

"I'm tired," she answered. How could she voice her doubts? This was to be their life together. Maybe it was simply a matter of nerves? Neither of them had much experience. It could get better . . . in time.

And it had been good—when he'd kissed her and touched her intimately. She'd glowed with burgeoning sensation, and it had lured her onward. But it had all been cut short, replaced by discomfort and awkwardness.

"Just a moment." He rose, nude, from the bed, and she allowed herself the simple pleasure of watching him in the glow of the fire and candlelight. He surely had a body made for sensuality—all lean, sinewed muscle, tight and firm without a trace of softness. His thighs and buttocks were taut and solid. Golden hair curled lightly over his hard chest, and trailed lower, down his belly in a fine line. Until it reached a thatch of tawny curls that surrounded his sated penis.

That made one of them who was satisfied.

Her mouth flattened into a line as she tried to suppress her feelings of being let down. They simply needed more time. Time to discover each other. What they wanted. What they liked. What didn't work.

Jeremy himself seemed quiet and preoccupied as he crossed the room, his brow furrowed. He did not strut like a proud, pleased man. He walked to the washstand and dipped a cloth in water. Then he returned to the bed.

When he moved to clean her between her legs, she reached for the cloth. "I can do that."

"Let me," he murmured.

So she lay back and widened her legs, a trace of shyness skittering through her—though there was no need. He'd seen her now, knew her body. Was there any mystery left?

She half expected his movements to be brisk and businesslike. Instead, he was slow and gentle, caressing her with the damp towel in careful swipes. She sighed and closed her eyes. This was pleasant. More than pleasant. Warmth crept along her veins with each touch of the cloth to her sore quim, both outside and . . . inside.

"I wanted it to be good for you," he said quietly. He exhaled. "Didn't quite work out the way I'd planned."

Should she lie, and say it was everything she'd ever wanted? They expected more from each other—and there were too many untruths between them already. "It will get better," she said without opening her eyes.

The cloth stilled and was removed. "You'll let me try again?"

She looked at him. "Of course. Why wouldn't I?"

"I was a beast," he said with biting self-recrimination. "I hurt you."

"To be expected the first time."

His eyes gleamed with more self-directed anger. "And if I hurt you again?"

She cupped the side of his face, feeling the stubble there against her palm. "You won't."

His gaze slid away. "I'm humbled by your faith in me."

"I have faith in *us*," she answered, gently guiding his face around so that their gazes met.

He kissed her, sweetly. Hotly. "I want no regrets between us."

"And I want the same." Yet she didn't quite have the confidence of which she spoke. Doubts continued to sting her, like needles. Would it be better? Would she come to lament her choice? Would he bemoan marrying her? Everything was so much more simple in books. The happy ending was a foregone conclusion. Not so with life. There were no guarantees. No Lady of Dubious Quality guiding the narrative toward a satisfactory finish.

She and Jeremy were silent for a long time. He finally spoke. "I meant what I said before. I've wanted you in so many ways for so long." His cheeks darkened. "I want to try again." He brushed his lips over hers. "Let me give you more."

She was sore, and tired, but the need and urgency in him lit a new flame within her. "What would you like?" Her voice had gone low and husky.

His gaze met hers. "Everything."

There would always be a part of her he could never know, never touch. She wanted to share the rest with him. To belong to another person, and have him belong to her. Mutual possession. She'd ached for it most of her life, and now it was being offered to her. She had only to claim it.

Taking a deep breath, she relaxed herself into the bed, her arms at her sides, her legs parted.

Setting the cloth aside, he bent down and took her mouth in a leisurely, deep kiss. Both languid and powerfully alive, she responded, her nerves sparking to life. A delicate, bright tension wove through her body as his kiss grew bolder, more sure.

Suddenly, she was naked. He whisked away her chemise and cool air touched her all over, stroking her heated flesh. For a moment, he simply looked at her, drinking her in as though she was his first sunrise.

His hands became very curious, exploring her body with a thoroughness that stole time. He touched her everywhere—along her arms, her neck, between and beneath her breasts. Then he stroked her breasts to needy points, gathering sensation at the very tips. The pleasure spread and built with each caress, echoing between her legs in warm pulses. His lips found one nipple, gently licking, sucking. She cradled him to her, arching upward. Yes, there—there was the pleasure she'd craved.

As he twirled his tongue around her nipple, one of his hands drifted down her belly, settling at her quim. His fingers probed and learned, stroking her. There was a moment of aching soreness—but it soon dissolved into sensation as he touched her with tender confidence. He found her clit and circled it. Golden light burst behind her eyelids as he caressed her there, a tenuous but marvelous pleasure. His own self-assurance grew as she moaned in response, as he came to know what she wanted. She showed him with her body—and he learned quickly.

She felt wetness slick her sex and his fingers. Everywhere was glorious sensation, and she writhed with it, heedless of everything but his touch.

He breathed against her damp flesh. "I want to . . . Let me . . ."

She did not ask him what he wanted as his mouth left her breast and trailed down her ribs, over her stomach. She lifted herself up onto her elbows, watching, amazed, deeply aroused, as he folded himself back and settled his head between her legs.

Was she to know this? Could she dare hope . . . ?

Yes.

His lips found her quim. He growled against her folds, and she collapsed backward at the touch of his mouth to her. Logic and words and comprehension all shattered apart, never to be found again. All she knew was feeling and response and brilliant pleasure. He traced her with his tongue, licked deeply, wetly. Stroke upon stroke as he swirled around her clit. He sank a finger into her, sucking on her pearl at the same time. Gone was the shy, uncertain vicar. This was a man of primal hunger and demand. Who knew precisely how to give her what she needed.

There was something vaguely familiar about Jeremy's mouth on her. The way he touched her with his tongue and his fingers . . . she dimly recognized it. Yet that couldn't be possible. She'd never done this before with anyone. How could she feel anything but amazement and ecstasy?

Thought broke apart and collapsed on itself as his finger stroked in and out, matching time with him gently taking her clit between his lips. He curved his finger slightly, pressing against a sensitive, full spot deep within her.

She splintered into a million shards of pleasure. Her climax was a wild thing, unstoppable. A cry broke from her lips, hard and unrestrained. She forgot everything. All she understood was this frenzy of sensation that rent her apart. She bowed up, clawing at the bedsheets.

But he wasn't done with her. Not until he wrung out another orgasm. And another. He was unyielding.

At last he relented and climbed up her body, kissing her skin as he ascended. When he stretched out beside her, he smiled down with a proud look.

"I'm only a scholarly man," he murmured, brushing her hair back from her damp forehead, "but I do believe you enjoyed that."

She managed to collect herself enough to speak. "Conceit is a dangerous thing."

"Not in bed," he said, grabbing hold of her hand and pressing his lips to her fingertips.

She felt his hard cock nudge her thigh. Glancing down, she saw that he was thick and curved. "Only one of us is quenched."

Despite the fact that he'd been licking and sucking on her sex not moments before, he blushed. "There are only so many demands I can make of you in one night."

"I want your demands," she said, and drew him down for a kiss. She tasted herself on his lips, and desire roared back to life.

He didn't ask if she was sure. In a swift movement, he was atop her again, settling between her legs.

"Can we . . ." She swallowed. "Let me be on top." She'd written that position so many times, with the woman in control of both the man and her own pleasure—and now she had her chance to experience it for herself.

His eyes widened, but he rolled over so that she straddled him.

"I like this," she murmured, eyeing him splayed beneath her, awaiting her command, her desire.

"You're not alone," he answered. His throat worked as his gaze moved over her hair, her breasts, then down to her sex pressed against his. He gripped her hips.

Sarah slid her hips back and forth, allowing his cock to slide between her slick folds. She was in complete control as she guided him precisely where she wanted him to be. At her entrance, against her clit. Both pleasure and power built with each stroke and swivel. Through hazed eyes, she stared down at him. His own gaze was heavy-lidded as he watched her.

"Yes," he growled. "Take what you want."

She did. She rubbed and glided. And when he brought up one of his hands to lightly pinch at her nipple, she felt the leading edge of another climax start.

Sarah moved, bringing his cock into her. With one swift, sure plunge, he was seated within her. There was only a fragment of pain, disappearing into a heavy cloud of pleasure that encircled her like an enchantment. Oh, this position was marvelous, allowing her to place him precisely where she wanted him to be. And there was wonder, too—that a strong, strapping man was hers to command, yielding to her willingly. She felt his strength, as well, as his hips rose to meet hers, the thickness of his cock inside her, filling her.

Her pace increased, her pleasure growing brighter and brighter.

"As fast and hard as you want, love," he groaned. "Take us there. Make us come."

Hearing this quiet, cultured man speak such earthy words—she couldn't last. Her orgasm took her, so intensely it was almost cruel. She tipped her head forward and moaned in release.

With a few more strokes, he followed her, growling her name as he came. It was a long, endless, too-brief moment. She splayed atop him, panting.

Now I know. What could be. What they could make together. The world opened up. Her heart was full. They had become the hero and heroine of their own tale.

The candle went out, and the only light in the room came from the fire and soft moonlight streaming in through the small window above the bed. The taproom below was silent—it was late, and everyone must have gone home to find the shelter of their own beds. Sarah had no desire to leave the bed she lay in now, wrapped close to her husband, aglow with the pleasure they'd made together.

He nuzzled her neck, his lips seeking, and she laughed throatily. "Again?" They'd made love once more—that final time, he'd taken her from behind, with her on her hands and knees. Like animals. It had been . . . wonderful.

"Again and again and again," he murmured. "Always. Forever." His hand trailed over her breast, stroking her flesh. Her nipple made an obliging point, roused by his touch, but she hadn't any strength left to do more but accept his touch.

"I want more," she breathed. "After a little rest."

"A *little* rest." He sounded only half serious. But he seemed to have spoken truly—too much passion existed between them, too much wanting to let more time pass before they loved each other again. "You've built a fire in me."

"And you in me. Though I had my concerns," she admitted, stroking her hand down his muscled back.

He grimaced. "All my grand plans for our first time. They didn't amount to much."

She smiled gently. Then, hesitantly, "Where . . . did you learn to do those things. With your . . . mouth. And your fingers . . . ?"

Despite everything, he still blushed adorably, sensuously. "Can I tell you a secret?"

She propped herself up on her elbows. "You can tell me anything at all."

"It's a little embarrassing to admit this, but . . ." Uncurling his body from around hers, he rose from the bed, then walked to his valise. She watched with a puzzled frown as he produced a small book. He sat on the edge of the bed and handed the volume to her.

"Pages one fifty-four and two thirty-six are particularly enlightening," he said as she flipped open the book to its discreet title page. "Though I'd like to try page seventy-five when you're feeling more rested."

She stared at the paper, dumbfounded. Shocked.

The Highwayman's Seduction, by A Lady of Dubious Quality.

For several long moments, she could only gape at

the book in her hands, frozen in fear. Did he know? Was this his way of telling her that he'd uncovered her other identity?

But perhaps he interpreted her silence as something else, because he said quickly, "My cousin gave it to me. The book, I mean. He thought I might find it . . . instructional. And I have."

"There's no other reason why you have it?" she finally asked.

His brow furrowed. Yet he hesitated for a moment. "Should there be?"

"No," she answered at once. "It's not usual for vicars to read such things."

"Not usual," he confessed, "no."

"I was just curious."

"It's harmless," he said, plucking the book from her hands and setting it aside.

"Harmless." An interesting choice of words for something over which she'd labored so intensely and with such purpose. But in this context, she couldn't be too concerned. He seemed unknowing of her identity as the Lady of Dubious Quality—and for that, she was grateful. The fear ebbed slightly.

"You think less of me for owning it," he said flatly, turning away slightly. "That I'm one of those sad, twisted men who lurk in dark alleyways and leer at women's ankles. Some filthy vicar who lusts after his congregation."

"Those words never left my mouth." Now that she knew about *The Highwayman's Seduction,* it made sense that there had been a vague sense of familiarity when she and Jeremy had been making love the second time tonight. His mouth on her, his fingers. Then the third time, when he'd mounted her from behind. They had all been acts described in *her very own book*.

She almost laughed, but she thought better of it and suppressed her smile.

"Actually," she continued, placing her hand on the firm curve of his shoulder, "I'm glad."

He glanced at her questioningly but said nothing.

"I think it shows you're broad-minded," she went on. "That you don't shut yourself off from the breadth of human experience. If you thought books like that one were repugnant or immoral . . . then we might have more to be concerned about. But the works by this . . . what's her name?"

"The Lady of Dubious Quality," he answered with a facility that said he was familiar with Sarah's pen name, which nearly made her smile again.

So, her husband enjoyed reading about sex. About the sex that *she* described. The irony wasn't lost on her—or her body.

"They're good," Sarah said. "Healthy. And, I think we've seen, they benefit both of us."

His face reddened, yet he said, "They did benefit us, didn't they?"

"The people down in the taproom surely heard how much I profited from your reading those books. I'm surprised we didn't break the bed."

He looked abashed, but also proud. "We can try again."

"In the morning." A yawn burst from her. "Now I can barely keep conscious—I blame my husband."

"And I thank my wife." He leaned forward and kissed her.

"What's on page one fifty-four?" she asked after they broke apart some time later.

He grinned wickedly. "You'll find out." He slid between the covers and gathered her close. "Fortunately, the Lady of Dubious Quality is prolific. We have a whole library to try out for ourselves."

He kissed her once more, and they lay back together. In a short while, he'd fallen asleep, his breathing deep and even. Despite her exhaustion, she couldn't drift off. She'd become a bride only yesterday. Soon she'd start her new life as a vicar's wife. Every moment filled with new understandings. The sort she'd only expected to write about. She had been two disparate parts, never fully united. A writer who'd never truly lived. But now she'd experienced those understandings for herself.

Tonight had been the most incredible of her life—thanks to Jeremy. And herself. The Lady of Dubious Quality.

Chapter 20

*The city had strangely lost its savor, though
every pleasure known to mankind could be
found there. My days were aimless as I drifted
hither and yon. I stood beneath the shadow of
my favorite statue—Eros riding a porpoise—
but could not feel joy . . .*

The Highwayman's Seduction

"**O**ver there," Jeremy said, pointing out the window
of the carriage. "That oak tree is where the girls gather
every summer solstice to see which men they're going
to marry."

Sarah peered at the oak in question. "How do they
do that?"

"They write the name of the man they fancy on a
leaf, then set the leaf on the nearby stream. If the leaf
makes it to the millpond, then they'll marry. If it runs
aground or sinks, then they won't."

Sitting back, Sarah nodded. She looked a little tired
around the eyes—but then, neither of them had slept
much last night. And they certainly hadn't this morning, when she'd woken him with her mouth on his neck

and her hand on his . . . Well, it had taken them at least an hour to get out of bed. By the time they'd made it down to the taproom for breakfast, they had been greeted by the other patrons with knowing smiles and winks.

Jeremy couldn't bring himself to be embarrassed. Not when he had a wife with a boundless sensual appetite. No longer did he dream of the Golden Woman. Sarah fulfilled his desires, his fantasies. She seemed to enjoy and desire lovemaking as much as he. Women weren't given their proper due when it came to sexual desires—as though they didn't have any, or merely endured men's touches. But that couldn't be the case. He had the Lady of Dubious Quality to reinforce this belief. And Sarah proved it. He was very, very lucky to have wedded her.

She was bold, open, curious. Almost indefatigable. And not afraid to ask for—or even demand—what she wanted.

Now she looked at him through slightly weary eyes, her mouth full and swollen from kisses. "A venerable ancient tradition," she remarked, referring back to his comments about the summer solstice rites.

"It may be the modern era," Jeremy said, taking her hand, "but in many ways, Rosemead hasn't changed much for several hundred years."

"I can't wait to be part of your home."

God, but he wanted her again. And again. He'd never tire of her. How could he? She was everything he'd ever wanted. More.

Thank good fortune for the Lady of Dubious Quality and her books. She gave him so much information about making love to Sarah. And bless whatever stars he was born under that Sarah hadn't been put off by his admission that he read those books. She'd seemed surprised, but not horrified, as likely many other young women might have been. In truth, she'd been remarkably accepting. Just as she'd been when looking at the Oriental art.

His father wouldn't allow him to put off his search for the Lady of Dubious Quality forever. Yet Jeremy found himself even less inclined to discover her identity now that she'd helped him so immeasurably.

But his father wouldn't be gainsaid. The earl had a will of iron. Once he set himself on a path, nothing could divert him. Not even his youngest son's recent marriage.

Sooner or later, Jeremy would have to resume his hunt. Now that he was married, he needed the income from his allowance more than ever. She had her own inheritance, but masculine pride smarted slightly at the thought of being entirely dependent on her fortune.

He and Sarah continued to look out the window, and he called attention to various landmarks they passed on their way to the vicarage.

There was a part of him, he had to admit to himself, that worried about her reception at Rosemead. What she'd make of the place. It was a simple English village. A far cry from the glamour and sophistication of London. Much quieter. Much more sedate. Would she be bored? Angry? He'd tried to be as honest as possible when describing it to her, and what her responsibilities would be as a vicar's wife. But there was theory, then there was reality. The two weren't often compatible.

At last the carriage rounded a bend, passing through a copse of ash trees. The vicarage came into view.

"Is that it?" Sarah asked, leaning forward, her hands on the frame surrounding the window.

"Your new home," he announced.

They watched the low building as they approached. It was a small, two-story redbrick building, built for the vicar of Rosemead during the Tudor years. The roof was sharply sloped, and the windows were abundant but small. A garden of wild roses adorned the front, showing the last of the blooms before the cold set in. A low gate enclosed the front yard and wended its way around the whole property.

Standing in front of the gate were Mrs. Holland and Mr. Wolbert. Both of them looked eager to meet the new mistress of the vicarage.

Sarah drew in a breath, as if steeling herself. The carriage came to a stop, and before either Jeremy or the coachman could open the door, Mrs. Holland was already doing it, chattering away.

"My goodness, but you've had a long journey," the older woman exclaimed. "Come all this way from London. You must be fair worn out. I've prepared cordials and cakes in the study and—"

"Sarah," Jeremy said, stepping out and handing his new bride down, "this is Mrs. Holland, my housekeeper."

Mrs. Holland dipped into a curtsy. "My lady," she murmured.

"It's an honor to meet you," Sarah said, holding out her hand. The housekeeper shook it gingerly. "Jeremy spoke of nothing but your stews and pies the whole trip. I was fair famished just to hear of them."

Mrs. Holland reddened appreciatively. "I'll be happy to show you how to make them, my lady. That is," she quickly corrected, "if you'll be wanting to know your way around the kitchen." A duke's daughter likely understood the stillroom, but not the oven.

"Anything you can teach me will be greatly appreciated," Sarah answered.

The housekeeper looked relieved. "Of course, my lady."

"And this is Mr. Fred Wolbert, my curate," Jeremy said, holding his hand out toward the man in question. He was slightly concerned, because Mr. Wolbert was a second-generation Briton, his freed grandparents having emigrated from Barbados. Jeremy had no idea how Sarah would react to being introduced to the curate.

"You're the man that keeps everything running smoothly while my husband is gallivanting in London," Sarah said, offering her hand.

"He leaves it in excellent condition for me," Mr. Wolbert answered, shaking her hand. His smile flashed white in his dark brown face.

Jeremy silently exhaled at the exchange. There was nothing to fear here. He should have known.

"About those cordials," Sarah said, turning back to Mrs. Holland. "The roads are so very dusty, and I know your refreshments will be excellent."

"Right this way, my lady." The housekeeper bustled ahead of them, with Mr. Wolbert following.

When the curate and housekeeper disappeared into the house, Jeremy pulled Sarah in close for a quick kiss.

"And the reason for that?" Sarah asked, leaning back with amusement and affection in her gaze.

"For being exactly the woman I knew you to be," he answered.

Did a shadow pass across her face at his words? He had to believe it was all in his mind, because in a moment, she was smiling again.

"Let's go inside, love," she suggested. "Much as I want to keep kissing you, I think I'd rather do it without an audience." She gazed meaningfully over his shoulder, and he turned around to see a herd of goats watching them from a field. One of them bleated in greeting.

With that welcome, Jeremy took Sarah's hand and led her inside. He hoped that the two of them would find perfect happiness within the vicarage's walls and that nothing could ever take that away.

Mrs. Holland refused to sit. She hovered in the doorway of the snug parlor as Jeremy, Sarah, and Mr. Wolbert took their tea and cordials. The housekeeper did consent to take a little sip of raspberry cordial, but she insisted that the cakes and other food were for the newlyweds—and the curate, though she sent him something of a baleful look as she said this.

"But surely you'll have just a bite, the merest bite of this lemon fairy cake?" Sarah pressed, holding one out to Mrs. Holland.

"I really couldn't," the housekeeper asserted. "I made those especially for you."

"And they are truly delicious." Sarah took an appreciative nibble. "You ought to go to London with these cakes. You'd give Gunter's and Catton's a run."

Mrs. Holland blushed. "Ah, some of us aren't made

for London's busy ways." She glanced at Jeremy pointedly. "Are we, Mr. Cleland?"

Jeremy took a drink of cordial instead of answering. He wouldn't have minded some whiskey instead, but he'd grown too acclimated to his father's excellent liquor. A simple country cordial would suit him fine from now on. It had to.

How could he answer his housekeeper? He glowed with pleasure whenever he looked at Sarah, sitting here in his own comfortable parlor, though it was a far cry from the elegant drawing rooms to which she had to be more accustomed. Anticipation thrummed through him at the thought of showing her around, introducing her to his parishioners, seeing her settle into her new life.

He had passion and excitement with Sarah. Yet he still couldn't lose this sensation of . . . incompletion.

He'd have to take up his responsibilities here in the parish again. Lead services. Counsel parishioners. Visit the sick and elderly. Listen to complaints and offer solutions. Manage the business of running the vicarage. It was, as he'd known for a long, long time, a quiet, uneventful life. One that would pass gently, calmly, with little to interrupt the shift of seasons. Births, marriages, deaths. The cycle of life endlessly perpetuating itself. And him at the center of it all, expected to serenely guide everyone along their preordained paths.

Something restless and not completely satisfied still gnawed at him. He'd thought it would go away after he married. After all, he'd found the one woman who suited him so well. Yet returning to Rosemead, he felt . . . edgy. Restive. As though energy pulsed through his legs, urging him to grab Sarah's hand and just run. Run far beyond the limits of the parish borders. Letting the whole of England swallow them up so they wouldn't be a vicar and his aristocratic bride any longer but simply husband and wife. Free to explore the country. Explore themselves.

Helping people did give him a sensation of usefulness and purpose. But life as a vicar restrained him, limited as he was to a single parish. He might try becoming a bishop—but they were much more managerial in their responsibilities. Besides, it took ambition to become bishop. He hadn't the kind of ambition his father wanted.

"I should bring your bags upstairs and unpack them," Mrs. Holland announced.

"I'll manage it on my own," Jeremy said quickly. He didn't want her finding his now well-thumbed copy of *The Highwayman's Seduction* amongst his belongings.

"As you wish, Mr. Cleland." Mrs. Holland threw back the last of her cordial. "Supper needs tending, so if you'll excuse me."

"Thank you again for making me feel so welcome," Sarah said to the housekeeper before she could take her leave.

Mrs. Holland glanced between Sarah and Jeremy. "A good woman is what this house needed. And by 'house,'" she added, pointing at Jeremy, "I mean 'you.'" With that, she walked off toward the kitchen.

After Mrs. Holland left, Mr. Wolbert spent the better part of an hour telling Jeremy about what had transpired during his absence. Despite all the domestic upheavals and dramas, not much—if anything—had changed. Sarah listened attentively and asked many questions about who was who.

Mr. Wolbert glanced at the clock. "It's nearly three. I ought to get back to my lodging house."

"And let everyone in the village know that we're home," Jeremy said.

The curate grinned. "I've been told I'll get nothing to eat for supper nor breakfast if I'm remiss in my duties as Rosemead's town crier. Hear ye, hear ye."

"I imagine the bell on the door will ring mightily within a day," Sarah said, rising.

"Expect some visitors, my lady," Mr. Wolbert said, also getting to his feet. He grabbed his hat from the nearby stand, bowed, then shook Jeremy's hand. "Good to have you back, Jeremy."

"Good to see you again, Fred," Jeremy answered.

In a few moments, Jeremy and Sarah were alone in the parlor.

"I love to look at you here," he admitted. "Never thought to have such a light in my home."

"Never thought I would be anyone's light," she confessed. "But I like being yours." She swayed over to him and threaded her fingers together behind his neck.

He kissed her forehead. "Let me show you around."

"The bedrooms?" A sly little smile played about her lips.

Ah. She was likely expecting the arrangement of most aristocratic households. "I have to warn you, love, this is a small, old house. There's only one bedroom."

To his relief, her smile was wide. "It will spare me having to walk to your room every night and back to mine in the morning. My feet will get so cold."

"Don't want any part of you getting cold," he said, voice low and husky as he drew her close.

"How will I stay warm?" she murmured, her gaze on his lips.

"We're intelligent people." He brushed his mouth against hers. "I know we'll come up with a reasonable solution."

She affected a pout—so very unlike her it made him smile. "But I don't want to be reasonable."

"Then we can be unreasonable together." He kissed her deeply. She tasted of cordial, cakes, and her own spicy sweetness.

As he kissed his wife, he glanced quickly toward the sofa. It wasn't especially large, but if he and Sarah were creative, they could find a way to fit on it. Mrs. Holland was busy with supper, and Fred Wolbert had taken himself off to his lodging house. They were alone. It had been hours since he and Sarah had last made love. Too long. The sofa might do very well . . .

A knock sounded on the door.

He and Sarah held each other, but stilled. They both waited. "Maybe they'll go away," he said lowly.

The knock rang out again. This time with more insistence.

"Very persistent, your visitor," Sarah murmured.

With an exasperated sigh, he let her go and strode toward the front door. He had half a mind to tell whoever was waiting to come back another time. But he had a responsibility to his parish.

As soon as he pulled open the door, however, he found himself facing nearly a dozen men and women of the village. They were dressed in their visiting clothes, and nearly all of them carried some kind of gift or offering, from loaves of bread to armfuls of lace and linens.

They beamed at him.

"Welcome back, Vicar," someone said. "We've come to offer our felicitations on your marriage."

"And get an eyeful at your new bride," an older woman added. The gathered crowd chuckled.

He felt Sarah hovering behind him. Debating whether or not to come forward. And then she appeared beside him. "Please, everyone, come in."

Murmuring their thanks, the parishioners filed in, shaking hands and bowing. Jeremy fought another sigh.

"I'll let Mrs. Holland know we have guests," he said above the din of the visitors. But as he moved to shut the door, more footsteps sounded on the pathway.

Jeremy suppressed a groan. A long queue stretched from his doorway all the way into the lane, with more people coming. They all seemed intent on paying a call.

In the parlor, he could hear Sarah laughing and chatting with the guests, welcoming newcomers and circulating amongst the visitors. Warmth filled him. She might have been a wallflower in London, but here in this humble village, she was a fine rose. And he was the lucky man who witnessed her blossoming.

What new aspects of her would he discover? He could not wait to experience this life with her, to learn all her ways and the depths of his growing affection for her. If he was ever restless or bored by his work as a vicar, he must find a way to overcome it. Together, he hoped he and Sarah could find joy.

Chapter 21

I found myself reading the newspaper often, piles and piles of them. They were quickly scanned, then discarded like so many autumn leaves. I searched for any mention of my highwayman. Time moved so slowly, as if happy to torment me. A fortnight passed, but there was no word . . .

The Highwayman's Seduction

Sarah stuck her head into the cramped little room off the parlor that Jeremy used as a study. She smiled to herself to see her husband seated at his desk, his shirt-sleeves rolled up, his hands cradling his head so that his blond curls poked up between his fingers.

"Can I fetch you anything?" she asked softly. "Tea. Wine. Something to eat."

"How about a blunt instrument to knock me unconscious?" He didn't look up as he spoke but kept his attention on the paper and quill in front of him.

She stepped into the room. "Sermon not coming along?"

With a sound of disgust, he leaned back in his chair.

"My mind is blank as this paper. Where's divine inspiration when it's called for?"

She seldom had difficulty finding a topic to write about, but then, human sexuality was a continuously evolving and wondrously fascinating phenomenon. Sex was inescapable and multifaceted. But it would make for a very scandalous sermon if Jeremy discussed lovemaking. However open-minded his parishioners had been in accepting her as the vicar's wife, they likely wouldn't take well to a frank and candid discussion of coitus. At least, not in church.

In her own writing, Lady Josephina and the professor continued their passionate liaison. Their appetite for each other seemed inexhaustible, Josephina's fidelity being especially surprising. But the lady showed no signs of tiring of her professor.

"Perhaps," Sarah said, coming to stand behind him and placing her hands on his tense shoulders, "you're approaching it too head-on."

"I don't understand," he answered with a frown.

"You're thinking of the whole sermon, all at once. Like a mountain you'll never be able to climb or a mural you cannot paint with a minuscule brush. But perhaps instead of contemplating the monolith in front of you, you take it thought by thought. Word by word." She nodded toward his quill. "Just a sentence. A single idea. Not a full treatise. Merely the kernel of a notion."

Obligingly, he picked up his quill. The nib hovered over the paper for several moments but didn't move. He cast it aside in annoyance. "It's no use. I cannot think of anything. My mind's a pudding."

She pulled up a chair and sat beside him. The desk

was covered in papers, letters, and books. A scholar's desk. "Is it always so difficult for you to write your sermon?"

"Not always. But I find myself distracted as of late." He picked up her hand and pressed a kiss to the back of it, smiling as he did so.

She cradled the side of his face. "Some distractions are worth it."

"Tell that to my parishioners on Sunday. 'Sorry, the vicar doesn't have a sermon for you today. He's been too preoccupied rogering his wife morning, noon, and night.'"

Sarah laughed. "*Rogering* is such a beautiful way of putting it. Besides," she added with a purr, "we haven't really explored that noon option yet."

He gave her a kiss—but it was all too quick. "More than anything, I'd like to make that exploration with you. However, I've less than twenty-four hours to finish this blasted sermon, and I can't budge from this chair until I get it done."

She banked her disappointment. After all, she would see him later in bed. "But you've already got your topic."

"I do?"

She grinned. "Marriage."

"Write about marriage," he mused.

"You've got experience with it now."

Slowly, he nodded. "That would do very well. I could start with Mark 10:7–9. 'And they twain shall be one flesh: so then they are no more twain, but one flesh. What therefore God hath joined together, let not man put asunder.' Yes. Yes." He quickly grabbed his quill and began to write. The nib flew across the paper as one sentence followed the next. He paused every now and then to think but soon was back at work, scribbling away.

Sarah rose and set her chair aside. Her husband was now deeply immersed in his task, and it pleased her to watch him at his labors.

"I'm going to catch up on some overdue correspondence," she said to his bent back.

His response was a distracted grunt. Quietly, she slipped from the room, and, with one last look at Jeremy hunched over his desk, she exited the study. Making sure that her steps were soft, she walked down the corridor to the narrow little chamber that had been cleared out for her use. It contained a small desk, a chair, and a cupboard.

It was very, very different from the Green Drawing Room—about a fourth of its size, and much less richly furnished. But the sun streamed in through a high window, and the space was truly hers alone. Her heart lifted every time she looked at it. At Jeremy's direction, Mrs. Holland had placed a vase with wildflowers atop a tiny table. The room was homey and humble, and she adored it.

Sarah sat and, after cutting a few quills into pens, pulled out several sheets of paper. She ran her hand back and forth over the blank pages, feeling their promise, their invitation. Soon she would immerse herself again in her world of flesh and pleasure. For now she knew what that pleasure was truly, and it would have to affect her writing. She greeted the change enthusiastically. Experience made for an excellent teacher.

Though she was eager to write, she let herself dally a moment longer, her mind drifting. In truth, she was a little muzzy-headed lately. But then, she hadn't been sleeping much this past week. She and Jeremy had been carrying on so much in bed that it was a wonder the sheets and blankets hadn't been reduced to rags. They were drunk on each other and what their bodies could create together. Every moment was an unfolding world, with new continents and seas to discover. Her body felt supple and sleek, replete yet always in demand for more. And more.

But the private world of the bedroom ended every morning, when they both had to rise with the sun and attend their duties. He to his parish business, and she to paying calls. Her visits to the people of Rosemead were far more important and useful than the visits she'd had to endure in London. Those had been full of empty talk, gossip, ways to fill time. Here in Rosemead, she had purpose, bringing food and a listening ear to those who needed both. She wasn't the Watching Wallflower here. She had meaning outside of being the Duke of Wakefield's daughter.

This would be her first time back at writing since her marriage. Would it be different? The only way to know was to try. She picked up her quill and began.

Lady Josephina stared at her nude, sleeping lover. She'd never expected to find such pleasure, and with such an unlikely man. Who would ever have believed that a university professor had such knowledge and imagination when it came to lovemaking? Yet more than his skill at loving her was the way he held her—tenderly. Reverently. As though they meant more to each other than a means to climax. None of her many, many bedpartners had ever treated her the same way. And she adored it.

She decided to wake him, in the best possible way. Carefully, she tugged the blankets down, revealing his . . .

Sarah glanced up some time later, only to discover that two hours had passed. Stretching, she looked down at the filled sheets of paper. If she had been worried that married life would rob her of inspiration, she'd been very wrong. A connection flowed between her and the page, as if the words poured from her like light.

Rereading what she'd written, she was struck by the difference in her work. Oh, there was still plenty of sex. But something else was there between the characters. Something more than the physical need of one body for the other. Was it . . . love?

She rubbed at her forehead. She hadn't thought about what she was writing as the words had come, but looking at it now, she saw that the hero and heroine cared for each other. They respected each other.

This was a *romance,* not just an erotic tale.

What would her readers make of it? Hopefully they would like the new direction she was taking with her writing. Because it simply seemed to happen without thought.

Her stomach rumbled, and she realized that it had been many hours since breakfast.

After a brief stop in the kitchen to talk to Mrs. Holland, Sarah returned to Jeremy's study. She tapped lightly on the door and was bid enter. As she stepped inside, she saw Jeremy standing beside his desk, stretching. He made a delectable picture, with his muscles straining against the fine lawn of his shirt, his long body on beautiful display. When he saw her, he grinned.

"The timing could not be better," he said. "I've just finished. A record time for me."

She stepped forward. "Wonderful!"

He looked slightly bashful. "Will you read it later, after I've reviewed it again, and give me your thoughts?"

The fact that he trusted her opinion with so important a task staggered her. "Of course."

He looked her up and down, wolfish. "What were you saying about some noontime exploration?"

"Sustenance first," she said, raising a finger. There was a rap on the study door, and Sarah went to answer it. As she hoped, Mrs. Holland was there, with a full picnic basket, which she handed to Sarah.

"A lovely day for it, my lady," the housekeeper said with a wink before heading back to the kitchen.

Sarah turned back to Jeremy.

"What's this?" he asked.

"A woven container that holds comestibles," she answered pertly.

"I know it's a picnic basket," he said with amused exasperation. "But what are you doing with it?"

"Isn't that obvious, my erudite and very observant husband? You and I are going to take some refreshment outside. The day is fine, and we've both been cooped up too long within these walls."

"Sounds pagan," he answered, stepping forward. "Don't know if my parishioners would approve."

"Fortunately," she replied, "none of them are join-ing us. Come." She held out her hand. "Let's you and I be pagan together."

After Jeremy grabbed a wide-brimmed straw hat, he and Sarah walked out of the vicarage hand in hand. She'd heard from Mrs. Holland that a tree-encircled meadow lay a small distance beyond the house. With a blanket tucked under Jeremy's arm, and her carrying the picnic basket, they wended their way along a barely used bridle path toward the meadow.

It was blissfully quiet and still, only the droning of the bees and sounds of the wind ruffling the tall grasses to be heard. A soft golden sun shone down over the barley waving slightly in the breeze. The last of the wildflowers dotted color here and there, like drops of paint from a paintbrush onto a canvas.

"London could never compare with this," she said as they walked, swinging their joined hands.

"It might not have the energy or pace of the city," Jeremy agreed, "but it's hard to find fault with the country on a day like today." He grinned at her. "Or with such company by my side."

"Ah, but you've picked up the flattering ways of the city," she chided with amusement.

"I am the perfect courtier." He stopped and made an old-fashioned bow. "They'll talk of me as far away as Paris."

"But I hope you remain here in England," she said. "With me."

His expression sobered. "Always. You tempt me so."

Though she wanted to pull him close for a kiss, she

continued on toward their destination. A thought had been brewing ever since she had finished writing, and she was intent to see her goal fulfilled.

They set an easy pace, climbing the stile of a fence, then wending along past a little creek before crossing a narrow footbridge. They breached a bank of trees, and there it was, the promised meadow. It wasn't especially large, but it sloped gently downward in a carpet of late grasses. A handsome old oak stood nearly at the center of the field, spreading speckled shade upon the ground.

"There." She pointed to the tree. "That's where we'll have our picnic."

"I do as commanded," he answered.

She sent him a cheeky smile as they walked toward the oak. "Married only a few days, and already he's learned the wisest course of action."

"Don't forget," he replied, "that I've counseled many a wedded couple here in the village. I've heard every sort of complaint there is. Most every grievance could be addressed by simply doing as the woman desires."

She laughed. "Is there no room for compromise? Surely the wife must accede to her husband's wishes every now and then."

"It's a peaceful household that bends to the whims of womankind," he answered. "'Husbands, love your wives, even as Christ also loved the church, and gave himself for it,'" he quoted. "Ephesians 5:25."

"No wonder the women of this parish adore you." They had reached the base of the tree, and Sarah watched as Jeremy spread out the woolen blanket upon the ground.

"As it turns out," he said with a small measure of

pride, "there are fewer husbands and wives living apart since I took on as vicar. Perhaps I've a little to do with that. But a very little."

"You are modest, Vicar. But then, 'Whoever exalts himself will be humbled, and whoever humbles himself will be exalted.' Matthew 25:12." She sat herself down, spreading her skirts around her.

"Been studying your Bible?" he asked, stretching out on the ground.

"I'd make for a poor vicar's wife if I didn't know my way around some Scripture. Besides," she added, "I have been going to church every Sunday since I was baptized. I should think I know a verse or two."

"Not everyone is attentive during services."

She rifled through the basket, producing a few meat pies, some apples, and a flagon of ale. Setting them out on the blanket, she said, "I imagine that there must be a bit of distraction at your own services."

He frowned. "Am I so dull?"

"So handsome, rather." She smiled. "I've seen the way the women of Rosemead look at you. Like a beam of God's grace has come to earth. There's been a few envious glares in my direction." She handed him one of the pies and took another for herself.

"An exaggeration!" He broke off a corner of the pie and popped it into his mouth.

"You really cannot see it?"

"See what?"

"Oh, husband of mine," she said with a sigh. "It is a good thing you are so blind to your own charms. Otherwise think of the trail of broken hearts and discarded underthings you'd leave in your wake."

He gave a full-throated laugh. "What an imagination you have."

He'd no idea of the depths of her imagination. But correcting him would send this ideal day into a dark spiral. "Suffice it to say that fortune has blessed me. And I will accept those blessings." She took a bite of meat pie, then chased it down with a sip of cold ale. "How does your sermon on marriage progress?"

"The first draft is already finished."

"Perhaps you were inspired."

His gaze was heavy-lidded. "My inspiration has been plentiful as of late."

Hers, too, but she could not say so. "Here's to inspiration." She raised the flagon, then drank.

He took the bottle from her and also took a sip. She enjoyed watching the strong column of his throat work as he swallowed. He'd undone his cravat, leaving a small glimpse of the golden flesh at the hollow of his throat. Though she knew precisely how that skin felt and tasted, she doubted she would ever grow tired of experiencing those sensations over and over.

"Tell me something of yourself, husband," she murmured.

"What would you like to know?"

Her lips curved. "A secret. Something no one would know about you."

He was silent for a long while, turning a thought over and over in his mind. As if in debate. But then, finally, he said, "I hadn't planned on going into the Church. It wasn't my idea."

She felt her brows lift in surprise. "Whose idea was it?"

"My father's." Jeremy's expression was distant. "He

checked off the boxes. A son to be the heir. *Check.* A son in an esteemed profession like the law. *Check.* And one for the Church. *Check* again." His finger made a little flicking motion, as though ticking off invisible boxes.

"You were the third son," she noted. "You weren't beholden to him."

His expression grew sardonic. "Clearly, you haven't met my father. He gets what he wants. Makes it impossible to refuse him."

"Is he so persuasive?"

"Not with rhetoric, but with threats. He made it clear to me that if I didn't become a priest, my finances would suffer and I wouldn't be welcome in his home."

Horror struck her. "My God. I'm . . . so sorry."

He shrugged, though by the stiffness of the motion, hurt still lingered. "That's how the earl does business."

"But you aren't business!" she exclaimed. "You're his son."

"Children are means to furthering goals. Or so my father has always believed."

She could hardly believe a man could be so cold to his own offspring. She imagined a young Jeremy being bullied into obedience, and anger surged. "What he did was wrong."

"His own father was worse, according to my mother."

"That's no excuse." Her hands curled into fists. "I'm glad I haven't met the earl. Because if I did, I wouldn't be very polite to him. In fact, I'd be decidedly unkind."

A corner of Jeremy's mouth turned up. "I'd no idea my wife was such a hellion."

"When it comes to things that matter," she said, "I am."

"And I matter?"

She leaned forward and cupped his face with her hand. "Very much so. Anyone who tells you otherwise will feel my wrath."

He took hold of her hand and pressed a kiss to it. "What of you?" His gaze searched her face. "What are your secrets?"

Panic seized her. She couldn't reveal herself as the Lady. Not yet. "I am entirely transparent."

"Everyone's got a hidden side," he pressed.

"Well . . ." She searched her memory. "I stole a fichu from my mother when I was seven. She blamed the servants, but I was too afraid to say anything."

"Children can't be blamed for their actions." He shook his head. "What else?"

"I used to hope that I was a foundling," she admitted. "A lost warrior queen."

"Who's to say that you aren't?" he asked.

"You've not seen my mother. We are duplicates of each other."

"So, she's beautiful."

Sarah gave his shoulder a playful shove. "We're married now. You don't have to say things like that."

"It's precisely because we're married that I do," he countered.

Sarah exhaled. Her darkest secret remained safe, but for how long? How could she keep it to herself when he continuously said things like that, things that made her body weak and her heart soften?

They ate quietly, continuing to murmur inconsequential yet deeply important things. She learned that he'd always had the desire to help others, which did not surprise her. Sarah confessed that she hated gardening and had little head or interest in domestic responsibilities, not when there was a whole world to explore.

An hour passed in serene nullity, filled with neither excitement nor action, yet pleasing nonetheless. She hadn't known until this moment how much she needed this in her life—the soft passing of time with a handsome, good man, who looked at her as though she was everything to him. She felt as expansive as the sky, and just as generous.

Another hunger continued to thrum through her as they took their outdoor meal. But she could be patient. There was something else she had learned as a married woman over the course of these past days. Sometimes there was pleasure to be had in delaying gratification, rather than diving right into it with reckless abandon. A fine thing to remember when writing—to have her hero and heroine frolic a little before getting to the business of bedsport.

The meal was summarily finished, and Sarah packed away all the leftovers and the empty flagon. As she did this, Jeremy propped himself up against the tree, his legs sticking out in front of him. He tipped his hat forward so that it covered his face, and he folded his hands across his midriff. Preparing for a nap.

She was tired, too. Worn out. Pleasantly so, however. Excitement built as her idea gathered focus.

Before he could drift off, she murmured, "Let's play a game."

"What sort of game?" he asked from beneath his hat.

"The sleeping farmer and the dairymaid."

He pushed the brim of his hat back with his thumb and raised an eyebrow. "There are rules to this game, I assume."

"The first rule is that you cannot look up from under your hat." Gently, she pushed it back down so that his face was once again covered.

"And the second rule?" he asked, slightly muffled.

"Don't call me by my name," she answered. "Just 'lass.'"

"You've thought this through," he said with amusement.

"It's that wicked imagination of mine. It can take flight from time to time."

He chuckled. "I think I like the sound of this game."

"You'll like it even better if you keep silent. Pretend to go to sleep."

He affected a snore.

She swatted his leg. "Not like that. Quietly. Don't move until the time is right."

"How will I know when the time is right?"

She grinned, though she knew he couldn't see her. "You'll know," she said with confidence.

When his chest rose and fell with slow, even breaths, she stood up. Glancing around, she made sure they were entirely alone and could not be seen. She walked away a few paces, then ambled slowly toward him. Anticipation hummed through her. She couldn't believe she was about to do this, yet the prospect of trying was far too thrilling to turn back now. She'd planned something along these lines ever since she'd written this morning, her blood high, her desire keen.

"What a long day I've had at the dairy," she said

aloud. "I'm so very tired. I could just lay myself down beneath this tree and sleep. Stop laughing," she added, giving Jeremy a nudge with her boot.

"Who talks like that?" he asked, snickering.

"Never you mind!" she insisted. "If you don't want to play, we'll just stop right now."

"I'll play," he said, raising his hands in surrender.

"No more interruptions," she commanded.

"I'm silent as the night." He resumed his "sleeping" position.

She cleared her throat. "This looks like a good place to have a little rest," she said. "But wait—there's someone already asleep there. A strapping young farmer."

Indeed, she could almost envision Jeremy thus, with his lean muscles filling out his shirt and his long, sinewed legs stretched out in front of him.

"He's not aware of me," she murmured aloud. "I don't even know who he is. But . . . I'm curious about him. So very curious. Perhaps no one will notice if I just kneel down here."

She did as she said, kneeling beside Jeremy's prone form. "I'll just have myself a little look," she said softly. "Never seen a man up close before."

Jeremy's chest rose and fell much more quickly now. He must have been getting into the spirit of the game.

"Never touched a man, either," Sarah continued. "Wonder what he feels like."

She stroked her hands along his arms, feeling the muscles tensing beneath her touch. Then she glided her hands up his calves, over his knees, along his taut thighs.

"He's hard all over," she murmured. With satisfaction, she noticed a growing bulge in his breeches lifting the fabric. "Mm."

Continuing to stroke and massage his muscles, she allowed herself the pleasure of simply feeling him, the energy and vigor of his young, healthy body. A body that responded to her touch. His legs shifted restlessly, but he didn't try to reach for her or speak. He continued to feign sleep as she caressed him.

"What's this here, that's becoming so thick and long?" she mused. She stroked between his legs and was rewarded with the feel of his hard cock beneath her hand. Though he didn't speak, he hissed in slightly at her touch. "I like the feel of this. I like it very much. I'd like to look at it, too."

One by one, she undid the buttons fastening his breeches. The placket fell away, and there he was, his erect penis jutting up from the opening in his drawers. Though she'd seen it in the morning light, never before had she beheld his cock in the full day, out here in the open. It was ruddy and full, veined and eager. The head was nicely round and plump, looking delicious as a little bead of liquid gleamed at the slit.

Arousal built in her breasts and between her legs, her own wetness gathering just to see Jeremy's naked penis.

She wrapped her hand around it, her fingers barely meeting—he was as stirred as she. "How soft it is," she sighed. "And how hard. Feels so wondrous in my hand."

He groaned as she stroked him, up and down. His hips moved, rising up with each pump. It was all the more exciting because she could not see his face, could only hear his sounds of pleasure as she caressed him. They could have been strangers. In a way, they were— she'd spent her morning penning tales of erotic adventure as he'd written a sermon.

"What must it taste like?" she mused to herself. Here, she wasn't playacting. So far, she had not yet experienced what it would be like to take him in her mouth. And she had been so eager, so ready for this moment, having written about it only today but never having known what it would be like to taste him.

Trembling a little, she bent low, her breath fanning over his penis. He strained toward her. She licked her lips, then gave the round head an experimental kiss. A groan tore from his chest. Feeling emboldened, she ran her tongue in a circle, tasting the musk of his flesh.

"Yes," he growled. "Deeper."

"He's awake!" she exclaimed.

"Aye, lass," he said, his voice taking on a rough country lilt. "And I want ye to suck my cock."

"So crude." But she loved it. Loved hearing him talk in such raw, earthy language, as if she'd written it herself for him. She felt exactly like one of her heroines— bold and unashamed. "Yet I must try."

She took the whole head into her mouth and was rewarded with his curse of pleasure. Sinking lower, she sucked his shaft, her hand grasping the base, wrapping tightly around it. She bobbed up and down. Women in books did this, simulating the feel of coitus with their mouths. He was exquisite, delicious. She'd never felt more powerful than she did at that moment, with him utterly at her mercy as she doled out pleasure.

His hand came up to cradle the back of her head,

gently guiding her. Her eyes closed in satisfaction, sensation pouring through her body. She was so wet, so ready for him. Judging by the way he growled and moved beneath her, arousal gripped him as tightly as it did her.

He grew yet harder in her mouth. Until he rumbled, "Fuck me, lass."

She couldn't keep up the pretense of the untried maiden any longer. Quickly, she stood and peeled off her drawers. Then she straddled him. And sank down, his cock filling her as she sat in his lap. She gripped his shoulders and moaned.

"God, yes," she breathed.

They could not go slowly. She rode him hard, bouncing as she ground her hips against his. Deep, hard thrusts that touched the very core of her. It was too good. Too wondrous. She felt her climax gather in hot gold streaks. Until it burst over her, racking her with pleasure.

He growled as he came, gripping her hips so tightly it nearly hurt. The slight pain only added to sensation.

At last, she collapsed against him, breathing heavily. He held her close, the hat still covering his face, but she heard and felt him gasping.

Finally he removed his hat. His face was red, filmed with sweat. He gazed up at her with awe and affection. She knew she looked down at him with the same expression.

"My lass," he said in his normal accent.

Fulfillment was a lazy river moving through her. Up to now, she'd only understood sex as something two bodies engaged in as a means of shaping individual pleasure, of reaching climax for its own selfish purpose. But this . . . what they made together . . . defied her capacious imagination. Went far beyond whatever she had known, or believed she'd known. Pleasure led to emotion, and emotion led to pleasure. They fed each other, and it grew and grew until it was the size of the universe.

This, she realized, was love.

Chapter 22

I went to Vauxhall, seeking diversion. There, I encountered one of my previous lovers, a sea captain on leave. I remembered how thick and delicious his cock had been, a crude instrument of passion. He offered to take me to bed, and though I remembered him fondly as a very energetic partner, my interest in pursuing our mutual pleasure was too minimal to accept his offer. I returned home alone . . .

The Highwayman's Seduction

Jeremy didn't mean to eavesdrop—yet as he walked down the hallway toward his study, he couldn't help but overhear the female voices floating out from the parlor.

"It's not that I don't *enjoy* being abed with my husband, Lady Sarah," sighed a woman who sounded suspiciously like Mrs. Edmonds. "It's just that . . . well . . ."

"It's all right," Sarah answered soothingly. "You needn't speak of it if you don't wish to."

"But I do. I cannot talk about this to anyone else, and . . . in truth . . . you've a way about you. I feel I can trust you to speak honestly. Yet you'll hold my secret."

Jeremy understood exactly what Mrs. Edmonds meant. Often, late at night, when he and his wife had temporarily exhausted their physical need for each other, they lay in bed and spoke of significant things, trivial things, the deepest secrets and the most mundane observations. He told her more of his wish to found a charity, of his desire for freedom that the Church—and his father—never permitted. She often found the beauty in small things, such as the silhouette of a cat sitting on a wall, or the color of wine held up to the light, and would recount them to him at these moments. She hated coconut. He loved the feel of silk. A thousand little intimacies.

He'd never talked to anyone the way he talked with Sarah. She held his heart in her capable hands.

"Anything you say to me, I will keep between us," Sarah assured the other woman.

"You won't even tell your husband?" Mrs. Edmonds pressed. "I've never seen a couple so lost in each other. The vicar has the world in his eyes whenever he looks at you."

Heat filled Jeremy's face. It was a good thing he didn't play cards—bluffing had never been his strength.

He could well imagine the blush that likely stained Sarah's cheeks at this statement, too. She concealed little from anyone; her honesty was humbling and inspiring.

"Nothing we speak of today shall leave this parlor," Sarah assured Mrs. Edmonds.

Jeremy couldn't resent his wife's discretion where this was concerned. He had to keep the confidences of an entire parish. Secrets overburdened him, but he had to keep silent. She never pressed him for more.

Which meant he really had to move along, lest he hear things he wasn't supposed to. So, as silently as he could, he crept down the hallway toward his study. He had lessons to plan for his thrice-weekly school sessions.

Teaching the village children remained a constant pleasure. Of all his duties as vicar, educating young minds continued to be his favorite. He loved watching their faces as they took in new knowledge, and he carefully answered every question that was put to him. He firmly believed in listening rather than grinding in education by rote. Dull obedience made for an even duller mind. This wasn't always a popular approach, yet he managed to retain most of his students even after their compulsory years had passed.

This, too, he spoke of to Sarah in the depths of night. And always, she listened.

He reached his study, crammed full of books and papers. It was a comfortable room, not particularly elegant or sophisticated. Propped up on one of the bookshelves stood a recent addition—a framed sketch, done by a local mercer who was also an artist, of Sarah sitting under an elm tree, reading. Jeremy often studied that drawing. Whenever he did, the restlessness that sometimes scraped at him calmed, and he felt both peaceful and expansive.

He stood before it now, admiring the strong line of her profile as she bent over her book. Mrs. Edmonds was not the only village woman to seek Sarah's counsel. Many of his female parishioners had appeared at their door over the past month, each eager to consult with her. At first, Sarah had been a little reluctant to offer advice.

"Who am I," she had asked at supper one night, "to tell anyone how to live their lives?"

"Perhaps they see a woman willing to listen without judgment," he'd answered. "Which is what many of us need."

She'd poked at her roast pigeon. "They think I'm some grand and sophisticated lady from London. But to many, I'm just a wallflower."

He'd taken her hand, gripping it tightly, and stared into her eyes. "You're not *just* anything. You are yourself, and that, my love, is everything."

She had kissed him, then. Hotly. And the rest of the meal had gone uneaten.

Since that time, she had received the women of Rosemead with grace and confidence. The visits took up a considerable amount of her time, like the copious amounts of correspondence she seemed to engage in. She often sequestered herself in her own study, writing letters every day, for hours. Her mother never wrote her, as Sarah's father had insisted, but that didn't stop Sarah from penning her own missives.

She had told him that she also occupied her time with writing a journal, and though he was surprised that a country vicar's wife could find so much to write about, he was glad she wasn't bored. He had feared that her new role would fill her with ennui, but that hadn't come to pass, and for that, he felt gratitude.

Turning away from Sarah's portrait, he moved toward his desk. He planned on reviewing geometry and history with his students this week, and both subjects required considerable planning. But as he sat down, he noticed a letter waiting for him, sitting atop a stack of books.

His father's handwriting on the exterior of the letter was unmistakable. A traitorous sinking pitched in Jeremy's stomach. He hadn't heard from the earl since his wedding, and his father was seldom one to simply jot off a note of greeting. Clearly, Lord Hutton wanted something.

After a moment's hesitation, Jeremy broke the red wax seal, marked with the insignia of the Earl of Hutton, and read.

It was, in fact, a command. The letter detailed that rumors circulated: the Lady of Dubious Quality was to publish a new book within the next few weeks. This, Lord Hutton insisted, could not stand. Jeremy had to return to London immediately to resume his search for the author and expose her before this newest novel could reach an eager, susceptible public. No reply to the letter was expected, as Jeremy was to obey it at once.

He set the missive aside, seething.

Jeremy was a grown man, with employment and a wife. He glanced at a blank sheet of paper and had the impulse to write his father back, refusing to journey back to the city. Anger surged at the imperiousness of the earl's tone, his expectation that he would be obeyed in all things. Yet if Jeremy disobeyed, his father would hound him mercilessly. Lord Hutton's tenacity was the stuff of legend. In Parliament, he ground down opponents with the force of his moralizing will. No one denied him anything. They couldn't. The earl refused any attempts to say no.

How could he tell his father that his life here in Rosemead was too full, too encompassing? Such notions would be rejected. Duty came first to the earl. And a son's duty was to his father.

And if he exposed the Lady of Dubious Quality?

He didn't want to. He wanted to preserve her secrecy. Through her, he'd learned the many ways of pleasing a woman, and for that, he felt profound gratitude. Sarah rose from bed—or the sofa, or the table, or the floor—with a smile on her face. A smile he'd put there. He'd not give up those smiles for the world.

How could he reconcile himself to this? The responsibility his father demanded, the threats he made, and Jeremy's own desires?

The cage seemed so small around him, cutting off freedom.

He would give this one last try. One final attempt to uncover the Lady's identity. And if he failed, he would tell his father, *No more*. Then his duty would be discharged, and he could return to his life with Sarah, though he would have to learn how to live with less money.

Perhaps then he'd have the freedom he longed for. Perhaps start a family—in a few years. He wanted to enjoy his time with her alone. But the thought of a daughter with her gray eyes made him smile.

Going to London meant parting company with Sarah for several weeks. A heavy weight settled in his chest. He'd been so used to being alone for so long, but now that she'd come into his life, he couldn't conceive of waking up without her beside him. Without her wit and sly smiles across from him at the table. Without her hand sliding into his when they walked. Letters home would have to suffice in her absence, but it was a paltry substitute. He'd need to wrap up his business in the city as soon as possible. Weeks without her seemed barren as a wasteland blasted by cold, desolate wind, lacking the sun.

Breaking the news to her was not a prospect he relished. He'd have to come up with some rationale—he couldn't tell her the true purpose of his errand, and the thought of lying to her, even as a means of protection, stuck hard in his throat.

After checking the parlor and finding it empty, he ventured toward Sarah's little study—she was there nearly half the day, so the odds were in his favor.

After tapping on the closed door, he heard the shuffle of papers, and then her call to bid him enter. He went inside.

Sarah sat at her desk, locking the top drawer. She glanced up with a bright smile at his entrance, and he returned the smile.

He crossed the small chamber and kissed his wife. "More of your wisdom dispensed to the women of my parish," he murmured, nuzzling her neck.

"I'm a paltry substitute for the vicar." She leaned into his touch, her eyes drifting shut.

"They can talk to you about things they'd never dare ask me," he replied. "They can trust you. You'll have to serve as their only source of counsel for a little while, I'm afraid."

She pulled back, frowning. "Leaving me so soon?"

"Only for a few weeks," he said quickly. "My father calls me to London."

"And you must go."

"Have you met my father?"

Her mouth turned wry. "The stern man with a back-bone of forged iron. But what does he want of you?"

Unease twisted in Jeremy's stomach. It had not been easy to prevaricate when he and Sarah had merely been friends, and now the pain of it was sharp and unrelenting.

"A matter of responsibility" was all he could manage. A more elaborate ruse refused to form in his mouth.

Sarah stood. "I'll come with you."

Panic sprang to life. How could he conceal his activities with her so close by? "It will be exceedingly dull. Not much time for parties."

"Parties have never been a particular delight of mine," she said drily. "I'll visit with my mother—or try to." Her look darkened, but she visibly shook it off. "I can go to the bookseller. I have an unusual capacity for entertaining myself." Another frown creased her brow. "Unless . . . you don't want me to accompany you."

It would be easy to find some excuse. The running of the vicarage while he was away. The tending of the sick and poor, which she'd taken on so admirably. Some vicars held multiple parishes and were often away—but Jeremy held just the one, and had been gone for too long. It would be a show of good faith to have his wife remain in residence while Mr. Wolbert took over spiritual duties.

But as he looked at Sarah, his chest clenched at the thought of being apart from her. Even an absence of a few weeks was too long. He wanted to bind her to him in every way, as he was bound to her. Going to London might cause some kind of change or rupture. Or were his concerns unfounded?

"I'd be honored if you would come with me," he heard himself say.

Because he was a lesser man when she wasn't at his side. It would take some maneuvering to keep his task secret, but he'd rather undergo a few factual contortions than face a day—or night—without her.

Her smile was wide and brilliant. She stepped into his arms and kissed him, long and deep. "I make for a very pleasant traveling companion," she said, finally surfacing.

"I'd rather we didn't have to go anywhere at all," he grumbled.

"But if we must travel," she said, "isn't it better that we do it together?"

"Everything is better with you and I together," he answered.

She grinned. "Oh, heavens, have we become one of those nauseatingly happy couples?"

"Afraid so."

"You don't sound the least bit regretful."

He pulled her close. "My lady wife, I think it's time we repair to the bedroom so I can show you how little I regret our current happiness."

Her mouth curved. "Why go so far as the bedroom?" She put her lips to his ear. "Lock the door."

Jeremy didn't hesitate.

After locking the door, he returned to Sarah and gathered her against him, determined to chase away his fears with shared pleasure.

Chapter 23

*I feared my time with Jacob had changed me
completely—not just my body but other parts of
my anatomy as well . . .*

The Highwayman's Seduction

Rows of new phaetons gleamed like promises of adventure. They stood side by side in the warehouse, ready to become some wealthy nobleman's latest toy or folly. Everywhere was the sheen of polished wood and metal, the scent of oil and privilege.

"Ever driven one of these?" Marwood asked Jeremy, standing in front of one soaring, impressive vehicle.

"The Earl of Hutton's son in one of these frivolous wastes of money?" Jeremy sent his cousin a wry look.

Marwood snorted. "Right. Stupid of me to even suggest such a thing." He moved on to another model, this one tall as the heavens, and likely just as expensive. "Thank God I never had the same expectations."

Expectations and threats had brought Jeremy back to London. Though he sometimes enjoyed the bustle and chaos of the city, being here now felt like an imposition. Yet again his father commanded him. Yet again

Jeremy was forced to comply. It barely mattered if he was only weeks into his new marriage.

Sarah awaited him at his parents' home. Her expression of concern had followed him out the door as he'd gone to seek his cousin. *Family business* he'd told her, unable to divulge the truth.

"Given that you aren't much of a phaeton enthusiast," Marwood drawled, "is there some reason why you asked to accompany me on today's outing?"

Standing beside Marwood now, Jeremy said, "I've run out of options. I *have* to find the Lady of Dubious Quality, but she's as elusive as ever."

"*Have* to?" Marwood raised an eyebrow.

"My father's putting the screws to me," Jeremy explained. "Find her, or lose my allowance."

"Surely your bride's portion is enough for you both," his cousin noted.

"Would you want Lady Marwood to support you both?" Jeremy looked dubious.

"Point taken," Marwood said drily. He shook his head. "Bloody damned shame, the lot of it."

"A situation of which I'm well aware." Jeremy ran his hand along the leather seat of one phaeton. It was durable, but satiny, and finer than any pair of gloves Jeremy had ever owned or handled. "But I'm at an impasse. She's kept herself well hidden. I don't know what other avenues to explore."

"Her publisher has been closemouthed about it."

"Why kill the golden goose?"

"Indeed." Marwood clasped his hands behind his back. "Maybe you're approaching it from the wrong end."

Jeremy frowned. "What do you mean?"

"You tried to work with her publisher," his cousin pondered aloud, "which is where the process starts, but perhaps we ought to consider the final product. The finished novels."

"There might be a clue there," Jeremy mused. "Someone in London must turn the manuscript into a printed book."

"Somebody there must know a scrap of information about the author of the books. An inkling of who she might be."

Jeremy exhaled roughly. "I'll track down whoever prints the books and see where that takes me. It's somewhere to start, at the least."

He wanted this search done, and now. He wanted to get back to his life with Sarah. There was no denying that an increased allowance would permit them to explore other options.

But at what cost?

London reminded Sarah of everything she had never truly been—a social success, a dutiful daughter.

Being back in the city was a bittersweet pleasure. She could not say that she had been particularly happy here, and aside from her mother, there was no one she wished to see. Further, she was barred from seeing the duchess for several more months, per her father's directive.

In Rosemead, she'd enjoyed her life. She'd come to more openly express herself away from the preconceived ideas of who she should and shouldn't be. And with Jeremy's constant support, she'd never experienced such a sense of well-being and strength. Her writing had been flowing strongly, even with the constraints on her time. It didn't hurt that she had an endless supply of real-life inspiration. Her husband didn't need the Lady of Dubious Quality books anymore. He knew precisely how to give her pleasure.

Hopefully, she and Jeremy wouldn't stay long in London. Whatever his "responsibilities" might be, she prayed they wouldn't last beyond a handful of weeks so they might return to the idyll of life in the country.

For the duration of their sojourn, they were to stay at the Earl of Hutton's home. She and Jeremy were, for now, unwelcome at her parents' house. A grim thought, and one that made London's smoke-choked skies even darker. Yet she couldn't regret her decision to marry Jeremy. That remained the beam of light puncturing the blanket of gray hanging overhead.

After the modest comforts of the vicarage, it felt strange to be back amongst enormous rooms and a surfeit of servants. Sarah had grown used to putting on clothing without assistance. Now she had a maid, and footmen to stand in attendance at meals. Even dressing for dinner was a strange, yet familiar, ritual.

But she couldn't write. While under her in-laws' roof, it was impossible to put pen to paper and write about the subjects that normally occupied her quill. Lady Josephina and her university professor were coming to an even closer emotional understanding. Unspent energy pulsed through her, thwarted from its usual outlets. At night, she practically attacked Jeremy in bed. The poor man staggered out the door every morning, worn out by her amorous attentions. And yet restlessness still goaded her.

Which was why she was taking a turn in the garden. Lady Hutton accompanied her—and Sarah was grateful for the company. Unlike her stern, cold husband, Lady Hutton smiled and laughed often, as though by her very existence, she balanced out Lord Hutton's cool reserve.

"What shall we do this afternoon while Jeremy is out, my dear?" Lady Hutton asked, walking beside Sarah as they wended through the garden paths. "Go and see a panorama? Visit the zoological gardens? I hear Catton's iced cakes will send a woman straight to Paradise."

"Whichever pleases you most," Sarah answered. What she really wanted was for Josephina to seduce her professor in one of the boats that glided up and down the Isis, but she couldn't. She had a letter from her publisher, which she had already read and reread, in the locked drawer of her traveling writing desk. According to him, her latest manuscript was with the printer and would soon be available for sale. Her first new book out since Jeremy had come into her life.

"You miss her, don't you?" Lady Hutton asked softly.

Her mother's absence felt like an invisible wound that would take months, if not years, to heal. Sarah had written the duchess numerous times, but she'd received no reply. Whether Sarah's letters were even read was something she didn't know.

"I wish my father wasn't so fixed on the difference between Jeremy and me," Sarah said, her voice brittle. "As marriages go, ours is far from the most unequal."

"Naturally, as Jeremy's mother, I am biased in his favor," Lady Hutton mused. "But I think that in a very short while, your father will see the wisdom of the union and revoke his embargo."

"I hope so." Sarah hadn't realized how much she would miss her mother's exasperating presence until it had been denied her. Yet there was comfort and even a kind of love in the duchess's frequent remonstrance. What her mother desired was Sarah's security and comfort, and Sarah couldn't fault her for that. If she had a daughter, she, too, would be preoccupied with her safety and happiness. Girls and women were so much at the world's mercy—it was a precarious existence, even for the most genteel lady.

Purposeful footsteps crunched on the gravel. Sarah turned to see Jeremy striding toward her and his mother. He looked preoccupied, yet he smiled as he approached. As if by instinct, he reached for her as he neared. She took his hand without thought.

"How fares your errands, my dearest?" his mother asked, after receiving a kiss on the cheek from her son.

A shade passed over his face, as it often did whenever his business in London was mentioned. It troubled Sarah, that shade.

"Things progress," he answered distractedly, "though not as quickly as I'd like."

"Eager to get home, I'd wager," Lady Hutton said with a wink. "To life with your bride. And the getting of an heir."

Sarah felt her face heat. It could hardly have escaped Lady Hutton's notice how Sarah and Jeremy frequently retired early and yet still looked tired in the morning. For all of Sarah's familiarity with bedsport, the subject was one she didn't particularly relish discussing with her husband's mother. Open-mindedness only went so far.

"Ah, but I've embarrassed Sarah," Lady Hutton trilled. "Newlyweds always have their little confidences to exchange. I'll enjoy your company later, at dinner."

She drifted off, an elegant figure full of good humor despite her years and her aloof husband. In truth, Sarah often wondered what drew Lord and Lady Hutton together, for their temperaments were so very unalike. But Lord Hutton was a handsome man, magisterial, and the possessor of a considerable fortune. Women had been lured into marriage with less.

Sarah took Jeremy's hand in hers, feeling the brush of skin to skin. They began to walk. "I didn't expect you back until later today."

"I can loiter outside the front door for a few hours if that will please you." He joked, yet he sounded pensive.

"What pleases me is having my husband beside me." She squeezed his hand. "I cannot like your errands. Every time you return from them, you look more and more unhappy."

"It won't be much longer," he said.

That was not much of an explanation. "I've tried to be understanding and not press you about details, but when I see something impact you so harmfully, I feel I must ask. What is it that you do? Where do you go?"

His eyes closed, and he stopped walking. That pained look crossed his face again. He looked as though he struggled with something, his mouth opening and closing, but no words emerging. His jaw worked, forming a taut line, and his lips thinned.

"Whatever it is," she said gently, laying a hand on

his forearm, "you know you can speak of it. Anything at all—you can tell me."

"I'm afraid," he rasped.

She frowned with concern. "Of what?"

"Of what you'll think of me if I tell you." He would not meet her gaze.

Carefully, she set her fingers beneath his jaw and turned it so that he faced her. "There is nothing you could say to me that would make me care for you any less."

"Is that a vow?"

"It is the truth," she answered. "I remember what the priest said at our wedding. That marriage was 'for the help and comfort given one another in prosperity and adversity.' Any adversity."

He exhaled. Then seemed to come to a conclusion. "We've nothing without honesty," he said at last.

A blade of guilt pierced her. Someday she might confide in him her deepest secret. But that was a long time off. Until then, for their happiness and security, she could say nothing.

He looked at her. "Do you remember that book I showed you on our wedding night? The book by the Lady of Dubious Quality."

"I remember."

He hesitated. "You were quite . . . open-minded about the fact that I'd read her novels. I hope you retain that same open-mindedness when I tell you what I must."

Dread climbed its way up her spine with cold claws. Pulses of fear moved through her body. "I'll try," she said, pushing the words out.

"The author of the novels is unknown," he continued. "Some suspected she is a man—some hack writer churning out lurid tales for the promise of quick, ready money."

Pride chased away some of her anxiety. Her back stiffened. "I should think not."

He nodded. "Clues in the writing make me believe otherwise, too. I think she's a genteel lady. Perhaps impoverished, perhaps not. But she must keep herself secret for the sake of scandal."

A blast of icy terror washed along Sarah's veins. "You've given this writer's identity considerable thought."

"I have to." He raked his hands through his hair, which normally charmed her, but she barely registered it now. "The reason why I've been coming to London is this—I have to discover who the Lady of Dubious Quality is."

The ground shifted and rolled under Sarah's feet. She thought she might be sick. She swallowed hard, then again, as she swayed on her feet.

"Why?" she said numbly. "She seems . . . harmless enough."

"That's what I believe," Jeremy said fervently. "But my father and my uncle think otherwise. They want me to uncover the Lady's identity. And expose her for the sake of the city's morality. If I don't do as he says, I'm to lose my allowance and have only my meager living to support us." He peered at her with concern, taking hold of her hands. "Are you all right? You look pallid."

"Feel . . . faint," she mumbled. Sarah allowed him

to escort her to a nearby bench. He sat beside her and wrapped one arm around her.

"I should fetch a physician," he said worriedly.

She managed to shake her head. "I'll be all right in a moment. Just got a little dizzy. City life has wreaked havoc with my nerves."

Absolute shock turned her limbs frozen, her mind sluggish. How could this be? Her own husband? The man who had been searching for her all this time. Who had inadvertently led her toward marriage through his pursuit of her hidden self. The man she'd come to love with her body and mind and soul.

One and the same.

"Once you e-expose her," Sarah stammered.

"Don't talk," Jeremy said soothingly. "Not until you're fully well."

"When you find out who she is," she pressed, "and reveal her identity . . . then what?"

He seemed displeased that she continued to speak when it was clear that she wasn't entirely herself. Yet he said, "The scandal will ruin her. Everyone will know who she is, and she'll have to stop writing."

"She'd lose everything," Sarah said bleakly. "Friends, family. She might be driven from England."

"I know," Jeremy answered darkly. "And I hate to do that to her, when she's done nothing of real harm."

"She's done *no* harm," Sarah said vehemently.

"But my father and uncle both think she's contributing to the ethical decay of Society, and they'll stop at nothing to make certain she can pen no more novels."

"Why do *you* have to go after her?" Sarah asked,

unable to hide the edge of bitterness in her voice. "If you think she's so innocuous."

"Don't want to," he growled. "But it's impossible to tell my father no. He'll cut me off if I don't obey," he added bitterly. "He'll hound me until I do as he wants. He's done so forever."

"This is a woman's *life* that's at stake, Jeremy!" She couldn't keep the heat from her words. "Surely you can find some means of denying your father. We have my dowry, my inheritance."

"My father stops at nothing to get his way."

"Perhaps it's time he learns that he doesn't get everything he wants."

He glanced down, looking ashamed. "You're right. Yet I have to perform due diligence. I've one more lead to track down, and then I'll tell him that I've done all that I can."

God, let that lead be a futile one. Let every path he pursued be fruitless. It was the only hope she had that their union could continue. And if he did find out that she was the Lady of Dubious Quality—would he expose her? Would he shame her publicly, and turn away from her? He'd have no choice.

There couldn't have been a more awful situation than this one. "Can't you give it up now?" she urged. "Think of that woman."

"Just one more possible clue to investigate," he soothed, without actually soothing her. "And then I'm finished." He looked at her with concern. "You truly look unwell, love. If I cannot call a physician, let me get you upstairs and resting in bed."

Her neck rusty, she nodded. She allowed him to help

her up from the bench and guide her gently out of the garden. The whole time, she leaned on him, aware of the irony that the man who supported and helped her so tenderly was the same man who could utterly destroy her.

Inside, they passed Lady Hutton, who exclaimed in shock and dismay when observing Sarah hanging limply on Jeremy's arm.

"She doesn't want a physician," Jeremy said when his mother insisted on summoning one.

"But what happened, my dear?" Lady Hutton cried.

"It's nothing," Sarah tried to insist, but her voice was weak. "A dizzy spell. It will pass."

"Perhaps it's a forerunner of good news," Lady Hutton said with a little smile, glancing at Sarah's stomach.

Oh, God—Sarah hadn't thought of that. She was fairly certain that she wasn't increasing, but there was always a chance. And if that was the case, then everything was doubly catastrophic. Even without the possibility of a baby, life as she knew it might be over.

She should have known the danger of the game she was playing. Except it wasn't a game. It was her livelihood, her purpose for being. Had she given up her writing before they'd married, not only would it *not* have solved the problem but she would also have suffered excruciatingly.

But soon, she might have to choose. Writing or love. And even that choice might be taken from her.

Chapter 24

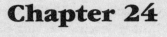

One night, three weeks after my adventure, I lay abed, too restless to sleep yet too exhausted to get up. The arms of Morpheus were denied me, as were the arms of my highwayman. The ecstasy we'd created fueled my most passionate dreams and filled my waking moments. More than once, I'd used my own hands to bring me satisfaction, but it was a pale echo of what pleasure Jacob had given me.

My fingers were trailing down my belly when I heard a tap on my window. Rising, too distracted to notice my nudity, I rushed to the window and threw open the casement. I could not believe what I saw . . .

The Highwayman's Seduction

Jeremy paced the length of the parlor set aside for his private use while in London. After yesterday's incident, Sarah had appeared pale and shaky this morning at breakfast, yet she'd insisted that it was nothing more than exhaustion from being in London. He couldn't help but think her ill health was somehow related to his pursuit of the Lady of Dubious Quality—though, when he'd pressed her about it, she had claimed otherwise.

"I only feel for that woman," she'd said. "I cannot help but believe that you're playing with her life."

"You think less of me for my task," he'd answered darkly.

"Of course not," she'd replied, though she hadn't been able to meet his gaze.

Now he brooded, certain that she found fault with him for searching for the Lady. Yet he meant what he'd said to her. He had one final lead to track down, and if it came to naught, then he would completely abandon his quest and give up his allowance. He and Sarah would return to Rosemead, there to resume their interrupted lives.

A footman entered the parlor, bearing a silver tray with a letter on it. Wordlessly, the servant handed Jeremy the missive before bowing and taking his leave.

Jeremy frowned over the letter. He didn't recognize the handwriting. His expression still dark, he opened it.

Sir,
   I have the item. Meet me at the park in Hackney in half an hour.

There was no signature, but none was necessary. Jeremy knew who it was from and what needed to be done.

After checking on Sarah, who napped in the bedroom, he donned his coat and hat and headed for the park. Soon all this uncertainty and strain would be over, and everything would go back to normal.

The unnamed park in Hackney was a small square of green, tucked away in a slightly shabby northeast corner of the city. As Jeremy approached it, he observed a man in a somewhat faded jacket sitting on a bench, a brown-paper-wrapped parcel perched beside him. Both the man and the parcel were the objects of Jeremy's mission.

Here Jeremy was, a man of God, on a clandestine errand. Granted, it was for moral purposes, but it was being carried out in a slightly immoral way. He now immersed himself in the shadier side of life.

Without looking at the poorly shaven man, Jeremy sat down, the package between them.

"Is that it, then?" Jeremy asked, staring out at the scrubby trees surrounded by low iron fences.

"The handwritten manuscript for the latest Lady of Dubious Quality book, aye," the man answered. "It's supposed to go straight from our printing house back to the publisher, but I did like you said and nicked it before it could make the journey. I'll say it went missing."

"Will you get into trouble?"

The man shrugged. "Might get a talking to, but you said you'd make it worth my while."

Jeremy handed over a purse heavy with coin. The man tested its weight in his palm before pocketing it. "That'll do nicely," he said with a wry smile. "What do you want with that thing, anyway, Vicar? Going to publish your own edition? Have a read and a frig?" He leered. "Think your congregation will want to hear it for Sunday sermon?"

"None of your business," Jeremy snapped. "You've got your payment, now our business is concluded."

"As you like, Vicar." The man stood, and then, after a mocking little bow, ambled off.

Jeremy sat alone with the paper-wrapped parcel beside him. After his outing with Marwood, Jeremy had checked on who printed the books, then gone to the printer's office and, after making discreet inquiries, found a clerk who was willing to go behind his employer's back.

Jeremy wasn't entirely certain what it might tell him—other than, perhaps, the true sex of the author, as revealed by the handwriting—but he was grasping at straws now. Searching for any clue he could obtain in order to appease his father.

Given Sarah's misgivings about uncovering the Lady's identity, he hoped that the manuscript would tell him nothing and that his search would finally be at an end. Especially now that he'd found contentment with his life, with Sarah as his wife. He didn't want to be his father's errand boy anymore. It was time to fully embrace his role as a husband, as a man with a profession.

He set the parcel in his lap. Strangely, his hands hovered over the twine used to tie it up. Coldness passed over him. He looked up, convinced a shadow had crossed the sun. But the sky remained pale and empty.

Pushing away the odd feeling of foreboding, he untied the twine and set it aside. He did the same with the brown paper surrounding the manuscript. He held the naked pages in his gloved hands.

Here it is. Now what?

Perhaps, as he'd suspected, there were some hints or signs in the writing. He didn't expect the author to write her name and address on the pages, not when she'd gone to so much trouble to ensure her privacy. The penmanship was distinctly feminine, so it was highly likely that she was, as her name indicated, a woman. But other than that, what did he learn?

It was peculiarly intimate to read the Lady's own handwriting. As though she was penning him a private letter, meant only for his eyes. A letter that contained the most earthy, sensual imaginings. Despite his intention to remain as impartial as possible, his groin stirred, and his pulse increased.

Dymphna cast a lascivious look at the groom. The man was strapping as the stallions he cared for, tall and muscular. He glowed with virility and barely contained sensual impulses. Dymphna could not wait to test his constitution. Her breasts ached for his touch and her quim dampened.

No, he had to stay focused on his task. Shaking his head as if to clear it, he continued to read, searching for anything—marginalia, notes to the editor—that might give some hint as to who the author was.

Yet . . . something seemed peculiarly familiar about the manuscript. As if he'd read it before. But that was impossible. This was a new book, never before printed. He couldn't have seen it at another time. What was it that seemed to ring so clearly in his memory?

. . . the handwriting.

The penmanship appeared painfully recognizable, as though the author lingered just at the fringes of his thoughts but kept herself obscured in a filmy cloud.

Where had he seen it? Whose handwriting was this? A friend's? A parishioner's? A family member's?

No—

He wouldn't allow the thought. He had to prove it wasn't true. His hand moved automatically toward the inside pocket of his jacket, where he kept one of Sarah's notes. He always carried with him a scrap of something that belonged to her. To keep her close at all times. The note was something simple and inconsequential regarding the tending of the glebe near the vicarage.

He reread the note now. Then looked back at the manuscript. Back and forth his gaze went. The truth hit him long before understanding did.

The handwriting was the same. Identical. Same looping *l,* same drifting dot over the *i.* Even the spacing between words and letters was exact. It was right there, in his hands. The proof he needed.

Sarah—his *wife*—was the Lady of Dubious Quality.

He ambled through the city streets for hours, too numb and stunned to do anything else besides walk. Every time he tried to wrap his mind around his discovery, his thoughts revolted, his mind rearing back like a horse refusing a bridle.

How could it be? All this time, for years, long before she'd ever known him, Sarah had been writing anonymous erotic novels. Risking herself, the reputation of herself and her family—all to write about sexual misadventures. *Why?* How could she take that chance? What provoked her to do it? How long had she been keeping this secret? Keeping it from everyone, including *him.*

A sick understanding hit him. She'd kept the truth from him when they'd married. Had deliberately deceived him.

Damn—if she was the Lady of Dubious Quality, then it stood to reason that she was also the Golden Woman. Another secret she'd hidden from him. Another identity draped in deceit.

No. *No.* He refused to believe it. They had given each other everything. They shared understanding and trust that existed between them alone.

She couldn't purposefully throw that away. She would not.

You don't have proof, his thoughts whispered. *Just a bit of handwriting. So they look very similar. Doesn't mean she's the Lady. Just ask her.*

Yes. He would ask her. When confronted directly, she would have to tell him the truth. She couldn't lie straight to his face. Not his Sarah.

And then she'd laugh and tell him he was being ridiculous—and whoever wrote that manuscript had been educated by the same governess or some other explanation that would turn all of his suspicions to ash.

He was being ridiculous. Utterly foolish. He made himself laugh aloud, though the passersby around him looked at him strangely, then gave the laughing vicar a wide berth as they proceeded down the street.

It was late afternoon. They would be getting ready for dinner at home. He'd simply go back, ask Sarah before the meal, she'd set his mind at ease, and then . . . then he'd throw the manuscript in the fire and go back to life as he knew it. A happy life full of love and honesty. He would make love to Sarah all night, both of them giddy with the absurdity that he could have ever suspected her of being the Lady of Dubious Quality. Yes. That's exactly what would happen.

He turned around and headed for home. Already the words were forming on his tongue. *I know this is completely ridiculous, love, but are you the woman who writes those salacious books?* He felt frenzied with the need to simply spill the words and have all his doubts thrown away. It would take a single question. A single response. And then it would be done.

He practically bounded up the stairs to the front door. The butler let him in, and Jeremy walked straight to his parlor. He hid the manuscript in a locking drawer of the desk, pocketing the key. Having the pages out and loose in the house seemed an invitation to disaster. Besides, he didn't need to show Sarah the manuscript. A simple question would suffice. He wasn't a Bow Street Runner, trying to gather evidence against a criminal.

After inquiring of a servant, he learned that Sarah was reading in one of the salons. He knew the route, so he took himself to the chamber. The door was open. He approached quietly, his footsteps slowing as he neared, as though treading on a fragile secret. He paused in the doorway and looked at her, unobserved.

Sarah perched on the edge of a settee, a small book in her hands. Late sunlight drifted in through the window, outlining her in gold. Little wisps of hair curled at her nape, giving her a deceptively fragile appearance. Experience had taught him that she was much more resilient than anyone credited her for. She was lovely to him, so lovely his chest and throat ached. Her strength made her even more beautiful.

He must have made a sound, because she looked up. Seeing him, a smile wreathed her face.

"Hello, love," he said, coming into the room. Words pushed at him. Just a question. And then it would be done. He had only to speak it.

Now.

Say it now.

"Do we know what's for dinner?" he asked.

He barely spoke through the meal. His food tasted of clay and sodden cotton. His unease soon spread to the rest of the table, and almost no one spoke. Even his usually cheerful mother could find nothing of which to speak. The only sounds were the clink of silver on china, or the pour of wine into a glass. Sarah kept glancing at him with a silent question, but he had no means of communicating what tore at him. He would look at her, then look away, his mind batting back and forth like a shuttlecock. Surely there had to be a mistake. She couldn't be the Lady of Dubious Quality. It simply could not be true.

It would mean that the entire time they'd known each other, she'd been deceiving him. Everything would be built upon deception and trickery. A house on shifting sands could never endure. It would crumble into rubble and dust at the slightest breeze.

But his question went unasked. All through the torturous meal—he'd never ask her in front of his father, anyway—and afterward, when dinner ended and the women adjourned, he kept quiet.

His father even took stabs at conversing with him over brandy and tobacco. Yet Jeremy's distracted re-

sponses were monosyllabic. At last, in exasperation, Lord Hutton retired to the drawing room, there
to seek better company. Jeremy trailed after him, but
not before undertaking one specific errand within the
house. He arrived at the drawing room a few minutes
behind his father, to find his mother embroidering, his
father reading, and Sarah staring out the window, looking at darkness.

Jeremy attempted to write a letter to Mr. Wolbert,
but his efforts stuttered into a page filled with half-
begun sentences. At last, he resigned himself to doing
nothing but gazing into the fire as his thoughts roiled.
His heart thudded heavily as he anticipated going to
bed, and what would follow.

Finally, his mother rose with a yawn. "It's been a
very long day."

"So it has," Sarah agreed, turning around. "I think
I'll retire."

"I'll join you in a moment," Jeremy said, his words
and movements deadened.

Sarah frowned at him, but, after saying good night
to his parents, she left the drawing room.

"Are you two quarreling?" his father demanded
once she'd gone.

Was it a quarrel? It would soon be nothing but an
empty query. But until Sarah put his mind at ease,
Jeremy didn't know what to call how he felt.

"Everything is fine," he said woodenly.

His mother looked as though she wanted to quiz
him on the subject, but she kept silent. He pressed a
goodnight kiss to her cheek, nodded at his father, and
headed for his bedchamber. Each step felt as though

he was climbing the stairs to the gallows. His footfalls were heavy and thudding.

He stared at his hand as it hovered over the doorknob to the bedroom. It was someone else's hand. Someone else's arm attached to his body—a body he couldn't even feel. He merely needed to open the door and find Sarah on the other side. Then he would have all his answers. Then his fears would be laid to rest, and he'd never have to think of this again.

He turned the doorknob. Slowly pushed open the door.

The room was in half light and half darkness, the fire casting dancing shadows over everything. His gaze slowly moved across the carpet, to the bed. To Sarah standing at the head of the bed, with a sheet of the manuscript in her hand.

She would look at him with a puzzled expression. Or she would laugh. Then he would exhale. Then his mind and body would calm.

But one glance at her face, and he understood.

She stared at him, her eyes wide, her face ashen. She looked as though someone had presented her with her own corpse.

It was true. His wife truly was the Lady of Dubious Quality.

Chapter 25

A man stood on my balcony. Moonlight limned his tall, broad-shouldered figure, turning him into an apparition from the depths of midnight dreams.

He was none other than Jacob Clearwater . . .

The Highwayman's Seduction

The world disintegrated around Sarah, and no matter how much she struggled, nothing could end her limitless fall.

In her hand, she held the means of her destruction. Standing in the bedchamber was the man bringing ruination—Jeremy. Her husband.

Everything she'd hoped would never come to pass had done so. In the worst possible way.

All she could do was stare at Jeremy, hoping, praying that he wouldn't be angry. But that was a futile hope.

"No denial?" he rasped. "No words of confusion or refutation?"

She managed to speak. "I wouldn't insult you that way."

He gave a hoarse laugh. "So now you've found your integrity." Stepping closer, he growled, "You've played me for a fool."

"That was never my intention."

"No?" he demanded. "You willfully imperiled my career. My family."

Carefully, as though it had been a lit bomb, Sarah moved the entire manuscript, putting it down on the nightstand. "I didn't know you were the man looking for the Lady of Dubious Quality, not until yesterday."

"That doesn't make it right," he spat. "You knew going into our marriage that your writing could destroy both of us."

"I . . ." What could she say? Nothing would exonerate her. All she could speak was the truth. "I wanted everything," she admitted. "To write, and to love you."

The word *love* seemed to cause a poisonous reaction in him. He reared back, a horrified look on his face. "Why?" he growled. "Why would you do something so foolish?"

"My books aren't foolish to me," she threw back, trying to make him understand. "Writing is who I am. I can't *not* write. If I did, I'd cease to exist."

He looked unconvinced. "It's pride that makes you say that."

"Are you disgusted that I wasn't the innocent you believed me to be?" she accused. Trapped, she could only lash out, like a wounded animal.

"No," he answered hotly. "I'm disgusted that you blatantly lied to me and used me. That's what you did, wasn't it?" He jabbed a finger toward her. "Marry me for the protection of my name."

"I wanted *you*," she insisted.

"Am I to be pleased by this?" His voice was low and soft, far worse than if he'd yelled. "You pursued me so ardently, and I was so bloody *flattered*. I should have seen it. The edge of desperation in your urgency." Pacing nearer, he spat, "It was because someone was looking for you, wasn't it? Because *I* was searching for you. That's what pushed you toward me."

"Partially," she confessed, knowing he deserved, finally, the whole truth. "But—I wouldn't have pursued you if I hadn't cared for you. I could never bind myself to someone unless I thought I could love them."

His mouth curled into a bitter sneer. It was so unlike him, so very different from the gentle, compassionate man she knew, that it made her heart wither.

"I cherished those moments with you," he rumbled. "But now everything is tainted by your dishonesty."

"If only you understood—"

"*Make* me understand," he demanded, almost desperately. "Because all I see before me is a woman who deliberately and without remorse imperiled herself, her family, and everyone around her." He stared at her. "It's like a shadow that envelops you, drawing everyone into its darkness."

"You're being melodramatic," she said despairingly.

"Am I? Or have you purposefully blinded yourself to the harm you have and could have caused—and for what?" he added with anger and confusion.

"For *myself*," she cried, uncaring of whoever might hear her. What did it matter now, with everything smashed to pieces? "I wrote these books for *me*. Because *I matter*."

Yet he shook his head. "I . . . am astonished at the level of your vanity."

"Yes," she said resentfully. "We all know how little you value yourself. Obeying your father like a frightened child." The moment she said the words, she regretted them, but they could not be called back.

Genuine fury gleamed in Jeremy's eyes. He whirled and strode to the fireplace. Bracing one arm on the mantel, he presented her with the wide, unmoving wall of his shoulders.

"I cannot ask you to leave," he said lowly. "Not so soon after our wedding. But I cannot be around you right now."

"Where will you go?"

He laughed bleakly. "This house is cavernous. I'll find myself another room and sleep there."

"Forever," she said bleakly.

"I don't know for how long. Don't ask anything of me right now." Voice rasping and sorrowful, he went on. "You've . . . broken my heart."

She reached out for him, but he was already gone, the door open and swinging behind him. The carpet muffled his movements, but with each footstep, she felt her own heart crumble into dust. Silently, she moved to shut the door behind him.

No tears came. Her eyes remained dry as she managed to undo her own gown and slip into her night rail. She took down her hair but didn't bother brushing or plaiting it. It hardly mattered if she failed to conform to the latest beauty standard.

Jeremy could expose her. Ruin her. Then she would

have nothing. She had to think. About how to proceed. Where to go from here.

But she could not plan for the future. She could think only of Jeremy and the boundless gulf that existed between them.

She gathered up the manuscript and walked it to the fireplace. Page by page, her face frozen into a mask, she consigned it to the flames. She felt as though she was burning her own flesh and blood.

When the last page was nothing but blackened ash, she stirred the embers with a poker. Making certain that it was gone, destroyed. Everything was destroyed now.

The fire died out. The room fell into darkness, and then, hours later, turned the color of ash as the sun began to rise.

Sarah sat beside the now cold fireplace, watching it all through dry, gritty eyes. She had barely moved during the course of the night, not even to put on slippers to warm her chilled feet. She moved through cold treacle.

The maid came in to build the fire, and she squeaked in surprise to find Sarah already up. The girl glanced at the bed—it was pristine. A far cry from the usual heap of bedclothes that signaled another night of passion.

"Don't bother," Sarah said to the maid as the servant bent to stoke the fire.

"But it's dreadful cold today, my lady."

"It doesn't matter," Sarah answered numbly.

"Shall I get the curtains?" the girl asked hopefully.

"Do or don't."

The maid left, though she looked uncertain as to whether or not she ought to go, with her duties not fully discharged.

Glancing at the mantel clock, Sarah noted that breakfast would likely be served soon. She dressed herself in a simple, front-fastening gown. Gazing at herself in the pier glass, she saw without interest the heavy dark circles under her eyes, the pale and drawn cast to her features. She looked sickly. But not bodily unwell. What ailed her went far beyond a cold or the ague.

What kind of night had Jeremy passed? Had he slept well, or poorly, or, as she had done, not at all? He must have thought of her—a million unkind, bitter things for which she couldn't fault him. She'd done him a devastating wrong. The kind of wrong from which there was no recovery. How could there be?

Like a wraith, she drifted down to the breakfast room. She froze when she saw Jeremy already seated, reading a newspaper. No one else was in attendance for the meal.

He stood stiffly when he saw her standing in the doorway. Gave her a little cold bow, which pierced her frozen heart.

"Good morning," he said.

"Good morning," she answered, barely able to get the words past her lips.

"Did you sleep well?" he asked as if by rote.

"No."

"Nor I," he said after a moment. He looked as though he wanted to say more, but he kept silent.

This was awful. How could she pretend to eat with him so close by, with the room full of mistrust and hurt?

"I'll leave," he said. "Not much appetite this morning."

"You stay," she said quickly. "I'll go."

Without another word, she turned and fled from the breakfast room. Back up to the bedchamber, where icy nausea knotted her stomach. She walked quickly to her portable writing desk and pulled out a sheet of paper. The quill trembled in her hand as she wrote, and sand scattered across the floor as she dusted the letter. In her missive, she requested an immediate reply.

A footman was summoned, and he took the letter without realizing the import of what it contained.

Sarah waited all morning, barely stirring from the settee. Jeremy did not come to see her.

Sometime around noon, Lady Hutton came to visit. "Beef tea always revives me," she proposed, setting herself down beside Sarah.

"Thank you for the suggestion, but no," Sarah replied, setting aside the book she couldn't seem to read. The same paragraph had swum before her eyes for the past fifteen minutes.

The older woman reached out and took Sarah's hand. "If there's anything you wish to discuss, I make for an excellent confidante."

Heat prickled Sarah's eyes. The one person with whom she truly wanted to talk was the source of her agony. She and Jeremy seemed to have exhausted their supply of words—and perhaps more.

"Your offer is most appreciated," Sarah answered sincerely, "but everything will work itself out." She did not believe herself, yet vapid palliatives were all she could seem to speak.

"Whatever it is between you," Lady Hutton said softly, "give it time. He's kind and gentle, but he possesses a surprising amount of pride. Always been that way, since he was a boy."

The pride Sarah had irreparably damaged. She knew he'd taken considerable satisfaction in the honesty between them, and she'd destroyed all vestiges of that illusion. There was no one to blame but herself, and no matter how much she brooded and stewed over the catastrophic situation, she could find no remedy. No way out. Only further darkness.

Sarah had no answer for Lady Hutton, so the older woman left her alone.

Meanwhile, the response Sarah waited for never came. Its absence spoke louder than any response.

Her mother would not allow her to return home, not even for a short while. Sarah had made her choice, the unwritten reply seemed to say, and now she must suffer the consequences.

That afternoon, Sarah vowed she would do *something*. Anything to alleviate this misery. So she donned her coat and bonnet, and, taking a maid with her, walked toward McKinnon's. Even on her gloomiest days, the bookstore never failed to give her pleasure.

London appeared to her at a great distance. Noise

and activity surrounded her on all sides, yet it was far away. She barely registered anything.

"Be careful, my lady!" her maid chided, pulling Sarah back from a cart that sped dangerously close.

Sarah hadn't seen it. She could hardly take note of anything, swaddled as she was in cotton wool and sorrow.

At last she reached McKinnon's. Despite the gray weather, the rows of books displayed on the sidewalk were bright punctuations of color, each containing its own world. They promised knowledge, escape, entertainment, information. All the things she loved.

"Afternoon, Lady Sarah!" McKinnon boomed cheerfully when she entered the shop. "It's been an age."

"So it has," she answered, trying her best to manufacture some enthusiasm. But even to her own ears, her words sounded flat and lifeless.

"You must tell me all about life in the country," the bookseller pressed.

"I shall—only not today," she managed. "I woke with a dreadful headache and haven't been able to shake it."

McKinnon nodded with understanding. "My wife enjoys a bowl of sugared pap whenever the headache has her. Brings her right back to the nursery."

"I'll take that under advisement."

Sarah could speak no more. With a wan smile, she drifted into the aisles of books. Here were her friends. Her solace. Her comfort. She'd lose herself in tales of adventure or romance—no, not romance. It was a bitter draft to drink, reading of someone else's happiness, when her own was lost. But a pirate tale, or maybe a gothic saga . . .

Yet, as she thumbed through volume after volume, nothing interested or pleased her. Everything rang hollow. It all felt trite. Even the sinister gothic tales contained pasteboard miseries. And her attention drifted. She could not read more than a few lines before seeking diversion elsewhere.

Coming to the bookshop had been a mistake. All it did was remind her even more of what was lost, and how far she'd fallen.

She could not even find it in herself to be frustrated. She felt only . . . nothingness. Absence and nullity.

Collecting her maid, she decided to hail a post chaise for the return journey. As she traveled back to Lord Hutton's home, she could not rouse any emotion in herself, not even dread. The world, and her own feelings, had retreated, leaving her in a barren plain where she barely recognized herself.

When they arrived, she went straight to her room. She did not inquire whether Jeremy was home or out. It didn't matter. His distance was assured wherever he was.

It was only a matter of time before he revealed to his father—and perhaps the world—her identity as the Lady of Dubious Quality. Yet she couldn't find it in herself to care. Everything was already ruined. What difference did scandal make?

There was one source of solace . . .

Yet when she picked up her quill to write about Lady Josephina and her playful, earthy professor, no words came. Her quill hovered over the paper, dripping ink. She tossed the pen down and cradled her head in her hands.

God. What had happened to her? Who was she?

A woman without purpose. Without love.

A woman lost.

Chapter 26

*My body, already primed by thoughts of him,
heated even more. I needed him on me. In me.*

"How did you find me?" I demanded.

*He said nothing, his expression hungry and
his eyes sharp. With feline grace he climbed into
my bedroom, shutting the window behind him—
all the while his eyes never left my face. There
was no mistaking the sensuous purpose or intent
in his gaze . . .*

The Highwayman's Seduction

In the predawn hours, Jeremy pushed himself through
the water. Harder, faster. Yet with every stroke, he
felt the shackles of his anger and sorrow pull at him,
threatening to drag him down to the bottom of the lake.

At last, bodily exhausted but still sick at heart, he
hauled himself out of the water. Slogging toward his
clothes, which waited for him on the shore, he barely
felt the cold. It didn't touch him the way the chill of
Sarah's deception did.

After toweling off, he began to dress. Nothing felt
quite as icy as the space between him and Sarah. He'd

been sleeping in a spare room, all too aware of the cold space beside him in the bed, knowing that she was somewhere else in the house but he was unable to talk to her, to touch her.

His routine these past few days had been grimly similar. Wake alone hours before dawn, walk the long distance to Hampstead Heath, swim until the sun began to rise, then wander the city aimlessly, wondering what was to be done.

He had the answer his father craved. He knew the identity of the Lady of Dubious Quality. But to expose her meant ruining his own wife.

Damp but clothed, Jeremy strode from the lake, back south toward the city. He felt hollow, ghostlike. He missed Sarah, and he was furious with her. He did not know a man could feel both emotions at once. He didn't know anything.

There were no solutions anywhere, only more conundrums.

Sarah sat upright in bed. A distant clock chimed half past two—not that it mattered.

She barely slept anymore and went to bed simply as a matter of habit. These past few days since the revelation, other than her visit to McKinnon's, she hadn't had the strength or energy to venture much beyond the threshold of her borrowed bedroom. Yet whenever she'd attempted to close her eyes and surrender to slumber, her mind had goaded her to wakefulness. Every now and then, she'd drifted off for a handful of minutes, or an hour, but nothing resembling real rest. Food, too, held no appeal. Nor did reading. Or writing.

Her only understanding of the passage of time was the maid coming in every morning to tend the fire and open the curtains. Sarah didn't bother going down for breakfast anymore. She'd only see Jeremy, and that was a fresh agony every time, the distance between them marking what they'd lost.

She had no husband. She was unable to write. Something had to change.

This cannot go on.

The thought rang in her head, loud as a bell, as she stared at the darkened bedroom. This situation was insupportable, intolerable. Unbearable.

Clearly, Jeremy hadn't told his father yet about her identity as the Lady of Dubious Quality, or else she would have been thrown out into the street. What was he waiting for? What was it that *she* waited on, for that matter? Action had to be taken, down one path or the other. He wasn't acting for some reason—so she had to.

Throwing off the covers, she rose from bed. The cold bothered her little anymore, but she donned her night rail and slippers as from rote. Opening the bedroom door, she peered into the darkened hall. No one was about.

She didn't bother with a candle or lamp. She knew the way because she'd walked it countless times but never had the courage to knock once she'd arrived. This time, she was determined to go in rather than lingering outside Jeremy's door.

Despite her resolve, she hesitated once she arrived at his room. Her hand hovered over the doorknob. What would he do? But the worst had already come to pass. Nothing could hurt her anymore.

That wasn't true. She had only to see the hurt and anger in his eyes or the stance of his shoulders, and it set off a round of sharp pain that would not fade.

But she could not hide from that hurt. She had to shape her fate, not wait passively, leaving it to providence or Jeremy or anything else to push her down the path. When it had come to her writing, she hadn't sat idly but had moved and decided her course of action. Now had to be the same.

No light shone from beneath the door. Pressing her ear to the wood, she heard nothing. Was he even within?

Sarah opened the door. She stepped into the blackness of the unfamiliar room, closing the door as quietly as she could behind her. It took a minute for her eyes to adjust to the darkness, the fire having gone out. When they did, she managed to pick out a dresser, desk, chairs, and, between two windows, a canopied bed. The draperies on the bed were drawn.

He was here. Asleep.

She took a cautious step toward the bed, her feet almost noiseless on the carpeting.

"Who's there?" he demanded, breaking the silence.

She nearly jumped. After taking a steadying breath, she answered. "Me." *Your wife,* she almost added.

"Sarah?" The curtains on the bed parted, and Jeremy looked out. It was too dark to read his expression, but his tone was puzzled. "What are you doing here?" Then, alarmed, he added, "Is something wrong?"

"Everything," she said.

He made a low sound, something halfway between a laugh and a grunt. "True enough. But you aren't ill?"

"No," she answered, though she wasn't certain if some kind of sickness hadn't overtaken her. A sickness not of the body but the soul.

"Why are you here?" he asked again.

She drew nearer to the bed. "Because I have to tell you something."

"At half past two in the morning?" So he hadn't been asleep but had heard the clock, just as she had.

"Don't," she cautioned when he moved to light a candle. "I need the darkness," she admitted, "to say what I must."

The bedclothes rustled as he drew back the draperies. In the halcyon days of their marriage, he'd slept either in drawers or nude, and a faint gleam of moonlight from the window now revealed the planes of his bare chest as he sat up, propping himself against the headboard.

He crossed his arms. "Say what you must."

Sarah continued to hover, trying to decide where to go. She sat herself gingerly down on the edge of the bed. At least he didn't try to move away from her. His body was solid on the mattress and his heat radiated near, but not near enough to touch. Several inches separated them, but it might as well have been a mile.

"These past few days . . ." she said, not looking at him. "I didn't know a person could suffer this way. Not without being killed by their suffering. But I'm still alive. We both continue to live. But *how* are we living? In misery. This . . . has to stop."

"You're right," he said after a pause. "Somehow, some way, things must alter."

"Before I continue," she murmured, "there's something I have to say." She took a deep breath. "I'm sorry. For the hurt I caused you. It was never intentional. That might not make it any better, but I am sorry, Jeremy."

"Because you did something wrong, or because you got caught doing it?" His voice was caustic.

She fought to keep from flinching. "A little of both. I knew that writing as the Lady of Dubious Quality was dangerous. Yet I couldn't stop myself."

"Why, for God's sake?" he demanded. "Why risk so much with your lies?"

Frustration with him and herself threatened to boil over. "I don't know if I can make you understand what those books—what *writing*—means to me."

"Illuminate me," he snapped.

She turned to face him, even though she could barely make out his features in the dim room. "Ever since I was small, since I learned to read, I've been drawn to writing. I used to scribble my own fairy tales. Stories of princesses rescuing princes. Young girls going on quests and becoming heroines. I would bring these fairy tales to my mother, who found them charming. Until I began to take them seriously. I wanted to turn them into books. I wanted to share my stories with the world. They made me feel . . . important. Significant. As though I was more than a pawn to be bartered to the highest bidder."

She drew a breath, recalling what came next. "When my parents both realized that my interest in writing was more than just an adorable little hobby, they forbade me from taking up a pen for anything but a journal, correspondence, or"—she shuddered—"planning gardens."

"But you didn't stop," he deduced.

"I kept it up, secretly," she confessed. "Started several not particularly good novels, all of which I burned when I realized how terrible they were. But despite that, I continued to write. Late at night, or when I was supposed to be writing letters."

"I remember all your letters," he said bitterly. "It surprised me how many people you wrote to."

"I couldn't have told you the truth," she said. "It would have torn us apart."

"That's come to pass," he said darkly.

"So it has," she said, sorrowful to her very marrow.

"It's a fair distance from writing fairy tales and novels to taking on the identity of the Lady of Dubious Quality," he noted.

"Not as far as you might think," she said. "My early writing efforts strived hard to be *significant.* I thought I wanted to be the next Maria Edgeworth or Fanny Burney. I believed I needed to write books that were *important.* But none of my attempts succeeded."

"Yet you kept on trying."

"I did," she said. "Even after my come-out, I kept going. Kept pushing myself. And would have gone on in frustration if it hadn't been for one misdelivered book."

"Which book was that?"

"*La secrete de la fille de laiterie—The Dairymaid's Secret* by Jean-Louis LeBrun." Even speaking of that slim little volume now made her smile. "I'd ordered a French novel from McKinnon's, and the LeBrun was delivered to me by mistake. As soon as I started reading it, I knew that my life wasn't going to be the same. Returning it was impossible—I devoured the book. Read and reread it a dozen times."

"But . . . it was filthy."

"Exactly." She nodded. "I'd known a little about sex—just overheard conversations, and I'd seen one of our maids kissing her sweetheart. My own body had its demands, but I never knew . . . I had no idea . . . the *bounty* of sex. How freeing the pursuit of pleasure could be. And the book itself was so . . . direct. Unapologetic. Just a taste of that, and I wanted more."

"More?" He sounded genuinely curious now. "Girls of good breeding aren't supposed to want more."

"As a vicar, you know as well as I do that that's ridiculous. If girls and women didn't enjoy sex, if they weren't curious about it, there would be far fewer people in the world. I daresay, there would be *no* people in the world."

"True," he acknowledged.

"So I ordered half a dozen French novels," she went on. "McKinnon never chided me. Never withheld from me, or threatened to tell my parents. I think he thought it refreshing that a woman would seek to further her own education. It wasn't long after reading so many of those books that it occurred to me: *I can do this.* I could write my own 'French' novel. So . . . I did."

She shook her head. "It was . . . revelatory. I loved to write but hadn't done it well. Not until I penned my own erotic novel. And then . . ." Her gaze turned inward, remembering the feelings stirred in her as she'd written her first sexual tale. "I *found* myself. My voice, at last.

Here it was, all this time, but I'd needed to find the right subject."

"Sex," he said flatly.

"Not merely sex, but women finding sexual fulfillment, finding themselves through the expressions of their bodies. We've been taught, us females, that we aren't supposed to know what we want, that men are supposed to guide us in everything sensual and earthy—but why? Why can't we know what we want, what we desire?"

"I don't know," he said tightly after a pause. "Fear of Eve, I suppose. Of women."

"If we women had as much knowledge as men, it makes us both stronger. It doesn't take away power—it adds to it."

He spoke, tension threading through his voice. "Why publish what you'd written? You put yourself in jeopardy." He accused her with his tone.

She mulled this over. "Because I wanted others to find the freedom I'd found in writing those books. What I wrote gave me release and pleasure. But more than that," she went on, growing in strength, "I wanted to stop living in the shadows. They called me the Watching Wallflower. Writing that first book . . . was a way for me to claim another identity." She smiled viciously to herself. "No one knew who I truly was. And I liked it."

He said nothing, so she continued. "I saw that there was a publisher of English-language 'French' novels," she explained. "I approached them with a query. They were intrigued enough by the notion that I was a lady of quality—we started working together. Through letters, of course. Never in person. Even then, I was careful. It was always dangerous."

The word *dangerous* reverberated. The quietness of her life was nothing but an illusion.

Running her fingers over the coverlet's stitching, she went on. "They couldn't keep copies on the shelves at booksellers'." She wasn't able to hide the pride in her voice. This was her accomplishment. Something she'd done entirely on her own, without anyone's assistance. "My publisher asked for more."

"And you gave him other books," he said with that same edge in his words.

"I did. I did, and I loved it." She exhaled. "It *was* a dangerous game I played, and that was part of why I did it. My secret. My thrill. But it was more than that. So much more." How to explain it, when she could not fully articulate it to herself. "It gave me purpose and . . . meaning. I *needed* it. So I kept going. And then . . ." She glanced at him. "You came into my life. Bringing a promise of a life I'd never thought I could have."

"Yet you didn't stop," he noted tensely.

"I had no idea what our relationship would become," she explained. "What it would evolve into. You were a vicar, I was a duke's daughter. It couldn't turn into something . . . more. And I couldn't give up the one thing that made me happy—made me more than happy. It gave me . . . value."

She drew in a shaky breath. Bracing herself for what was to come.

"Now . . . I've decided," she said after a moment. "It all ends now."

"I don't understand," he said.

This was it. No turning back. She said, as boldly as she could manage, "The Lady of Dubious Quality will never write again."

Chapter 27

Without speaking a word, he seduced me. It wasn't precisely a seduction, as I desperately craved his touch, but he left no part of me untouched. He carried me to the settee before the fire, pulling off his clothes as he went. Naked, my lover was magnificent, hard all over, wanting me. After laying me down, he gripped my thighs and . . .

The Highwayman's Seduction

Despite the darkness, Jeremy could only stare at Sarah, certain that he'd misheard. Or there was another explanation for her announcement. She had just told him all the reasons why writing meant so much to her, yet here she was, telling him she would give it up. Heat and anger continued to tear through him, yet she'd revealed her deepest secrets to him.

He was pulled toward her. He wanted to push her away.

"Why?" was all he could manage.

"Because . . ." She paused, as though gathering her

thoughts. "These days without you have been excruciating." Another long pause. "When I was a little girl, I was standing behind a dog cart, and it backed up, rolling over and breaking my foot. The pain was everywhere in me. I couldn't escape it. It encompassed everything. But that hurt is nothing, *nothing,* compared to the time we've been torn apart."

His heart beat faster and faster as tears thickened her voice—he hadn't been at peace ever since she'd come unexpectedly into his bedroom. In truth, he hadn't been calm or easy for days. The torment she described was precisely what he felt.

"I haven't been able to write," she went on. "Not a sentence, not a word. And I realized . . . what was the point of writing when it gave me no pleasure, no purpose, anymore? It was worthless. I was worthless."

Those words from her sent a stab of alarm through him. He'd heard such despair from parishioners on the very brink. "Sarah—"

"I've thought about it," she continued, talking over him. "Turned it over and over in my mind until I've worn the thought down to a shiny pebble. None of it matters, none of my joys or achievements, if I cannot share them with someone. If I can't share them with *you.*"

She reached over and took hold of his hand, her own faintly trembling. It was their first touch in days, and it rocked him to his depths. It had been agonizing without her, being torn between wanting her desperately and roiling with fury at what she'd done. He needed her so much, yet her betrayal continued to burn him. She was hurting and he wanted to gather her close, shield her from the pain. Yet it was an injury that she had caused with her recklessness.

"There's that story about Solomon," she whispered. "With the women and the baby."

"The Judgment of Solomon," he recalled. "Two women fought, each insisting that they were mother of a baby boy."

"King Solomon called for a sword," Sarah went on.

"He said the only solution was to split the living child in two, and each woman would get one half. One said to go ahead and carve the child in two, the other said she'd give him up to spare him the judgment."

"Because she'd rather the boy lived, even if it meant being raised by another." Sarah exhaled. "If I must choose between writing and you, I choose you. I won't kill the love that we shared. And I hope," she went on, her voice shaking, "that in time, you'll forgive me, and we'll find a way back to what we once had."

The enormity of what she said she would do struck him hard, as though he'd been thrown by an explosion. Writing was *everything* to her.

"You cannot give up the most important thing in your life," he protested. "Not for me."

"I have to," she said firmly. "I need you to trust me once more, and this is the only way I can show you that I will not hurt you again."

"Sarah, love," he choked. Reaching out, he pulled her against his body. She wrapped her arms around him. They held one another for a long, long time. Time moved onward, but he paid its passage no mind. He cared only for the feel of her in his arms again. It felt right. Like coming home after a long, wearying voyage.

"Life without you has been a miserable, shriveled thing," he murmured into the cascade of her hair.

"I can't do this without you," she breathed. "I can't—"

"You don't have to." Pulling back slightly, he cupped her face with his palms. "It will be us, together."

"But your father . . ."

"I'll think on that. Later. Let's just have this moment." He kissed her, slowly, cautiously.

They lay side by side. Unable to truly touch. Something very precious had been lost forever.

They had made peace, but there would be no going back to the way things had been. That life was gone now. Moving forward, all he could see was murky haze and more uncertainty.

What was to become of them?

Jeremy tucked Sarah's hand into the crook of his arm as they left Astley's Amphitheater. The happy crowds exiting the theater after the performance were thick, threatening to force them apart. But he held on to her tightly as they made their way toward the street.

He glanced down at her. "Didn't know horses could dance," he said above the din of the throng.

"Or that dogs made for superior equestrians," she said with a smile. "Of all the things I thought I'd ever see, a pug atop a gelding ranks toward the bottom."

"The wonders of London are manifold," he noted. "Hope they don't make Rosemead seem tedious in contrast."

"I'd never feel that way about Rosemead," she answered at once.

This was the first they'd mentioned their home in some time. Neither of them seemed willing to discuss their return—though it would have to happen eventually. There were many things that needed to transpire, but both he and Sarah avoided all these topics. Avoidance was the way things went, lately.

Ever since she had come to his room a week ago, he'd embarked on a campaign to revivify their marriage. Work and anything resembling work had been shunted aside. Everything had been about entertainment, enjoyment. He'd taken Sarah all over London, to as many amusements as possible. Astley's displays of horsemanship were just one of innumerable diversions they'd attended.

They had strolled in countless parks. Attended a fair on the outskirts of Town, where they'd seen acrobats and racing. Visited museum after museum displaying everything from antiquities to Mr. Turner's most recent paintings. They'd paid a call on Catton's, stuffing themselves on cakes and tea. For entertainment, London could not be surpassed, and Jeremy was determined to take Sarah to everything. Whatever it took to make her smile.

And she did smile. Yet, while her lips curved and she sometimes even laughed, the gestures seemed . . . hollow. Sterile. Much as they did now, leaving Astley's incredible performance. She looked up at him as they finally made it out of the theater, but only a shadow of Sarah shone in her eyes. She was somewhere else. This woman with him now was a changeling.

He'd managed to hold his father off, telling the earl that he'd been tracking down leads. Yet his father wouldn't be deterred for long. He'd want results. Soon. Jeremy still didn't know what to say, but he prayed nightly for solutions.

"Catton's?" Jeremy suggested.

She shook her head. "The drums and hoofbeats fatigued me. Would it bother you overmuch if we went home?"

"Not at all." He hailed a post chaise and carefully helped her inside. Her energy remained minimal lately. She slept late and could barely be roused for breakfast.

She was always too tired to make love, and a cold strain continued between them whenever they climbed into bed. Strangers had taken their place in the bedchamber.

They were silent for the ride home. Sarah actually dozed along the way and hardly stirred when he gently awakened her.

"Come, love," he murmured, escorting her out of the carriage and up the front stairs. "Let's get you to bed."

He saw her inside, then helped her up to their bedroom. After tucking her in for a nap, he softly made his way downstairs. His destination was the study, but as he passed the drawing room, his mother's voice called out.

"Please," she entreated. "Come in."

He did so, finding her sitting with her embroidery on a settee. After giving her a kiss of greeting, he sat beside her, fighting restlessness.

"It's no better, is it?" his mother asked gently.

"What isn't?" he wondered.

His mother shook her head. "I'm a month away from my fifty-second birthday, Jeremy. Far too old for games." She set her embroidery hoop aside. "The situation between you and Sarah—it hasn't improved. I'd thought that once you two had started sharing a room again, things would recover. I'd see you both happy again." She sighed. "But that hasn't happened."

Jeremy glanced away, knowing his expression would reveal the depths of his grief. "No," he finally said. "It hasn't." For all that he'd done, despite the countless hours spent escorting her from one diversion to another, Sarah was miserable. There was no denying it.

"Why?" Lady Hutton pressed, clearly bewildered. "She's got a husband who loves her, a fine home. I cannot understand it."

Jeremy swallowed. "She's suffered a loss. I can't discuss it, but it's devastated her." Rubbing at his brow, he said in unhappy exasperation, "All the books I've read, all the theosophical texts I've studied, all the parishioners I've counseled—I can't think of one thing to do to help my own wife."

"You'll figure something out," his mother said with a consoling pat of her hand.

Yet her words and gestures gave no comfort. Nothing did.

Chapter 28

*Many hours later, we lay together in my bed,
intertwined from the acrobatics of our exertions.*

"How did you find me?" I asked.

*"Not without difficulty," he answered with a
smile, "but I am a resourceful man."*

*"Have you come for this?" I held up my hand,
showing where the pearl ring adorned my finger.*

*"Ma'am, if that's what you believe, then you
are far less clever than I'd believed you to be."*

*"For me, then," I said, my heart beating
quickly, half in dread, half in hope of his
answer . . .*

The Highwayman's Seduction

"**Y**our guests have arrived, my lady," the butler announced to Sarah as she sat in her bedroom.

She rose, smoothing down her skirts, and readied herself.

This would be the first time she had received calls on her own, as a married woman, here in London. She'd always been in the company of her mother, who'd always acted as the perfect hostess. Sarah had been her wallflower daughter, watching, but never truly participating.

Perhaps once she might have been afraid to invite a woman as celebrated as Lady Marwood to tea. Now . . . she had much more experience. As Sarah made her way toward the drawing room, her hands didn't tremble. Her breathing was steady and even.

It had been her idea to invite Lady Marwood. Despite all of Jeremy's efforts to engage and amuse her since she'd given up writing, a part of her was going mad. Needing something, but not certain what. Perhaps a social call might help.

Jeremy had deliberately gone out, leaving her to receive Lady Marwood on her own.

"I think this is an excellent idea, seeing Lady Marwood." He'd pressed a kiss to her cheek before heading out the door. "Besides," he'd added with an attempt at lightness, "if you can solve Mrs. Edmond's marital woes, an hour of charming conversation with Lady Marwood should be quite pleasant."

"So you *were* eavesdropping!" Sarah had exclaimed.

He'd reddened. "Only a little. My feet carried me away before I heard too much."

Despite the attempts at banter and normalcy, this past week and a half had been awful, with her abandonment of writing. She'd found no pleasure in anything. No joy. Even her time with Jeremy had felt muted and hazy. She had thought that once she'd made a decision, *any* decision, she would have felt better. But that hadn't happened. She'd sunk even deeper into a formless gray mist.

Sarah stepped inside the room. But two women awaited her, not one.

There was Lady Marwood—a petite, dark-haired woman with large eyes and a penetrating gaze. Sarah had seen her briefly a handful of times and was thus able to recognize her. But the other woman . . . Sarah didn't know.

"Do forgive me," Lady Marwood said, "but I've invited my friend Eleanor . . . I mean, Lady Ashford . . . to join us. I hope it's no trouble. Lady Sarah Cleland, may I present the Countess of Ashford."

"A pleasure," Sarah answered by rote, nodding at the taller blonde woman.

The countess had a lean, angular face and possessed a gaze as astute as Lady Marwood's. But a ready smile played about her mouth as she dipped into a curtsy.

"You're very accommodating to our rudeness," Lady Ashford said with that wry smile.

"Nothing rude about it," Sarah answered. "I'm glad of the extra company. Won't you sit? I'll ring for tea."

She gestured toward the settee. As Sarah pulled the bell, her two visitors took their seats. Both of them were very elegantly dressed, though she noticed that Lady Ashford had neglected to wear gloves. Ink stained her fingers.

The smell of ink came flooding back, dark and wet. Sarah had always been careful to keep it from tinting her own fingers.

Countesses didn't have dried ink all over their hands—did they?

After calling for tea, Sarah sat opposite her guests. The women looked at her with mild expectation. But no words seemed to come to Sarah.

Viscountesses seldom wielded a pen for anything other than writing invitations and guest lists. How had Lady Marwood managed it? Marriage to a nobleman and maintaining a career? A career doing the thing that Sarah loved and needed more than anything.

Clearing her throat, Sarah said, "I understand that *The Last Scoundrel* is doing very well at the Imperial. Sold-out audiences every night."

Lady Marwood, rather than basking in the accolades, merely nodded. "It's a bit of unexpected good luck, I think."

Lady Ashford made a very unladylike noise. "Nothing lucky about it. You wrote a blessedly good piece of theater, and the crowds are showing up for it."

"Thanks to a good review in *The Hawk's Eye*," Lady Marwood pointed out.

"That wasn't my doing," her friend answered. "I always tell my reviewers to be impartial, no matter who's performing what."

A maid came in with the tea things and set them down on the table in front of Sarah.

But Sarah didn't pour the drink and serve cakes just yet. "Just a moment." She lifted a hand as she looked at Lady Ashford. "Are you affiliated in some way with *The Hawk's Eye*?" The paper was one of London's most popular sources of news—and gossip. Sarah often read it to keep abreast of the scandalous goings-on about town.

"'Affiliated?'" Lady Marwood chuckled. "Eleanor owns and edits it."

Shocked, Sarah stared at the blonde woman. "The paper is *yours*?"

"From scribbled page to printed sheet," Lady Ashford said with a not-insignificant smile.

"Do you . . . write for *The Hawk's Eye,* as well?"

Lady Ashford smoothed her skirts. "Not as much as I used to, since the staff has expanded considerably these past months and I'm more managerial than creative. But I do have a regular column once a week. The Hawk's Talon. It's a new feature."

Good God. *Both* these women were also writers? What was the likelihood that they would not only be friends but also sitting in Sarah's drawing room right this moment?

They were so damned *lucky,* these two women. Did they know the depths of their fortune?

She felt a pained expression cross her face, unable to stop it.

"Do you find my calling distasteful?" Lady Ashford said coolly.

"No! Not at all," Sarah said quickly. "It's only . . . well . . ." She wasn't sure how to explain it. She couldn't tell these women the truth—she barely knew them, and she wasn't certain they could be trusted, even though the three of them had something in common.

"I'm something of a dabbler at writing, myself," Sarah finally said. It was as close to the truth as she could get without jeopardizing everything.

Both Lady Ashford and Lady Marwood brightened.

"What do you write?" Lady Marwood asked.

"Stories, mostly," Sarah prevaricated. "But . . . I don't do it anymore."

"Why not?" Lady Ashford demanded.

"Oh . . ." Sarah feigned a shrug. "Married life keeps me so busy."

"But if you enjoy it," Lady Ashford said firmly, "you should keep at it. No matter what."

"It's not that simple," Sarah answered. "I should think that both of you would know that. You're women of title, of consequence. Writing doesn't fit into that equation."

Lady Ashford and Lady Marwood exchanged a glance. "We *make* it fit," Lady Marwood said.

"And if Society sneers at you?"

"Let it," Lady Ashford declared. "My marriage to Daniel cost him friends, but only those of little value. Those that mattered, stayed."

"Cam never gave a fig what the *ton* thought of him," added Lady Marwood. "My own position in Society has always been on the outside. If a few snobs fell away or stopped coming to my shows, I couldn't bring myself to care."

"Forgive me, but . . . you both married into the aristocracy, didn't you?" Sarah remembered now the minor scandal that had happened when Lord Ashford had taken a commoner, and a woman who *worked,* for a wife.

"We did," Lady Marwood said. Her accent wasn't the most genteel, but it did have the rounded tones of one who was in the theater. "But we had just as much to lose as our prospective husbands. Our livelihoods could have suffered severely because of the unions. In truth, the decision to marry wasn't an easy one, not for either of us. I broke it off with Cam, thinking I had to choose. Writing or love."

"And I thought that a commoner and an earl could never be married," Lady Ashford noted. "I'd never give up *The Hawk's Eye*. I believed I had to pick one or the other."

It was as if Sarah had been struck. Though she wanted to cover her face with her hands to hide, she couldn't. Yet she felt shaken down to her very core.

"What . . . changed your minds?" she pressed.

Both Lady Ashford and Lady Marwood smiled. "Very persistent men," said Lady Marwood. "They both let us know that they wouldn't be deterred. They were determined, and, in truth, both Eleanor and I were miserable without them."

Sarah had deliberately given up the thing that gave her life meaning to show Jeremy that she was trustworthy. Yet these women had their husbands' faith as well as their work.

"Why do you write?" she asked them.

"What do you mean?" asked Lady Marwood, plainly baffled.

"What makes you do it?" Sarah pressed. She shook her head. "Especially in the face of societal disapproval."

"*Your* condemnation?" Lady Ashford asked sharply.

The question made sense. After all, women like Sarah, from her class, her station, were precisely the sort who would turn their backs on women like Lady Marwood and Lady Ashford. Again, Sarah shook her head.

"Not mine," she answered. "I've nothing but admiration."

Lady Marwood smiled wryly. "We've both been

called the worst words. *Hack, virago, peddler of trash.*"

"*Unnatural harpy* is one of my favorites," Lady Ashford said with a dry smile.

Their casual reaction to these slurs stunned Sarah. She'd fielded her own share of polite insults at being a wallflower, but at considerable cost. Yet Lady Marwood and Lady Ashford had no trouble brushing off the hurtful words.

"Then why pursue it?" Sarah pressed.

The two women fell into their own pensive silence. After a moment, Lady Marwood said, "It validates me. Makes me feel like I make a difference."

"It's like I'm a ghost without form or substance," Lady Ashford added. "But when I write, I become corporeal. I have substance. I can move objects—I can change the shape of things." She shook her head. "I'm sure that makes no sense."

Sarah had never spoken to anyone about what it felt like to write, and to *not* write. It had always been a private, secret understanding she hadn't been able to share. But these women were giving voice to all the feelings she'd never articulated, not even to herself.

"No, I understand you completely," Sarah quickly said.

"Even if we didn't get paid to write," Lady Marwood continued, "I think both Eleanor and I would continue to do it."

"We've got stories to tell, don't we, Mags?" Lady Ashford said fondly.

"Heaps of stories," her friend agreed, "and nothing can keep them inside."

Sarah turned this over and over in her mind. She

wished, *oh, she wished,* that she could tell these women the truth. Because they, more than even Jeremy, seemed to understand what writing actually meant to her. As a person. As a woman. They could truly comprehend what it was like, the joy of writing, its sorrows and victories, its importance, and the devastation of its loss. But she'd silenced herself—to preserve peace.

At what cost?

"What if, for some reason, you couldn't write anymore?" she asked.

"I'd find a way," Lady Ashford said immediately.

"But if you *couldn't,*" Sarah demanded. "If it simply wasn't possible."

Expressions of horror crossed the ladies' faces. They turned pale, as though someone very dear had turned to ash right in front of them.

"I . . . don't know," Lady Marwood finally said. "It would be like . . . losing a part of myself."

Sarah absorbed this. She had felt as though a part of her had gone missing but she felt its phantom pain.

"Is Mr. Cleland keeping you from writing?" Lady Ashford asked gently.

"If he is . . ." Lady Marwood looked fierce, as though she would battle Jeremy herself.

"Oh no," Sarah said quickly. "The decision was entirely mine."

Lady Marwood appeared unconvinced, but she nodded.

"And the choice," Sarah went on, "between love and writing? If you had to pick one or the other, what would it be?"

"I thought I had to," Lady Ashford said soberly.

"But I was fortunate. Very fortunate. I didn't have to select one or the other."

"If you *had* to pick," Sarah said, almost frantic, "which would you choose? Love? Or writing?"

Neither Lady Ashford nor Lady Marwood spoke. They looked like the mother from the Judgment of Solomon. Horrified at the decision.

A decision Sarah had to consider.

Chapter 29

"You've stolen my heart, ma'am," Jacob said.
"I find myself unable to exist without you." He
stood, gathering his clothing. "Run away with
me . . ."

The Highwayman's Seduction

Jeremy woke suddenly, coming to full consciousness in an instant, as though plunged in a polar sea. He sat upright. Shadows swathed the room around him, painting the chamber in shades of indigo and black. The fire lay silent and dark in the fireplace, its coals barely smoldering. A chill turned the air thin and breakable.

Had he been dreaming? Had a nightmare roused him from his sleep? A cloud enveloped his mind. But a deep, profound sense of *wrongness* pervaded him.

His hand slid across the covers as he reached for Sarah, seeking her warmth, her softness.

But his hand continued to move across the bed finding . . . nothing.

She was gone.

"Sarah?" He peered into the darkness, searching for her. Perhaps, unable to sleep, she'd seated herself beside the now-cold fire. Maybe she dozed in one of the wingback chairs. "Sarah?" he called again.

No answer. She wasn't in the room.

He bolted, naked, from the bed, fear immediately chilling him down to his marrow. Ever since she'd had tea with Lady Marwood and Lady Ashford, she'd been even more withdrawn, more silent and remote, as though her body remained but her spirit was distant.

Jeremy quickly threw on a pair of breeches and a shirt, and stuffed his feet into a pair of shoes. Half-dressed, he lit a candle, then stepped out into the corridor.

Waking the house was a possibility he did not entertain. He didn't want his parents involved. There wasn't time for explanations, and he'd no desire to give any. He needed to find his missing wife.

If he raced hither and yon, without any strategy or structure, he'd go mad. Drawing a breath to steady himself, he decided to start at the bottom of the house and systematically work his way upward.

He began with the library. But all hopes for finding her curled up with a book died quickly when he discovered the chamber lay empty. Each parlor and drawing room yielded the same results. Room by room, he went through the house, urgently whispering her name while praying feverishly to find her safe and well.

He refused to think about any other possibility.

The other floors, however, proved just as empty. Hope began to perish, little by little, curling at the edges like burned paper as he found himself yet again in another unoccupied room.

She wasn't in the old nursery, or his other childhood

rooms. Unless she was in the kitchen or the servants' quarters, Sarah had left the house.

The kitchen glowed with a banked fire, where a boy slept in front of the spit. The lad stirred a little when Jeremy looked inside the kitchen, but he didn't awaken. Jeremy considered rousing the boy to ask if he'd seen Sarah, but he didn't want to raise the house alarm. Not yet.

But there seemed no alternative. He was about to pound on his father's door, then wake the entire household to look for Sarah, when he remembered one final place in the immense house. He raced up the stairs, hardly bothering to muffle his frantic footfalls as he climbed higher and higher, staircase after staircase. Until he reached the very top of Hutton House, and its cupola.

One of Jeremy's stargazing ancestors had built the small chamber half a century ago as a way to feed a love of astronomy, when the study of it was nascent and all the rage for the fashionable elite. It was a compact, round room, surrounded on all sides by windows that could be unbolted to accommodate a large Galilean telescope, which continued to stand proudly in the cupola.

Jeremy skidded to a stop at the top of the staircase opening onto the observatory. His heart also slammed to a halt.

Sarah stood in the cupola, trying to work the telescope. She resembled a wraith in her long white night rail, her hair down around her shoulders. But she wasn't a ghost. She was real, and relief poured through him so aggressively that he nearly staggered with it.

His wife glanced up at his entrance. A look of surprise crossed her face, as if she little expected to find him here. The feeling was mutual.

"Jesus," he swore, not caring that he took the Lord's name in vain. He rubbed his knuckles in the center of his chest, trying to calm his thundering heart. "You scared the hell out of me."

"I didn't want to wake you," she said quietly.

"Better that than have me tearing through the house like a Bedlamite." He took a tentative step toward her, as though she might take flight through one of the open windows. The chamber was bitterly cold, yet Sarah didn't seem to notice. "I thought . . . I don't want to say what I thought."

"I'm sorry." She didn't move toward him but kept space between them. A protective barrier. She glanced out at the dark sky. "I've been trying to look at the stars. Sky's too smoky to see anything."

He reached a hand out toward her. "It's fit to freeze Hades in here. Come back to bed."

But she didn't move. She only looked at his hand. The murky light traced the familiar lines of her face, suspending her in an aquatic half-illumination. It was too dark to see much, but he knew her so well that he barely needed any light to know that the expression she wore was one of profound sadness.

His heart pitched. What could he do to heal any wounds she suffered?

"Before we do," she said, her voice soft with sorrow, "I need . . . to tell you something."

"We can talk in bed." He wanted her away from this cold height, where it seemed as though the fathomless universe would swallow her whole.

She shook her head. "I'm uncertain if we'll share a bed again."

Fresh panic shook him. "You don't know that."

"No, but I realize that after I speak, things will change. They'll never be the same again." She sounded bleak but resigned.

"Just tell me," he urged.

She stared at him, then looked away at the hazy night sky. "The sky's so different from the sky in Rosemead. Here it's choked with smoke and dull with the lights of the city." She exhaled. "Heaven seems very far away in London."

"Sarah . . ." he said warningly. "Promise me. Swear to me you'll do nothing foolish."

She let out a sad laugh. "Define *foolish*."

"It's a sin to hurt yourself." He hated even saying the words, but he forced them out.

Her eyes widened. "No. Oh, no. I would never . . . I couldn't . . . Oh, Jeremy." She took a small step toward him. "I'm so sorry if I ever led you to believe that I'd done something like that. Please. No."

Thank God. A small thread of relief wove along his spine. But he couldn't feel easy. Not yet. "Say what it is you have to say. And then we'll go to bed. I swear we'll share a bed again."

"That's something you cannot know." She exhaled once more. "Jeremy. My love. That will never change. I will love you . . . forever."

"So why do you make this sound like a good-bye?" he demanded, cold with fear.

"Because it might be. Because . . ." She looked down at her slippered feet, then back up again. "Neither of us is happy. There's a pall of misery hanging over us, and no amount of theatrical performances, botanical gardens, or tea shops can ever change that. You've tried. I know you've tried so hard. But there's only one solution. One way to make this right."

He kept silent, but his pulse drummed in his ears.

"I have to write," she said with finality. "I have to be the Lady of Dubious Quality again. She's who I am. I cannot refute that any longer. I can't deny who I am. Not for anyone. Not even," she added mournfully, "for you."

He shook with the force of her words. It resounded in his flesh, his muscles. His ears rang. Everything quaked.

No words came to him. He opened his mouth to speak, but silence reigned.

She'd made her choice. And her choice wasn't him.

Sarah spoke quickly, filling that void. "If you desire, we'll live apart. To protect you from scandal. I don't want to endanger you in any way."

"Is that what you want?" he asked hoarsely.

"I want everything," she answered. "I want to write. I want you. But I know . . ." She gulped back tears. "I know I cannot have everything. Only a lucky few get their every wish. In time, maybe, I'll look at this decision and curse myself. But I can't go on this way. I can't be who other people want me to be."

"You were yourself with me."

She shook her head. "Never fully. There was that secret between us, and I hoped to be the good, devoted wife. I wanted to be what *you* wanted."

"I always wanted you," he said hoarsely.

"You didn't," she answered. "Not when I revealed that I was the Lady of Dubious Quality."

"Because you didn't trust me with the truth."

"And if I had from the beginning, would you have accepted me?"

"We'll never know."

"You're right, she acknowledged, "and for that I'm sorry. But perhaps it *was* her you cared for," she wondered aloud. "Because she is me. All those aspects are part of who I am—the lady, the writer, the woman. You *know me,* deeper than anyone does. You've always known who I truly am."

He scrubbed his hands over his face, then dragged his fingers through his hair. Grounding himself with his touch. Realizing that everything he'd ever learned, his every experience and scrap of knowledge, all the philosophy he'd read and bit of wisdom and guidance he'd ever dispensed—it all led to this moment. This defining time.

He stared at her. She had her arms wrapped around herself. Either from the cold, or to protect herself from what she surely thought would be his wrath and disappointment. But she didn't look afraid. She looked, finally, resolute. As sure of herself as he'd ever seen her before.

She'd made her choice. That choice wasn't him. Yet he knew that it was the right one. She needed to be herself, entirely. Not to pretend or cut off a limb just to prove something to him or to assuage his pride. This was the woman he'd come to care about so deeply. The one with conviction. Who knew what she wanted and took it.

"Thank God," he said finally. "This is the right choice."

"What do you mean?" she demanded.

His voice was thick, rusty. "I mean . . . that I've always wanted to be with you. The complete woman you are. Lady. Writer." He stepped closer to her. "I've known, I think for a long time, the truth of you. That secret self." He continued resolutely, "That night, at that private masquerade."

She went cold all over. Had someone spied for him? How could he know she'd been there?

"You kissed a stranger," he went on, relentless. "The kiss made your heart speed and your blood heat." He stepped closer still, a sharp, intense look upon his face.

"I—" What could she say? It had happened during their early days, but still she felt the dark sting of her infidelity. How could he forgive her?

"I know all this, because I felt it, too." He gazed intently at her. "That man in the blue mask—that man was me."

She gaped at him. "*You?*" The stranger had had dark hair, but that could easily have been changed. He'd had the same height as Jeremy, the same rangy physique.

He nodded. "I was looking for the Lady of Dubious Quality, and I found her. I found you."

"Oh, God." She didn't know whether to be appalled or overjoyed. Both emotions crashed against each other, leaving her dizzy. Her anonymous lover was actually her husband.

"It felt right," he pressed. "We both knew it. But, not knowing the truth, we both believed we were betraying the other." He spread his hands. "On every level, we are exactly right for each other. The vicar and the duke's daughter. The man in the blue mask and the Golden Woman. The libertine and the Lady of Dubious Quality. They're *us*." He blazed. "To hell with what Society dictates—we can be all of those things."

She couldn't catch her breath, and her mind raced. "I must be able to write."

"And I want you to. God, Sarah—when I think how I stood by, doing nothing, dumbly accepting it when you gave up the thing you needed and loved most in all the world . . . I've been in touch with McKinnon," he continued. "Your newest book is amazingly successful. Women and men both purchase it. That's . . . extraordinary." He clenched his fists. "I didn't fight hard enough for you to keep writing. I hope you'll forgive me."

"We each have need of forgiveness," she said softly.

"We'll find it," he answered with conviction. "If anyone can weather the tempests of life, it's you and I." He swallowed hard. "Write anything and everything. Write of sex. Of love. Of whatever you want. Only," he reached for her, "never leave my side. Never be apart from me." He opened his arms to her.

"Jeremy." Would he truly stand beside her through all the twists and turns?

"Don't make me wait a second longer, love."

She crossed the distance between them. Wrapped her arms around him, feeling his solid body, the body she loved beyond all reasoning, and the man himself. Relief tore through her so hard that tears streamed down her face. "Jeremy."

"My Sarah." He kissed the top of her head as he cradled her close.

She sniffled a little. "But . . . your parish. Your status as a vicar."

He was silent. But then, "I'll think of something. Some way for us both to have what we need."

"We'll think of it together," she insisted.

"Together." He cupped her face with his broad hands and stared deeply into her eyes. "I love you, Sarah."

Though the night was dark and hazy, she could still see the love and passion in his gaze, warming her from the inside out. Her heart brimmed, and everything within her aligned, becoming exactly right. "I love you, Jeremy."

He brushed his lips over hers, gently, sweetly. As if learning her anew. She trembled beneath his touch. It had been so long, and she needed him fiercely.

Gradually, his mouth became more demanding. She opened for him, tongues caressing each other, savoring their midnight tastes. Pressing her body closer to his, she felt the warmth of him, his solidity and strength. This man who had enough will to let her be herself. She felt entirely consumed by him, yet wholly her own woman.

Gripping his hard shoulders tightly, she deepened the kiss, discovering again what they created together. A perfect balance between softness and potency.

His fingers threaded in her hair as he tilted her head back, taking the kiss hotter. Here was what she craved. This man.

"I need you," she breathed into his mouth. "Now."

He held her wrist when she moved toward the buttons of his breeches.

"Not here," he rumbled. "Want to take my time. It's been too long to hurry, love."

Threading his fingers with hers, he led her down the stairs, out of the cupola. Quiet as dreams, they moved through the shadow-strewn house, everyone around them asleep. It was as though they were in some magic story, in a bewitched castle where everybody within slept beneath an enchantment, and only they had escaped the spell. Yet they were within their own kind of sorcery as they strode purposefully toward their bedroom.

He closed and locked the door behind them, his gaze always on her, rich with intent. He came forward, enfolding her in his arms. For long moments, they merely held each other. Trembling shook both their bodies.

Slowly, he pulled away. Then he knelt beside the fireplace and built the blaze up. The room filled with warmth and golden, flickering light. He pulled all the blankets off the bed, then spread them with care on the carpet before the fire.

Kneeling on the blankets, he gripped the bottom of his shirt and drew it over his head. He reached a hand out toward her. With the firelight behind him, touching blond curls with a line of brightness and outlining the long lines of his body, he looked mythic, like some golden god offering promises of eternal passion and pleasure. Promises he fully intended to fulfill. But he was a real man—*her* man. And that made his strength all the more potent.

Sarah kicked off her slippers and tossed her night rail aside. She had no idea what would follow next, but it didn't matter. All that signified was that they were united now, their hearts aligned. She crossed to him.

Their hands wove together, palm to palm, as she faced him, also kneeling. Her breasts brushed against his chest, and she shivered at the contact.

"Missed you," he murmured as he nuzzled her neck. "So damned much."

"I missed us," she answered, tipping her head back to give him further access to her flesh. "I ached with it."

"Everything hurts without you." His mouth made a hot trail along her skin. He nipped at her collarbone, dipped his tongue in the hollow of her throat.

"And now?" she asked breathlessly.

"Now . . ." He bit her shoulder through the thin fabric of her nightgown. She felt claimed in the best possible way. "I can't think. Only want you. Want to feel you. To taste you."

His hands gathered up her breasts, stroking them, teasing them to points. He growled in appreciation as she moaned softly with pleasure. She caressed his body, relearning it through touch. This was Jeremy. Her husband. Her companion. Her champion.

"You're so beautiful," she breathed.

"For you." He tugged at the ribbon threading through the neckline of her nightgown. It pulled free, causing the neck to gape. Easing the thin fabric down, he revealed her straining breasts. "Only for you."

His lips fastened around one hard nipple, drawing on it, licking. Her hands came up to weave through his hair, pressing him closer as he licked and sucked. Shining pleasure built, centered in her breast but radiating out like summer. He brought the same attention to the other nipple, until she writhed with sensation.

"I want you inside me," she gasped.

"Not yet." He was carved and hard in the firelight, a creature of sensual demand.

With gentle but commanding hands, he urged her backward, until she lay upon the blankets. Feral but intent, he loomed over her. He swept her nightgown off, throwing it to one side. She forgot about it at once, reveling in being naked before him. Especially the way he looked at her, as though she was everything—the moon, the tides, the sun, the seasons. She wasn't just Sarah anymore. She was Sarah and the Lady, and all the different parts of herself. Naked, exposed.

He prowled down her body, kissing and caressing her as he went. Her sensitized skin responded at once. There was no part of her that went untouched.

Until he brought his long body down, positioning his head between her legs. Holding her gaze, he spread open her willing thighs. Then brought his mouth down onto her.

She arched up at once, at the first touch of his tongue between her slick folds. Softly, but with purpose, he licked and tasted. He discovered her. He created her. He drove her deliberately toward madness with each stroke and every sweep. His tongue swirled around her bud, and he gently took it between his lips, drawing lightly on the sensitive flesh. She cried out with ecstasy, then once more as he dipped into her entrance with muscular, slick intent.

The pleasure nearly blinded her. Yet she hungered for more.

"I want . . ." She moved down his body, her lips trailing along his torso.

"What do you want, love?"

"The scene in *A Wicked Liaison* . . . you know the one . . ."

He moaned with approval, then knelt back to pull at his remaining clothing. In an instant, they were both nude. Primal creatures of desire. Here they were, honest and genuine. She could at last be the Lady, in every way.

As sensual as a satyr, he lay down on the blankets. His cock formed a beautiful shape, curved and upright, hard with need.

Sarah knew exactly what she craved. She straddled his head, positioning his mouth close to her quim, while she faced his cock. "Yes?"

"Yes," he growled.

She bent down. Took his cock between her lips at the same time that his mouth found her sex. Her eyes rolled back with pleasure as she and Jeremy tasted and feasted on each other, an endless circle of sensation, her to him and back again. She sucked and licked while he did the same. Ecstasy suffused her, down to the smallest part of her, every fragment, every piece.

She loved his taste, musky and masculine, and lapped eagerly at it. She adored the feel of his most male part in her mouth. His hips bucked and rose as she sucked him, and he groaned against her damp, intimate flesh. Pleasure built, demanding release.

When he sank two fingers into her passage, she came apart, screaming around his cock. The orgasm shook her like a storm, threatening to uproot her. But he didn't yield with her climax. Instead, he continued to lap at her, his fingers deep within her, pressing against that one exquisite spot, until she came again.

She sucked on him, intent to wring pleasure from him, too. His groans and moans, and the movement of his hips, were her reward. They fed on each other, the world narrowing down to just the two of them.

Finally, he pulled himself free of her mouth.

"I need you," he growled.

"Yes."

He moved swiftly, arranging their bodies so that he lay on his side, with her in front of him, facing away. He gripped her thighs, widening them.

She looked down, eager for the sight of him entering her.

"Look down," she whispered. "Watch us."

The position gave them both a view of his cock as it sank into her. They both moaned at the sight. He drew back, then plunged forward. And they could watch every stroke. Every thrust.

One of his hands continued to hold her thigh, while the other drifted down to stroke her bud. She refused to close her eyes. Instead, she watched it all. His hand on her sex. His cock within her. They were elemental beings, raw.

He took her neck, holding her with his teeth, as he loved her. He was a beast. He was her animal. For her alone he became a wild creature, barely tamed by her hand. Jeremy pounded into her, frenzied, and she reveled in his lack of control.

She cried out in ecstasy, the orgasm ripping her apart as it formed her into something new.

The vibrations slowed in her. As soon as her breath caught, he paused for a moment, then shifted, moving them so she was on her back. He placed himself between her legs, his cock at her entrance, his gaze locked on her face. His jaw was tight, every muscle hard as iron, but the tenderness in his eyes undid her.

He thrust into her. She bowed up, receiving him. Her legs wrapped around his hips. They lost themselves in the creation of more and more pleasure. He groaned and snarled from sensation—a gentle man turned wild with need.

He froze as his release poured from him. He threw back his head, letting out a growl of triumph and surrender. He'd never been more beautiful than in his abandon.

When the last of his climax receded, he gently lowered himself down. Still inside her, he gathered her close and kissed her deeply.

Wordlessly, they stroked each other's faces, their damp bodies. Sealing the bond of their union. They belonged to each other—forever.

Chapter 30

"But my life here!" I exclaimed, watching him dress. "I cannot simply leave it."

"Then I'll join you here in the city," he answered.

"And give up being a highwayman?"

"I'm not giving up anything by being with you."

Laying back, I mulled over the prospect. "Why can't we have both . . . ?"

The Highwayman's Seduction

Jeremy was able to wait until just after he and Sarah finished breakfast. They'd slept much later than usual and drifted down to the morning room holding hands, their gazes lingering.

But not everything was exactly as it should be. There was much left uncertain. And that uncertainty lingered like a shadow in his chest.

It relieved him to see Sarah tuck into her morning meal with a good deal more enthusiasm than she'd shown for eating these past weeks. Hopefully, the hollows in her cheeks would soon fill, and the shadows beneath her eyes would disappear entirely. She was on her way, though, and smiled at him over her eggs and tea. He returned the smile, but inside, his stomach churned and his heart thudded in anticipation of what was to come. He both dreaded and embraced the ensuing confrontation. It had to be done.

As soon as Sarah drained her teacup and finished the last bite of her toasted bread, Jeremy asked, "Are you ready?"

"For what?" She lifted a brow, curious.

"There is unfinished business we must attend to."

"Will we be together?" she wondered.

"Of course."

"Then I'm ready," she answered at once. "When?"

"Now." He took her hand in his, kissing the back of it. Then he stood, still holding her. She rose, smoothed down the front of her dress, exhaled once more, then followed him from the morning room into the hallway.

"Dare I ask where we're going?" she ventured.

"My father's study." At her alarmed look, he said, "Trust me."

She gave him a slightly tremulous smile, but there was conviction in her gaze.

Jeremy directed her through the corridors, toward the back of the house. Lord Hutton preferred quiet, and many years ago had transformed a little-used parlor into his study in order to take advantage of its remote location. How like him, to isolate himself in order to strengthen his agenda. Jeremy remembered a time, not that long ago, when he'd been summoned to the study to receive commands from his father and uncle. So much had changed since then. Especially himself.

Once he might have felt trepidation to approach his father. But now, with Sarah beside him, her love and conviction gave him strength to believe in himself. No matter the consequences.

They stopped in front of the door to his father's study. He knocked, then received the directive to enter. After taking a breath, preparing himself for what was to come, Jeremy went inside, bringing Sarah in with him.

His father sat, as usual, behind his desk as he perused a sheaf of documents. He stood and removed a pair of spectacles at Jeremy and Sarah's entrance. Those were new. A rare concession to growing older. It startled Jeremy to realize that his father was subject to the same rules of aging as the rest of humanity, that Lord Hutton wasn't only an earl but also a man, of fragile flesh and bone and blood.

"You woke late," his father noted.

"We are newly wed, after all," Jeremy answered.

His father seemed less inclined to broach the topic of marital relations today than he had been in Rotten Row so long ago.

"I'll ring for tea," Lord Hutton announced, striding toward the bellpull.

"We've just breakfasted," Jeremy said, "so that's unnecessary."

"Then sit." His father gestured toward the chairs arrayed before his desk.

Sarah did sit, but Jeremy shook his head. "I'll stand."

"As you like." His father took his seat behind his desk. "But whatever it is that brings you here this morning, it needs to be discussed without delay and as expeditiously as possible. I've a substantial amount of parliamentary bills to review this morning."

"This won't take long." Jeremy stood beside Sarah, his hand on her shoulder. "I have to tell you something. To tell you both something. About the Lady of Dubious Quality."

Sarah stiffened beneath his hand, and only he heard her sharp inhalation. With an unspoken question, she glanced up at him, her eyes wide.

He gazed down at her in reassurance.

"That subject isn't fit for your wife's ears," Lord Hutton said censoriously.

"Anything that you and I discuss can be heard by Sarah," Jeremy insisted. "We don't keep secrets."

His father looked annoyed, and Sarah was pale, but neither of them left the room or demanded that Jeremy wait or stop.

"Out with it, then," the earl clipped.

Jeremy bristled at his father's commanding tone, but that had never changed, regardless of Jeremy's age. Some things might never alter. It was up to *him* to change.

"Not that long ago," Jeremy began, "you started me down a path. It wasn't a path of my choosing. It was of your design and intent. Yours, and my uncle's. He isn't here, but I trust that everything I say to you now will be communicated to him."

"I'm not your errand boy," his father muttered. He glanced at Sarah with a fraction of unease, as though uncomfortable being gainsaid in front of her.

"And I am not yours, sir," Jeremy returned. "As of now, this moment, I shall no longer hunt for the identity of the Lady of Dubious Quality."

Sarah looked up sharply at him. "Truly?"

"The search is done," he said to her gently but firmly. "I am finished with it." He gazed at the earl, who reddened with anger. "I am not the boy you can command anymore, Father. I'm a man grown, with a wife—a *life* that belongs to me alone."

"You are familiar with the penalty should you not continue with this?" his father demanded.

Jeremy squared his shoulders. "I am. It doesn't matter. My pride isn't as easily wounded as it once was. I can accept the costs of my decision."

Lord Hutton looked shocked. He curled his hands into fists and set them on the desk. "That trollop's books are dangerous. They must be stopped. To hell with your pride."

"*Trollop*?" Sarah repeated incredulously before Jeremy could speak. "A harsh word, Lord Hutton."

The earl looked affronted at Sarah's having the temerity to speak to him in that fashion. After gathering his composure, he retorted, "A deserved one."

"You are wrong," Jeremy said firmly. "She is a woman of skill and determination. I admire her. More than she will ever comprehend."

Sarah stared up at him, her gaze brimming with emotion.

Jeremy continued, "Her books harm no one. In truth, Father, they *help* people." He reached into his pocket and pulled out a copy of *The Highwayman's Seduction*. Setting the book on the desk, he said, "Read it."

"I will never read such salacious garbage that contributes to the decline of morality." The earl glared at

Jeremy. "You're a man of God. You cannot support that . . . that *scribbler*."

"You cannot condemn what you willfully don't understand," Jeremy said determinedly.

The look of sheer amazement on his father's face was one Jeremy would not ever forget. Perhaps in the whole of his life, this was the first time someone besides his own father had actually denied him.

At last the earl spoke. "And the reward I'd offered? You'll cast that aside? You'll take the loss of your allowance."

"I will and I do," Jeremy replied. "I have everything I need."

He looked at Sarah as he spoke, squeezing her shoulder. She clasped his hand with hers, returning the squeeze.

Glancing at his father, Jeremy saw something he'd never anticipated. His father was staring at him as though staring at a stranger. Not a child, not his son. But a *man*. A man with his own opinions and resolve. Who would not bend to someone else's will.

"The scandal nearly ruined me—it will do the same to both John and Mark if they take up the task. It is done now."

"And what of you?" the earl pressed. "Can you face yourself, knowing you've failed?"

"You cannot understand," Sarah answered. She looked at Jeremy. "He didn't fail. He prevailed."

Jeremy's heart rose upward.

Lord Hutton fell into a baffled silence, staring at them.

"I've concluded my business here," Jeremy said,

helping Sarah to her feet. "Continue on with your parliamentary bills. We're leaving this afternoon."

With that, he escorted Sarah from the study. They walked straight out the front door together, down to the street, where they strode arm in arm. The world passed in streaks of unformed color. Jeremy barely noticed. He might not ever be received back into his father's home. The anchor had been raised, and he sailed on unexplored waters. Would there be tempests ahead? Or unknown lands, ripe for exploring?

He would find out. On his own. But not alone.

Sarah seemed to float beside him, wearing the same dazed expression that he felt. "Why?" she asked after several moments. "Why did you do that?"

"There wasn't any alternative," he replied.

"Untrue," she answered. "You had a choice. Me, or your family. And you picked me," she said wonderingly.

He stopped walking, heedless of the pedestrians around them. All he saw was her. Taking hold of her, he said, "*You* are my family now."

"Jeremy," she said, then pressed her lips together, as if to stop herself from weeping.

"My happiness and my love," he continued. "That's what you are. That's all I need. I need you. And the Lady. All of you. And," he went on, "we'll work together to make certain we have everything we want. Everything we need. Because I love you, Sarah."

She cradled his face in her hands. Gems of tears glinted on her eyelashes. "What of the future?"

He smiled. "We are the authors of our destinies. If there's anybody's quill I trust, it's yours."

Epilogue

And so, dear reader, for many months, Jacob and I decided to live part of the year in London, and part of the year in the country. We knew unending ecstasy, having found it in the most unlikely place.

The Highwayman's Seduction

One year later

Opening night of one of Lady Marwood's new burlettas at the Imperial Theater always caused excitement and anticipation. Crowds packed the theater's lobby as well as the street outside, where people jostled to secure tickets to another eagerly awaited production.

Jeremy and Sarah wove their way through the throng, maneuvering past the hordes of would-be audience members. They didn't have to worry about being admitted to the theater, as Maggie had made certain to set aside tickets at the box office.

In one of their twice-monthly gatherings at Catton's, Maggie had confided to Sarah and Eleanor that she never grew tired of looking out from behind the curtains of the theater and watching the seats fill.

"After all this time," she'd confessed, "I still can't believe that a ragman's daughter like me could draw a crowd—for the right reasons."

"That's sham humility, Mags," Eleanor had chided with good humor.

"So speaks the woman whose scandal rag has a circulation of thousands," Sarah had laughed.

"Thus decrees the lady with readers on the Continent and the Americas, let alone here in soggy Britain," Maggie teased. Sarah had lately begun publishing fairy stories under her own name. She continued her anonymous work as the Lady of Dubious Quality— but Eleanor and Maggie didn't know that. The Lady's story of Lady Josephina and the professor, *A Study in Love,* outsold all her other titles, with the emphasis on romance generating even more readers. She had been quite inspired in writing the book, and she continued to enjoy her inspiration.

Sarah sometimes felt bad for not telling her friends about her other writing activities, but it was for the best to preserve the security of her identity. There was always the chance of scandal if it was revealed that Lady Sarah Cleland, duke's daughter, married to a former vicar turned publisher, wrote such salacious material.

Every other Thursday, Sarah met with Maggie and Eleanor at Catton's. The three of them made most unladylike sounds over their cakes and tea, causing more than a few heads to turn in their direction. But none of them cared, especially Sarah. She had friends now, *true* friends who didn't pity or insult her. Who shared her love of writing and understood the difficulties and joys of the work.

She hadn't realized how much she'd needed the friendship of other women until she'd finally possessed it, and now she counted the two female writers as honorary sisters. Better than sisters, because they didn't have the burden of family connections.

Maggie had been worried about the reception of her newest work, *Along Came Love*. It was a matter of course that Sarah and Jeremy would be present in the theater to support her on opening night.

"It's a crush," Sarah said now over the din in the lobby.

"That'll make Maggie happy," Jeremy answered, raising his voice.

"One would think so," Sarah replied. Maggie was a terrible perfectionist, holding herself to higher and higher standards the more successful she became. Thank goodness for Cam, who kept his wife grounded through his dry wit and ardent devotion.

Finally, Sarah and Jeremy breached the lobby and made their way up toward the box held in reserve. Jeremy looked devastatingly handsome in his dark evening dress—though ever since he'd left the Church, he'd continued to wear sober, plain clothing, as if he couldn't quite adopt the life of a layman. Though his departure from the Church had been entirely voluntary, he'd confessed late one night that there would always be a part of him that remained a vicar. She didn't mind—not when he still had the sensual appetite of one devoted to pleasure.

Reaching the theater box, Sarah smiled when she beheld Eleanor, Daniel, and Cam already there. Everyone greeted each other warmly.

"Maggie's backstage?" Sarah asked, taking her seat.

"I can never drag her away for long," Cam answered. "Though," he added with a wolfish grin, "I try."

"A true lover of the arts," Jeremy said wryly.

"How fares the latest book from Cleland Publishing?" Daniel queried, shaking Jeremy's hand.

"Reports are back from bookstores across the country." Jeremy grinned. "They can't keep copies of *Little Fairy Stories for Big People* on their shelves. And our other titles are doing just as well."

"I would never have guessed that the reading public had such an appetite for moralistic bombast," Cam drawled.

"They're mostly philosophical treatises." Jeremy shook his head with mock sadness. "Yet I'd never expect an untutored barbarian to make that distinction."

"You've truly fallen from grace," Cam returned with as pious an expression as he could muster.

"Into the arms of my wife." Jeremy's look for her was intimate, ripe with possibility. She fanned herself, though the gesture was only partially playful.

Eleanor said, "Cam, if you read anything other than plays, you'd know that his books are aimed to help those with the most rudimentary education find their footing in the world."

Sarah glowed with pride at Jeremy's work. He'd transitioned from assisting a few hundred people in a parish to several thousand across the country. The books he published were an unusual amalgam of philosophy and instruction. He'd written two volumes himself already, but he also had a stable of writers—men, women, highborn, commoner, and Sarah herself—who provided writing that, it seemed, readers devoured. The first few months had been shaky, with Sarah and Jeremy's income generously supported by her dowry and income from her novels. But since that uncertain time, profits had steadily risen, as had readership. They had a staff of half a dozen already.

They lived in London most of the year, with a little cottage near Rosemead for the summer months. The arrangement suited them both exceptionally well, giving them necessary solitude from the rest of the world. Whenever they went to church, they were still greeted warmly by the villagers, even though Mr. Wolbert was now the vicar.

"My apologies," Cam said with a bow, though he spoiled the effect by grinning.

"You can't help being a boor." Jeremy spoke with affection. The past year had seen him change so much. He was still a reserved, thoughtful man, but he spoke and moved with more confidence now. His laughter came more frequently. He wasn't afraid to speak his mind.

Neither of them saw their parents, despite the duke's earlier decision that relations would thaw in six months—but Sarah still hoped that the situation might warm in time.

"Maggie tries to reform me," Cam answered despairingly. "Yet even she knows when a task is impossible. But, quiet! The burletta's about to start."

Jeremy sat beside Sarah, their hands automatically finding the other's. As the crowd quieted, Sarah glanced over at her husband, who looked back at her with a warm, promising smile. Her heart overflowed in palpable waves. She had discovered so many valuable things in the last year and nearly lost them all. Yet she'd held on, and now possessed more than she'd ever believed possible. She had friends. Writing. A man who loved her, and whom she loved. Two people who allowed each other to be fully themselves. There was no last page, only another and another, their story ongoing and unfolding, chapter by rich chapter.

The curtain rose.

*G*ive in to your Impulses!

**These unforgettable stories only take a second
to buy and give you hours of reading pleasure!**

Go to *www.AvonImpulse.com* and see what we
have to offer.

Available wherever e-books are sold.

AVONIMPULSE

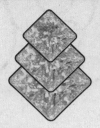